IMPERISHABLE BLISS

A Novel

by

D. E. Tingle

to CLB

the first cause

TABLE OF CONTENTS

CHAPTER ONE
EROS

I put pen to paper with no thought of justifying myself, but with the single purpose that has guided me since my rebirth in God many years ago: to glorify Him and his Son Jesus Christ. I'm a humble man, conscious of my shortcomings. If I'm also strong, my strength arises from my faith and I don't apologize for it. Yet my story seems, at the outset, impossible to tell, marked by trial after unfathomable trial, by failure and embarrassment, by the world's scorn. But I will tell it, because in the end my Faith abides, and for this I give all glory to the Father.

I wasn't always a man of faith, even though born in the American Midwest between the world wars to God-fearing parents, and under the religious influence throughout my childhood of a kind, loving, Christian grandmother. I was conventionally religious until my teens, when I fell into some kind of untutored doubt, which was abetted by four years of a highly secular college education, then marriage, the birth of children, and preoccupation with building a career. Those were my years in the wilderness. As will happen in the wilderness, I lost my way. Losing my way, I fell into isolation and despair. And my despair led to the miracle through which, by the astonishing grace of God, I was saved.

There was a young girl working in a flower shop near the office where I was employed in those days as an administrator in a large company. Her name was Marie, a Catholic, with dark hair and large, green eyes, a soft face and body, and a look of isolation that reflected mine. We might never have met, but one day I got the idea—inspired by nothing I can remember—to bring one red rose home to my wife. I stopped in the flower shop on the way from work, and some signal passed between Marie and me in the five minutes it took to choose, wrap and pay for the rose. She knew I wore a wedding ring—saw it when I handed her the money—but some shared need made us stop and look each into the other's face with an intensity that I have never experienced in a first meeting, before or since. I was haunted. I took the rose home to my wife. She was touched and happy. But the sense of isolation that had been growing in me for years seemed to balloon at that moment. My wife was young and pretty, but I felt as if I were looking at her through the wrong end of a telescope. Our two small daughters, playing nearby, were beautiful. But I felt myself shivering and abandoned.

The following day, after work, I went to the flower shop again and bought another rose from Marie. As she handed me the rose and I handed her the money, I bent close and asked quietly, not to be overheard, to meet her somewhere away from the shop. She looked frightened but whispered "Yes."

"I'm married," I said.

"I know," she said. "And I'm engaged to be married."

I thanked her for the rose and, very agitated, left the shop. I couldn't take this rose to my wife; I carried it back to my office, deserted after hours, and left it in a vase on my desk.

In the days that followed I struggled to think of some means of meeting Marie—whose name I didn't yet know—without being detected by my wife. Lying was difficult for me. My religious upbringing had imbued me with the conviction that lying was a sin as grave as any, and—irreligious as I may have been at that time—the requirement to lie filled me with such anxiety and guilt that I felt sure I couldn't lie and be believed. I couldn't share my anxiety with my wife, who I was certain loved me. My despair and isolation deepened.

Eventually I thought I saw an opportunity to meet Marie without disrupting my family. Because the flower shop was open weekends, I guessed that Marie's work schedule provided for days off during the week. I was in a salaried job, with some latitude to make my own schedule. So one day at lunchtime I found Marie alone in the shop and, with great anxiety on both sides, arranged to meet her at mid-morning the next Tuesday, her day off.

What followed has seemed to me in later years the very epitome of allegiance to a false god. We met as arranged, drove out of the city in my car in order to avoid being seen by acquaintances of either of us, and fell into hellish circumstances that seemed a Heaven then.

She was only twenty years old—nearly ten years younger than I—and the only woman other than my wife I had ever been intimate with. I tell this story in some detail, not because I approve of what we did, but because the entire experience was unique in my life, events out of time, an object lesson in wrong behavior. From it I learned how seductive a false god can be, and how hard it can be—impossible, really, without Grace—to tell a false god from the true One.

We fell into a terrible, harrowing love that first day, each knowing barely more about the other than a name. She was engaged to be married in six months, the date and the place already chosen. She and her fiancé were taking prenuptial instruction from their priest. Marie knew I had a wife and daughters. But a vast longing, an inexplicable loneliness, an impression, though false, that God had forsaken us, drew us irresistibly together.

We drove to the country, stopped by woods, walked into them, removed each other's clothing and would have made love, but Marie was *virgo intacta* and resolved to protect this sign of innocence until her wedding. Mad with irrelation and thwarted need, we tore at each other's bodies, kissing, biting, crushing, but never penetrating. We talked and talked. We had nothing to say that wasn't of hunger and loss. She was an uneducated shop girl; I was a relative sophisticate, with pretensions to ideas and a nagging certainty of the importance of things unseen. Really, we couldn't communicate, and this failure sharpened our anguish and our sorrow. And it seemed to me we were both beautiful: she with her long, black hair spread on the pine needles covering the forest floor, her white body with its pink nipples and vivid thicket of pubic hair, her huge, green, beseeching eyes; I young then, with a slender body and broad, well-wrought shoulders, vibrant with physical strength and electric with sexual force, priapian, graceful. By an unspoken agreement, we did nothing that first day to give ourselves or each other physical relief. We strained for hours at the verge of detumescence, kissing and clinging to each other. Her virginity, immense and totemic, stood between us like a wall. Her fear was manifest: fear of losing her virginity, and with it any hope for the plans she had ordered for her life. I felt the complementary fear: that if I took her virginity I'd be responsible for whatever life was left for her, and would lose the life I had with my wife and children. We lay together in an agony of challenged trust, tormented by love and desperate for a shared peace and safety, while our moral irresolution turned into the physical pain of thwarted release. I could see in her eyes the pain in her congested pelvis, a reflection of the debilitating ache in my own lower torso and testicles. So we suffered. So began our passion.

Late in the afternoon we dressed and drove back to the city, and I dropped Marie where I had picked her up. Parting was cruel; we were in several kinds of pain, sunk in confusion, burdened with a mighty secret, foreseeing only difficulty. Circumspect, afraid of being observed, we kissed and separated, she to keep her own counsel with her family and fiancé, I to go home to a new regime of secrecy, lies by omission, the attendant guilt.

In the weeks that followed, Marie and I continued to meet. We found a motel and moved indoors. Each meeting consisted of hours in a bed conserving Marie's hymen. The fear and diffidence of our first meeting slowly gave way to such trust that by our third meeting we could engage freely and happily in fondlings and manipulations that, without endangering Marie's intactness, gave both of us sexual release. But in that process we lost any hope of falling out of love.

Even in our ecstasy there was just one topic between us: our loneliness and isolation. We talked about the flower shop and my work, but the invariable subtext was Marie's interior estrangement from her fiancé and my felt distance from the world and the nearest part of it to me, my wife. In our motel room we clung together, not knowing where to go or what to do, neither of us willing to forsake the other or our other lives. When we tried to imagine keeping and living our secret even after Marie was married, anxiety overwhelmed us.

Then, rather soon, we got caught.

One day when Marie and I had been meeting for about two months, my wife phoned my office and was told by a co-worker that I was out for the afternoon on an unspecified errand. When I arrived home that night she asked where I'd been, and I had no answer.

If the moral training of my childhood had not disabled me as a liar, her question would have been easy to deflect. She asked it without suspicion, almost without curiosity. But the only idea that came to me when she asked was the idea of my guilt. My face discomposed itself; she saw. Her own face registered fear and shock, and we both began to cry.

Then followed what seems in retrospect an absurd series of gestures by the three of us—Marie, my wife and me—to save everything and lose nothing. First my wife wanted to meet Marie. I think she felt sure of the sanctity of her own relationship with me, and believed that she could convey to Marie a sense of the fitness of Marie giving me up. I loved and wanted both women; I hoped a meeting between them would inspire tolerance in my wife and confidence in Marie, so that I could love them both without guilt. Accordingly I went to Marie, told her my wife had discovered us, and asked if they could meet. Marie shrank in terror. Her green eyes started in her pale face and she seemed about to faint. I took her in my arms and held her while she regained her strength.

"Are you crazy?" she asked me. "You're crazy." We had been walking in a city park. She collapsed onto a bench. "What happened? How did she find out?"

"She just did," I said. "She asked me and I told her."

"If Kevin found out, he'd kill me. Really, I think he might kill me."

"Well," I said. "Beth won't kill anybody. She just wants to talk."

Marie sat on the park bench pressing her hands together in her lap and looking stricken. Guilt assailed me. But I sensed her poise, her courage and devotion, and I loved Marie more than ever. Finally she said, "I'll meet her if you want me to." I was thrilled and relieved. Recreant that I was, I foresaw plain sailing.

The meeting took place one evening at my house, after our daughters were in bed. Marie arrived in her old car, pale, pretty and nervous, deferential when I introduced her. Her hair was down and she was wearing shapeless clothing calculated to disarm a woman, not the modish dresses I was used to. Beth was informal but almost imperious, as convinced of her territorial hegemony as Marie must have been of her own foreignness. Seeing these two women, lovely, vital and my sexual intimates, facing each other across the kitchen table and preparing negotiations to share me, filled me with pride and awe. I slipped away to the living room and tried to occupy myself with a newspaper. Not more than ten or fifteen minutes passed, though, before I heard their voices in the hallway, the sound of the front door, and Beth returning to the kitchen. I caught Marie at the door of her car. "What happened?" I asked.

"What do you think?" she said. "She wants me to stay away from you."

But for the idolatry I'd fallen into, this might have been the end of a misadventure that threatened destruction for so many innocents. I might have thanked Marie for her goodness to me and her courage in facing my wife, kissed her farewell and gone back indoors to my family. But when I thought of giving her up, a pit of isolation, loneliness and terror yawned in me. Marie was my necessary and only resort. I hungered for her like humanity in search of Faith. "This can't be," I said.

"What are you going to do?" She stared at me, her eyes forlorn but dry under the street lamp.

"My best," I said. I kissed her. She drove away and I went back indoors.

Our next gesture was to separate, my wife and I. This was the upshot of two weeks of densely concerted introspection and debate. In these circumstances she was the rationalist and I the hysteric. The less sure I seemed of my intentions with Marie, the more determined Beth became to forge some kind of certainty for herself. She would not let me temporize: I either had to declare my affair with Marie at an end and return to the *status quo ante*, or I had to move away from home and make up my mind. But I knew, whatever my intentions, that I could not give up Marie just then. So I asked for time to think, and we separated. I agreed with Beth on a schedule to visit my daughters and I went away and rented a tiny apartment—a sitting room with a bed.

All at once I was relieved of the logistical difficulties inherent in carrying on an affair from one's place of work. I no longer had to devise sites and schemes for meeting Marie on weekdays. Subject to her own ability to evade detection by her fiancé, we could meet at my apartment virtually at will. Neither of us had ever had a trysting place before. Our shared loneliness, our predilection for secrecy, the risk we were running of the loss or devastation of others we loved, the necessity to preserve the signs of Marie's virginity: these made our hours in the apartment poignant beyond imagining. We were in a continuous state of sexual and spiritual longing. This was my first—Godless—experience of ecstasy.

The last, best gesture was Beth's. When I came to our house to visit my daughters a few times each week, my wife let me back into our bed. I don't know what she felt. My own experience, in spite of the secrets I carried, was of greater closeness to her than ever before. It was as if, for the first time, I had in Marie a gift so privately and particularly my own that I could afford to give all of myself—except my secrets—to Beth. And so sex with my wife became an ecstasy as well.

I was in a precarious paradise. If ever a life of bliss teetered on the brink of doom, this was it. My—(*my!*)—happiness depended entirely on the maintenance of secrecy, supported on my side by lies of omission and on Marie's by lies of every kind—to her fiancé, to her parents, to her friends. My happiness even seemed to depend on the stoppage of time. We were now within four months of the date of Marie's wedding. It seemed impossible that we could continue our affair indefinitely. But we had no plans to give it up.

The crash came with no warning except for our anxiety. In my Faith, I agree with the dictum that God works in mysterious ways. In my apostasy, it was painful to see my fate being worked in sacramental ways. One Saturday Marie and her fiancé, holiday shopping a few weeks before Christmas, passed a Catholic church and at Kevin's instance went into the confessional. Marie had not confessed in several months and didn't want to confess then, but she was trapped. She could hide and wait while Kevin confessed, but the next morning at Mass, unshriven, she would not be able to take Communion, and Kevin would want to know why. So she made her confession to an unsympathetic priest.

She told me that story on Monday evening while we lay fully dressed on the bed in my apartment. Her forlorn green eyes searched my face for advice, and as usual I didn't know what to do. If I had been two people, one of them would have undressed Marie and consummated our love, body and soul. The other would have lifted her to her feet, wept to express the depth of that love, and let her go forever. I did neither. We lay there immobilized by our sorrow and my fear. But I knew she would leave me. And soon after Christmas she did.

At the saddest season of the year for a Christian apostate, I found myself alone in a bed-sitting room, suddenly unaware of any reason to live. I still had a wife and children, but I felt helpless to go back to them. With the loss of Marie, Beth became strange to me again and I was impotent. We wept. I couldn't tell her what was wrong, because I couldn't tell her what had been right before. My depression was profound. At work I was barely able to maintain appearances. Compulsively I walked past the flower shop for a glimpse of Marie. I feared death, but I feared living more. I consulted a psychiatrist.

Like most of his fraternity in those days, the doctor's training was Freudian, and by the second meeting we had begun to construct an edifice of myth and symbology around my agony. The myth was a lugubrious one and made me weep, but none of its insights conduced to make me well. My depression deepened; it governed my waking hours and disturbed my sleep. I must have looked as gaunt and terrible to the doctor as I looked in my mirror; after a few more meetings he resorted to medicating me.

The medication he prescribed was one of the recently developed mood elevating drugs, fifty tiny, oblate, reddish-brown pills in a plastic cylinder. I began taking these according to instructions, three per day at eight-hour intervals. My despondency did not remit; I even exacerbated it by driving past the flower shop. After four days I emptied the remaining pills onto a table top and counted them; there were thirty-eight. I gathered them back into the palm of my hand. And then, whether impatient or insane, I swallowed them at a gulp. I took a glass of water to sluice the last few down my throat.

That God intervened in my life in those hours is beyond doubt, but I have never known whether He did it before or after the overdose. I lay down on the bed that Marie would never visit again. I felt calm, satisfied to have acted and indifferent to danger, and mourned my loss. A kind of dizzy anesthesia curled around me, my body numb and heavy and my mind sinking into it, as if by gravitation. I might easily have slept then and had no second chance. But as I felt the drug overcoming me, in a wave of pity I remembered my little daughters. I had not made up my mind to die; I had acted impulsively, and now I seemed likely to die a death that could never be justified to them. I had to stop. I found the telephone and gave the dial one full turn for help.

I don't remember that call, but it succeeded. I remember the remote crash of my apartment doorframe breaking before the onslaught of a police ambulance crew, the paramedics shouting in my ears and slapping hard and harmlessly at my face, cold air, snow under my dragging feet. I vomited into the snow, thinking: "My body is trying to save itself. My mind doesn't care."

I was unconscious for two days, from Friday until Sunday. I awoke very hungry but well rested, and not surprised, as soon as I remembered myself, to see that I was in a hospital bed. Outside the window it was dark; a lamp burned beside me on a table. In a chair nearby, Beth sat sleeping. She looked sad, distant, exhausted, pathetic and vulnerable. I felt great pity for her, but no longer any love. I thought of Marie and felt no love for her either. It seemed to me my life had started over. I didn't know exactly where I was, or how long ago my old life had ended, but I felt something like exaltation—a calling to a life of Perfection. In the silence and subdued light of the hospital room I sensed the presence of Divinity. After years of my neglect of Him, it was clear that God had saved me, and for some purpose.

I resented Beth's sleeping attendance then. I wanted to be alone with my experience of God, without this unwelcome residuum of the sinful existence from which I knew I had been saved. I thought of my children; they seemed unimportant next to the enormous certainty of Duty and Salvation. I understood that my previous life was over. God had ended it, forgiven me for it, and presented me with a new and thus-far sinless one, and for this I owed Him my devotion and my constant effort to follow a Christ-like path of faultless dedication to His Truth. I felt humble and exalted at the same time—whereupon God tested me.

Beth stirred, awoke, raised her head and saw me looking at her. She started, gasped, burst into tears and threw herself on me, clasping her arms around my neck, kissing my face and sobbing violently. I sought to comfort her by holding her to me and patting her shoulder, but I could not share her emotion. I was in such awe of my covenant with God, and of His expectations of me, that my survival to see my wife and children again seemed trivial.

I foresaw at that moment that my life of faith would entail obligations incompatible with the obligations of my old life. To think of getting lost again in the quotidian particulars of a secular job, family breadwinning and superficial friendships—this oppressed me. The idea of pursuing an illicit love affair filled me with disgust. I believed that my covenant with God required a clean break from old entanglements, so that the burden of any new fault or failure would be entirely my own. I resolved to be divorced from Beth.

The news, when I conveyed it on the day of my release from the hospital, seemed to devastate her. She wept miserably, and I felt tremendous regret. But for my determination to keep faith with the God of my Salvation, I might have faltered in this first step. My daughters, too young to appreciate their parents' struggle, had their mood subsumed in their mother's, and they wailed and clung to my legs when they understood that I was to leave. The tribulations of those first few days were vast.

I returned to the bed-sitting room long enough to pay the landlord for the damage done by the ambulance crew, and then I left, driven out by the unhappy associations of the place. I found another, as small and monkish as the first, but I consecrated this one to my quest for the Godly perfection I could never attain, and the Covenant I would never forswear. I devoted much of my time at home to prayer and meditation. For many years nobody, man or woman, visited me in that place.

Although I knew that I had been saved and that God was real, I struggled to see His face. The war then under way in Vietnam caused me particular distress. I understood that Communism, as a militantly atheistic force, had to be defeated if God's hegemony were to be realized on earth. But I saw the sacrifice of thousands of seemingly innocent noncombatants; I saw friendly-fire accidents in which the righteous killed the righteous; I saw horrendous suffering where quick death would have been the merciful alternative. I prayed to God to understand His purpose in that war. I didn't for a moment doubt His goodness or His mercy, but I longed to see it whole, the better to bear witness among doubters, of whom there were plenty around me.

In some ways I felt more lost at this time than I had felt during my period in the wilderness. I knew that God expected everything of me and that I owed everything to God, but I felt unsure of the path. At night in my tiny apartment I removed my clothes and looked at myself in a long mirror. I was quite beautiful: tall, blond, with a high forehead, deep-set blue eyes, a straight nose, a fine mouth in a line that bespoke my earnestness, a strong jaw, broad shoulders and well-muscled arms, a deep chest tapering to a narrow waist and hips, long, well-formed legs, graceful ankles, gracefully arched feet. It was easy to believe that God had made me in an image close to His and that He had made me for His purposes. But near the geometric center of this beauty was my penis, pale and smooth and rather large, surmounted by a pale shock of pubic hair. I looked at my naked image in the mirror and I shivered. I felt my soul and body at risk. I had no confidence that my penis would not of its own volition rise up against God. I knew that God could break and burn my fragile body whenever He liked. My penis glimmered in the lamplight like a slumbering threat, its role in my salvation problematic. I understood that I must banish every manifestation of sexuality until God had made his purpose plain.

This understanding became the source of my greatest trials. I was young and vital, and my physiology seemed to have a life apart from my will and the life of my spirit. It was the rare morning when I didn't awake with an erection and have to clasp my hands in prayer until the hazard passed. I had lurid dreams of sexual encounters with Beth or Marie, or with women I didn't know but had seen on the street. Usually I'd awake from these dreams in dread and physical frustration, but sometimes I'd sleep through a consummation and awake later with the sticky evidence of my unwilling onanism. My confusion on these occasions was complete. I loved God and was faithful to Him, but the body He had given me seemed to rebel against us both. Yet however weak my flesh, or however strong the Devil's habitation of it, I vowed that my Soul, at least, would never surrender to temptation.

CHAPTER TWO
AGAPE

When I met Solveig, she appeared first as a doer of God's work. There was a rally against the war in Vietnam, and I went out of curiosity, still watchful for the meaning at its center. Solveig was one of half a dozen speakers on the dais; she had gone to South Vietnam as a medical doctor and worked in a children's clinic until the South Vietnamese government discovered her previous stint as a medical volunteer in North Vietnam and revoked her visa. She spoke in musical, Swedish-accented English about the damage the war was doing to Vietnamese children in the North and the South. The rally was outdoors. Her voice arrived out of phase with itself from several sets of loudspeakers. I pushed through the crowd and stood closer to the platform. She seemed as tall and blond as I was, and nearly as beautiful, as if God had set her apart. I felt sure that God meant us to be allies in the work of justifying His purpose in the war; I felt sure that Solveig would help me to see the parts of the mystery that so eluded me up to that time. And I was lonely.

Before I ever spoke to her, I had assigned a significance to Solveig that I saw later was more from myself than from God. She had the same name as the faithful woman in Ibsen's play. I had read *Peer Gynt* and knew the ending; I had seen as much adventure as I wanted. I thought: Maybe this is the woman I'm to come home to.

When the rally was over, I waited for the small crowd that had gathered on the platform to disperse, and then I approached her. She was crouching, collecting an assortment of books and papers from beneath a chair. Her hair was straight and blond, and it fell over the eye nearer to me as I stood at the right distance for speaking to her, but unsure of myself. She must have sensed my presence, because she pulled her hair aside and glanced up. Her eyes were of a limpid, unsaturated blue; they seemed to size me up faster than I could think to frame a greeting to her; she smiled at me before I could speak.

"Carry your books?" I blurted.

She laughed. And I realized with a thrilled sense of unearned intimacy, as if I were being admitted into a secret, that she was laughing in Swedish. It was a warm, musical, rising laugh. She stood up and handed me the books; "You are so nice to ask!" she said. The lilt of her laugh invested her speech.

She threw a purse strap over her shoulder and we began to walk. She was my height—nearly six feet— and wore a blue jersey a little lighter yet than her eyes, a denim miniskirt and leather sandals. It was spring; we were walking in the green campus of the university; her hair gave back golden highlights from the slowly northering sun. From the quietly charismatic presence I had first seen on the dais, she had become— effortlessly—my companion, walking at my side and waiting for me to speak. I told her my name and made one hand free from the books I was carrying so she could shake it. Her hand was as large as mine. She felt like an equal. Neither of us gripped.

On the street a block down from the campus gate we sat at a sidewalk cafe table and ordered croissants. It was a relief to unload Solveig's books onto the tabletop. It was an innocent pleasure to sit across that white surface from her and admire her smiling beauty glowing in the sun, all blues and yellows, the colors of her country's livery.

"Are you living in the States?" I asked her.

"For a few months only," she said. "I have to go back to Sweden for my work."

"What do you think is happening in Vietnam?"

Her smile became less dazzling but didn't entirely disappear. "Did you hear my speech?" she asked.

I nodded. "You talked about the effect on children. But is anything good happening there?"

"Some people are fighting for freedom," she said. "That might be good."

"Which are the people fighting for freedom?"

"The Viet Cong are fighting for freedom. They get help from the North and the Soviets, but they are fighting for freedom."

"But the Viet Cong are Communists. If they were to win, who would be free?"

"It's a good question." Her smile had still not disappeared. "What is your interest in the war?"

"That of a sponsor, I'm afraid."

"Then you like it."

"No. I hate it. But I pay for it. And I've voted for it."

"Time to repent," she said, and laughed again in Swedish. I was stunned. She seemed to know of my rebirth. She even seemed to be challenging me to find my vocation.

"What must I do?" I asked.

"Everyone must do what is right. I do whatever to help the little kids. Nobody can do everything."

Many years later, as I write down my best recollection of Solveig's words, they seem less than a clear call to a lifetime of privation, temporal failure and ultimate spiritual triumph. But the injunction to do right so resonated with the decision I had already made that I felt an alliance with her. I imagined us yoked together, animals of the same size and strength, preparing the ground for God's kingdom on earth. I even dared, there at the cafe table, to imagine us equally yoked in the sight of God, a couple in Christ, and myself no longer lonely. I felt powerfully moved and excited. I saw that her golden hands were bare of jewelry, as now were mine. So much matter for thought and process swelled in me that I was confused and knew that I needed to withdraw for a while.

"I want to think about what you've said today," I told her. "May I call you? This stuff seems very important to me."

She tore a scrap of paper from a sheet among the pile of books and wrote her name and a telephone number on it. I folded the scrap and put it in the breast pocket of my coat. I put down money for the croissants. I stood and took Solveig's hand in both of mine, shook it again, and thanked her for her company. "I'll call you," I said, and hurried away to my apartment.

I spent the next couple of days in considerable agitation. I had a vivid dream in which Solveig and I were traveling in an unfamiliar country. She walked ahead of me, although I tried to keep abreast. Her straight, blond hair lofted from her shoulders, and I had a quartering view of her face—and then only the cheekbone and forehead. I realized I didn't remember what she looked like. I hurried to catch up, but my feet dragged and my body felt heavy. The land was gray and featureless and the sky overcast. In the far distance, crepuscular rays penetrated the cloud cover and picked out something on the ground. I understood that the war was there and we were going to find it. Solveig stretched a hand back to me. "It's God," she said. "We've got to hurry." I reached for her hand. I awoke in my bed.

I spent much of each workday in my office with the door shut, preoccupied. For the first time since my initial employment out of college, I felt sure that I had missed my vocation. I suffered in nervous anticipation of phoning Solveig. It seemed to me that I had reached another of many recent crises in my life. If I were to call Solveig, it would have to be for reasons of the Holy Spirit working in me, and I would have to dedicate myself entirely to whatever project He, through her, might reveal to me. I foresaw that I would have to resign my job. After much struggle, I girded my loins for spiritual battle and phoned the number on the scrap of paper.

Her voice when she answered was even more musical than I recalled, and her accent more pronounced. I identified myself. She remembered me and sounded pleased that I'd phoned. Rather keyed up, I proposed to meet her sometime in the course of the following weekend to talk about her work.

"Oh, I so sorry I can't," she said. I was simultaneously stung with disappointment and bemused by her childlike ellipsis. "I going away for the weekend with my friend. We're going car-racing."

"Your friend."

"Ya. He's one of your nice American guys."

I felt cold and foolish. A moment later I was ashamed of my feelings. I had not called Solveig as a prospective lover, but as an aspiring ally and co-worker, and I believed that the spiritual importance of my relationship with her could not be jeopardized by a relationship of whatever description with some other person.

"Well. What a disappointment," I said as cheerfully as I could. "Maybe we could meet sometime next week."

"There is anti-war group Monday at seven p.m. We could meet there and talk afterwards." She gave me the address and I hung up with my morale a little tattered, but unswerving in my purpose.

I went home that evening from work, kept to my tiny apartment, and prayed at length for guidance in the next part of my life. God seemed to be requiring me to give up my job. The thought gave me great anxiety and I prayed harder. I had a good income, much of which went to support Beth and my children. I knew, if

God had a plan for me that entailed quitting my job, that He would provide. I knelt on the floor at the edge of my bed, squeezed my eyes tight shut and prayed aloud, hoping to see Him. I grew tired and fell asleep. I awoke sometime later, stiff and still kneeling, the right side of my face hot against the bedspread. He had not spoken yet, and I felt as far as ever from seeing His face. I crawled onto the bed and continued to pray. Late in the evening I got up, undressed, brushed my teeth, put on pajamas and got into bed for the night. I prayed then for patience. God granted me patience and I fell asleep.

The next day God answered me with a sign. In my mail at work there was a letter from Beth telling me of her plans to remarry. It was formal and somewhat cold, but it meant I would be released from alimony payments. The balance of disbursements allocable to child support was small. God had begun to show me how He would provide. I asked the receptionist to hold my calls, closed the door of my office, fell on my knees and prayed silently beside my desk. My fear evaporated. I thanked God, climbed back into my swivel chair and spent the rest of the morning composing my letter of resignation.

The weekend was a trial. I found myself thinking of Solveig, away somewhere with her friend, engaged in something she had called "car-racing". All I knew of this subject was that it existed and could be seen from time to time on television. My impression, based on very little exposure, was that it was a blood sport and obscenely dangerous. Except when something went spectacularly wrong, the activity seemed boring and idiotic, a parade of impractically loud vehicles jostling one another for what—judging by the space allotted in the television listings—must have been hours at a stretch. I tried to imagine Solveig's interest in so unedifying and irresponsible a sport, but I couldn't. Even less could I imagine her in the company of what I visualized the devotees of "car-racing" to be: hulking troglodytes with defective hearing and a degraded sense of the sanctity of human life. But I shamed myself and—I'm sure—disappointed God with these uncharitable judgments of people I hadn't even met. It occurred to me that the secret underlying my confusion might be charity itself—Solveig's charity, which I knew to be great, at the service of worthy sufferers. I imagined her volunteering medical assistance to the battered survivors of the frequent crashes. But the cheer in her voice on the phone had not suggested any such dolorous scenario. And then I realized that I didn't know if she had gone racing as a spectator or as a participant. Could she herself, strapping blonde that she was, be a driver?

I got my answer on Monday night at the anti-war gathering, convened in the basement of a Unitarian church near the university. Solveig appeared with her friend in tow, and oddly transformed since our first meeting. From her Swedish blue and yellow she had become—American?—red, white and blue. She was sunburned, as was her friend, and the sun seemed to have bleached her hair. The eyes were still dramatically blue, and she was wearing red slacks and a white blouse. I had not noticed before how white her teeth were. She smiled happily when she saw me, took my hand and introduced her friend. "This is Bartley," she said, and she told Bartley my name.

"Bartley," I said, shaking the hand he offered. "Bartley what?"

"Rob Bartley, actually," he said. "Most people call me by my last name."

"Why is that?"

"I have no idea." He smiled inconsequentially.

It seemed we might be about to run out of conversation, but Solveig provided a dynamic by taking Bartley's arm in hers and squeezing him to her side. She tilted her head and bumped it lightly against his; they turned their faces to each other and exchanged a kind of loopy grin; they behaved as if they were in love.

I inspected Bartley, trying to apprehend the nature of their attraction. He was a little shorter than Solveig; he had nondescript brown hair, slightly receding; his face was open and pleasant but not handsome. Watching their body language, I realized all at once that they had just come from bed. I was desperate to change the subject.

"What's this racing you were doing on the weekend?" I asked neither of them.

"Bartley has a sports car," Solveig said.

Bartley told me the name of his sports car, but it was just a series of letters and meant nothing to me. "We drove it in time trials upstate," he said. "Solveig's pretty good." Solveig smiled happily.

I was riven with disappointment at this hint that Solveig might be capable of frivolity. The evening was starting badly. I thought of excusing myself and going home to my apartment to be spared whatever pain might be in the offing, but my dedication stayed me. As I hesitated over how and where to steer this unsatisfactory conversation, the meeting was called to order and the three of us settled onto folding chairs near the front of the room, with Bartley and me proprietary at Solveig's flanks.

The chairperson of the meeting—or chairman, as he was still known in those days—was a young, bearded academic of some sort. Because there were only about two dozen people present, the chairman proposed to have each of us stand, identify himself and give a précis of his position on the war. Considering that no one at all stood to defend the American policy, there was a remarkable divergence of opinion as to what was wrong with it. Some thought Vietnam a just war with the United States on the wrong side. Some thought the war was simply unwinnable. Some thought that all American government declarations were lies, and that America was therefore under a moral obligation to fail. A pudgy fellow with a lower-middle-class accent and a look of paranoia had to be cut short before he was well begun on a Marxian analysis of war in general. Bartley, when his turn came, cited the so-called "domino theory" of Communist expansion from country to country through Southeast Asia as the only rationale he'd been offered for the American war in Vietnam, and he rejected it as not equal to the occasion.

Solveig stood next, beautiful and impressive again, and offered the opinion that no political program justified the killing of children. Then all eyes turned to me and I stood, perhaps beautiful, said my name, and then heard only a silence echoing in my head. I looked down at Solveig. Her eyes were turned up to me; she smiled expectantly. I couldn't meet her gaze. I raised my eyes and looked past the attentive faces of strangers to the far wall, gripped by stage fright. The silence grew louder. And then I said to the wall: "I have no opinion about this war. I don't understand the first thing about it. It's a mystery to me. I hate it." There was applause, the first I'd heard. I sat down. Solveig kissed me on the cheek.

The rounds of the audience continued, but my mind was no longer on what was being said. I had expressed what was in my heart, without knowing in advance what I would say; I had moved an audience and Solveig had kissed me. All at once it seemed that I might be called to preach. I closed my eyes, bowed my head and prayed silently. After several minutes, when I had finished praying and felt encouraged by God, I opened my eyes and glanced at Solveig, who must have been watching me. She nodded. She smiled. For the first time I knew my vocation.

CHAPTER THREE
PHILIA

The news that I was resigning my job to enroll in seminary created a small sensation at my employer's. My record there was excellent; most people assumed that I was on a career path to the top of the company. My boss tried to keep me on by offering an immediate promotion; it was clear he had no idea of what was at stake. The demands of duty and conscience that had made me such a good employee now called me away.

Anxiety to begin my task tormented me. I felt sure that Solveig was to be yoked with me in the work, but she had said that she was going home to Sweden at the end of the summer. There would be no opportunity for me to enroll in seminary until the fall. I chose a non-denominational Christian seminary within a few miles of my tiny apartment, applied and was accepted for admission. I looked carefully for any sign of doctrinal divergence between the seminary's Confession of Faith and my own convictions about the nature of God and His Son and Their relation to the world, and I was satisfied that there was none. We believed in the inerrancy and Divine inspiration of Scripture, in the historicity, deity and virgin birth of Christ, in the reality of His miracles, that He atoned for man's sins with His death, that He was resurrected in His body and ascended into Heaven, that He will return. We professed the Heidelberg Catechism.

The spring continued to warm and summer came on. I stayed at my old job, having given enough notice to complete tasks I'd made myself responsible for and to leave in good order, with my successor ready and able to carry on. But I attached myself to Solveig's projects. When she appeared at a rally or a teach-in, I was there. I attended the same weekly anti-war organizing meetings that she attended, and usually in her immediate company. But as often as not, Rob Bartley was in her company too. I wished he would go away, but I didn't pray that he would. Jealousy is the province of a God jealous of idols, not of a mortal man seeking to be Godly. I would not make an idol of Solveig, even though I loved her, and sexual jealousy was out of the question, although I had to pray long hours to fend it off. I hoped that God would lead Solveig into a narrower path of virtue. I prayed for Solveig in that spirit. I wanted her to be as good as I wanted myself to be. But Bartley seemed to be a fixture in her life, and the physical pleasure they took in each other's company was unmistakable. Their hands were rarely out of contact; they touched, bumped and butted each other constantly. Their displays caused me anxiety, regardless of the childlike innocence that surrounded them. They smiled, laughed and fondled like Adam and Eve before the fall. It was almost possible to imagine that the fruit of the Tree of Knowledge had passed them by entirely. And it was impossible to dislike them together. And because I loved Solveig and Solveig appeared to love Bartley, I supposed that I must love Bartley too, just as my faith told me that God also loved Bartley. But my trials at that time would have been less if Bartley had been absent.

Vietnam remained an enigma. Solveig characterized it as a proxy war between two equally unworthy Great Powers, fought on the territory and in the bodies of a dispossessed people who only wanted to be let alone. Bartley's main objection seemed to be that his government was fighting under false pretenses. He regarded every official pronouncement as a probable lie, and he was as resentful as if the lies had been addressed personally to him. He presented himself as cheerfully disposed, but I sensed some anger, subterranean and non-specific, that Solveig's sunny presence regularly disarmed before it could rise up. One evening after a war-resistance meeting, we sat on a sofa before the television in Solveig's apartment and watched the President, Lyndon Johnson, address the nation. From Solveig's opposite side I heard Bartley grumble: "What an oleaginous, smarmy, murderous, hypocritical sleaze-ball! Don't you just want to...?" As he groped for the appropriate sanction, Solveig leaned away from me and snuggled Bartley with such conviction that the sofa shook.

"Hit him in the face with a pie?" she ventured. "Yes, Bartley, I do!"

I peered sidelong to see if Bartley was soothed. He had his arm around Solveig's shoulder and their heads were together. They gazed with dreamy smiles at the President, as if he were not the actor at the center of the world's woes. I smiled too. Solveig seemed capable of bringing the lion to lie down with the lamb, of initiating the Rapture all by herself. (To hear myself say this, these many years later, I realize again how dangerously close to idolatry I came in my relations with her.) I was determined that we should work together.

But how and to what end? I was fiercely anti-Communist and a committed Christian; Solveig seemed indifferent to political categories and behaved like some kind of Nordic pagan. I had not actually broached the subject of religion with Solveig, even though I thought of little else, and it seemed crucial for my salvation that I evangelize her. One day in June I invited her to the Sunday service at the church I attended.

"Would I have to wear a hat?" she wanted to know.

"Most of the ladies do," I said.

"Okay," she said.

Still equipped with a car in those days, I picked her up at her apartment at 10:45 a.m. and drove her two miles to the church. She looked stunning: taller than ever—and taller than I—in heels, a dark blue dress longer to the hem than was usual for her, but still above the knee, nylon stockings (or pantyhose?) with straight, dark seams, and a summer straw bonnet with a wide brim that framed her head like a halo, made her blue eyes dramatic, and reduced her clearance in doorways by a further three or four inches. "Do you go to church when you're at home in Sweden?" I asked her as we drove.

"Sometimes," she said. "We have a church in Stockholm that performs a whole Bach cantata every

Sunday as part of the service. It's very nice. I go for the music."

"Bach," I said.

"Ya," she said, "it's beautiful. Bartley took me to a Negro church once with a black friend of his. That music is so great too."

My church in those days, the Gospel Church of the Redeemer, had for music an organist and a congregation singing traditional hymns. I offered a little prayer that Solveig might find our music appealing. We parked in the lot, arrived at the church door just on time and went inside, turning heads. I led us to my usual pew; the congregants there smiled and shook hands and made room for Solveig and her hat.

I no longer remember much of the specifics of that service. A few of the flock went forward to witness. Solveig joined in the hymn singing; she may have known some of the numbers already, but I think she sight-read from the hymnal. At least once I followed her strong, bright voice singing the alto part. I've entirely forgotten the subject of the sermon, although our pastor was charismatic and compelling as always. I thought of myself in the same role in years to come. My introduction to homiletics was to happen that fall.

Out of a sense of pride in my friend that was not altogether appropriate and may even have been sinful, I felt impelled after the service to introduce Solveig to the pastor, who in his smiling progress down the center aisle during the recessional hymn had looked twice at her. We greeted him at the exit. He called me Brother, then took Solveig's hand and squeezed it as I presented her to him. He nodded his head in a courtly half-bow and said, "God bless you this beautiful morning. Thank you for joining us." She said something in reply and he heard her accent immediately. "Will we be seeing you again?"

Solveig's smile shone down from on high like the sun upon Gibeon. "Maybe not," she said. "I'm a visiting Lutheran."

"Our sister in Christ," the pastor said, and handed us down the church steps. "Bring her back, you hear?" I felt somewhat giddy, and conscious again of the attention Solveig attracted by her height and coloring. Faces in several parts of the parking lot were turned toward us. I took her hand and stopped her.

"I think the ladies are serving lunch in the basement. Would you like to eat?"

"Oh, I can't, I'm sorry," she said. "Bartley is coming for lunch. But you could have lunch with us."

"I don't want to crash your party."

"Don't be silly," she said. "I cooking eggs Benedict and Bartley is bringing orange juice. He thinks it's breakfast."

"Gosh, thank you," I said. "I'd enjoy that. Is there something I can contribute?"

"Maybe more orange juice. In case Bartley doesn't bring enough."

On the way back to her apartment we stopped at a convenience store and I ran in for the juice. There were bouquets for sale in a refrigerated case. I bought one of those too. "How nice!" she said, and smiled happily when she saw the flowers. There was no doubting her sincerity then or at any other time. Her candor was complete. I felt thrilled by her friendship, grateful that she had gone to church with me, and hopeful of the outcome.

"What did you think of the church service?" I asked her.

"I had fun," she said. "I like those hymns. It's interesting to see how different churches can be."

"Did you hear anything you especially liked? I mean in the testimony or the sermon or the prayers. Anything that seemed very true to you?"

"It was familiar," she said. "The testimony was different. I have never seen that before."

When we arrived at Solveig's building, Bartley was sitting on the front steps reading a book, a supermarket shopping bag beside him. He stood and embraced Solveig; they kissed quite a lingering kiss, their limbs intertwined more than would have seemed possible for people standing upright. Solveig had removed her bonnet for the ride in the car and not put it back on. She dropped it on the pavement, but held on to my flowers, when Bartley kissed her—or when she kissed him: she was distinctly the taller of the two and could have been construed the aggressor. After several seconds Bartley disengaged his right arm, planted his chin on Solveig's shoulder so he could see me past her blond hair, and offered his hand. "Hi!" he said. "How was church?"

I shook his hand. "Ask Solveig," I said.

"Okay," he said, "I will."

Bartley hoisted his shopping bag, Solveig retrieved her hat, and we went upstairs. Solveig kicked off her heels and we all went into the kitchen, where Bartley spread the contents of his bag on the counter top: a half-gallon of orange juice and two bottles of champagne. "Mimosas for throats parched by joyful noise," he said. I believe he meant no disrespect; nevertheless I took some offense, which I didn't show, and which I promptly forgave. He mixed the mimosa cocktails, distributed them and offered a toast. "To human love and friendship," he said. We clinked our three glasses and sipped.

"To Divine Love," I said. We lifted our glasses and sipped again. It occurred to me that I had never offered a religious toast, nor—on second thought—ever heard of one. I felt all at once that I'd committed a terrible act of profanation. One invokes God for His help in all things, not to congratulate Him on the quality of His mercy. I felt cold with shame. I closed my eyes for a few seconds and prayed silently for forgiveness. But then things got worse.

I should mention that my church held no position on the question of the drinking of alcohol. A substantial minority of my friends in the church—or it may even have been a majority—disapproved of drinking and never imbibed. I had always drunk in moderation and found the sanction for it in many places in Scripture. But this day, without my volition and regardless of my preference, something went wrong.

Bartley and I sat on stools at the kitchen counter while Solveig cooked, and Bartley asked me about my church. This seemed at first a God-given opportunity to begin the work of bringing Solveig to my faith, and perhaps to bring Bartley, whom I liked and God loved, along as well. He asked me to repeat the name.

"The Gospel Church of the Redeemer."

"So—" he said. "Christian, Protestant, evangelical."

"That's right. We believe—I believe—that Jesus died on the cross to atone for our sins, and that I have the obligation as a believer to tell that good news to everyone, because knowing it and believing it and acting on it is the only way in the world to salvation."

"Man!" Bartley said. "Your work is cut out for you. You're operating in a society where everybody has a Constitutional right to his own theory. What do you do to sell yours?"

"I tell the story and trust the truth of it to do the selling. And I try my best to exemplify it in my own life."

"How's it going?"

"I fall short."

Bartley sipped his drink and surveyed me with an indulgent smile. "From the little I know, I'd say you meet or exceed most people's standard for virtuousness."

"I'm a sinner."

"How can you tell?"

"I fall short of Godliness in more ways than I could hope to enumerate. I know what He wants of me, and I fall short in thought and deed."

"Gee," Bartley said. "That's tough."

I reviewed the tone of that remark. I replayed it in my head, listening for the inflection of irony. There seemed to be no trace. Bartley sipped again and said, "You know, I feel quite virtuous. I may be one of the happiest people in the world. And I couldn't be happy if I didn't feel virtuous. And I don't believe that you're in any way a worse man than I am. Is my standard so low? Or are you measuring yourself against a standard not meant for human beings?"

"I'm measuring myself against a standard that isn't worldly."

"But isn't the world where the action is?"

"The world is where the fight for salvation is. The action is in Heaven."

"This is funny," Bartley said. "You're the unhappy Christian, and I'm the blissful secularist trying to shrive you of the conviction of sin. Who will save whom?"

I felt a stab of fright. Satan adopts any guise necessary to outflank the wary Christian. I looked at Solveig, who was puttering happily at the stove, and saw her for the first time as the Other. I set down my mimosa glass, bowed my head and prayed to God for guidance and protection. I asked Him to show me if I had stumbled into the den of the Adversary. I shook with fear. After several seconds the fear passed, and I understood that God was with me as always, that I was safe, and that my task was to witness to Bartley and Solveig, who were not Satan's agents but his targets. I picked up the glass and moistened my dry throat.

Bartley was still talking. "Solveig likes you. I like you too, but it's not the boon that being liked by Solveig is. That's why I'm knocking myself out trying to come up with the formula to convince you that you deserve to be happy."

"I am happy," I said. "Joyful, actually. My faith gives me joy."

"Really? I hope so."

"I hope so too," Solveig said.

"Because I'm thinking," Bartley said, "that maybe you've tied into a set of metaphysical obligations that the human mind was never meant to confront or designed to understand. I mean, if God is running the world, how do you account for Vietnam? I want to retire God and put Solveig in charge. On the strength of the evidence before me, Solveig is kinder and more loving than God."

Bartley's monstrous, unexpected blasphemy took my breath away. I glanced again toward Solveig, almost hoping not to see her there. But she was there, seemingly oblivious to Bartley's remark and assembling the egg servings. I asked God to forgive the three of us and to sustain me.

"But Bartley," I managed to choke out, "there can't be any comparison. Solveig's love is human love. God's love is Divine love. They're just not understandable in the same terms. When God was on earth in Jesus, He appeared as a man filled with love that was recognizably human, even though it was subsumed in the Divine. But God's love is not human. You can't look at it and say you understand it."

"Amen," Bartley said, and laughed. He laughed! Then he climbed down from his stool and sat at the dining table, leaning back, placid, with a smile of seeming contentment. After a moment his face grew serious and he said, "Do you understand it?"

"No, of course not," I said. "But I hope to."

"Here's what I don't get," said Bartley. "If we are made in God's image and God requires certain behavior of us if we are to be called good, why is the world he's given us to live in such an ethical nightmare? I mean, shouldn't it make moral sense to us? Shouldn't we, as God's simulacra, be able to see the pattern of his commandments for us reflected in the human condition?"

"Don't we?"

"I don't think so. Tornados chop up trailer parks and kill children and poor folks. Their survivors weep and wail, lie awake nights for months or years afterward, wondering why they were punished. What is that about? What lesson are we supposed to learn from such an example? Surely God doesn't want us killing children and leaving their parents to suffer indefinitely. He's told us he doesn't. So why does he do it himself? Why does he sponsor a world that seems utterly indifferent to human happiness, where there's no detectable correlation between virtue and reward, where his creatures go to war, mistreat and murder one another in generation after generation? Why does he require me to believe in his goodness if I'm to be saved, but deny me the capacity to believe? That's what I don't get."

"It's a profound mystery," I said. It would have been better if I had ignored the generality of Bartley's observations and remonstrated instead that God denies no one the capacity to believe, that He has imbued every human creature with free will; but I was oddly off my form.

Bartley stretched in his chair, folded his arms behind his head, and turned to watch Solveig at work. "You know," he said, "I don't think I've ever been happier in my life."

I felt somewhat dizzy, as if my mind had projected itself partway out of my body and uncentered me. I looked at the glass on the counter and saw that it was empty. I realized too that I had emptied it once or twice before in the course of my conversation with Bartley, and that Bartley had refilled it each time. Now I looked at him and tried to organize my thoughts. I felt quite engaged with Bartley, as if he were my friend and ally, and that some exalting revelation might be imminent. I turned to look at Solveig. The turning disoriented me; I felt myself tipping. I placed a steadying hand on the counter top until I could regain my balance and focus my eyes, to discover Solveig looking back at me. She flashed her dazzling smile. Without forethought, and to my own amazement, I reached for her, took her hand and kissed it. The revelation that I had anticipated seconds before now struck: that I yearned for her, body and soul. Her face seemed so beautiful that tears welled in my eyes. Something like a sexual wind swept through my body, and I felt stirrings of an erection. Fear seized me and I dropped her hand and sat back, folding my arms across my chest, aware of my heartbeat, my head suddenly clear. Solveig reached out with the hand I had kissed and patted my cheek. "Are you ready for food?" she asked.

We sat at the table and Solveig served. I offered to ask the blessing and was accepted, then ate mostly in silence, although Solveig's eggs Benedict were done to perfection, and Solveig told Bartley about her morning in church. I had switched from mimosas to orange juice, and I had promised God that I would not drink alcohol again until the Work was finished.

I watched my two friends talking happily together. But for the solemnity of my covenant with God, their intimacy might have made me envious.

CHAPTER FOUR
WAR

After the failure of my gesture to bring Solveig to Jesus, I withdrew a little and submitted the problem to constant prayer. I spent almost every hour when not at my job sequestered in my tiny apartment, agonizing with God. He seemed more distant from me, as if reflecting my new isolation from Solveig. I prayed hard to bring Him close, but I felt bereft. It seemed that I had tried to bring the objects of my love together, failed, and forfeited some of my intimacy with both.

I had a kind of reprise of the dream I'd had right after I met Solveig. We were in the same featureless landscape under the same gray sky, but this time Bartley was present. He and Solveig were talking together and to me, but I couldn't hear their voices. Bartley's sports car was there, although no road could be seen, and Solveig was leaning over the raised engine cover, removing parts and placing them in a row on the ground. I raised my hand to my brow—but not to shade my eyes, because the sky was dark—and gazed into the distance, looking for a sign. The gray land stretched away unmarked in every direction. I closed my eyes, and I could see the insides of my eyelids. They were of the same gray as the landscape, but they loomed in a way that oppressed me. I opened my eyes again, but now I could see nothing. I sensed that I was supposed to be in the presence of God. I looked carefully, nearby and at a distance, but I detected nothing, not even a variation in the intensity of the pervasive gloom. I felt that I was at the center of an infinite space. I could hear my thoughts swelling into the emptiness, but no sound came back. I tried to think louder. I tried to swim in space. I scrambled up out of sleep and found myself alone in the darkness of my room.

I now felt more forlorn than at any time since my drug overdose. Either God had seen fit to leave me temporarily a little more on my own, or I had forfeited my intimacy with Him through my pursuit of Solveig. I hungered for the sympathetic human contact and counsel of a Christian mentor, so I arranged a visit with my pastor. He received me on a Saturday afternoon in the church vestry, extending his hand.

"God be with you, Brother," he said, and waved us both into seats. "What do we need to talk about?"

"I think I'm in a spiritual crisis," I said.

"Tell me," he said.

I was silent, considering where to begin. I looked the pastor over. I had known him only for several months, since soon after my decision for Christ. In that time my attitude toward him had been the reverential attitude of the acolyte; I had depended on his example of a Godly approach to life, and thought of him as a source of moral leadership, should I need one. But at this moment he seemed reduced: less exemplary, smaller, his complexion paler, his well tailored suit less assured in its fit. I worried all at once that he was little older, no smarter and no more God-fearing than I. I felt again that all of my ties to the Godhead were being loosened and attenuated, regardless of my earnest wish that they be strong. But I plunged ahead. "Have you ever seen the face of God?" I asked him.

"Yes," he said. "On the occasion when I was saved. And since then I've known what He looks like."

"What does He look like?"

"Oh, it's impossible to describe," the pastor said. "Like perfect Love. Peace. Beauty. Not like anything you could see on earth."

"But does He have eyes and a nose and a mouth, for instance?"

"Oh yes, I would say so."

"Ears? Hair?"

"We are made in His image, so yes."

"What color are His eyes?"

"I don't know. They could be of every color. It's a very non-specific beauty. It's not describable. But I've seen it and I know it."

I was silent again, filled with doubt. The pastor seemed sincere. I tried to understand why it was given to him but not to me to see God.

"Has God ever drawn away from you? Have you ever had the feeling that He was distancing Himself in spite of you?"

"Spite?" His complexion grew paler.

"In spite of your best efforts to know and understand Him."

"No," the pastor said. "Never." He paused. "Has something happened to your faith?"

"No," I said, "not my faith. My ability to communicate it. To people and to God."

"You communicate it to people by witness and by example. You communicate it to God through prayer."

"I know, Pastor," I said. "I'm having trouble being heard."

"Not hardly," the pastor said. "Not by God. Shall we pray to Him right now?"

"Yes," I said. I clasped my hands together, shut my eyes tight, and let the pastor choose the manner of address.

"God in Heaven," he said, "help our brother here to know Thy presence. Speak to him. Make Thy face to shine upon him. If he is in doubt, reassure him. If his spirit is troubled, soothe it. He is Thy faithful servant, maybe in a moment of crisis that he doesn't understand, but Thou surely dost. Draw him into Thy presence. Amen."

"Amen," I said. I opened my eyes and looked at the pastor. Nothing important had changed. The pastor's color was back, but his carriage seemed mundane and uninspired, his feet profoundly in and of the clay. My faith in God was not in doubt, but I had lost faith in the pastor. I saw that my rapprochement with the Lord would be up to me; I took heart.

The pastor must have sensed the return of my courage, because he placed a hand over mine, favored me with a benign smile, withdrew his hand and changed the subject. "Thank you for bringing your Lutheran friend to services," he said. "Evidently a lovely person in every way."

"She is, Pastor," I said. "The kindest woman I ever met. And a medical doctor."

"Will you bring her again?"

"I hope to. I think her Christianity may be more practical and nominal than a matter of tested faith. I pray that God will intervene with her. She's probably the best person I ever knew that wasn't certainly saved."

"Are her sins great?"

"I don't know."

"Are you very attached to her?"

"She's going home to Sweden in a few weeks."

"To stay?"

"I think so."

"We'll pray for her," he said.

I took my leave, went back to my tiny apartment and prayed sedulously for many hours. I presented the history of my life to God, Who already knew not only the part I could recount, but also the part I had yet to live and about which I could know nothing. I told my story to Him complete and without excuses, but I asked to be forgiven for each of my sinful acts as I recalled them. I asked for forgiveness for years of sinful ideation, for my adultery with Marie, for attempting suicide, for wasting part of Beth's life by invading, occupying and finally leaving it, for disappointing my children. I prayed to be brought nearer to God's presence. I prayed for Solveig to be saved, but for the first time I expected to play no part in that drama. I prayed for Bartley to be saved as well. I confessed my incapacity to bring the two of them to God and foresaw that I would have to let that go. I re-dedicated the energy I had devoted to their case to delivering myself more fully into God's hands. It seemed to work. I felt relief. I felt once again that I was being heard.

A couple of weeks passed, during which I made no effort to see Solveig. I worked at my job by day and studied the Bible at night. I attended no meetings on the Vietnam War, but looked in Scripture for clues to its meaning. In the Old Testament, examples of war abounded. For cruelty, any one of them seemed the equal of Vietnam. The answer to the riddle was that now, as in antiquity, war was the means by which the people of God sacrificed themselves and their wealth through collective action in times of historical crisis, just as martyrdom was the means by which the individual sacrificed himself in times of spiritual crisis. Both were pleasing to God, Who knew their votive significance. The suffering attendant on both was part and parcel of the human condition: mortal, devotional and temporary. The reward for such acts of faith outweighs the sacrifice as greatly as Godhead does mortality. So the meaning of Vietnam became clear to me and I thanked God and prayed for victory.

Independence Day fell on a Tuesday that year. With the day off from work, I studied the Bible, looking in the concordance for as many references to war and battle as there was time to read, and at dusk I walked by myself to the park and watched the fireworks display. Couples and families in festive mood sat or lay on blankets spread on the grass and exclaimed at each Roman candle bursting overhead. I sat on a bench and concentrated on the remoteness of these explosions with their delayed popping sounds, like rumors of war rather than war itself. The backdrop of stars, farther away still in the darkening sky, reminded me that the God of Battles was watching also. We were the United States of America, blessed by God and most likely chosen by Him too, of all nations in this century, to champion His purposes. In my lifetime we had rescued Christian Europe from demented pagans bent first on the annihilation of the race into the midst of which God had sent our Savior, and then on a thousand years of statist enslavement; we had rescued a fledgling Christian Asia from initial enslavement by the Japanese; and now we were the bulwark against the hegemonic spread of the first avowed state atheism in human history. The signs of our fealty burst gorgeously above my head; they whistled sometimes in the air like breath drawn in panic on a battlefield. Spent ash drifted down.

I looked around me at the smiles of pleasure on the faces of the spectators and regretted their failure to appreciate the solemnity of the occasion. A Holy War was under way in Vietnam and everywhere else on God's Earth, but my fellow citizens seemed to think they were watching an innocent light show. At the end, dozens of rockets went up simultaneously, their polychromatic starbursts cluttering a sky enfiladed with the yellow-white flashes and unsynchronized thumps of aerial bombs. The crowd cheered and applauded as wildly as if the Victory had been achieved. I walked alone back to my room to read and pray some more.

Solveig phoned my office a few days after that. "Bartley invites you to an auto race," she said. Her musical voice thrilled me less than it had, but I felt less stress, too, now that I had given over the responsibility for bringing her to God. It was still possible to see her as an ally and a friend, since her wish to save children was in no way at odds with my wish to save Christianity. But our evaluations of the war must now at least diverge a little. I imagined that henceforth we'd talk about it less.

"What do you mean?"

"There's a race close to town. Bartley's going to take the car on a trailer and leave it for the weekend. We can take you along either day."

I had no interest in auto racing apart from an uncompelling curiosity, but I cared for Solveig and Bartley and enjoyed their company, and my weekends lately had been lonely ones, so I said yes and picked Saturday. I didn't suppose that for an auto race I could gladly miss the Sunday services.

My friends called for me in front of my building at eight a.m. Bartley was driving a somewhat wrinkled black pickup truck with a trailer in tow. On the trailer was Bartley's sports car, and in the bed of the pickup truck was an assortment of tools, boxes, tires and wheels, fuel cans and other automotive paraphernalia unfamiliar to me, whose total volume appeared to be more than that of the sports car itself. The combination was too big to park. Bartley stopped in the middle of the street and Solveig, in Levi's and a halter-top, jumped down from the pickup cab before she spotted me waiting at the curb. "Hey!" she said. I think we were happy to see each other. She climbed back aboard the truck and I followed, and there we were again: Solveig flanked on one side by Rob Bartley and on the other by me. Bartley extended his right hand to shake mine, then moved it to the gearshift lever, which was between Solveig's knees, and we drove off.

It was a sunny, mild morning, promising to be hot, and we headed out of town on the main road. In the side mirror I could see Bartley's car jiggling behind us as the scenery slid past. Small boys along the way took an interest. Some of them waved. I waved back, but I doubt that this adventure engaged me as much as it was engaging them and my companions. For the entire hour and more that we were on the road, Solveig and Bartley were quite jolly. I was urbane, but watchful and subdued.

At the racetrack there were cars, trucks and trailers by the dozen. We stopped in queue at the front gate. "Got to sign in," Bartley said, and to me, "Be sure to sign all the releases. Solveig'll take you for a ride."

Beyond the gate and its adjacent bleachers I could see the track. It was not the closed circular thing I'd imagined, but the semblance of a scenic highway meandering away and disappearing into wooded hills in the middle distance, then reappearing from another direction closer at hand. From the top of the grandstand, as I discovered later, it was possible to see nearly the whole length of the course—a couple of miles of asphalt road rising, falling and twisting through the natural landscape. But the circulating traffic was manifestly not composed of weekend sightseers. It was moving much too fast, making too much noise, and all traveling one way.

At a reception booth we filled out forms, and Bartley passed some cash across the counter in exchange for plastic identification bands for our wrists. We climbed back into the truck, the gatekeeper waved us through, and we followed signs to a large, gravel paddock filled with towing rigs. Bartley parked the truck and unloaded the car from the trailer. "Want to take it through tech?" he said to Solveig. "I'll get dressed."

"Okay," she said, with that happy smile she seemed to display in response to virtually everything. "Get in," she said, pointing me to the passenger seat. I had never been in Bartley's sports car. It was a close fit. Solveig twisted the ignition key and the engine started with a loud, blatting roar that took me entirely by surprise. "Bartley took the muffler off," she shouted. She put the car in gear and we moved noisily off, picking our way at knee height through wandering crowds. "Taking it through tech" consisted of waiting in a line of cars while some people in white shirts and caps inspected and approved various things, including a pair of helmets stowed behind the seats, and applied a sticker to the steel hoop over the cockpit. When we arrived approved back at the pickup truck we found Bartley resplendent in a fireproof jumpsuit.

"Are we legal?" he said. "I'll warm it up." He climbed into the seat vacated by Solveig, fastened a belt around the seat vacated by me, and strapped himself in place with belts across his lap, over his shoulders and between his legs, all anchored by a single steel latch at his navel. He donned one of the helmets, handed the other to Solveig, restarted the engine and drove blatting off toward the entrance to the track. Solveig and I climbed up the grandstand to watch his progress.

Bartley's car was dark green, and for the occasion he had applied white circles with the black numerals "64" to the doors. We saw a man with a flag wave Bartley onto the track, and then we watched as Bartley's car joined the traffic and snarled into the distance. In less than two minutes Bartley was passing under us again and proceeding once more into the distance; it all looked and sounded like the first time. Solveig fished a stopwatch out of her Levi's pocket and hung it by a lanyard from her neck. When Bartley appeared in front of us again, she started the watch, and when he came around the third time she stopped it, read the face and wrote the number on a clipboard. She seemed practiced. After twenty minutes or so, during which Bartley circulated quite regularly around the track and Solveig timed his passages, the general roar of engines began to subside and I saw the cars parading through an exit to the paddock. In a minute the track was empty and there was relative quiet. Solveig danced down the bleachers and I followed. We met Bartley at the truck.

"Ready for a ride?" he asked me. "Solveig's going to drive the next practice session. She'll take you." He unstrapped and lifted off his helmet, mopped it inside and handed it to me. On the back I read, in embossed tape, "Robert Bartley, DOB 2/8/38, O-positive, tetanus 6/66." A slight frisson, which I discounted. I tried on the helmet, which was too big, but I discounted that too.

We unbelted the passenger seat and I climbed into it and deduced how to attach the harnesses. With everything in place and cinched snugly, I couldn't move. My arms were free, I could rotate my head and I could shuffle my feet, but my torso was immobilized. Solveig put a denim jacket on over her halter-top, buttoned it to the neck, strapped on her helmet and, sitting behind the wheel, raised her arms in the air and let Bartley attach her belts. She restarted the engine. Bartley kissed the top of her helmet, slapped the top of mine and stood back. Solveig pushed the gear lever forward and we bumped away over the gravel to join a line of cars waiting for the track. At the head of the line we were stopped by a man who tugged at our seatbelts, and then by a man with a furled yellow flag who never looked at us, but held his left hand palm-outward in front of us and peered intently over our heads and the low wall that separated us from the track. When he turned his hand palm-inward and waved us on, I was subjected to the first of a series of intense and unexpected physical sensations. The engine roared and we accelerated rocket-like onto the track. I gasped and turned my head to look at Solveig. A band of golden hair visible between the edge of her helmet and the collar of her jacket gave back the sun, her eyes darted to the rearview mirror and then ahead, she snapped back the stubby gear lever on the console between us, and another surge of acceleration banged my helmet into the headrest behind me. I turned my attention to the front and saw that we were accelerating into a diving, sweeping right-hand turn. The car seemed to be going sideways, and Solveig seemed intent on running off the road to the right, but no sooner had we reached the inside edge of the track than we began to drift outward again and slide up the gradient toward the outside of the track, at whose edge was a concrete wall. I was in sudden, total and abject terror. I watched fascinated as we approached the wall at a shallow angle, still accelerating. The wall was smeared with black tire rubber and long streaks of paint that I realized had once decorated cars like the one I was in. By some amazing dispensation, our trajectory became parallel to the wall at the exact moment we reached it, so we never actually struck, Solveig slapped the gear lever forward again and the acceleration continued with barely an interruption. The track ahead, bounded on the left by the wall and the grandstand, was now wide, flat and straight for several hundred feet, a space occupied only by a yellow car some distance in front that had been waved out just before ours. That car was crossing the track from left to right at a shallow angle, and we followed exactly in its wake, still accelerating. The yellow car seemed to be keeping its lead. As it reached the right edge of the track I saw a brief flash of brake lights and the yellow car veered leftward and disappeared. Solveig switched the lever to what I guessed was fourth and hoped was the last of our gears, and the frantic pitch of the unmuffled engine fell a bit. I peeked at the speedometer and saw the needle wavering unconfidently between 95 and 105 miles per hour. At the same moment we arrived at the end of the grandstand. The track bent left and slightly downward. This was where the yellow car had used its brakes, but Solveig evidently didn't so much as lift her foot off the throttle, because there was no change in the pitch of the engine. I felt a tremendous force trying to throw me into the undergrowth on the right, but I was pinned in place by my harness. Ahead and downhill I saw the yellow car again, less than half as far away as before, its brake lights flashing on, a wooden platform on the right mounted with a green flag and two or three white-clad people, and beyond them no sign whatever of a continuation of the track. I closed my eyes, lowered my head and wondered that I had forgotten to pray. My oversize helmet wobbled and I cringed to remember the possible mark of the beast Dymo-labeled to the back of it.

God knew my intention, which I offered wordlessly. I began to feel sick. A tremendous decelerative force dragged my head and arms forward and loaded my shoulders, chest and groin against the harness. I heard the engine blat twice, then begin rising in pitch, and the forces on my body suddenly switched leftward. I felt sure I would vomit. I opened my eyes and the crisis seemed to pass. We were still on the track, which was flanked on the right by swampy ground and on the left by a chain-link fence and bleachers. We were accelerating hard through a long, left-hand bend. The yellow car was now less than fifty feet ahead. Solveig shifted up from second to third gear, I suppose, and a moment later there remained less than a car length between us. A few hundred feet ahead I could see the track turning sharply to the right at the foot of a hill. Inside the corner was another wooden platform with a green flag and personnel, and at the left, just before the corner, was a series of equally spaced signs marked 150, 100 and 50. As we reached the sign marked 150, the yellow car moved across our nose to occupy a line just to the left of the track center. As we passed the sign marked 100, the brake lights flashed on. Out of the corner of my eye I saw Solveig's hands dart clockwise and then back, the yellow car fell away on our left and we arrived ahead of it at the 50 sign. The deceleration I'd felt with my eyes closed I now felt again. The engine blatted, Solveig shifted down, the howl rose and we scrambled around the corner, Bartley's sports car pointed a little to the right of our actual direction of travel, and accelerated up the hill.

I was quite uncomfortable, partly on account of the physical forces and partly on account of my physical helplessness. I imagined that pitched battle in a war must be like this: no time to reconnoiter, no time to reflect, no time to make orderly provision for anything. Bullets were flying at me and there was no time even to center my mind on prayer. I glanced leftward at Solveig, a warrior to my helpless civilian. She was even busier than I, her eyes, hands and feet moving constantly, as if she were heavily armed and carrying the battle to the enemy. What she was doing looked like criminal insanity. She was putting me in terror of my life, without reflection or apology, and I was afraid to interrupt her concentration by screaming at her to stop. Later I thought I must have been seeing an epitome of the soldier in combat, too intent on survival to entertain a moral scruple. I understood then for the first time how, in emergent circumstances, anyone, Godly or not, might murder another person.

We crested the hill and were momentarily weightless; I heard the engine overspeed as the driving wheels left the ground; then we plunged downward into a bowl-shaped curve that turned back on itself, and we were in view of the grandstand once again, now far away on our left, bright-colored cars reduced by distance rushing along the wall in front of it. We reached another bowl-shaped curve, this one announced by another trio of numbered signs, plunged and reversed direction again so that the grandstand was at a distance on our right, then accelerated over a long, nearly straight stretch through three gears, and suddenly I saw that we had arrived back at the place where we had first driven onto the track. This time, instead of accelerating, since we were already traveling a little over one hundred miles per hour, Solveig stepped hard on the brake, and then we were recapitulating exactly our previous trajectory through the first turn, complete with the slide, the feint to the inside of the track, the drift up toward the grandstand wall with its rubber and paint marks, the acceleration through gears in a straight line toward the far side of the track at the far end of the grandstand.

This degree of familiarity with what on the previous lap had been entirely new sensations, and the knowledge of what to expect ahead, increased my confidence just a little, but it was enough to let me offer a prayer of thanksgiving for our safety thus far, and to ask God that if it were His will, we should be delivered safely back to the paddock, and soon.

Out of curiosity, to prevent nausea, and with growing confidence that Solveig would not kill us, I kept my eyes open for the renegotiation of the blind turn at the flag station, and learned that what had seemed a solid berm with no exit was really the left edge of the track where it made a 120-degree turn to the right between sandbanks. From that cul-de-sac we emerged once more onto the sweeping left-hand section where we had overtaken the yellow car. This time, as she completed the upshift to third gear, Solveig lifted her arm high and pointed over my head, and I was startled two seconds later by an explosion of noise and motion at my right elbow as a car I hadn't seen before rushed past, dodged leftward directly in front of us, drew away quickly, braked somewhere after the sign ahead numbered 100, turned rightward up the hill, crested it and was gone by the time we arrived at the bottom. I was astonished. I had thought we were traveling as fast as it was possible to go without crashing. By the time we had crested the hill and negotiated the bowl-shaped switchback on the downgrade, the fast car had already exited the second switchback and could be seen rushing away below us in the direction opposite ours. Solveig's hands, feet and eyes were as busy as ever, but the world had changed. This activity that had seemed so exhilarating, frightening and bizarre, now seemed frightening, bizarre and futile. So much for secular wars with secular aims. Bartley's helmet, too big for me and with the Satanic tetanus booster date documented on the back, wobbled on my head and dropped globules of perspiration on my neck and face. We accelerated, engine screaming, to the second switchback, slowed precipitously and carouseled down the bowl to the long straightaway. This time, instead of following the straightest line toward the distant first turn, we hugged the left side of the track, Solveig lifted her right arm, and we drove, slowing, onto a road that I hadn't noticed before, separated from the track by a low wall, and proceeded into the paddock. We were delivered. I bowed my helmeted head and thanked God.

Other cars were whizzing over the parts of the track I could still see. I was surprised—but relieved— that Solveig had driven only two laps before bringing me back in. As sensitive as I knew her to be, it seemed possible that she had detected my discomfort and taken pity, even though she seemed not to have looked at me even once while we were out.

We bumped along slowly on the gravel. Solveig undid her chinstrap, lifted her helmet and shook out her hair, golden in the summer sun. "What do you think?" she called above the unmuffled noise of the exhaust.

"It made me very nervous," I said.

She nodded and smiled. We arrived at the trailer and stopped beside it, and Solveig switched off the engine. The relative quiet was a further relief, although the droning *continuo* of circulating cars could be heard from the track. Solveig smiled again and gave my arm a chummy pat. "Don't ride with Bartley," she said.

CHAPTER FIVE
DISEASE

The rest of that day yielded not much more than sunburn and a measure of chagrin. Bartley and I sat in the grandstand and ate hotdogs from a concession stand and watched Solveig practicing on the track. Then Solveig and I sat in the grandstand, eating hotdogs, and watched Bartley. Then there was a break for lunch, during which the white-suited people from the wooden flagging platforms here and there around the track rode to the paddock in pickup trucks and ate hotdogs from the concession stand. In the afternoon, I sat alone in the grandstand and watched the cars— dozens of them in batches of four—rushing one by one around the race course in time trials, no car ever closer to another than two or three hundred yards. It was ineffably boring. Bartley and Solveig drove Bartley's car separately, two or three times each. As I learned later, Bartley drove faster than Solveig and won a trophy for second place. Solveig won a trophy for first place, but in a separate class for women. Late in the afternoon, after the time trials, Solveig joined me in the grandstand and we watched a dozen cars, one of them Bartley's, line up in front of us in alternating ranks of three and two, to swarm away, at the drop of a green flag, in a single, roaring mass—an actual race, like the one Solveig had imitated in the morning with me aboard. This was the only automobile race I had ever witnessed on-site, and it seemed much more violent, frightening and loud than anything on television. After my experience in the morning, I could appreciate the vertiginous flight of these little cars as they dodged about, at quite disconcertingly close quarters, looking for an advantage. Bartley had started the race near the back of the pack, but he forged his way toward the front as the cluster of cars became a train and the intervals between cars increased. Each time Bartley overtook and passed another car, Solveig danced like a dervish. After several laps it became clear that Bartley had passed as many cars as he would ever catch and that no one else on the track was challenging for a position. The race had become a sparsely-concerted parade, fully as boring as the time trials (aptly named!), and then the man with the green flag displayed a black and white checkered flag, and one by one the cars passed under it and slowed, Bartley finishing in third place. The skin of my face, arms and neck felt like seared vellum from my day in the sun, and I doubted I would ever attend another motorsports event.

Solveig bounded down the grandstand steps and I followed. Her blond hair fluttered on her shoulders as it had in the first dream after I met her, but now we were in a bright landscape, although the sun was lowering, and we were hurrying to meet Bartley. My disappointment was complete. I no longer believed in our alliance. I felt lonely in company. I wondered if I were good enough to sustain a love that was not requited.

By the time Solveig and Bartley had collected their trophies and covered Bartley's car for the night, it was nearly dusk. Hunger gnawed at my stomach, my exposed skin burned and I felt grimy. In the cab of the pickup truck, riding away from the track and barely two miles along the road, I fell asleep and dreamed I was wearing Bartley's helmet.

Much later a sudden stillness startled me awake. We were stopped in the street in the darkness in front of my building and Bartley had shut off the engine. I lifted my head from Solveig's right shoulder, embarrassed that the corner of my mouth was damp, and certain that I had been snoring.

"You with us?" Bartley said. "We were going to stop for dinner but you seemed whipped."

"Oh, no, thanks," I said. "What an outing." I wished to be anywhere but in the company of people. I opened the truck door and climbed down.

"Thanks for coming along," Bartley called. "Get some sleep!"

"Good night," Solveig said.

I raised a hand in valediction and went indoors.

In my apartment I raided the pantry for something to soothe the griping in my stomach, then I drew a tepid bath, undressed and sank into it. My body looked like alabaster bracketed between the carmine of my sunburned arms and hands. I ached throughout. Once again I felt that my attention to Solveig had sent me off the course of my devotion to God. I listened for signs of Him in the room, in my head, in my intentions, but I seemed to be alone. It was as if the guns had temporarily fallen silent and I was left in no-man's land, out of the sight of my enemy, but abandoned by my Ally, who had retreated. I was exhausted and had no wish to fight. I knew I couldn't stay where I was, but I didn't know where to go.

I washed the day's sun-baked dust out of my hair, soaped my body and rinsed off. The water in the tub had grown murky and now was growing cold, but I felt too weak to lift myself out. I reached the handle for the hot water with my left foot and turned it on, to buy time. For no reason, there flashed in my memory the image of my feet dragging in the snow on the night when the ambulance crew interrupted my death. I felt as if I had come full circle and was near to death again. More out of duty than conviction, I closed my eyes and prayed that God would save me. I struggled up, shut off the water, climbed out of the tub and let it drain. I toweled myself dry, put on pajamas and went to bed.

The next morning, Sunday, I awoke refreshed, but stinging with sunburn, and went to church. In those familiar surroundings and circumstances I was at home again, and the previous night's apostasy seemed unaccountable. God was present; the congregation was there to confirm the faith of our community; the pastor, finite and human though he was, reassured me. I sang the hymns, read the responses and joined in the prayers. God had restored me with sleep after my exhaustion and with peace after—what? Not doubt, surely, but discouragement. At the door following the recessional, the pastor noted my sunburn and asked after Solveig. I thanked him for the sermon and told him she'd be leaving soon for Sweden.

Late in August she phoned to say goodbye. Her cheerful voice, full of lilting, Scandinavian music, once more made me think of God's grace. I was glad to know that the world harbored such a person—tall, blonde, lovely, kind, generous, intelligent and devoted to the service of humanity. I regretted that her appreciation of the Godhead was not rigorous and that she and I could not be yoked together to do God's work. But I foresaw that I'd remember and pray for her for the rest of my life.

In September, without regret, I left the job that was to have been my career and began my theological studies at Divinity Bible Seminary. It was good to be immersed in the matter that was most vital to me, and to be surrounded by like-minded people. With the other first-year students I enrolled in what was known as the Foundation Curriculum, a series of courses basic to understanding the living of an evangelical and Christian life: the meaning of Christ's passage on earth, the certainty of His return, the meaning and practice of prayer, baptism by water and the giving of tithes, and the means of witnessing and living in the Holy Spirit. Beyond the Foundation Curriculum and the course in preaching that had called me to seminary in the first place, I enrolled in courses that interested me, confident that God would reveal His purposes more exactly as I went along.

Of my fellow students, most were five or ten years younger than I; two or three were about my age; another handful were substantially older. I felt somewhat solicitous of the welfare of the younger students, but not much attracted to a dialog with them. The older students excited me more, and I might have looked for a friend and mentor among them, but willy-nilly the school faculty supplied me with just such a person. This was Randall Lang, a man of about fifty, very intelligent, of medium height and shaped like a barrel, the instructor in a course I chose on the significance of wilderness in Scripture, and my faculty advisor.

Randall was deeply charismatic. Meeting him put me in mind again of the question of war. He had powerful qualities of leadership, but one felt them more in face-to-face conversation than when he spoke in public. He was a good teacher and a competent preacher, but when he sat or stood opposite you and fixed you with his black eyes, he was magnetic. The first time we spoke I hoped he'd tell me where the battle was, that I might follow him into it.

His discourse was not like that of anyone else. Considering he was a member of a seminary faculty, his speech was remarkably lacking in Christian rhetoric, although its substance was Christian enough. His words were allusive and pythonic. At times their meaning eluded me.

Randall was married to a small, blonde, green-eyed, pretty woman about halfway in age between Randall and me. Joanna was a journeyman pianist and organist, and frequently, in a bright soprano, sang solo pieces at our chapel services.

"Come to dinner," Randall said to me a few days after our first meeting. "You have a wife or a friend to bring?"

"Neither," I said.

"Come anyway," he said.

I arrived at their door on the appointed evening with a potted plant for Mrs. Lang. The house was large, comfortable and attractively furnished, its Christian iconography muted. I had to reach down to take Joanna's hand, surprised on this first acquaintance that she was not over five feet tall.

"I'm pleased to meet you," she said. "Now we'll find out why Randall likes you so much." If her enthusiasm was only polite and a social gambit, I was flattered anyway. To be liked by Randall was a boon.

The Langs gave me the freedom of the house and disappeared together into the kitchen to put finishing touches to the meal. I wandered about the living room, scouting the bookcase and admiring a large, original painting over the mantelpiece. It was evidently a depiction of Christ in Gethsemane, but in a realistic style, its only concession to the popular tradition in religious painting being the halo at the head of Jesus; but this was so subtly wrought that it seemed an effect of ambient light in the natural scene. The figure of Jesus was small in the scale of the painting, subsumed in the larger business of the canvas, praying at night in a wild garden. It was the least ambiguously human representation of the Son of God I had ever seen, and as melancholy as any Pietà.

I was not surprised to see that the bookcase contained a lot of Biblical commentary and history of the Holy Land, but I hadn't expected to find the sacred texts of traditions other than ours. I counted a couple dozen of them, ranging from the Bhagavad-Gita through the Koran and the Egyptian Book of the Dead to the Douai Bible and even the Book of Mormon and the Pearl of Great Price. Superfluous stuff, it seemed to me, in the context of a life of Faith—unless one needed familiarity with these source materials in order to combat effectively the error they propagated. I leafed through the Pearl of Great Price, regretting the ease with which modern prophets can suppose that God inserts Himself into their politics with the kind of particularity that might be expected of a big-city ward heeler. My own struggle to understand the great questions of war and public morality was on another scale entirely, and—up to that point in my life—far less well requited than Brigham Young's.

The blond head of Joanna Lang appeared around the corner of the bookcase and invited me to table. In the dining room I sat down facing her; Randall stood at the head of the table and offered a blessing. Roughly, it went like this: "Father, we thank You for what we are about to enjoy: food to sustain us and the company of a new friend—neither very rich, but both, we believe, pleasing in Your eyes. May all of us be truly worthy of these gifts."

Joanna murmured "Amen" and so did I, although I found myself reviewing what had just been said, to make certain I wanted to subscribe to all of it. I was to learn, in the time I knew him, that many of Randall's utterances needed to be heard twice.

He served us from a platter at his elbow. The main dish was a humble pot roast, moist and inclined to disintegrate, but richer, it seemed to me, than Randall had represented it in his blessing. It was garnished with vegetables and new potatoes, all steeped in the juices of the meat.

"Something happened to you," Randall said. This statement, whether rhetorical or—as it sounded— simply declarative, came without preamble and while the meal's first forkful was on its way to my lips. I looked at Randall and glanced across the table at Joanna. Her eyes were directed at her plate and she was chewing. I looked at Randall again.

"Yes," I said. "I nearly died."

"And why didn't you?"

"God saved me. I did a terrible thing, and God gave me the chance to make up for it."

"To atone."

"Yes."

"And you're atoning now."

"Every day is a day of atonement," I said. Joanna looked up and smiled at me, and I took my first bite. It was rich. I felt I was in the company of friends, and more at home than at any time since before I met Marie and lost my family.

"Talk about it whenever you want to," Randall said.

"I'm ashamed," I said.

"Haven't talked enough to God about it, then."

This remark took me by surprise. I felt I had done nothing but talk to God since that awful, transforming event, but when Randall said it, it sounded true. Then he added, "Something's gotten away from you."

"What do you mean?"

He shrugged. "I don't know."

There was a long silence, during which the three of us continued to eat. "You know how you get shriven of a thing," Randall said.

"Tell me," I said.

"First," he said, "you don't do it anymore."

"Of course," I said.

"Second, you compensate your victim. If that's possible."

I waited.

"And then you ask God to forgive you. Which He will."

"And if God is the victim? If the sin is against God?"

"All sins are against God."

There was another silence.

"Something's gotten away from you," Randall said again.

"Yes," I said. But I didn't know what it was. Nobody spoke.

"Who did the painting over the mantelpiece?" I asked.

"My pa."

"He's an artist?"

"He passed when I was still a boy. But no. He was a bricklayer."

I looked at Randall's hands. They might have been the hands of a bricklayer too: broad and strong, with short, stubby fingers. "How did your father die?" I asked him.

"Heart disease. Kills the men in my family at about the age of forty."

"You're fifty."

"I'm the rare survivor. When I made my commitment, I figured God and I both knew I'd die at forty. Now I guess only I knew it."

"A deliverance."

"A different life. You think you'll live only to a certain age and you have no example of how to live beyond that age. When you do, it makes you kind of a stranger in the world."

I thought about that. I looked forward ten years and tried to imagine that my death then was certain. I looked across the table at Joanna, who was about forty, and tried to imagine no earthly future for her. It was easier to imagine an indefinite—but long—future for all of us, one that evolved into distant old age, transcendence and eternal reward.

"My own experience was just the opposite," I said to Randall. "I was a stranger before I died—or didn't die. It was when I didn't die that I made my commitment."

"And yet something's gotten away from you," Randall said for the third time.

Now I was lost. The remark, having gone from oracular and recondite on first hearing through true on the second, had become nonsensical. I couldn't imagine what he was talking about. "What do you mean?" I asked.

"I told you before," he said. "I don't know."

I looked at Joanna for help, but she only smiled and shrugged.

We passed the evening in talk about the seminary, the Langs' friends, people I could expect to meet while I was enrolled there. At our first conference I had told Randall, as my advisor, about the vocation to preach that came to me at the anti-war gathering in the church basement near the university. In the living room after dinner, over coffee, while Randall smoked one of his pipes, Joanna told me she was glad I intended to take the pulpit. "You'll be very impressive," she said. "The power of the Lord is easier to see when it's expressed through a strong and handsome man." I may have blushed. I had no sense of myself just then as a preacher, but I felt magisterial in the presence of this small woman, and worthy in the company of her strong and charismatic husband. I had virtually no experience of public speaking, and for most of my life a phobic reaction to the very thought of it, but I felt confident that God would provide me with the words and the courage I would need. Joanna Lang sat before me as the embodiment of the hungry I could hope to feed. My heart leaped up.

CHAPTER SIX
PESTILENCE

If since committing myself to seminary I had felt doubts and insecurity about learning to preach—and I had—I now felt the power of my vocation redoubled, and I looked forward with an eagerness I felt for no other part of the curriculum, to the meetings of my class in homiletics. Whatever fear I had had of the crowd staring, my mind a blank, and the terrible, clangorous silence communicating only shame and pity—that fear was now replaced with a passion to stand up and exhort, to tell the entire Truth to the people of God, so that they could hear it in all of its vivid joy and clarity, perhaps for the first time.

My professor of homiletics, George Woodrick, was a small, lantern-jawed man in his sixties. Dynamically, his personality was a near-inversion of Randall Lang's. Where Randall was almost seductively charismatic in close quarters, Woodrick was amiable but unimpressive. And while Randall could speak plausibly and with authority to a room full of people, Woodrick could launch the same room—or a large auditorium, or a tent meeting of thousands—into an orbit of pure ecstasy, weeping, laughing, shouting, crying in tongues, falling on the ground. Every time he preached, he demonstrated the truth of the proposition that the Word finally is transmitted—as we said in the gender-elliptical language of those days—from man to men. No amount of Bible study or reading of the commentaries could convey with the same force the truth that struck the heart of the listener when it was dispensed from the bosom of a preacher like George Woodrick.

I never discovered whether Woodrick was also— beyond his marvelous example—a good teacher, because my vocation so overtook the process of learning the craft that the rankest pedagogical incompetence could not have prevented me succeeding; but the same preaching course that trained me, trained some very indifferent preachers too. I believed that if God called us all to preaching, He had called me most emphatically, and it was this that made the difference.

Woodrick's course design required each participant to become familiar with and to deliver to the class an example of each of the categories of sermon heard in the evangelical church—one meditating on a particular Biblical text, one exegetical, one intended to evangelize the unsaved. My own devotion was such that every sermon I composed became evangelical when I delivered it. Whatever the subject, and however sophisticated those first, academic congregations might be, I felt I had more to convey than they could know by any other means than through my preaching. The vocation was so strong that my spirit wanted at every moment to leap from my body and over the pulpit, to drive out every vestige of error, resistance or indifference lurking in those hearts.

Outside the walls of the seminary that winter, while I became a preacher, the world gave signs of falling apart. The minority of Americans opposed to the war became more strident and appeared to grow. At the end of January, when the President and General

75

Westmoreland were telling us that the war would soon be won, the Communist enemy suddenly rose up and threatened to overrun every provincial capital in South Vietnam. Vietcong soldiers breached the outer perimeter of the US Embassy in Saigon. Inside the seminary the ground was covered in snow. It was one year since I had been dragged through that other winter's snow by an ambulance crew sent by God to save me to be His witness and to preach His Truth. My life had changed more profoundly in that single year than in all the rest of the time I had been on earth. It was right to say I had been born again. My authentic life, the true one that God had called me to, was only one year old.

My friendship with Randall Lang continued and deepened, although he was in many ways an enigma. His personality had a warmth, immediacy and candor belied by the arcaneness of his speech. His role in my life was triple: as my faculty advisor, in which role I experienced and revered him almost as a father; as my instructor in the course on the theme of wilderness in Scripture, in which role he stimulated me intellectually; and as my best friend, in which role he gave me plain companionship, treated me as his peer, and shared his thoughts, secular and sacred.

As the winter term progressed, my gift of preaching began to be talked about, even though I had preached only within Dr. Woodrick's course. I was offered a Sunday service in the seminary chapel at the semester break—very rare for a first-year student—and I accepted it gladly and without trepidation. I knew I had only to pray to be filled with the Spirit, and I knew I had only to see the faces uplifted in the pews to utter the Truth.

In any case, my subject came to me instantly and effortlessly, suggested by the public events of that winter. I remembered the words of the psalmist, "Blessed be the Lord my strength, which teacheth my hands to war, and my fingers to fight," and a few verses later, "Send thine hand from above; rid me, and deliver me out of great waters, from the hand of strange children; Whose mouth speaketh vanity, and their right hand is a right hand of falsehood." These verses seemed addressed to the growing generational difference over the war, and to the Godless trajectory of political, social and sexual rebellion being followed and proclaimed by the generation—only ten years younger than mine— just reaching adulthood. I composed a sermon on the text, "Deliver me from the hand of strange children."

When I stood in the pulpit on the Sunday morning to preach, I saw a congregation well salted with people of the generation I was about to belabor. Faculty and community were represented too. I spotted the Langs in a pew near one of the side aisles; I think they tried to make themselves inconspicuous, afraid their presence might make me self-conscious. But I was prepared—eager—to preach to as many and as diverse people as could be crowded within range of my voice. The text of my first public sermon is lost—burned or mislaid in some Satanic intervention years later—but I departed so often from the words I'd written that it hardly matters. The people in the pews that day seemed, after the first five minutes, to anticipate me. My excitement was great, but theirs was greater. I established the truth that Vietnam was a battle in the Holy War against atheism and the rule of man over men. I showed that Satan was marshaling his forces where we were most vulnerable—among our impressionable and idealistic youth—and that he was exploiting their sexual vitality to bind them together in an alliance against their elders. I quoted the slogan, "Make love, not war," then glossed it as "Christian soldiers! Abandon the field to fornicate!" I warned that the strangeness of our children was a Satanic work in progress, and that God willed us to bring them to Him by any moral means. At the end of half an hour I was shouting, the congregation was shouting in response, and some were weeping. Among the weepers, I saw, was Joanna Lang.

When the Langs came to congratulate me after the service, something had happened to Joanna. She offered her hand; I took it, and I felt something mesmeric surging in her flesh. Her eyes were huge and excited; she seemed electric with fear. I couldn't look at her. I turned to Randall, who threw his arms around me and crushed me in a bear hug. He seemed as excited as Joanna, but with what I took to be avuncular pride and frank admiration of craft. I had done well and I thanked God for it: all glory to Him. I was glad that Randall was proud, but I felt no pride myself— only joy in this confirmation that I was truly called.

The Langs had been inviting me to dinner two or three times per month throughout the fall and winter term. Sometimes I was the only guest; sometimes there were as many as six of us at table. Once or twice an uncoupled and probably eligible woman was included in the party, but I never took more than a brotherly interest in any of the guests. The first dinner at the Langs' following my preaching debut, I was once again alone with my hosts.

Joanna was still not herself. There was a giddiness about her that made me think less of fear than of contagion. Her eyes were unnaturally bright and her skin unnaturally flushed, as if she were consumptive and had a degree or two of fever. I told her I hoped she was feeling well. A look of dark tragedy flickered behind her eyes, but so briefly that I wasn't sure I'd seen it, and then she smiled brightly, squeezed my elbow and turned away without speaking. In the living room after dinner, while Joanna was in the kitchen out of earshot, I mentioned her unfamiliar affect to Randall.

"She's at a spiritual crux of some sort," Randall said. "I think she wants to talk with you."

"Really?" I said. "Of course, I'd be glad to talk."

"She's been agitated since you preached. Want to talk with her now? I thought I'd fill a pipe and take a walk. The weather's fine."

"Of course," I said again.

Randall fetched a light jacket from the hallway closet, tucked a pipe and tobacco pouch into a pocket, poked his head past the swinging door to the kitchen and said something to Joanna. In the vestibule he stopped, packed the bowl of his pipe and lit it up. He waved away a cloud of aromatic smoke. "I know I can count on you," he said, and he left the house.

I felt a little off balance, but pleased and humbled to think that the Langs had such confidence in me, their junior in every way. I stood for a moment rooted to the spot I'd been occupying when Randall closed the front door. The house was quiet; no sound came from the kitchen. I walked into the living room and hovered tentatively in front of the mantelpiece and the painting by Randall's father. After a minute or two, with no further sign to guide me, I walked to the kitchen door, swung it ajar and looked in. Joanna was standing in the middle of the room with her arms folded across her breast, her head lowered and her eyes downcast.

"Randall said you wanted to speak to me," I said.

She looked up. "Come in," she said.

I pushed through the door and let it swing behind me. Joanna walked the few paces to close the distance between us, wrapped her arms around my torso and laid her head against my chest. The difference in our height was such that, although she was standing upright, her arms naturally enclosed me at the level of my lower ribcage and her head rested over my heart. Utterly surprised, I folded a hand over the back of her head and pressed lightly, hoping I was offering whatever reassurance she might be seeking. But at that instant her body went limp and I found myself supporting her whole weight from her head and the nape of her neck. I relaxed my grip and she slid downward, her encircling arms passing my waist, my buttocks and my thighs, until her mass stabilized on the kitchen floor, her head just bracketed between my knees, her arms folded behind my calves. I stood amazed and—a moment later—terrified. I felt a shock of sexual energy more forceful than any I had experienced since my near-fatal love affair with Marie. I thought I might lose my balance and fall on Joanna. I backed away from her; her arms went slack and let me escape; she sagged on the floor, still on her knees, with her forehead on the tiles as if she were kowtowing. "Please," I said. "Get up."

She didn't move.

I knelt beside her, afraid she might be suffering some physical debility. I could hear her breath, shallow and rapid. "What's wrong?" I asked.

"You've got to help me," she said, her voice escaping muffled from the contortions of her body. "Tell me about the Rapture."

I recited to her from Corinthians: "For the Lord Himself will descend from heaven with a shout, with the voice of the archangel, and with the trumpet of God."

"Yes," she said. "Is it possible that He's here already?"

"No," I said. "We'd know it. All of the End Time things that are to follow would be happening now."

"But something is happening," she said. She seemed unable to catch her breath. "Lift me up," she said. "Please, lift me up."

Frightened and confused, I put my hands under her arms and lifted. She offered no help. I hoisted her dead weight off the floor. She moaned and seemed to faint.

Her eyes were closed, her head lolling back. I pressed her body against mine to stabilize us, and immediately her vitality returned. I felt the same animal magnetism surging from her body that I had felt when I took her hand in the chapel after my sermon. She clung to me; her head bobbed forward against my chest and she bit me hard through my shirt. The pain shocked me. She wrapped her legs around mine; I lost my balance and we fell on the kitchen floor.

Sexual *force majeure* overwhelmed me. However bizarre the circumstances, I was lying with a woman for the first time in more than a year, and she was tearing at my shirt. As small as she was, she seemed to be everywhere at once, clambering over my body, dragging her fingers over my scalp, grinding her pelvis against the straining penis that I had been battling so long to overmaster. And she was nipping my neck with her teeth and whimpering in my ear, "Help me, Jesus! Help me, Jesus!"

Hearing those words in those circumstances compounded the horror of what was happening to me. I tried to organize my mind to pray, but my mind gave back Joanna's words. I grabbed her wrists and pinned her arms against my chest, immobilizing her. She screamed out the name of the Savior, and at that moment, to my everlasting sorrow, I was wracked with such a series of detumescent explosions that I thought I might lose consciousness. I felt Joanna thrashing against me and heard her scream. I was as helpless as I had ever been, abandoned by reason and seemingly abandoned by God. I lay on the hard kitchen floor, depleted and ashamed. Joanna quaked beside me. I released her wrists and she wrapped her arms around me and kissed my chest where she had opened the buttons of my shirt. She licked droplets of blood where her teeth had broken my skin. "God hears me," she said.

I was appalled and miserable. The unforgiving floor, the clamminess of semen in my clothes, the loss of my hard-won virtue, Joanna's invocation of the Divine as the sponsor of sin, this terrible misprision of Randall's confidence—these misfortunes made me so wretched that I fell for a moment into doubt of the certainty of my salvation, and thus I became guilty of yet another sin.

I struggled out of Joanna's grasp and picked myself up from the floor. I felt dizzy; I sat on a chair and rested my head in my hands. Joanna lay on her side in front of me. "We still have to talk," she said.

"May God help us both," I said. I left the kitchen, walked to the half-bathroom on the first floor and locked myself in. By the fluorescent light from the medicine cabinet, my reflection in the mirror was wan and tentative. I felt divided from my image, but my image seemed more real than my self: it was watching me. I heard my soul echoing at a distance and saw my reflection gazing in judgment. I wasn't sure where I stood, whether in my body or in the mirror, but I felt unprotected. I looked down into the washbasin and concentrated on the reality of my surroundings until— after a few seconds—I stopped hearing that second self.

I tugged my shirttail loose from my pants, opened the front of my clothing and tried to mop myself clean with a dampened washcloth. My semen had a flat, ashy, stale smell, and there was a lot of it. I tried to understand what had happened in the kitchen, but it was inexplicable. That I had semen to spill in this way was inexplicable. In the midst of a Godly life, without the least hint of danger, I had been ambushed and virtually killed. If, as I believed, God and His angels were my outriders, they had inexplicably been absent when the danger threatened. The mystery that I struggled every day to understand was deeper than I had thought.

I dried with a towel and tucked and zipped my clothing back together. There was a small tear where one of the buttons was sewn to the front of my shirt, and there was a tiny bloodstain from Joanna's bite, but I felt presentable. I would have to face Randall. I had no idea what I would say to him.

When I unlocked the door and emerged, Joanna was waiting for me in the hallway. She reached for my hand but I pulled it away.

"Please don't be afraid to touch me," she said.

"We mustn't touch the way we did before," I said. "It's wrong. It's unfair to all of us. Unfair to Randall. God doesn't want it. It's the plainest sin."

Tears welled in her eyes. She blinked. The tears squeezed past the outer corners of her eyelids and traveled in smooth, symmetrical, convex arcs down her cheeks and into the corners of her mouth. The end of her nose looked damp. She lifted the hand I had spurned and drew the back of it across her face and fetched a deep sigh, a brief paroxysm of caught breath that made her shoulders jump. I felt sorry in the extreme. "I have to touch you," she said. "I've never felt more that someone was from God."

"But the way we touched. It wasn't of God."

She sat suddenly on the floor and began to cry. I stood over her helplessly, knowing that Randall was counting on me, wishing for a sign from God, unsure of how to ask for one. God and I had been disastrously out of touch since I walked into the kitchen. Joanna sobbed at my feet, wiping her hand from time to time across her face. "How can this not be from God?" she said. "You're so young. Maybe you have all the truth in you but you don't know yet what all of it is. Maybe I understand more of it than you do."

My disorientation was complete. I tried to order my thoughts. All at once I felt the same fear of a Satanic presence that had seized me the day I came under the influence of mimosas with Solveig and Bartley. The most plausible explanation for the events of the past half hour was that Satan had somehow invaded Randall's house and shut God out. I felt an impulse to run. I wished Randall would come home immediately. But then the picture flashed in my mind of Randall waving smoke away from his face, and my fear increased. I closed my eyes, bowed my head and called out to God. I stepped around Joanna's huddled body, retreated to the living room, sat on the edge of an overstuffed chair and continued to pray. When I opened my eyes, Joanna was opposite me on another chair, watching with the look of dark tragedy that I had nearly missed earlier in the evening. God had answered me to the extent that I was no longer afraid. No fetor of evil wafted from Joanna. She was small, lovely, vulnerable and sad. I reached a hand to her and pressed her fingers.

"I want to follow you," she said. "I want you to teach me."

"I'm called to preach the Truth to everyone," I said.

"But there's more," she said. "I'm called to follow you. I know it. You can preach to everybody, but God wants me to have my communion with Him through you."

"I'm only a man. God wants you to take Communion through Jesus Christ, the flesh and the blood of the New Testament."

"Jesus was a man," she said.

"Jesus was God."

"God is in you," she said.

I sagged inwardly. Joanna's enthusiasm for my vocation had come, in this dialectic, perilously close to sacrilege, and it had probably risen to the level of actual idolatry. But she was right that God was in me.

"I'm older than you," she was saying. "God has given me experience that illuminates the truth you preach. I know what it is to love." And then she added, "Randall loves you."

I sat silent and perplexed. I nodded my head in assent. I knew that Randall loved me in Christ, just as I loved him. But I sensed that Joanna had meant to convey something different. I waited but she said no more.

A minute passed. Joanna sat opposite me, seemingly calm for the first time that evening, as if she had staked out a position and could rest in it. I was not calm and not ready to rest.

"What have you said to Randall about needing to talk with me?" I asked.

"I told him what I've told you."

"Everything? Does he accept it? It's a strange thing for a woman to say to her husband."

"He believes me."

"Does he approve?"

"He believes me."

"Has he seen this before? Have you tried to follow someone to God in this way before?"

"No," she said. And then she said again, "No."

I felt quite awkward—cast simultaneously into a number of roles, none of them familiar. Joanna had explicitly defined me as her spiritual advisor, but she was talking to me from her ten years' seniority as if I were a child. She had embraced me as carnally as if she were my wife, but by the evidence of her words, it was her husband that loved me. And she was tiny—a fact that made me feel physically protective toward her.

I had no idea how to proceed. She had been resisting my spiritual advice with advice of her own that sounded parental but felt dangerous. As protective of her as she made me feel, self-protection seemed in order too. I was afraid to touch her. Finally I said, "You've been a Christian all your life?"

"Yes," she said.

"But not born again?"

"Yes—born again."

"When did that happen?"

"Soon after I married Randall. Jesus was immanent in our life together. We were very close—the three of us. When it happened it was like a rebirth and a remarriage all at once."

"And when you were reborn—or at any time—did you see His face?"

"The face of Jesus?"

"The face of the Father. The face of God."

"I think so, yes," she said. "I've thought so."

"And what does He look like?"

"You don't know?"

"What does He look like to you?"

She paused. "Not like any person. Not a face, really, but colors—beautiful, pure, shining colors that glow and melt. Very beautiful and thrilling."

"Do you see Him often?" I asked.

"Not often. But when I do, I know it's Him."

"And do you remember when and where you saw Him last?"

"Oh, yes," she said, and her eyes grew moist. "Tonight. When we talked in the kitchen."

CHAPTER SEVEN
FAMINE

To my relief, Randall came in from his walk a few minutes later, stopping on the porch to knock his pipe empty against the heel of his shoe. Joanna put her arms around his shoulders and kissed him on the cheek—the first outward sign of their mutual affection I'd seen in the time I had known them. Randall smiled and kissed the top of her head. "Good talk?" he said.

"Wonderful," she said.

"Anything we should all talk about?"

"I guess not," she said.

I thanked the Langs for their hospitality and took my leave as expeditiously as seemed graceful and decent. I told them I was tired, and it was very true. I went home to my apartment to pray and reconnoiter.

I found myself in another of those periods when God seemed distant and my prayers seemed to dissipate into the void. My question for God had to do with my role in the religious life of women. The religious life of men, and my duty to them in the body of Christ, presented no insuperable challenge to me. In my relations with men, the spiritual was a realm of shared ideas, rich, familiar and unproblematic. With women it had proven to be different. My best efforts to engage Solveig spiritually had yielded nothing. She had not resisted me; she had simply not heard me. And now Joanna seemed to be hearing messages different from the ones I meant to convey. She was not the spiritual ally I had hoped to find in Solveig; she was instead a kind of acolyte, but a rebellious one. I badly needed to hear God's counsel. I poured out my prayers and listened.

I fell asleep that night listening, but it was too soon. I dreamed circumstances that put me on guard against what I now took to be a frontal assault by the forces of the Devil. Awake, I felt confirmed in my belief that God had called me to be a great weapon in His arsenal. The Enemy, in his desperation, was using every fleshly device at his disposal to annihilate me. Asleep and without my rational defenses, I dreamed I was lying naked with Joanna. She was tiny except for her vulva, which was huge and swollen, large enough to admit my huge and swollen penis. I pushed into her and her entire body expanded to accept me. She was crying, and crying out. Her legs spread wider apart as I pushed, and she began to split in half. I closed my arms and legs around her, trying to keep her intact. I realized I was about to ejaculate. I realized also that I was asleep and dreaming, and that the dream was sinful and to be despised. But in my stupor I believed that I had to keep clinging to Joanna in order to save her from disintegration. I ejaculated then, and it was too late to wake up. I fell deeper into sleep, and into other dreams.

My vexed relations with Joanna seemed to have no effect on my relations with Randall. I had thought at first I'd have to confess to him and ask his pardon, but I realized there was nothing for me to confess. Any abuse of Randall's trust had been Joanna's. To broach the subject at all would be to expose Joanna, thus to violate the confidence that both of the Langs had placed in me when Joanna asked for spiritual advice. Randall's conversation was as cordial, allusive and oblique as ever. His only comment on my meeting with his wife was unsolicited and ambiguous: "Joanna thinks a lot of you."

"I'm glad," I said, conscious of ambiguities of my own.

Spring advanced; the snow melted; gray squirrels decapitated the crocuses. What I had to preach was informed largely by political events, none of them of a stripe to make Christians complacent. Eugene McCarthy, an anti-war insurgent of the President's party and hero of the distempered youth I had rebuked from the pulpit, won the primary election in New Hampshire. At the end of March, the President seemed to lose his courage and resigned from the campaign. A few days later, Martin Luther King, a man whose great gifts as a preacher were diluted by a tendency to subordinate God's Truth to the assumptions of his own social program, was murdered while in Tennessee supporting a strike by garbage handlers. I prayed to God to knit up the fabric of our American society, and I preached that atheism would steal a march if we failed to meet our obligations at home and in Vietnam.

In the first warm days of April I happened to meet Rob Bartley on the street. He had just climbed out of the little sports car that Solveig had so terrified me with the summer before, and he was accompanied by a young woman, very pretty, a few inches shorter than

Bartley and therefore substantially shorter than Solveig. This woman had dark hair, large, brown eyes, and a general look of Mediterranean softness. Bartley introduced us; the woman had a Jewish name that I never remembered. Her interaction with Bartley, even on the street, was as physical as Solveig's had been. I looked at Bartley and tried to appreciate his appeal, but, aside from his amiability, it was lost on me. I asked if he had heard from Solveig.

"I got a letter from her a few days ago," he said. "She's back in harness and doing medicine in Stockholm. She asked if I'd seen you. Now I can tell her I have."

"Please say I asked after her."

"I'll do that," Bartley said. "How's it going in seminary?"

"By the grace of God, it's going extremely well. I've discovered a vocation to preach."

"Congratulations!" Bartley said. "I'm impressed. That's got to be a daunting activity."

"Not daunting," I said. "Uplifting. Exciting. Very rewarding."

"I'd like to hear you," Bartley said.

"Most of what I've done is inside the classroom," I said. "But I expect to be given a pulpit a couple of times this summer. I'll invite you."

"And I'll come," Bartley said.

We shook hands and he sauntered away with one arm around the Jewish beauty. I watched them recede down the street and wondered at Bartley's seeming lack of focus. He reminded me of a man at—and the irony struck me at the time—a smorgasbord. He had sampled Solveig, and now he was evidently sampling this Mediterranean. He gave a dilettante's attention to racing his little road car. He appeared to be irreligious, but he wanted to hear me preach. It occurred to me that I didn't actually know what line of work he was in.

As the academic year drew near its end, I reviewed my accomplishments. I had learned to preach. I had distinguished myself as a student in my other courses as well, and what I learned in those courses I regarded as at the service of my preaching. I had found a friend and a mentor in Randall Lang, but I had also found a moral challenge and a mortal hazard in his wife, who made no secret of her devotion to my example but seemed not to care that her interest in me could be understood or misunderstood as sexual by anyone bothering to notice. Surely Randall must have noticed; but if he did, he never alluded to it. I sensed that some of the faculty wives had noticed, but if they did, they never spoke of it within earshot. The constant threat posed by Joanna's failure to distinguish between sex and spirit troubled me both awake and asleep; it made me wish that God would either take away the temptations of my flesh entirely or else send a mate suitable to be yoked with me in His work. I prayed for either outcome, but neither happened. I found myself wondering again, as I had in other crises, if some willfulness of mine were causing me not to hear God's real intentions for me. I prayed and listened, but much of what I heard was my own voice urging me to preach. I tried to make my mind a blank, hoping that God in

His purity would fill the void with clear and certain evidence of His intention, and that He would let me see His face. Instead I tended to fall asleep, to dream my unsatisfactory dreams.

I considered going to Randall for advice. I felt allied with him, and that we could discuss the problem of Joanna without touching on specifics that might violate Joanna's confidence. The agapic love that flowed from my Christian heart now fell most particularly on Randall anyway; it seemed to me that of earthly things nothing could be more important at this time than to resolve whatever was ambiguous in the relationships among the three of us, their pivot being the woman who was loved by and bound in Holy Matrimony to Randall, but whose fixation gave me no rest.

I passed a couple of weeks in interior debate about the best way to broach my subject; finally I just prayed for wisdom and determined to leave the upshot to the grace of God. I presented myself to Randall at the end of a meeting of his wilderness course and proposed that we go for a walk.

"Glad to," he said. He filled a pipe and lighted it and we set off.

It was a fine spring day, mild and sunny, much like the one a year earlier when I first walked with Solveig. We wandered, silent at first, through the seminary campus, glorious just then with leafing and blossoming trees. Randall didn't offer to speak, evidently satisfied to enjoy the beauty that surrounded us. Eventually I risked breaking the mood.

"I wonder if you find Joanna's enthusiasm for my pastorate completely appropriate," I said.

He clenched his teeth around the stem of his pipe and spoke past it in a way that could have been disguising a smile. "I will, as soon as you have a pastorate."

"Maybe that's what I mean," I said. "I don't have a flock. But since I preached, Joanna has been treating me in a way that seems...idolatrous. Don't you think? Has she talked to you about me?"

"She hasn't stopped," he said, still talking past the pipe stem.

"Well, what do you think?"

"I think she thinks you'll be a great conduit for God's Truth."

"You think she's right about that?"

He took the pipe out of his mouth. "The Truth is definitely in you when you're up there preaching."

I nodded; we walked on silently for several seconds. "Do you think women experience God's Truth differently from men?" I asked.

"Shouldn't," he said. "Not systematically. Would naturally be small differences from person to person, but systematically between the sexes? I wouldn't think so."

"Hm," I said, not sure where to go next. This diffidence, under the circumstances, might equally have arisen from fear of Randall's anger or fear of violating Joanna's unwelcome trust, but in fact I felt out of my depth, though quite calm. I wasn't sure I had the insight to do justice to my subject. Finally I said,

"Her understanding of God's love seems a little sexualized."

"I know that about her," Randall said.

I was suddenly breathless. For the first time in my friendship with Randall, I was afraid to be in his company. My mind scrambled to find continuity back to the safety of the earlier part of our conversation. I heard in his remark, "I know that about her," the echo of an invasion of the Langs' deepest intimacy. It was as if I had awakened to find myself in bed with the two of them. He was telling me about their marriage, and it was identical to the Godhead that Joanna had insisted she detected in me. I wanted to be far away. In my panic, I felt for the first time since my near-death that I was losing my faith. All color must have left my face; I thought I might faint.

Randall gazed at me quizzically. "You all right?"

"I'm not sure," I said. I tottered to a concrete bench nearby and sat down. Randall joined me there and smoked, not talking. Eventually his pipe went out. He knocked it against the sole of his shoe and put it away in his coat pocket.

"Did I ever tell you how much I love Joanna?" he asked.

"No," I said.

"A lot," he said.

I tried to think of a suitable reply, but nothing came. I seemed to be trapped inside Randall's marriage, and now Randall was perhaps conducting a tour. My discomfiture was complete. I turned my thoughts inward and tried to pray. God was surely testing me; I prayed to understand the nature of the test. I felt lonely; God seemed distant. I felt an impulse to embrace Randall but I was afraid to do it. I thought of the three of us, Randall, Joanna and me, clinging together. It was easy to believe that we loved one another. I began to cry.

Randall put an arm around my shoulder. "Something's gotten away from you," he said. This was an echo of something he had said to me before. At that moment I couldn't recall the old context, but the meaning to me now was explicit: God had gotten away from me. If Randall was trying to console me, he had made me inconsolable instead. My chin fell on my chest and I wept helplessly. Randall gripped my shoulder once, then lifted away his arm. "Take your time," he said.

I wept.

"Have you read anything about the Jewish Kabbalah?" Randall asked me presently.

"Nothing," I said.

"They're mystics," he said. "They have the idea, among other things, of *Deus condatus*—something else in Hebrew, I forget—of God hidden from us."

"From us?"

"From them. From all of us. They think God purposely created us unable to perceive Him."

"It can't be true," I said. "Plenty of people have seen God. I've felt Him as real as anything in my experience."

"I suppose the Kabbalists were trying to account for experience that was general enough to them that they must have thought it was universal—that God never revealed Himself. Only His works could be seen— nature, people, the self—and those were the occasion of suffering. They asked why God required us to follow Him, but never showed Himself. Why our experience of His Creation is so full of pain and cruelty."

As frequently happened with Randall, just as he had posited an idea that I could understand, he fell silent. I was afraid he was about to change the subject, or to cloud it with allusions to matters of a significance known only to him. I interrupted his silence. "And what was their answer? The Kabbalists."

"Is the question familiar? You've thought about it yourself."

"Of course. And had the answer through Scripture and Revelation. But what was the Kabbalists' answer?"

"Their answer's tricky, because it requires you to entertain two opposed ideas simultaneously. One idea is that you seek God through your human understanding. The other idea is that you surrender your understanding entirely, in an act of faith utterly beyond reason."

"Why both?" I asked him. "Why not one or the other? Might not either course get you to God?"

"No. See, here's the trouble: if God created us unable to perceive Him, as the Kabbalah says, then no amount of rational inquiry will lead to Him. On the other hand, the act of unreasoning faith requires a sense of God that's entirely outside of human experience. According to the Kabbalah, God is pure altruism. Man is not made in God's image; there are no elements in common. So we're trapped in our egos, mistakenly thinking we can reason our way to God, while our experience of the physical world makes the pure altruism of the spiritual world incomprehensible."

"Why are you telling me this?"

"Wait. Don't you want to know how the Kabbalists square the circle? Don't care to know how they get from egocentric blindness to transcendent Godliness?"

"I'm not certain I understand the problem," I said.

"The problem is: our life in God's Creation is hard, troubled, full of misery and injustice. Somehow, in the context of so much disaster and disappointment, we have to discover the will of a loving God."

"A simple act of faith won't do it?"

"Evidently not. If in spite of your faith the world goes on being a harsh place, you can't be said to have found the will of God in it."

"Precisely," I said. "That's the reason to have Faith. Faith will keep me until God calls me home. Then I'll understand."

"You're not a Kabbalist."

"I'm a Christian."

Randall fixed me with his black-eyed stare. He made a fist and punched me lightly on the shoulder with the flat of it. He said, "What were you crying about a minute ago?"

"Trials of faith," I said.

"God hidden from us," he said.

I nodded.

"The Kabbalah has it that our soul comes from God—is a piece of God—but that He's devolved us from pure Spirit by putting us into a physical body in a physical world with rules different from the rules of the spiritual world. And not just different. Contrary."

"Then He's hiding from us on purpose?"

"So they claim."

"And why?"

"I don't think there's a 'why' as such. They don't say God's testing us, challenging us to lift ourselves by moral bootstraps. As I read it, their account is purely descriptive. An attempt to explain why the world looks the way it does."

"And do you accept their account?" I asked him.

"No," Randall said. "I'm a Christian. Like you."

"But if God were hiding from me—how would the Kabbalists say I could find my way to Him?"

Randall smiled. "By suffering so long and so deeply at the separation from Him, that finally you abandoned every worldly claim of reason, common sense, self-interest. At that point your ego would cease to be separate from God's, and you'd have regained the spiritual unity with Him that your soul enjoyed before it entered your body."

"It sounds a little like the Buddhist nirvana."

"Yeah, it does. And it shares some of that elitism. Probably more so. I think the Kabbalists believe that only a tiny handful of God's favorites in any generation can achieve the transcendence. And those few probably have to be intellectuals."

I tried to imagine abandoning my common sense. The idea seemed preposterous. In any case, nowhere in Scripture or in our tradition did God ask us to be anything but responsible. "Are you telling me all this as my spiritual adviser or as my teacher?" I asked Randall.

"As your teacher," Randall said.

"Well, it's at least interesting," I said.

"But not compelling," Randall said.

"No," I said. "God doesn't play games with us. He sent us His Son. The message is plain and simple. It doesn't take an intellectual to understand it."

"And yet, something has gotten away from you."

"How many times are you going to say that to me?"

"Every time it comes to my attention."

The conversation ceased. I had lost track of its direction; I found myself without ideas. Each time Randall spoke of something getting away from me, he seemed to be referring to a different thing. "Something has gotten away from you." Randall never inflected it as a challenge; it was descriptive, nothing more than the statement of a truth, more or less sad from time to time. He reached into his pocket and began to repack the bowl of his pipe.

"Do you have an idea what it is?" I asked him.

"No," he said.

"But it comes to your attention."

"Yeah. I hear it and see it in you. But I can't identify it. I imagine you ought to pray about it."

"If I knew what to pray about."

"Pray in general. It'll come to you."

We sat on the stone bench and Randall smoked his pipe. I tried inwardly to retrace the course of our conversation, back to its first subject, Joanna.

Something had deflected me from my purpose, which had been to neutralize Joanna's power to frighten and distract me. I had broached the subject. Randall had engaged me on it. We had strayed into metaphysics. Now I had neither the moral strength nor the mental discipline to attempt it again. I looked sidelong at Randall where he sat slouched on the bench, his forearms on his splayed knees, his hands clasped between them, the pipe clenched again in his teeth. Smoke wreathed his head; he gazed into the middle distance. Except that envy is sinful, I'd have envied him his understanding, whatever it might be.

CHAPTER EIGHT
PRIDE

With the end of the academic year I emerged a little from the intellectual and social cloister of the seminary and took a closer look at the progress of the world. My old employer, perhaps hedging against the possibility that my religious vocation was not real, took me under contract to work for the summer. Without a course load, I was once again reading a newspaper at my desk, and what I read was edifying only if it could be understood as signs of the approach of the Millennium, still more than thirty years off. The spirit of mayhem and rebellion was everywhere. In Prague, the government and the people rebelled against their Soviet masters and—after a breathless time when it looked as if a piece of the Communist hegemony in the East might at long last be reversed—were crushed. In Paris, students seemed to rebel against authority in general. They closed the Sorbonne and interrupted the civil polity, although Paris survived. At home the angry rebellion of youth against age, and of skepticism against received wisdom, continued and grew worse. It found a champion in Bobby Kennedy, but no sooner had he declared himself and set a course to wrest power from the old order than he was killed—ostensibly gunned down by a Moslem extremist rebelling against the Jewish occupation of the Land of Abraham. It seemed as if every person, every race, every cohort of age, occupation, income, class, sex, confession or national origin had a grievance, and that no grievance anywhere was susceptible of mediation. I found as I sat at my desk and worked at the projects of my old employer that the outlines of new sermons were taking shape in my head. I smiled to remember the aggrieved Rob Bartley a year earlier mollified by Solveig while we sat on the couch and watched the President. I wondered if I could deliver a sermon—when and if Bartley came to hear me—that would mollify him as well.

I had been in my summer job less than a week when the office receptionist buzzed me to answer an incoming call. I pushed the flashing line button and was surprised to hear the voice of Joanna Lang. "Can you come to dinner?" she said. "I have a letter for you from Randall."

I caught my breath. "Joanna? I don't understand. You have a letter for me from Randall?"

"Yes. He asked me to give you a letter."

"Where is he?"

"He's on a walkabout," she said.

"A walkabout."

"Yes. He's walking westward—thinking, he says— meditating. Looking at the country."

"When did he leave? How long will he be gone?"

"He left yesterday," she said. "He could be gone for as little as a few days or as long as the whole summer."

My mind reeled in trepidation and confusion. "Is he all right? Are you all right? Was anything said that prompted him to do this?"

"He's fine," she said. "He'd been thinking of doing this for a long time. For at least a year."

"I'm amazed," I said.

"The last thing he did, night before last, was to write you this letter. Can you come to dinner? I can give it to you then."

"Under the circumstances, maybe it would be better if you mailed it to me."

"Randall asked me to hand it to you."

I closed my eyes and asked God to calm and instruct me. At the other end of the line, Joanna was silent.

"You know how important it is that we avoid the occasion of sin," I said.

"I know that God has His purposes and that His purposes will be fulfilled."

I was dizzy with fright. In her remark, unexceptionable as it was if one simply parsed it, I heard the thunder of a monstrous possibility. I was as confused as a child. I had no fixed idea of my relationship with Joanna. I had felt the satisfaction of the faithful shepherd when it first appeared that she wanted me to oversee her spiritual welfare, but now I found myself ceding my moral primacy like a minor of age before an imperious adult. I was thirty years old, but I felt like a hapless adolescent.

"Randall is walking west?"

"Yes," she said. "He's walking. You know it's one of his favorite activities."

"And you'd like me to come to dinner when?"

"Tonight would be fine. Or tomorrow. Whenever you can get away. I'll just cook for the two of us when I know you're coming."

"Tomorrow," I said.

"Oh, good," she said, and named a time.

"That's fine," I said, and thanked her, and hung up the phone.

The rest of my workday was not productive. I wondered why I'd agreed to have dinner alone with Joanna, and why I had agreed to go as soon as the following night. I must have believed that the meeting was unavoidable, that it could be postponed but not cancelled, and so I had postponed it. To postpone it was the most I could do by way of protest. I left the office promptly at quitting time and went straight to my apartment to begin gathering strength for the trial to come. I had never before felt in its literal sense the need to gird my loins, but I did then. Had I been able to devise a physical means of locking away my private parts and the danger they represented, I'd have done it. Instead, I set about perfecting my moral armament. I prayed long and assiduously, but I felt the remoteness that had been tormenting me for several weeks.

I tried ungirding my loins. I removed my clothes and looked at myself in the long mirror, hoping that observation would somehow lead to understanding. There was no doubt, by the standards of the world, that God had given me a body of unusual beauty. I tried to understand His purpose in endowing me like that. I had no use for my own beauty, and if it was a factor in Joanna's immoderation, I'd have preferred to be without it. The irony that I looked for all the world like a Greek god—or like one of the late classical statuary representations of a Greek god—perhaps Hermes—

heightened my frustration. To have been endowed by the true God with the features of a false god, and then to be tested by having Godliness imputed to me on the basis of such false appearances—it seemed a cruel joke. I couldn't laugh, and I couldn't fathom where the joke had come from. Satan was clearly hovering about me, intent on stealing my Truth, intent on strangling my vocation. God had given me a physical presence and a sexual vitality that exacerbated the stringency of the test I was to undergo. As I stared at my image in the mirror, Satan assailed my mind with the memory of certain recent dreams, and the genitive part began without warning to swell and rear out of control. I closed my eyes and turned away, praying aloud, feeling my way along the apartment wall to the bath. I stepped into the tub and, without taking time to pull the curtain about, turned the water on full cold from the showerhead to mortify my flesh.

The combination of prayer and cold water was effective, and the danger passed. I shut off the water, swept the film of it from my body and toweled myself dry. Tomorrow I would face a greater test. I wrapped myself in a warm robe and knelt in the living room to pray for guidance, resting my head on the seat of the overstuffed chair. I had begun to think of Joanna as demonically possessed, although I couldn't think badly of her as a person. I asked God to intervene with her, to make her mindful of my weakness and the danger that she put me in. It was inconceivable that I could be allowed to betray God, myself and my dear friend Randall. The power of my flesh to distract me with temptation was appalling. I remembered the dream of sexual congress with Joanna, when I had been tricked into consummation by the illusion that her body would fall apart if I let her go. I had no confidence that Joanna couldn't trick me as well when I was awake. The claims of my body had become more powerful than at any time since my affair with Marie. I foresaw that it would be easy, if I let the blandishments of Satan and Joanna capture my imagination, to go entirely, orgiastically, insanely bad, and so to lose my life.

I struggled up from my knees and walked to the kitchen, where I found a butcher's knife. I opened my robe and set the sharp edge of the knife against the root of my penis. I realized I wasn't sure which parts needed to be removed to make me safe. I knew that God didn't want me to mutilate myself unnecessarily— that He didn't want me to mutilate myself at all, if there were a better alternative. I placed the knife edge experimentally under my scrotum. In the life I intended for myself, surely my testicles would be useless to me. I could cut them off without interfering with any of the housekeeping functions. I was less certain about the penis. It was hard to imagine urinating gladly without it. Irresolute, I put the knife back in its drawer and returned to the living room to think.

I was not ready to mutilate myself. I thanked God for being with me on this night. He seemed closer once again, and I thanked Him for that. I prayed that He would see me whole through the coming trial with Joanna, and that He would help Joanna to see who I truly was—neither a false god nor a vicar of God, but a servant of God, faithful but weak.

I got up and went to the kitchen again, much restored in my heart, and this time I opened a few cans and prepared myself a supper. I thanked God for the supper too, before I ate it at the kitchen table. One or two new sermon ideas came to me and I wrote them down. I was on the path once more.

I went to bed early that night and slept better than I had in several weeks. The twin facts that I had beaten down temptation quickly and emphatically when it threatened, and that God had drawn closer to me in my hour of danger, gave me confidence that I would be able to meet Joanna, receive Randall's letter, have a polite dinner and leave Joanna unsullied, to the great moral edification of us both. If I dreamed, the dreams were modest and unmemorable.

Fortified in my faith, I was able all the next day to give my employer value for money. I ate lunch at my desk and took advantage of the break to add particulars to the notes for my sermons. After work I went home to my apartment, traded my suit and tie for an open collar and a sport coat, and went to the Langs' house at the appointed hour, carrying a small book of Christian poetry as a gift. At the front door I asked God once more to be with me and to instruct Joanna, and then I rang the bell.

Joanna let me in and left me in the living room, where I stood and sampled the air. The dominant odor was the rich one of whatever she was cooking in the kitchen. There was less of Randall than I was used to;

the masculine smell of his tobacco was barely detectable. I stared again at the painting of Jesus in Gethsemane. The smallness of the figure in the scale of the painting made me think of Randall walking alone. It occurred to me that Randall's interest in the wilderness must be more than academic.

When Joanna called me into the dining room, I saw that places were set where Joanna and I regularly ate. Randall's place at the head of the table had no setting. I was glad Joanna hadn't put me there. On the other hand, the table was set for wine, and there was a bottle in a bucket of ice on the sideboard. I lifted the bottle far enough to read the label, hoping there was no alcohol, but in fact it was a bottle of wine.

This was the first alcohol I had been offered since the disastrous brunch a year earlier with Solveig and Bartley. I considered protesting; I considered refusing the wine when it was offered; but I was certain that God would not have me be ungracious—just as I had been certain the night before that God would not have me mutilate myself—except in extremity. My great success the night before in defeating Satan through prayer and action gave me confidence that I could do as well tonight, however unruly Joanna might become. She looked as pretty as I had ever seen her, and I sensed willfulness in the way she moved as she brought the cooked dishes from the kitchen, but I felt myself well armed. I would drink the minimum amount of wine consistent with not offending Joanna, and I would promote the best interests of Randall, Joanna and me by heeding the manifest will of God, that I should bear witness to His Truth at all times and in all things. When I offered the blessing I had those thoughts in mind, and I did mention Randall and his absence, but I did not mention the wine.

The main dish was breast of chicken on a bed of rice pilaf and mushrooms, with young peas and a salad of spinach greens with hard-boiled egg. The menu struck me as much less homely and workmanlike than what I was used to eating with the Langs. The wine— something white and French—made the food, which was very good anyway, seem almost ambrosial. I felt confused. Such pleasures of the table were undoubtedly a gift from God, but they seemed extravagant when nourishment could be had without them, and they seemed something taken unfairly from Randall, who was not there to enjoy them with his wife.

I praised Joanna's cooking sincerely and thanked her for it, and she smiled, evidently pleased. My confusion increased, because I had thanked God for the same food a few minutes earlier without actually having tasted it, and now that I had tasted it, my gratitude to Joanna felt more vivid, more emotional than my blessing had been, as if the food and all the loving kindness it represented had come from her. I felt again that Randall should be with us.

"Randall left a letter for me," I said.

"Yes," Joanna said.

"Where is it?" I asked.

"In the desk. Don't you want to wait to read it until after dinner?"

"Of course," I said. "I don't want to interrupt the meal. It's wonderful."

Joanna only smiled.

"Did Randall show you the letter?" I asked a moment later, unsettled by her reticence. "Do you know what's in it?"

"No," she said. "But I know he loves you."

"He's a wonderful man," I said.

"Wonderful," she said.

I was hearing echoes of myself. I began to be embarrassed.

"He hadn't told me he was leaving," I said.

"I think he made up his mind in just a day or two. But it's something he's thought of doing for a long time."

"So there was no precipitating incident? He's well? You're both fine?"

"Never better."

"Thanks be to God," I said.

"He's looked forward to being able to take this walk. With the summer break he can do it."

"It's a surprise to me."

"I imagine it'll be a surprise to our other friends as well."

I listened to Joanna's half of our conversation with a degree of circumspection. I realized I didn't trust her. I believed the truth of every statement she made, but I didn't trust her not to surprise me with maneuvers as unforeseen as Randall's walkabout. "I love Randall too," I said. "I care very much for both of you. I take the physical and spiritual welfare of all of us very seriously."

"You're much younger than we are," Joanna said.

"Well. Not very much," I said.

"Randall was already a seminary student when you were born."

"Golly. I suppose he was. But don't we all hope to be equally responsible in the sight of the Lord, regardless of our age?" Joanna let my question pass, rhetorical construction that it was. She also refilled my glass, which I had emptied in my enthusiasm for tasting the wine with the food. I undertook mentally to drink no more, and I pushed the glass a little away from my plate, for the mnemonic value.

"You don't like the wine?"

"I like it very much," I said. "But I allow myself only a small amount."

"You allow yourself only a small amount of everything."

"I think that's true."

"Would you allow everybody else as little?"

"No, I don't think so. Jesus promised a more abundant life to those that follow Him. There's nothing wrong with abundance."

"In moderation, of course."

"You're being satirical, but I don't think it's inconsistent to allow things to others that you don't allow to yourself."

"But in denying things to yourself, sometimes you deny others the pleasure of sharing them with you."

"Pleasure. Is pleasure important?"

"Is our earthly life important? God gave it to us. He must have wanted us to do something with it."

"Yes. He wants us to use it to glorify Him, not to glorify ourselves." I stared across the table at her. She stared back, her eyes sad. I was struck again by how small she was. I felt like a bully, although I knew I was right. She was more willful than rebellious; I was more certain than triumphal. It made me as sad as Joanna that God found us at cross-purposes. I'd have liked to love her with as little circumspection as I loved Randall.

"You're very strong, very smart. Very beautiful," she said. I nodded, solemn but wary. "It's a lot to bring to a vocation," she said.

"In some ways it's not an advantage," I said. "I'd be glad to have my faith and nothing else."

"But God must know what He's doing."

"Yes, He must. That's part of my faith."

"When you're ready to leave, I'll give you Randall's letter; then you can read it in peace." Her eyes looked a little teary, as if she had lost something. I wished I could help.

"Did he give any indication how long he'd be walking?"

"He'll be back for the fall term, I'm sure."

"That's nearly three months."

"He'll probably be back sooner."

We finished the meal in some combination of silence and small talk. I touched no more wine. Joanna finished a second glass before corking the bottle and setting it aside. I helped her clear the table into the kitchen dishwasher. She offered coffee and dessert, which I declined. It seemed a good idea to take Randall's letter away and learn as much as I could as soon as I could about what had happened to my friends.

CHAPTER NINE
SLOTH

Randall's letter said this:

June 10

My friend:

I apologize for leaving you under an obligation without discussing it with you first. I count on you to look after Joanna while I'm gone.

I'm headed for the desert. In this you'll hear echoes of Jesus' 40 days, but don't think I think I'm Jesus, or that I expect to meet the Devil. I want to see whatever there is to see with a mind unclouded by familiarity & duty. I hope to come back a better man & I ask you to pray that I will.

This pilgrimage, if it turns out to be that, might only have happened years from now, or never, if you hadn't come into Joanna's & my life & given me confidence that Joanna would have moral recourse for a time without me. I've told her that she may not hear from me at all for days or weeks, or I may write or phone from the road. I'm walking without an itinerary or any preconception of what the wilderness will

mean to me—even tho I've spent 25 years
telling our brothers what it means.

A few weeks ago you mentioned that you
thought Joanna had God & sex conflated—
something to that effect. You're right—she
somehow never got the message that sex is a
trouble to be driven down & resisted. She was a
virgin when I married her in Christ, & we were
both self-identified spiritual Christians, but
from the beginning our physical experience of
each other was almost Tantric—Christ
intoxication & sexual practice occupying the
same space. I've never thought of it as anything
but a gift from God, although I haven't found
anything in our Judeo-Christian scripture
approving it or even alluding to it. I wonder if
the fact that it happens inside a Christian
marriage puts it beyond second-guessing.

I've left you in a bit of a bind, but I trust you to
work it out & learn something from it. I don't
know which to emphasize—how unwilling I
am to put you through a trial that by rights
should come from God or the Adversary, or
how willing I am to trust in God to guide you
& Joanna through it. She told me what
happened the night I left the two of you alone
to talk. I don't doubt that God was present &
at work.

The same God that saw us through that night
will watch my progress on the road & hear me
pray for your safety.

God bless, guide, protect & love you.

Randall

I read his words within two minutes of arriving
home, and for ten minutes I sat stunned and
motionless in my overstuffed chair, confounded by the
challenge that Randall had set for me, willingly or not.
On the one hand, I had long since lost any confidence
that I could be a spiritual guide for Joanna; on the
other, every meeting with her—indeed, every thought
of her—made me fear for my immortal soul. And now
Randall seemed to be asking me to continue in that
fruitless task, hazarding that awful risk, and for an
unknown time.

Once again I felt that God had distanced Himself
from me. I prayed to understand how my dearest friend
could become the agent whereby was renewed a test
that I had faced and passed several times already. As I
prayed, the distance shortened, and I came to realize
that I had not yet really passed the test—not even once.
If I had passed the test, Joanna would no longer have
the power to frighten me. I realized that all my
response thus far to the danger had been defensive
counterpunching, that to succeed I would have to go on
the attack. I set aside the sermon I had been writing, to
begin a new one.

It was a Godsend that I had met Rob Bartley on the street and invited him to hear me in the pulpit. In my mind, I made Bartley the congregation to whom I would preach certain truths ordained by God for right relations between the sexes. These were truths that Bartley—otherwise a seemingly decent man—appeared to have no awareness of. Here was an opportunity given by God to organize my thoughts on the challenge embodied in Joanna, to mobilize Scripture for my battle, and to carry the war beyond my own little theater and into the wider world, where it desperately needed to be waged. I saw Joanna, Solveig and Bartley's Jewish friend as avatars of the same misprision of God's design: they had been made sexually vital and attractive, and without the interposition of God's love they were ripe for plunder, as I had plundered Marie, and she me. Remembering Marie, I prayed for the health and safety of her soul, satisfied that my Protestant devotion could compensate for any deficiency inherent in her Roman confession. I prayed for Solveig too, a kind-hearted Lutheran, the quality and degree of whose sexual abandonment I didn't know. I prayed for Joanna, who had made a Christian marriage by the grace of God, but whose sexuality did not remit. I prayed also for Bartley and all of his conquests. And then I began to write.

I began where most commentaries on my subject begin: with first Corinthians. Paul warns his flock that the body is consecrated to the Lord, and that to use it for immorality pollutes the body of Christ, of which each of us is a part. I tried to anticipate Bartley's objections. Probably they would center on some defense of the right of consenting adults to behave as they liked in private: this was the current direction of the civil and criminal law, and Bartley was nothing if not current. The answer, of course, is that there is no privacy that excludes the body of Christ, whether among believers or non-believers. He came for the remission of all sins, that finally all men and women should acknowledge His Divinity. There could be no hiding from Him. I imagined Bartley *in flagrante* with the Jewish beauty and I quaked with fear for him. I came near to imagining him with Solveig, but my mind rebelled, and I doubted that they had had a sexual relationship.

I foresaw that to reach Bartley I would have to make him feel and share my fear. It is a monstrous and terrible thing to disgrace the body of Him who let His own body be tortured and killed for our deliverance. If I could make Bartley see that in gratifying his fleshly desires he was contributing to the death of his own soul and to the chagrin of the world, I could appeal at once to his fear of death and to what I believed was his better nature. If Solveig had liked and approved of him, that better nature must be a large part. Then maybe it was a large part as well of the congregation I'd be preaching to in Bartley's name.

I banged something together rather quickly, because the issues were so stark and compelling to my mind. I found I had fewer scriptural references to consenting heterosexual partners outside of marriage than I had supposed, and none at all from the Old

Testament. Paul seemed to be the major authority on this narrow subject. So I was forced to expatiate on Paul's words alone; but a good effect of the scarcity of source material was simplicity in the message. I foresaw that my passion for the subject would do far more than exegetics to carry the day.

I thanked God for providing the message and its expression so freely, and then I re-read and girdled myself in it like armor. I was pretty sure Joanna would be among the congregation when I delivered it—surer, in fact, than that the seemingly guileless but inscrutable Bartley would be there. This sermon would be my continuing answer to her overtures, should there continue to be overtures. I undressed, said my usual prayers and went to bed encouraged.

To my surprise, I lay awake longer than was typical for me at that time of my life. In general I had slept easily and well ever since the night of my near-death and spiritual rebirth. But now I found myself alert and my mind refusing to give up the business of the day. Composing the sermon had kept me up an hour past my regular bedtime; the next morning I was to be in my summer office at nine for a meeting, and I worried that I wouldn't function well on little sleep. I tried to lull myself into slumber with such psalms as I knew by heart, but my brain would not relax. I remembered this phenomenon from the troubled time at the end of my affair with Marie. As I lay in my bed, I felt lonely and without recourse. I prayed for peace and sleep, and after a long time the sleep came, but with it came dreams that gave no peace.

Once again I was in the featureless, gray land I visited often in my sleep. I was climbing, because all of the land was sloping upward. Ahead of me I saw Randall, also climbing, too far away to hear me if I called. I sat down to rest and opened my Bible. There were tipped-in plates, pastel-tinted half tones of scenes I didn't recognize, although they had the look of the Holy Land. The figures in them looked Biblical but not familiar. Bartley's Jewish girlfriend sat beside me and looked at the pictures.

I realized that the Bible was not mine. I dropped the marker ribbon between the open pages and closed the book. I placed it on the ground between us and waited for Bartley's friend to pick it up, but she only smiled at me and folded her forearms over her knees to rest her chin. Her dark hair fell on her wrists. Her skin was nut-brown and smooth, and all of her surfaces were round. She looked edible, like some exotic fruit. She stood up with the Bible already in her hand and walked away from me with Bartley, whom I hadn't noticed before. He lifted her into his arms and folded her into his clothing until she disappeared.

I stood up and saw the land, now flat, empty to the horizon. I stared and squinted, hoping to find Solveig, but visibility was poor. I began to walk in the direction I thought Randall might have taken, peering as deeply as I could into the gloom, but there was nothing to see. I pressed on, conscious of some obligation. I felt tired and wished I could sleep.

In the midst of this cold desert I saw Bartley again, seated in my overstuffed chair, holding my ex-wife Beth by the hand. She stood upright beside him while he reclined. Beth asked me where I was going. "To work," I said. I saw that she'd been crying; her face was puffy, her cheeks streaky with tears. I stopped in case she wanted to speak again, but she turned her head away. At the nape of her neck I saw brown hair that I remembered. Anxiety gripped me and duty urged me on; I believed I was late for my meeting. I walked in a large circle around Bartley's chair, anxious to correct some wrong. Beth now stood beside the chair dressed in bib coveralls, her hands plunged deep in the coverall pockets, and Marie stood beside her naked. The chair was empty. My anxiety was unbearable. I hurried away after Randall.

I awoke in great distress and looked at the lighted face of my alarm clock. It was three a.m. I had slept for forty-five minutes at the most.

Something had gone badly wrong with me; I felt worse than at any time since my overdose. I was desperate to sleep. I heard my pulse beating in my ears. I sandwiched my head between pillows and my pulse grew louder.

I crawled out of bed, knelt on the floor and prayed, bereft of company. The night seemed darker than any I could remember in years, although an overspray of urban lights framed the window shade and made a pale gloaming in my room. I felt utterly alone. God was not hearing me, as far as I could tell. I tried to catch my breath but couldn't. I was afraid, but I didn't know of what.

I struggled up and went to the living room and switched on the lamp beside the overstuffed chair, to read the Bible. The chair was not warm from Bartley's occupation, and there was no hint that Beth, Marie or any woman had stood beside it, either recently or ever. I tried to re-read the material gleaned for my sermon from the epistles of Paul, but their tone made me feel more isolated still, and less likely to sleep. I read from Psalms and the Song of Solomon. Little by little I grew calm, and I fell asleep in my chair.

Again I dreamed, but now I was in Stockholm with Solveig. It was nighttime, but the sky was bright with midsummer twilight. We were walking in empty streets, looking for a place for me to sleep. There was no shelter, only bare streets and locked, deserted buildings. I lay on the sidewalk beside a stone foundation wall while Solveig covered my body with a blanket. My neck hurt and my head bumped on the pavement. She sat with her back against the wall and drew my head into her lap, singing to me as her namesake had sung to Peer Gynt. I began to cry. The sun rose and went down again. I thought I was happy but I knew I was not. Solveig sang and cradled my head, and again the sun rose and set. I was desperate to sleep and I had missed my meeting. I was tempted to die, but I knew that to die willfully was a sin. I was afraid that I would never die, that I would never sleep, that I would never see God. I wept helplessly. The sky grew dark. I could see nothing. Solveig continued to sing.

I awoke in my chair. My neck was stiff; the lamp was burning and the Bible was open in my lap. I closed it and lifted myself up and shut off the light, but the room didn't go dark, because dawn had come. The alarm clock in the bedroom now said 4:30. I had not missed my meeting, but I was exhausted and there were only three hours remaining before I had to get up. I crawled into bed, thought of Solveig and prayed to God. I fell asleep.

The alarm woke me at 7:30, groggy and distressed. I shut it off and would have slipped out of bed and knelt on the floor for my regular morning prayers, but the shortage of sleep made me heavy, sore and stupid, like an ox with a headache. I remained supine and began my prayers like that.

Lassitude made my communication with God more problematic than ever. My prayers seemed rote effluence; I had no sense of their immediacy; they were words without force or direction. I sagged in my bed and tried to connect the language in my brain with the God to Whom it was addressed.

Next I found myself up and out, headed for the office, but I felt unprepared for the meeting and unable to remember its subject. Instead of the usual city bus, I was traveling on foot in an unfamiliar neighborhood. I checked my watch; the time seemed all right, but I knew I'd have to hurry. I ran several yards but my feet felt heavy, so I slowed again to a walk. The sky seemed abnormally dark. I came to a street corner and there I stopped, unsure of the direction. Randall Lang crossed from the opposite corner and placed an arm around my shoulder. I was surprised to see him, but glad to have him to guide me. Even so, although I was sure he knew I was lost, he said nothing. I looked in every direction, hoping to see a familiar landmark, but the visibility was poor. I looked at my watch and saw that it was nine o'clock. I hurried away to the right along the intersecting street and soon reached the building where my office was, but the door was locked and I realized that the meeting had been cancelled. Across the street I saw the flower shop where Marie had worked, unaccountably transplanted from its real location on another block. I crossed to the plate glass and cupped my hands around my eyes to see inside. There were no flowers; the shop was bare.

Behind the counter where I had met Marie, a very old woman stared back at me and pointed. She fixed me with her knotty, arthritic finger in a gesture of accusation and menace. I turned from the glass and ran away.

Sometime much later a noise awoke me in my bed: I heard the echo of it as I jerked awake. I looked at the alarm clock. It was 9:14. I had overslept and was missing my meeting.

I hurried out of bed, splashed water on my face and went to the telephone, disoriented, embarrassed and chagrined. My treasured self-mastery all at once seemed lost: I was unable to sleep; I was unable to wake up; I was incompetent and under siege in either state. I dialed the office receptionist, who was surprised to hear me.

"They're in the meeting," she said.

"Can you patch me through?"

"I think they're waiting for you," she said. "I'll buzz."

A few seconds passed and my boss's voice came on the line. "Where are you?"

"Embarrassed and humiliated. I overslept. I think you know how unlike me this is."

"Not to worry," he said, perhaps embarrassed too. "How soon can you be here?"

"Not very, I'm afraid." That was an understatement. I was unwashed, undressed, unfed and a half-hour bus ride away. "But I have the material with me. Can we do this on the speaker?"

"We can try."

"Give me three minutes," I said. "I'll call you back."

I hung up the phone, fell to my knees and thanked God. I rushed to the bathroom for certain lavings and purgations, collected my briefcase and a carton of orange juice, and had joined the meeting telephonically by 9:20. My manifest defects and the weakness of my flesh had created an emergency that I was now being delivered from by the grace of God. My boss's speakerphone gave a ghostly timbre to the voices of the half-dozen participants; I could interject when appropriate and still enjoy, myself unseen, the luxury of observing the meeting with my mind's eye. If Satan had intervened in the night to disable me, God had intervened in the day for my re-edification. The strongest part of me, my voice, was present at the meeting. No one had to know the depleted vessel it issued from.

When the meeting was over and my boss picked up the handset to speak privately, he was gracious in accepting my apologies. I told him I'd be in after an early lunch.

But I felt off-balance and insecure. I heard Randall's voice repeating that something had gotten away from me, and I began to think he was right. It was not God, though, that had gotten away from me. On the contrary, God had come to my rescue in that very hour. (I stopped and fell on my knees once more to thank Him for it.) Something else had gotten away from me—something that was isolating me from all except the Lord. I wished Randall would come home. I made a mental note to discuss this topic at length in my evening prayers, because it was a complex and subtle one, with ramifications to my moral safety, to Randall's spiritual growth, to Joanna's companionship and comfort, to matters I supposed I had yet to imagine.

I took a shower and dressed, then I bused toward work, stopping to fortify myself with a businessman's ninety-nine-cent luncheon special, widely available in those days. I reached the office a little past noon, still dopey from the sleep shortage, and found a phone memo from Joanna asking me to call. I didn't want to. I felt unequal to whatever challenge she might present, and unwilling to engage her with any agenda of my own. I closed my office door and tried to work, but my brain was performing poorly, caroming from thought to thought. I had to read text twice to understand it once, only to lose the sense and have to read it again. I considered taking a sick day and going home, but I lacked the energy to make that decision. At last I picked up the phone and dialed the Langs' number, believing that my indisposition would provide an excuse for refusing any overture of Joanna's that might be worrisome. She sounded predictably happy that I'd called.

"Have you heard from Randall?" I asked.

"Yes," she said. "That's why I phoned. Just to tell you he's well and says hello."

"Did he call?"

"No; he wrote. A short letter. I'd read it to you, but it's rather private."

"A letter." Even in my stupor, this bit of news seemed anomalous. Randall had departed on Tuesday; this was Friday. It seemed a short time for the writing, posting and delivery of a letter from a man who had announced his withdrawal, perhaps incommunicado, into the wilderness. "A letter," I said again. "What's the postmark?"

"June twelfth," she said. "The day before yesterday." And she mentioned the name of a town not more than forty miles away to the west and south.

"Does he say what his plans are? Does he say how often we'll hear from him?"

"No," she said. "It's a very short letter."

"I see."

There was silence on the line.

"I read Randall's letter last night after I left you," I offered. "He wants me to look after you while he's away."

"I'm glad," she said.

"I had some trouble sleeping."

"Really? I'm sorry to hear it."

"Yes. I was working on a sermon rather late. I think I just overstimulated myself. I ought to have wound down a little earlier in the evening—meditated instead of writing."

"You're not worried about the responsibility of looking after me, then."

"I don't think so... I don't think you require any serious looking-after." This denial echoed in my head. It was false, of course. I was surprised and distressed that I'd let Joanna coax me into lying. I tried in my befogged brain to reformulate my answer, to make it true without broaching issues that I felt unprepared to tackle just then. "Well," I said. "Well, I take seriously any responsibility conferred by Randall. And of course I take you very seriously. You're a dear and important friend. But I don't think the prospect of looking after you was keeping me awake." I wasn't sure of the truth of this last statement either. I seemed to be wallowing in moral quicksand. "I'd better hang up and try to concentrate on work I'm being paid for," I said, and instantly I heard resonating a space for the inference that I resented not being paid to look after Joanna. Such an idea was too ludicrous to entertain, but my mind had identified it. I hoped (and reflexively prayed) that Joanna had not heard it that way. I couldn't tell; she was silent. "I'll call you when my brain is working again," I said. "Is there anything you need immediately?"

"No," she said. "God bless. I'll talk to you soon."

I hung up the phone and rested my forehead on my desk. I felt quite stupid and afflicted. My best efforts to do right by God, myself and my fellow man were failing, and my physical strength seemed to be ebbing. I listened for God to speak to me, but I heard only the beating of my heart through my breastbone and the edge of the desk, and the soughing of my breath against the desktop. I hoped for a sign that would point to a new idea. I hesitated to pray just then, thinking I might have been going about it wrong. If God was displeased with me, I should listen for Him to tell me why. But I knew if He didn't speak to me soon that I'd fall asleep at my desk. So I sat up and tried to work.

CHAPTER TEN
GLUTTONY

It's impossible even now to recall that summer of 1968 with equanimity. Around us all, the world we had known was disintegrating. The youth rebellion that culminated later that year in riots at the Democratic convention in Chicago had its manifestations everywhere. Sexual anarchy was being practiced on a public scale unseen since the days of Sodom and Gomorrah. Shameless homosexuals were declaring themselves, demanding imagined rights to offend the public conscience. The flag of our country was burned in the streets and desecrated as material for underwear and tendentious collage.

But more terrible for me than the virtual tottering of civilization was the fact that, as dangerous and unsettled as I felt the world to be, it was only the backdrop for a corresponding siege of my soul by dark forces that tormented me with feelings of insecurity and panic. As the Sunday appointed for the first of my guest sermons approached, there were days when all the physical concomitants of fear coursed through my body: my heart raced, my mouth grew dry, my hands shook. I doubted then that I'd be able to preach at all, let alone impress God's Truth on the congregation. It was clear that Satan was pursuing me with all his forces. But the knowledge that the Adversary was afraid enough of my evangelism to hound me in this way gave me strength, and on some days I exulted in the faith that with God's help and my own constancy I would rise above the worst the Devil could impose. I prayed to God for stability, and I asked Him at least to raise me up on the day of my sermon, for Jesus' sake. I believed I could bear any trial except failure in—or the loss of—my vocation. My sleep suffered too: there were nights when I was too fearful and depressed to sleep, and there were nights when I was kept awake by my excitement over the battle that I had been called to join. My mood at work ranged from dread to distraction, and my performance was irregular, depending on how well I had slept the night before. But I think nobody noticed.

On a day of particular exaltation I phoned Bartley and invited him to hear me on the Sunday. He thanked me and said he would come. That day I believed God's purposes were being served, but the next morning I awoke once more depressed. I could point to no reason for it. I had suffered no important reversal at work; my sermon was polished and ready; the news of the world was no worse than usual. Evidently Satan's campaign to undermine my confidence and blunt God's message was proceeding with renewed force. I understood, perhaps for the first time, how it would feel to be possessed by demons. My meditation before breakfast was on the total war I must fight with the Devil, and my prayer was that God would interpose Himself between me and this powerful but nameless melancholia.

The site of my guest sermon was the same Gospel Church of the Redeemer where Solveig had accompanied me to services a year before. I wished for a strong Christian to pray with during the troubled days before I was to preach, and I'd have asked the regular pastor to pray with me, but I remembered the indifferent outcome of our prayer session during the crisis that followed my failure to convert Solveig. And now, with a year of seminary behind me, the pastor seemed further diminished. I knew I was the better preacher, and I supposed I was the better scholar as well. I took no pride or joy in either of these facts: they were neutral truths; but they made me doubt that the pastor and I would be praying from the same page. In my soul's ferment I thought it very possible that the pastor was a better man before God than I was, although it was not possible that he could be trying harder. I wished again that Randall were in town. However inscrutable he might be, I could pray with him and know that his voice would dignify and magnify my intention.

Thinking of Randall reminded me that I had probably neglected Joanna during these weeks. I blamed myself, but I felt I couldn't risk exposure to her manipulations while I was already under siege by the Adversary. The idea that I was letting Randall down contributed to my anxiety and self-doubt, and so I was caught in a vicious circle. I thought of breaking the circle by going to pray with Joanna, but it was impossible. My doubts centered on her. I would have to petition the Father without a human ally or any earthly comfort except the knowledge of Christ's sacrifice. But to the faithful that is enough.

I devoted the entire afternoon and evening of the Saturday before my sermon to prayer and to meditations on grace, and I went to bed early and by the grace of God slept well enough, soothed by dreams of Messianic sponsorship. I awoke rested early on Sunday morning and stayed in my bed to pray until it was time to get up, dress and go to church.

This Sunday was the fourth after Pentecost, and the altar was bedecked in the green of that liturgical season. Sitting behind the pulpit in my black cassock, waiting for the sermon, I was gratified to see Joanna in a pew near the front. I could see no sign of Bartley, but I asked God to grant that Bartley should be there and that I'd find him looking up at me when I took the pulpit. I had taken as my lessons for this Sunday texts from Deuteronomy, Psalms, first Corinthians and the Gospel of Matthew, and I meant to weave these lessons together to spare no one guilty of real or contemplated insults to chastity, myself included. Deuteronomy 22:22 was a warning for Joanna and for me, and for any like us: "If a man is found lying with the wife of another man, both of them shall die, the man who lay with the woman, and the woman; so you shall purge the evil from Israel." I added verse 23 in penance for my sin with Marie: "If there is a betrothed virgin, and a man meets her in the city and lies with her, then you shall bring them both out of the gate of that city, and you shall stone them to death with stones." 1 Corinthians 6:18-20 was for Bartley and his ilk: "Shun immorality. Every other sin which a man commits is outside the body; but the immoral man sins against his own body.

Do you not know that your body is a temple of the Holy Spirit within you, which you have from God? You are not your own; you were bought with a price." I selected the Gospel text from Matthew 5:27-30 to challenge my hearers with the very high standard I had adopted for myself, and to remind myself of that standard: "You have heard that it was said, 'You shall not commit adultery.' But I say to you that everyone who looks at a woman lustfully has already committed adultery with her in his heart. If your right eye causes you to sin, pluck it out and throw it away; it is better that you lose one of your members than that your whole body be thrown into hell." And then the leaven, from Psalm 119:1,9-10: "Blessed are those whose way is blameless, who walk in the law of the Lord! How can a young man keep his way pure? By guarding it according to thy word. With my whole heart I seek thee; let me not wander from thy commandments!"

When I stood to preach, I saw immediately that God had favored my prayer. Bartley was installed, dressed as I'd never seen him before, in a suit and tie, about two-thirds of the way back along the center aisle, his face lambent and benign. He seemed not to be accompanied, but it was impossible to tell.

God was with me and I preached well. I had only the lesson texts before me, and the barest outline of the sermon I'd composed. I knew what God wanted me to say; my notes were there to remind me only of the order in which I meant to say it. I intercut one commentary with another. I lifted the congregation into my hands and swept them about, running fore and aft over the lessons, revisiting one when another had illuminated it, extolling progressively the urgency of the Word, weaving a fearful tapestry of Divine intent. And then, when the mood had reached the highest pitch of fear of the wrath of God, I returned to the Psalm text with a meditation on the goodness of Him Who gave His commandments clearly enough for His children to follow them, and then sent His only Son as hostage to our human failure. There were more than a few tears among the assembled.

As I offered the prayer at the end of the sermon I thought Joanna looked chastened. Bartley, on the other hand, seemed to have emerged from the experience of my preaching in the same mood in which he entered. Each time my gaze fell on him in the course of the sermon, I found him smiling and enthusiastic, as if I had been leading him, not through the valley of the shadow of death, but through a garden of delights. And when he shook my hand at the door of the church after the service, he seemed positively elated. "What a terrific sermon!" he said. "I loved it!"

I thanked him. As I had thought, he had no woman on his arm. I invited him to the same ladies' church luncheon that Solveig a year earlier had turned down in favor of that scarifying brunch. He hesitated for a moment, seeming to consider options that I could only imagine, and then he accepted. "Great!" he said. "I threw a buck into the plate. Now I guess I get it back."

That beatific smile, a frequent feature of Bartley's kit, so belied the crassness of his remark that even a non-Christian would have forgiven him. I smiled in spite of myself and pointed the way to the church basement, but Bartley proposed to wait in the sunshine nearby while I greeted the congregants yet to exit. Among these was Joanna, who took my hand in both of hers, smiled in a wan, stricken way, and asked if she could join me at lunch. I gestured toward Bartley, now lounging against the trunk of a tree, his arms folded over his necktie, and urged Joanna to walk down and introduce herself. "His name is Rob Bartley, an old friend of mine. He'll have lunch with us." Joanna set off in the direction of Bartley, and I continued shaking hands and receiving congratulations.

Ten minutes later, when I was able to join my friends, Bartley's recondite charm had already won Joanna. She was laughing comfortably with him, and they both turned to smile as I approached, as if they were looking at me from inside a single frame. I could overhear their appraisals, in what I took to be a spirit of badinage.

"He's an imposing-looking guy," Bartley was saying.

"I think he's beautiful," Joanna said.

I may have blushed. Being blond, I blush very detectably even now.

We repaired to the church basement, filled plates from the buffet, and sat on folding chairs with other congregants at one of two long tables covered in the green of Pentecost. I introduced Bartley, who must have been unfamiliar to every churchgoer in the city, and Joanna, whose regular congregation was elsewhere, to a few of the diners sitting nearest, accepted some more compliments for my preaching, and watched to see how the conversation would go.

Bartley's enthusiasm for my sermon had seemed genuine, and now I sensed his eagerness to talk about it, but the first word broached around the table was an observation about the weather, and then momentum drove the colloquy into the shallows of incident and personality, and Bartley grew noticeably quiet. He ate heartily enough, however, and he went back to the buffet for seconds and thirds.

I was disappointed that the urgency of my subject, plainly granted by the assembly while I was actually preaching, could have been forgotten so soon. I hoped the message that God had wanted me to convey was now printed indelibly in every heart at that table, regardless of the lack of an outward sign. I appreciated the need for social intercourse, but I wished for a world where chatter and bonhomie were only the leaven in a loaf of earnestness, rather than the loaf itself.

Bartley must have wished for the same, because as people finished eating and the population at the tables began to thin, he re-established eye contact. "You are some preacher," he said.

"If I am, it's a gift and I thank God."

"But I thought to myself while you were preaching: where's the percentage in trying to short-circuit human nature? People are highly sexual. Everybody tries to keep it a secret. But it keeps popping out."

"Popping out."

"Yeah. It may be the one interest that virtually everybody has in common, but polite people never talk about it. They talk about the weather. But get them alone and they're sexual. Always."

"Really?"

"In my experience."

I stole a glance at Joanna, to see how she was registering this surprising discourse from Bartley. She looked rather prim, I thought, but Bartley had all of her attention.

"Of course," I said, "sex is a powerful influence in human life. That's why it's important that it be kept under control and never abused. The potential for harm is very great."

"So people say," Bartley allowed. "But I don't believe I've ever seen sex do anything but good. It makes people happy. Women look better after sex. It's good for the skin tone."

I examined Bartley's face for evidence that he was jesting, but he seemed sincere. "Of course," he went on, "it's certainly possible to be abusive in the context of sexuality, but that's not sex; that's abuse."

"Don't you think that sex outside of marriage is abusive *ipso facto*? It's a perversion of God's purpose."

"Gee, I hope not," Bartley said. "I know Paul takes that position here and there in the epistles, but Paul was kind of a crank, wasn't he? Jesus seems to have been a much nicer guy."

I think I flushed. "It wasn't God's purpose that either of them should be 'nice'," I said. "Jesus came to redeem humankind. Paul preached the Truth."

"Yeah, but it always seemed to me to be a truth that flies in the face of everything I know about people.

140

I read Paul and I have a picture of a really sour, self-important, bean-counting kind of guy who's trying to get all the Christian ducks in a row before Jesus comes back and cancels the world."

"Paul does write about the End Time."

"There's the problem, it seems to me," Bartley said. "Paul thought the Second Coming was maybe a week off, so all of his instructions have to do with dying, not with living. The best people I know have a fund of loving-kindness that's got nothing to do with fear or death. Solveig has it."

I glanced again at Joanna. Now she was looking as intently at me as she had been looking at Bartley. I didn't know by her look whether she meant to endorse Bartley's challenge or to encourage me to a telling response. "God's love is the love that matters," I said.

"How do you know?" Bartley said.

"By my faith."

"Strong medicine," Bartley said. There was a beat, and then he smiled. "Many things have been revealed to me," he said amiably, as if oblivious to the mockery in his choice of words, "but the love of God hasn't been one of them."

"Is it possible that you haven't been looking?"

"No, no," he said, "I've been looking. Nothing interests me more than to find out what makes the world tick. That's why I was delighted to hear your sermon. I'm doing research."

I may have cocked an eyebrow at him.

"Well," he said after a pause, "maybe 'research' is a bit of an overstatement. I'm collecting impressions."

"Impressions can be misleading," I offered. "If you want to know for sure, read the Bible."

"I've done some of that," he said. "It's a text. I find it requires some interpretation."

"Certainly it benefits from exegesis in its particulars, but I think the truth it has to tell about the world is unmistakable. God exists. He takes an interest in our lives. He expects certain things of us."

"Well," Bartley said, "I'm not sure. Even a fairly non-rigorous reading turns up a lot of problems. One of my favorites is this purely mechanical one of the shape of the earth."

"And how's that?" I asked him.

"There's a passage somewhere about four angels standing at the corners of the world."

"Yes," I said, "in Revelation." Then I helped him by quoting the scripture: "`... I saw four angels standing at the four corners of the earth, holding back the four winds of the earth, that no wind might blow on earth or sea or against any tree.'"

"So you have a description of the earth as planar. And to be exact—because the four winds of the earth are given elsewhere as north, south, east and west—it's a more or less rectangular slab with its corners pointing in the cardinal directions of the compass."

"Is that important?" I asked him.

"Well, I don't know," Bartley said. "Is it important to you? How much poetic license can you tolerate in the Bible and still claim inerrancy? Because if you want to read that passage unambiguously, it says the earth is flat. And that's evidently an error."

"I feel safe in accepting the inerrancy of God's word, undivided. I believe it all."

"Then you accept that the world is flat?"

"If that's what it says, yes."

"Your faith is strong," Bartley said.

"And for that, I thank God," I said.

Bartley smiled and stretched in his chair, as I had seen him do at brunch in Solveig's apartment. I didn't envy, but I was struck again by his ease in the world. I stared at him in frustration and with flagging courage. He seemed eminently worth saving, but the way was obscure.

CHAPTER ELEVEN
LUST

In the days following my guest sermon, my mood deteriorated again. I missed Randall and wished he had been able to hear me preach and give me the benefit of his perspective. I wished he had been present to meet Bartley. I imagined a conversation in which Randall confuted Bartley's errors and so brought Bartley, chastened and undeceived, into our circle.

I looked forward with some discouragement to my second and final guest sermon, scheduled for mid-August. My sermon on chastity had gone well and been received with enthusiasm, but I doubted that it had done any lasting good. Bartley had been impressed by my preaching but unimpressed by the message, as if style mattered more to him than substance. And Joanna had barely responded. I hoped her subdued manner meant that she had heard God's warnings and taken them to heart. But in my growing despondency I thought it equally possible that she had taken as a rejection the parts of my sermon directed especially to her, and that the relationship of trust that I so valued—her trust of me—was at an end.

I took these worries to God in long nights of prayer, Bible study and self-examination. I prayed with a growing sense of loss and abandonment, a growing burden of guilty doubt that God was listening. When I examined myself I disliked what I saw: an isolated man—so physically well-favored that had I been only a beast of the field I should have been regarded as blessed by God—and morally feckless. However upright and steadfast I tried to be, I failed to convey the power of my faith beyond myself. I might as well have been a coward. In my darkest moments I thought that God was right to ignore me. I couldn't imagine ever again standing before people and preaching God's word. I was afraid to try, but utterly forlorn at the thought of such a loss. In my solitude I remembered a piece of music I had listened to when I was married: a beautiful song sung by a baritone in a minor key, about a man alone at midnight, assailed by moral doubts and fears. In the final verse God comforts him, and he sings:

> At midnight,
> Unto Thy might
> Deliver I my strength.
> Lord, life's breadth and length
> Guard'st Thou in sight—
> At midnight.

And as he does so, the music changes from the minor to the major key. The effect is gorgeous and triumphant. I poked through my small collection, found the record and put it on my phonograph, hoping to be comforted as well. But the music only made me cry.

In the midst of this time of trouble a letter came from Randall. It was postmarked from a small town three states away to the west.

July 3

My friend:

God made the world very large & his servants
very small. This trip is all I had hoped for—
solitude, weather, the kindness of strangers.
Also growing fitness. I think I've lost weight,
but haven't been on a scale. I've stopped
smoking the pipe, but suppose I'll take it up
again when I get home.

This paved and posted American wilderness is
evocative of God's interest in us in a way that
untracked wilderness could never be.
Everywhere I go there is the evidence of people
at work. Even where people are scarcest there
are fencerows nearby & farm buildings in the
distance. Cars & trucks rise right out of the
land, first as distant sound, then as louder noise
& color. I step off the pavement when they pass.

America is all signs—road signs, advertising
signs, Keep Out signs. It's busy. I see people
living lives that I'll never see again—just the
instant's tableau as I walk by. I see a few
seconds out of a whole lifetime of work, see
what they've built so far, see where & how
they're living today & I keep walking. It's
amazing & awful to know that God sees as
deeply into each of them as He sees into me.

I guess Joanna is sharing with you the few
notes I've written to her & I guess you'll share
this one with Joanna. You & she are the two
people closest to me in this world. I pray that
when we meet next time we'll be closer still &
also better & closer to God.

May He bless you until then,

Randall

I finished this letter with a feeling almost of self-
loathing. I had let him down badly. I had been so
lacking in the courage to face Joanna that I had
neglected my duty to both of them. And the news that
Joanna had received letters that she hadn't even
mentioned to me, let alone shared, made me ashamed.
Now I felt such humiliation that my courage flagged
some more.

I prayed to understand how my life in God, which
had begun in such promise and progressed so
brilliantly through my first year of seminary, could now
be sinking into a pit of fear and failure. I prayed that if
it were God's will to test me in this way, I could learn
to accept this sign of His Grace, struggle on in the
perfection of my faith, and emerge triumphant in God's
good time. But I hurt terribly.

For several days after I received Randall's letter I
tried to gather courage to visit Joanna. Whereas before
I had been afraid of her sexual predisposition, now I
was afraid of her scorn. And I found this conviction, not

entirely rational, that Joanna had come to dislike and disrespect me, spilling over into my relations with co-workers. At my summer office I felt humiliated and barely competent, although there was really nothing wrong with my work. I kept my office door closed all day in dread of telephone calls and visitors. My hands trembled when I took a cup of water at the cooler, and my embarrassment at trembling caused me to tremble more.

Alone in the evenings in my sad, small apartment, I alternately prayed, read the Bible and tried to compose my next guest sermon. I felt I knew nothing of God's Truth that I could transmit to a congregation. The thought of trying to preach filled me with anxiety and fear. For the first time since I stood up at the meeting of Solveig's anti-war group, I knew stage fright. I looked at the calendar and tried to estimate how long I could temporize before phoning my pastor to cancel.

I knew I could not be whole again until I had confronted Joanna, but I was afraid. Prayer came to my rescue only in the act of praying. I'd ask God for the strength to face Joanna and I'd feel the strength coming into me, but as soon as I stopped praying and reached for the telephone, the fear returned in time to stop me from dialing more than three or four of the seven digits. Finally, one evening when Randall's letter had been in my hands for several days as a constant rebuke, I swallowed my fear—which made me go cold in the stomach—and dialed through.

"Oh!" Joanna said when she heard my voice. "How are you?"

"I have a letter from Randall that he thinks I should share with you."

"Do you?" she said. "I'm glad you called. I'm in the middle of something right now. Can I call you later tonight or tomorrow?"

"Of course," I said, relieved by the lack of censure in her tone. "I'll be up until eleven-thirty."

"All right," she said. "I'll call you back."

I hung up the phone feeling better than I had at any time since my sermon. I thanked God for having given me the strength to persevere in spite of my terrors. I re-read Randall's letter. This time the lines about our closeness resounded not as a confirmation of failure but as a call to action. I folded the letter back into its envelope, tucked it into the breast pocket of my jacket, and set off for Randall's house.

It was the worst mistake of that summer. When I arrived on Joanna's street at about nine p.m., the first thing to catch my eye was Bartley's little sports car, the emblem to me of everything strange, unwelcome and ungovernable, parked at the curb in front of Randall's door.

These many years later I remember vividly, and feel nearly as keenly, the shock of that discovery. Bartley had ruined my peace again. I understood immediately that he had taken advantage of my neglect to exploit Joanna's weakness. He was inside Randall's house, perhaps even in Randall's bed, taking his sexual pleasure. The man was a monster. I remembered the mark of the Beast encoded in the date of his tetanus booster shot. I had been deceived by Bartley's affability more times than I could count.

I crossed the street to the side opposite the Langs' house and concealed myself in the shadows along the sidewalk. There was a light on in the living room and another in a room upstairs. I stood irresolute and helpless, the weight of a huge, uncertain moral duty bearing me down. I felt I should intervene before God in His wrath took Joanna. I felt equally that I should intervene as the very instrument of God's wrath: cross the street, break into the house, drive Bartley out and scourge Joanna's flesh. The despondency of recent days possessed me again like an intimation of Hell, and my courage left me entirely. I turned away and went back home.

In my apartment I uncradled the telephone and buried it under pillows. I was afraid Joanna might make good her promise to call me back. If she did, it would mean either that Bartley had finished with her and left, or that she had the audacity to speak to me while Bartley was in her house. I couldn't bear to hear her under either condition.

Although it was not yet ten o'clock, I turned out the lights, undressed and went to bed to pray and try to sleep. I felt cold, although it was July, and I huddled under covers. The lights of the city glowed through the drawn shade of my bedroom; my breath came fast; I felt the chill of panic clutching at my heart. I closed my eyes and prayed to be comforted, and little by little I grew calm. But the melancholia remained.

I dreamed that I was on the road with Randall. Neither of us spoke. I watched him out of the corner of my eye, afraid that he would ask me to find Joanna. We walked along the edge of a narrow highway. No cars passed. The sky was dim and colorless and there were no shadows, except for catenary curves of telegraph wires projected on the ground ahead of us, reaching away toward the dim horizon. We approached a farmhouse and climbed the steps to an open veranda, where two small children were riding on a porch swing. Randall sat with them; I withdrew to a far corner and watched for traffic on the highway, but none came. There was a large, dark window near where I stood. I approached to look through it into the house, but there was no glass, only a curtain. I pushed the curtain aside and saw a large room furnished in the comfortable, outdated, rustic style I remembered from visits to my grandparents during my childhood in the Middle West. The woman of the house stood beside a dining table and stared back at me. It was Beth. There was no sign of recognition in her eyes or manner; I thought she didn't see me. There was a place set at the table and food on the plate, but no one was eating. I realized that Bartley had been there and gone. I turned back to the highway and saw Randall waiting with a child at each hand, preparing to walk. I vaulted over the veranda rail and landed on the ground noiselessly and with no shock to my feet, and hurried after. When I reached Randall the children were gone. We pressed on along the highway, following the wire shadows. I looked at Randall again from the corner of my eye and saw that he was crying. "I'm very sad," he said, and I began to cry also. We walked on, shedding tears, until that dream ended.

Sometime later I awoke from a different dream, one that I couldn't remember. It was dark and I had no idea of the time. I felt sad, haunted and weary, and I avoided looking at the clock, hoping to fall back to sleep, but I lay awake wondering where Bartley was. After fifteen minutes perhaps, I looked at the clock and saw with surprise and a sinking heart that it was barely one-thirty. In my head I heard again the music of the song "At Midnight". I tried to lull myself to sleep by recalling the words of the minor-key stanzas, but I could remember only the sense: isolation and the remoteness of the stars. I lay awake distressed and praying. About two a.m. I slipped out of bed and knelt on the floor. I was too tired to organize my thoughts; I wanted God to see me praying continuously, even if I should fall asleep. But I was awake all night.

CHAPTER TWELVE
COVETOUSNESS

The next day I stayed at home, consuming eight of the forty hours of paid sick leave that my summer employment entitled me to. I left the telephone buried under pillows, napped and tried to think of what to do about Joanna. Prayer was not giving me the answer. God seemed to have left me temporarily on my own, as if He now wanted me to struggle. My life in Him had had its tribulations, but they had been minor up to this point. Usually I had been guided by prayer and by signs, and the knowledge of what to do had come easily. My ability to preach had come as a gift outright, but now it seemed that I would have to struggle to keep it. I thanked God for the Love that such an important test implied, and I asked Him to be with me in the trial.

Sometime after lunch I found the courage to uncover the telephone, but not the courage to call Joanna. Late in the afternoon she called me.

"Are you all right?" she asked. "Your office said you phoned in sick."

"I've been sleeping badly," I said.

"Nothing else?"

"A lot of spiritual trial," I said.

"Well," she said. "God help you." There was a silence, then she said, "You got a letter from Randall?"

"Yes."

"I'd like to see it," she said. "Are you well enough to come over? Or I could visit you there."

"I thought I saw Rob Bartley's car parked on your street."

There was another, longer silence.

"You know," she said at last, "this makes me very angry."

"Tell me why."

"Because I think you abandoned me."

I had no ready answer. The depth of sin into which Joanna had evidently fallen seemed out of all proportion to anything I had either done or failed to do. But I felt an immense burden of guilt before God, Randall and Joanna too.

"I'm sorry," I said. "I've prayed for forgiveness."

"Why did you do it?"

"I don't know," I said. "I'm not as strong as I seem. I'm not as strong as I look."

Joanna didn't answer.

"But regardless of my shortcomings—did Randall deserve this?"

"I love Randall," she said. "No harm can come to him.

"I love him too," I said. "I've never felt worse. And Bartley. I'm convinced that Bartley is an evil man."

"He isn't," she said. "He's very kind."

"He's a womanizer."

"Women love him."

"Can you say that with a straight face? His life is selfish and sinful. He's practically a poster boy for the sin of lust."

"We're all sinners," she said. "Some of us do more harm than others."

"All sin is harm."

"You are an unhappy man. Randall says that something has gotten away from you."

"Is that what he means when he says that? That happiness has gotten away from me?"

"I don't know," she said.

"I'm not unhappy," I said. "I take joy in my vocation. God has rewarded me far beyond my deserts."

"I'm glad," she said. "You're a marvelous preacher."

All at once I felt too tired to continue the conversation. I no longer felt any urgency about sharing Randall's letters, or any curiosity about the letters he had written to Joanna. "I'll pray for you," I said. "And you must pray for guidance. I have to hang up now. I'll talk to you again after I've prayed."

"All right. Thanks. 'Bye." And she was gone, supplanted by a dial tone.

The extent of my failure to help Joanna and to vindicate Randall's trust now weighed on my mind both day and night. I prayed for guidance in undoing the harm, but I felt weak, frightened and unequal to the challenge. I was glad I had no way to communicate with Randall. I wondered what I would say to him when he eventually came back.

I considered calling Bartley to try to impress upon him the wrongness of his conduct. I even thought of trying to arrange a pastoral meeting among the three of us, where I could appeal to Joanna's Christian understanding, and perhaps to Bartley's ethical intelligence, for remediation. But Joanna increasingly presented herself to me as a stubborn child, and

Bartley was evidently an accomplished moral relativist, more interested in excusing behavior than in regulating it.

I examined my face in a mirror. In the two weeks since my sermon, something had happened to diminish the look of command that was normal to me. My complexion had gone from ruddy to china-like, and my blue eyes were large and diffident in that bloodless field. My weakness and incapacity were written there for anyone to read. Each day I dreaded going to the office. And the thought of facing a congregation, speaking to them, enduring their appraisal, was by now unbearable. I began looking for some means of escape. I imagined setting off into the wilderness on the track of Randall, but I was afraid to give up the security of my apartment and the income from my summer job. I imagined becoming sick and helpless, so that the onus of maintaining myself and meeting my social and work obligations could pass from me. I imagined dying untimely and going home to God.

When ideation finally brought me to the point of contemplating my own death as a welcome event, I stopped short and prayed for forgiveness. I had let myself sink into defeatism, as if Jesus Christ had not trodden the hardest path to make me safe. I felt more worthless than ever, my existence on earth and my hope hereafter justified by my faith and my faith only. But it was hard to live from day to day when my faith gave me certainty without comfort.

I was still isolated, still struggling and still not re-engaged with Joanna when another letter arrived from Randall. He was now four states away.

July 12

Dear friend:

I'm writing to you from the front step of the house we lived in when my pa died. It's even smaller than I remember & the neighborhood, which used to be on the edge of town, is now in the middle. The lady of the house invited me inside to look. My brother's & my room is tiny & belongs to a girl—it's pink & full of stuffed animals. My ma & pa's room has a bed in it exactly where the bed was when my pa died.

If I had a destination in mind when I started to walk, this was it. Now I have to decide whether to push on or turn back—also whether to keep walking or catch a ride. Maybe I'll pretend this is home again & explore the neighborhood. The school will be closer than I remember & I guess the grocery where I used to buy candy won't even be there. From where I sit I can see they've tucked some new houses into vacant lots.

I haven't mentioned my pa to you much. After he died I kept looking for ways to get him back. At first I thought if I prayed hard enough he'd come back, or that it would turn out a mistake had been made & he hadn't died at all. After a while I gave up on that & prayed that my ma would marry our preacher, until I figured out that the preacher was already married. Now I look at this house, which is the only place I ever knew my pa, & it's hard to remember he was ever here, he's so long passed over & the town is so changed. I went on missing him until I met Joanna, then I stopped wishing I had somebody taking care of me & turned my attention to taking care of her.

The first time I laid eyes on you, I had the feeling somebody had died on you too. It's what I meant when I said something had gotten away from you. You looked like me in the time between my pa dying & me finding Joanna. You've said you don't know what got away. I imagine we'll figure it out sooner or later.

Tell Joanna I said this trip is also a search for her. It's a search for everybody & everything I love.

May the two of you care for each other & God care for us all until we're together again.

Randall

I refolded the letter immediately after reading and hid it in a dresser drawer. I felt utterly unequal to its demands. I sat down in the upholstered chair, closed my eyes and bade my brain go blank. I waited for God to show me how and for what I should pray. But nothing came.

It was as if God had left town with Randall. For the time being, I didn't know where to look for either of them. It was a pity that Joanna's behavior had foreclosed any chance of finding communion through her, because of all people she was closest to Randall, and of all people she had been the first to call on me to be a shepherd. I might have had recourse for spiritual guidance to the pastor of my church, but I had lost confidence in him a year earlier when we prayed over Solveig, and now I anticipated a terrible failure of my own, in that same church and in full view of the pastor, if I didn't regain confidence in myself before I was to preach again. I was ashamed of my judgment of the pastor and ashamed of my fear of being judged by him; but I didn't want to face him then.

I thought of going to Dr. George Woodrick, if I could find him in town during the summer. I had been his star student the winter before. Although I had never consulted him on spiritual matters, I knew he was a strong man of God and that he would help me if he could, both in my spiritual crisis and with the practical difficulties surrounding the preparation of my sermon. I found his home phone number in the book and dialed it from my office.

The professor's wife answered. She remembered my name as soon as she heard it; she was sure that Dr. Woodrick would be glad I called, but he couldn't be disturbed just then. I offered to phone later; she suggested I try again in two hours.

I hung up the receiver and kept to my office, haunted by a growing sense of isolation. Quite unreasonably, I felt Dr. Woodrick's temporary unavailability as a rejection. The world seemed a place of loneliness and alienation. Everyone I had ever befriended was now absent or estranged: Randall on his walkabout, Joanna and Bartley in a liaison that I could never approve and that excluded me anyway, Solveig gone to Sweden, Marie married and gone, Beth remarried and gone, my co-workers uncomprehending and adrift outside my door. And God, Who had been as close and comforting to me as any physical presence, now seemed to have withdrawn as effectively as Randall himself.

While I waited to phone Dr. Woodrick, I tried unsuccessfully to concentrate on my work. I realized that circumstances would compel me to be less candid with Dr. Woodrick than I might be if the only thing at stake were my spiritual welfare. I would have to protect Randall's and Joanna's privacy, because Woodrick knew them both. It almost seemed that there was no point in talking to Woodrick, because Joanna was at the very center of the current crisis; without Joanna I had no coherent story to tell. Finally I decided to go to Woodrick and tell a story anyway, coherent or not, and hope that God would give him the understanding to appreciate the nature of my pain, if not the immediate cause, and to help to guide my spirit. When at last I was able to speak to Woodrick on the phone, I asked to meet him for a conversation in Christ.

"Of course, my dear fellow," he said, "of course. Is there a particular subject?"

"No, Sir," I said, "just some spiritual uncertainty that may be interfering with my capacity to preach."

"Tomorrow during the day, or in the evening?"

"I work during the day," I said.

"In the evening, then. Can you come to my house at eight?" I had the address from the telephone book; he gave me directions to find it.

The house was grander than the Langs' by a factor of roughly three. I gathered that the ministry Woodrick operated in addition to his teaching duties had rewarded him well. I considered whether it was in me to take material advantage of my own gift of Holy Truth telling. I conceived there was nothing wrong in living comfortably in exchange for giving comfort to God's people, but I didn't envisage myself preaching for material reward. Nevertheless I admired the Woodricks' house. It was large and in the Tudor style, with as much bare wood inside and out as any wilderness imagined by Randall.

George Woodrick answered my knock and ushered me into the high, beamed living room long enough to introduce me to Mrs. Woodrick, then we retired to the den, which smelled of cigars, although Woodrick was not smoking one. The den was larger than the Langs' living room, wood-paneled from floor to beamed ceiling, and decorated with dozens of framed photographs of Dr. Woodrick posing with notable people, among whom I recognized the Reverend Billy Graham, General Edwin Walker and two Vice Presidents of the United States. Woodrick waved me into one of two overstuffed leather chairs and took the other for himself.

"I understand you've been given a couple of guest pulpits this summer," he said.

I nodded.

"How's it going?" he asked.

"Well enough so far," I said. "I'm having some difficulty preparing for the next one."

"And that's when?" he wanted to know.

"August eighteenth," I said.

"Eleventh Pentecost," he said. "You can't be having trouble finding a text."

"No, no," I said, and to my great surprise and embarrassment, my voice broke a little. "I'm having trouble finding courage."

Woodrick stared with something that looked and felt to me like disappointment. "I don't understand," he said.

I hesitated. I felt that whatever I might say next would be unwelcome. I actually thought for a moment of turning and running, but I told myself that Woodrick would hear me in a spirit of Christian fellowship, and that l owed it to both of us to share the generality of my tribulation, if not its sensitive particulars. "Yes," I said, "some personal events are testing my faith. Making it hard to set aside my own preoccupation in order to preach to other people. To address any doubts that they might have."

"Preaching is not an activity that you take up or drop according to the mood of the moment," Woodrick said. "It's a profession. The Good Lord knows I've preached at times when I was too tired or distracted to make sense to myself, but I've preached. Leaders don't lead by being temperamental; they lead by being dependable. You have the Truth. You give answers. You don't give questions."

"What would be an adequate reason to forgo giving a sermon, then?"

"Too sick to get out of bed."

It seemed I was in no danger of being asked to reveal secrets. The subtlety that so fascinated me in Randall was absent from Woodrick's personality. Woodrick was granting no latitude for weakness. I doubted he was aware of weakness, except as a concomitant of the sinful condition that he freebooted against in tents and stadiums. It also seemed that I was in no danger of being subjected to a feminizing sympathy. But I hadn't come to Woodrick seeking sympathy—only guidance—and it was guidance I was getting. Already I felt much better and stronger, sitting opposite Woodrick, than I had when I came in. I redirected the conversation to the subjects of preaching in general and of Woodrick's career, and after that to the subject of his house. He spoke knowledgeably about real estate as an investment. After an hour or so I thanked him for his advice, let him see me to the door, shook his hand and took my leave.

Once outdoors, I found myself wondering at the inconsequential tone of the meeting I had just left. I had gone into it feeling vulnerable and anxious for learning and fellowship, and I had come out feeling poor and diminished in wisdom. It was as if George Woodrick, who could move populations to God wholesale from the pulpit, had no gift for retail. I looked upward at the pale suburban sky. The night was balmy and caressing, the sort of night that reflects in nature the essential goodness of a loving God. If I'd been a pantheist and not a Christian, this weather by itself might have restored me from the sense of spiritual pilferage that remained from my meeting with Woodrick. I looked up into the sky for signs of the Christian God. There was no moon and few stars; beyond the silhouettes of leafy trees the sky was blanched in urban light. I could hear the sounds of motor traffic from the major road a few blocks away, and I could see amber lamplight behind windows of the large houses on Woodrick's street. God is with us always, whether we sense His presence or not.

I began to walk toward home, a matter of fifteen or twenty blocks. I had come by bus, but the weather was fine and I wanted time to reflect.

The meeting with Woodrick had been both easier and much less gratifying than I had hoped. The example of his professionalism as a preacher would help me, but I wondered if, brilliant as he was from the pulpit, his vocation was equal to mine. I wished I had his single-minded confidence, and I'd have prayed for it then and there, but I was still in the mode of waiting for a sign from God that He was ready to engage me again, so I walked on meditatively and in all humility, receptive to any indication.

A few blocks from my apartment, another of that summer's reversals caught me up. I happened to see by the light of a street lamp, lying against a curbing, a thick manila envelope, evidently fallen from a car: a single dusty tire track crossed it lengthwise. I picked the envelope up to look for a mark of ownership, but it was plain brown paper, unautographed, its flap sealed. I turned it over several times without learning anything more about its provenance or contents. I looked up and down the street, hoping for a clue to its owner or its home. But I was on a commercial street, the nearest residence a block or more away, and I didn't associate any of the nearby businesses with such an envelope. If I was not to leave the packet abandoned in the gutter, the only option was to open it and be guided by the contents. I lifted the flap at one of its corners and tried to peel as non-destructively as possible, but the paper tore. Finally I just inserted my index finger and ripped across the top of the flap.

By the streetlight I discovered a pack of eight-by-ten black-and-white photographs—perhaps twenty of them. The first photograph—the only one I looked at then—was crudely, grossly, explicitly pornographic. I clapped the envelope shut and pressed it against my chest. I scanned the street again, this time for a trash barrel or dumpster where this material could be disposed of securely, but the sidewalk waste containers were of open steel basketwork. I tucked the envelope under my arm and hurried the last blocks home.

CHAPTER THIRTEEN
ENVY

The wide divergence between what we know to be right and the actions and inclinations that our earthly flesh impels us to is a constant trial. In that summer of 1968, transgressive sexuality was becoming a mark of the popular culture. Behavior that had formerly been secret and shameful began to be lauded and lionized by the generation born ten years after me. There were millions of them, noticeably richer and more privileged than I had been at the same age, the girls toy-like with their disproportionately large heads of glossy hair, their eyes painted oversize and their skirts so short that one was surprised at how high up their legs remained separate, the boys even taller than I was, unshaven, arrogant and open-faced, mooting revolution and—we understood—exploiting the girls *en masse*.

The iniquitous youth pictured in the pornography I found that night and brought home to destroy seemed cut from that bolt. They were perhaps a little older than the members of that demographic swell known then and since as the baby boom. I can't say, because in my kitchen I tore the photographs one by one into small pieces as fast as I could confirm the pornographic nature of each. But one of them stopped my hands. It was a naked couple in the act of sexual intercourse, the woman reclining in a chair, her legs draped over the chair arms, her eyes under drooped lids gazing directly at the camera, her lips slack in a moue of listless surrender. She had Marie's face. I caught my breath. I looked again at the woman's eyes and set the photograph aside.

I tore the remainder of the pictures to shreds, one by one, when no familiar face appeared in any of them, and threw the scraps into the garbage bin beneath my sink. The one intact photo remained on the counter top. I walked away and sat in the living room to gather my thoughts.

I felt haunted. In spite of my constant devotion through the past two years, the onslaught of circumstance had brought me full circle and confronted me, barely defended, with the fact of my deadly sin with Marie. She had suddenly invaded the very apartment that I had consecrated to sexual abstinence. The hand of Satan was unmistakable.

And God had never been so quiet. I was still waiting for a sign from Him, and while I waited Satan had broken into my house.

My best defense would have been to destroy the Devil's photograph without ever looking at it again, but something made me wait. Even though God continued to be quiet, I tried praying, but my thoughts became filled with vague images of Joanna and Bartley in some intimacy or other—perhaps nothing more diabolical than a walk together hand in hand—and of Joanna and Randall together, and of myself with my arms around Randall. The more I tried to invoke the Holy Spirit, the more the love of human persons supervened. In my mind's eye the woman with Marie's face grew large. At last I decided I could learn no more until I looked again at the photograph. I brought it from the kitchen counter to my desk, turned on the desk lamp and sat down to study.

The woman was not Marie, of course, but she could have been. The content of her look was content I had seen in Marie's face and had not thought of again until that moment. The man having intercourse with her was turning his body to give a quartering view of himself and to allow the camera to see his erect penis half-buried in the woman's vagina. They were posing. But a small detail of the photograph disturbed me more than its entire freight of unregulated lust; it distracted me from the unwanted but inevitable effects on my body of the picture's eroticism; and it stopped me again from destroying the photo, even though there was no question that the woman was not Marie. The detail was the interplay of her right hand and his left, the only parts of their bodies, except where she had him invaginated, that were actually touching. Their fingers were interlaced as delicately as if the two of them had been school children, or Adam and Eve before the fall. I stared transfixed at these fingers, examining every geometric particular. There were seven separate points of contact along the line where the planes of their hands intersected, and an eighth point of contact where the pad of his thumb rested against her open palm. Her gaze, hooded by lust, was still directed at the camera— or at me—but the sum of all human connection in the picture was not in her look or in their naked, copulating parts, but in those interwoven hands. I leaned close over the photograph and tried to understand it through the hands. I dug in the desk drawer for a magnifier I kept there and examined the fingers through the glass. They hinted at a kind of intimacy that I had once known but had forgotten. In the glass I could see magnified the white meniscus of the man's thumbnail, and the soft depression the thumb made in the woman's palm. Anxiety rose in me like the threat of unshriven death and I felt unspeakably sad and lonely. I hid the photograph and the magnifying glass away in the desk.

I went into the bathroom, undressed and took a cold shower, although my undesired erection had subsided by itself. I watched the water cascade down the hairless planes of my body and stream off the end of my penis, shrunken by the cold. I had come to doubt that I knew what God expected of me after all. But I dared not cease to inquire.

After the shower I knelt at the side of my bed and prayed to God that, if it were His wish, He might reveal Himself to me in a more prescriptive way than He had ever done. I didn't mean to instruct God in the conduct of my spiritual life, but I asked Him to tell me exactly what I ought to do about Joanna. I asked whether He expected me to go to work every day, even though—as I now suddenly realized—the work was becoming a torture. I asked what message He wanted me to deliver in my next sermon. I asked to be assigned to a Crusade. Or I asked Him to give me a plain and simple task to carry out for His glory, so that I might remember what it was to experience success. But there was no immediate response to my petitions.

I knelt beside my bed desperate for any kind of companionship. But my nearest friend, as long as God was silent, was Randall. I wanted to ask God to send Randall home immediately, but I didn't want to risk His wrath by seeming to place Randall before Him. Once again I thought of trekking west in Randall's footsteps. I crawled into bed and covered myself with a sheet and turned out the light.

It was almost predictable that Satan would invade my sleep. I was lucid but dreaming, and I found myself with the woman in the photograph, or with Marie. Her soft, sad face stared out at me and we linked our hands. I remembered what I had forgotten entirely since my religious awakening: that I had loved Marie to the extremity of death. I felt exalted by her touch, as if the force of life and knowledge and final understanding flowed into me from her fingers. We twisted in space, like God and Adam on the Sistine ceiling. I knew I was dreaming but I didn't wake up. We interlaced the fingers of our four hands, so that it was impossible to tell where one of us ended and the other began. Our bodies flowed together like tributaries of a stream, and I saw that we were swimming in our own tears, breasting the current, going away. We clung together tightly, and the more our bodies interpenetrated, the more I was exalted and the stronger grew my sense of understanding everything that was and everything that could be. We swam higher, weightless, electric, suffused in a light that grew whiter and more intense until it burst, and burst us with it; and then we—I—

fell down, still weightless, into darkness and peace. And still I didn't wake up.

Sometime later I dreamed again, but this time I was not lucid, and I believed I was on the road with Randall. We had found his father alive and praying in a landscape that looked like the painting on the wall of the Langs' living room. We sat together silent on the ground and shared a large, ashy-looking cake of no particular color or flavor. Randall and his father looked alike, although the father seemed older and wore a plain robe or gown of the same texture as the cake. They talked, but I understood none of the words. I walked away and stood beside a river that flowed nearby, watching the sun glisten in the water and looking for fish. I squatted down and passed the fingers of my left hand through the reflecting surface. There seemed to be nothing beyond it. I turned my gaze back toward Randall, who was still sitting on the grass. He lifted one arm toward me in a slow, hieratic gesture, and I saw that his father had disappeared. Now he was accompanied by two small children in summer dresses. They flanked him on either side, only as tall standing as Randall was sitting. I expected to hear Randall's voice calling to me, but there was no sound, the raised arm his only sign. I lifted my own arm in reply. Still there was no sound, and no one moved. The tableau remained.

I awoke rested but somewhat depressed, a few minutes before my alarm was set to go off, and said my morning prayers. I understood that lacking specific guidance I would have to carry on working at my summer job, and proceed, whether aware of divine inspiration or not, to prepare and deliver the August sermon. I knew that God existed and that He wanted me to do the right thing, but I had no information at all about what the right thing was. And so I would have to do what I had been doing. I could not change course without an obvious sanction. I switched off the alarm before it could ring, and got up to face the world.

For several days I spent lunch hours in the library at the seminary, looking in volumes of collected sermons for some hint of what I should preach. Eventually I settled on a topic of some urgency to me just then—that of man's individual relationship with God. I was so desperate for reassurance and so lacking in spontaneity that I borrowed the armature of an existing sermon for the eleventh Pentecost that had been composed and delivered hundreds of miles away and many years earlier. I took the scriptural lessons selected by the original writer, hoping they would speak to me as well as to my congregation. Of course I would rewrite the sermon in my own voice, without which it could not come from my heart or speak to any of us.

The first lesson was from Exodus 16, where the children of Israel are fed in the wilderness with manna from God, which they mistakenly believe was provided for them through the intercession of Moses and Aaron. The second lesson was from Psalm 78, which recounts the story of Israel in the wilderness and laments the failure of Israel to acknowledge Him. In the third lesson Paul challenges the Ephesians to put away every un-Christ-like deceitfulness that can alienate them from God; and in the fourth lesson John describes Jesus pursued to Capernaum by the multitude, hungry again, whom He had fed with the miracle of the loaves and fishes. The sermon writer saw in all of these lessons a common theme: man separated from God by preoccupation with quotidian things and failure to form and nurture a personal relationship with the Lord.

I read the sermon hungrily but received no sustenance. The failure of the Israelites to recognize God in the manna was not a failure of mine. Paul's appeal to the Ephesians to eschew licentiousness and accept God in Christ was not one that needed to be addressed to me. The clamoring of the multitude for a free lunch instead of Faith was not a defect I shared. It made me sad to think that I had avoided all of these spiritual shortcomings and still failed to grow close to God. I was determined to discover another meaning in these lessons—one that could account for my own spiritual isolation. I was finding it harder and harder to appreciate the spiritual disengagement of so many nominal Christians. I now imagined myself one of a disappointed spiritual elite, and as such I deplored the negligent, lackadaisical adherence of my coreligionists. What was worse, and culpable, was that I also despised it. I fell on my knees in the seminary library and asked forgiveness. But there was no clear answer.

I found myself thinking I was the only authentically religious person I knew, except for Randall. Was this a delusion similar to the one that led to the apostasy of Satan? Would my desire to attain perfection be the agent of my fall? I didn't know what to believe. The choice appeared to be between two deadly sins: spiritual sloth and meliorist pride. I was stymied. Of all of God's creatures then struggling on earth to know and understand Him, it seemed unlikely that any could be struggling harder than I. I prayed for a sign. Still none came.

I told God of my faith and promised Him that I would do His work forever, sign or no. I told Him that I would be vigilant, ever aware of the ingenuity of Satan. I affirmed that I would be His witness as long as He willed me to live, even if no other Christian could be found on earth. As I prayed, I wept with mixed frustration and relief—frustration that no answer came, and relief that my mind was still made up, that my faith was intact. I photocopied the sermon and carried it home for study and recasting.

When I got it there I was surprised again by the fatuousness of its argument, which seemed to be that God makes Himself distant only from the simple-minded and the self-absorbed. I knew better. In His profound mystery and the particularity of His intention for each of His children, He may hide Himself indefinitely from the most assiduous man of faith. I sat and read Exodus 16 in a new way. I saw that it was a mistake for the man who would be faithful to let a third party, however holy and astute, interpret God to him. Luther had had the same revelation about the Roman Church. Now I was having it about myself and everyone I knew. My vocation from God now seemed to be to put myself out of a job. I would preach to my community that they must look past me, and past every other person professing to know God better than they. I would challenge them to stop their ears, or else to get up and walk out of church, to meet God outside in the street. I would challenge them to go directly to God, not to Moses, for the proper recipes for the keeping of bread and the cooking of quail. And God—or Jesus, Who is God—would have to attend to them one by one, because the priests would no longer be holding their proxies.

The lesson I drew from Psalm 78 was a new one too. When God grew angry with Israel, "He slew the strongest of them, and laid low the picked men," just as He had earlier smitten all the first-born of Egypt and visited plagues, pestilence and natural disasters on that unhappy bumbledom. There was no safety in numbers; on the contrary, there was risk in numbers. There could be safety only in a high profile and a firm, private understanding with the Lord.

Of course I now saw Paul as the very archetype of the apostle who should endeavor to make himself superfluous to the faithful, and as soon as possible. And in Ephesians 4, Paul is uncharacteristically non-prescriptive, as if for a moment he shared my distrust of priesthood. I would mention this to my congregation, although I doubted there was much mileage in it.

And finally I read the Gospel lesson from John. The genius of God-on-earth in Jesus is precisely the personal relationship it's possible to establish with God when you meet Him in the body of a man. But still one must meet Jesus man-to-man, not Jesus as described by a third party or captured by a hired runner with an autograph book. The aspiring freeloaders who followed Him to Capernaum got to hear from His own lips what would be required to save their souls. I myself wanted to hear from His own lips. I wanted to plead with everyone to hear God, and when everyone understood, I could stand aside. I longed to do that. And I longed for Randall to come back, because I thought he was the only person I knew that understood already. Once more I began to cry.

It seemed to me that this recent weepiness could not be a good sign. Evidently I was not entirely in control of myself. I thought of Jesus weeping for Lazarus, only to resurrect him an hour later, and of Mary the mother weeping over the crucified Jesus in a thousand Italian paintings. These were tears shed over circumstances that would be put right. But I wasn't sure what I was crying about, or what would be needed to put it right.

I composed the first draft of my sermon in only two evenings, then set it aside, so that I could come to it again fresh. I put in my eight-hour days at the summer job, interacting with my co-workers as amiably as I could in my state of doubt and preoccupation. I scanned their faces, listened to their talk and watched their body language for clues to whether they, too, might be doubtful and preoccupied. I tried to see them as creatures conscious of their distance from God, but they seemed untroubled and thinking of something else.

On at least one evening I took the pornographic picture out of the desk drawer and studied it again. I was perfectly aware of the danger it posed, and I would have torn it up like the others, but the woman who looked like Marie had excited my sympathy. I stared into her eyes and she stared back. There was some hint of tragedy there, but it seemed equally possible that the depth and intensity of her gaze were due to sexual transport. One couldn't tell by looking whether she was happy or sad, sexually excited or anesthetized, intelligent or dim-witted, a willing harlot or a pathetic victim. But the most thoroughgoing pagan would have admitted that she had a soul: it called out from her eyes. I wished I knew what it was saying.

I thought of my co-workers in the summer office. I had applied the same scrutiny to them and detected no passion. It was a measure of my growing isolation that this photograph was better company. In my loneliness I even imagined that I might try to find Marie and speak with her. She had been married only a little more than a year. I knew her husband's name; I supposed they still lived in the city and could be found through the telephone directory. But when I tried to construct our conversation, I saw that it was impossible. The basis of the friendship on which I could presume to call her had been a ruinous affair, and now I was not the needy sinner she had known, but an apostle of Christ, obligated by faith and duty to evangelize her to the flock, and she already a member of the Roman church and married in it. I thought immediately of half a dozen reasons why any overture would be unwise, and I could think of no way, if I did speak to her, of avoiding a counterproductive awkwardness. Seeking Marie was out of the question. So I contented myself as well as I could with looking at the eyes of the woman in the picture until I felt I could learn nothing more from them, and then I returned the picture to its drawer.

And about this time, in the midst of life and its small trials, the thing happened, terrible and inexplicable. On Sunday afternoon, July 28, the telephone in my little apartment rang. I picked up and heard through the receiver the cries of an hysterical woman. Until she spoke the name of Randall I didn't know who she was.

"Joanna! What's wrong?"

"There's been an accident! Randall has been killed!"

How can I convey the immensity of the chasm between what I heard Joanna saying, and my understanding, up to that time, of the nature of the world? I didn't believe in accidents, although I heard them reported every day. I didn't believe that Randall could die, although I knew it was the way of all flesh. A huge void opened where my heart had been, and in my disorientation I heard myself exclaim idiotically, "No! Randall killed? For good?" Tears burst from my eyes and I fell to the floor, the heavy black body of the telephone tipping off its table and crashing after me. I clutched the receiver to my ear, praying desperately, but not with words, that I had misunderstood and that Joanna would say something different. I heard her wailing, unable to catch her breath, and I despaired. I gave myself over to crying and just lay there, at the beginning of a very, very long—perhaps endless—process of acceptance. At that moment I was not curious to know how Randall had died. I only wanted to know that he had not died. But if he had died, the manner of it was of no importance.

I lay on the floor for several minutes, distraught, listening to Joanna's paroxysms while she listened to mine. My abject failure in the service of my friend now weighed on me a hundred times more than all dying. I had abandoned my responsibility to his wife; I had neglected to follow him when I might have; I had failed to save him from death. The weight of my guilt crushed the breath out of me.

And then I thought of what must be Joanna's guilt, and pity for her crushed me again. In failing her I had failed everyone; I had failed God. Perhaps I had even failed Bartley. The sound of her helpless keening at the other end of the phone tore at my soul. When I thought she could hear me I asked if she had called anyone to sit with her. "No," she sobbed. "Can you come? Randall would want you to be here." That was certainly right. I was inert with sorrow and so weak with shock that I couldn't imagine lifting myself off the floor, let alone finding the energy to go to her house. But I told her I'd come immediately.

I washed and dried my face and phoned for a taxi, then waited in front of my building. The day was sunny and moderately hot, the trees along the street leafed out in deep green, some Sunday traffic moving. I looked for any hint that Randall was no longer in the world, but there was none. I felt giddy, as if I might pitch forward on my face at any moment. A light breeze stirred the branches. I stared up into the blue sky and understood nothing. Sunlight sprinkled down through the foliage and splashed in irregular, wandering patterns on the surfaces beneath, but buildings across the way were variously bright or in deep shadow, according to the geometry of their walls and the altitude and azimuth of the sun. These were signs of the abiding order in the universe, unaffected by the passing of my friend and indifferent to the appalling fact that an accident had killed him. I tried to reconcile the bland ordinariness of the Sunday afternoon with the anguish in my heart, but my head was too light. After some vacant, comfortless time, the taxi came and took me to Randall's house.

CHAPTER FOURTEEN
ANGER

In the ten minutes transit from my door to Joanna's I tried without success to re-center myself in the world, now terribly changed. I knew that if I was to be of any help to her I'd have to accept that Randall had died. But my mind continued to rebel, tempting me with the idea of a great misunderstanding and a happy, tearful reunion. I resolved to be a source of strength for Joanna, regardless of the facts, but I had no idea of what I would say.

I rang and she let me in. She looked wretched, smaller than ever, her face red and wet; she was mopping her nose with a soaked handkerchief. We embraced at the door and said nothing; she quaked and sobbed, and I cradled her head helplessly against my chest. I must have looked wretched too. We walked to the living room and sat on the couch opposite the mantelpiece and the painting by Randall's father. Its setting was the dream landscape where I had last seen Randall, flanked by two little girls and raising his hand to me, but now only Jesus was there, praying alone. Joanna was wearing a gray sweatshirt and matching pants; she drew her bare feet onto the couch, folded her knees against her chest, rested her head against my shoulder and continued to weep. I stared at the painting, remembering that in my dream the sun had been shining, but here it was night. After a long time Joanna grew quiet and I thought it was safe to speak. "What happened?" I asked.

"Randall fell from a bridge," she said, and began to cry again. I folded my arm around her, hoping to comfort, and waited. After a few minutes she said, "It happened yesterday. They called today. From the sheriff's office." And she mentioned the name of a county in the state where Randall had written me his last letter. I waited, mystified and disbelieving, for her to say more, but she only wept quietly.

"Did they say what the circumstances were?"

"No," she said. "Only that he fell. And was killed."

"Were there witnesses or anything?"

"No," she said. "I don't think so."

"And did he fall into water?"

"Onto a railroad track." And she shook again with sobbing. I sobbed too, helpless in the face of this strange news.

"Would you feel better if we prayed?" I asked after a minute.

"I've been praying," she said.

I tried to imagine what might have happened to kill Randall. I tried to visualize an accidental fall, but no version involving a sound bridge over a railroad track seemed plausible. I saw him being pushed to his death by a malicious stranger. I saw him leaping to his death, a suicide like me. I couldn't believe it of Randall, any more than I could believe his death an act of God, or the mindless act of an unknown person. Once again I considered whether we were dealing with a mistake, a false report.

Joanna continued to cry quietly in my arms. I couldn't share with her the forlorn hope I was harboring; it was far too likely to be groundless, too likely to interrupt for no reason the process of acceptance she was undergoing. I felt desperate to know more of the truth. I felt pity for Joanna and would have changed the subject if I could, but there was no other subject. I hoped she knew more and would volunteer more, but she only lay and wept.

Time passed. I wanted to ask Joanna's permission to phone the sheriff out of state and get some clarification, but I hesitated, unwilling to quibble with the terrible, overarching fact that Randall was evidently dead. The particulars could hardly matter to Joanna at this moment; the only reason they mattered to me was that my mind could not accept the truth of a narrative as elliptical as this one. Until I could see the logic of Randall's death I would not believe in its inevitability. I imagined this late Sunday afternoon in the sheriff's office of a small Midwest town. There was information there about this dolorous event, no doubt the saddest of Joanna's life, and I felt I needed it before I could proceed to help. I asked God to guide me and I believe He did. I stayed where I was, ignorant as I was, and gave Joanna as much comfort as I could.

Days later it came to my attention that Joanna had spent some or all of the previous night in the bed of Rob Bartley—this while Randall lay alone and dead a thousand miles away. Her torment while she lay weeping in my arms must have been terrible. Mine would have been too, if I had known.

It wasn't until the next morning that Joanna's anguish had stabilized enough for her to communicate practical information to me. I stayed with her that night, afraid to leave her alone and unwilling to be alone, God with me or not. Her sexuality had disappeared entirely, even though she clung to me and made me sleep beside her on Randall's bed. She felt tiny as a child, and she shuddered in her sleep like a child recovering from a tantrum. I slept fitfully, fully clothed, disturbed by dreams, awaking frequently and knowing each time where I was and what had happened. We both awoke finally at dawn and I got up and sat in a chair, stale, bleak and stupid from lack of rest.

Barely speaking, we picked breakfast from the refrigerator. We sat at the table in the kitchen, doing little more than looking haggard. I gave thanks silently for my portion of the food, diffident to involve Joanna. Eventually I asked her permission to telephone the sheriff. She gave it with a wordless nod. But when I called there was only an operator to take my name for the deputy, who was due at his desk at eight a.m., so I had to hang up the phone and wait some more. I could not go to work that day; I called my company and left a message for my boss, pleading Joanna's emergency.

She went alone back up to the bedroom; I sat reclining in Randall's chair and tried to sleep. At eight o'clock I phoned again. The deputy wouldn't talk, but asked my name and phone number and returned the call. "Who are you, Sir?" he asked as soon as I picked up.

"I'm a friend of the family," I said.

"You're with Mrs. Lang, I take it?"

"That's right."

"What can I do for you?"

"I hope you can tell me what happened."

"How long have you known Mr. Lang?"

"Only about a year. But we grew quite close."

"Were you aware of anything wrong with his health?"

"No. Was there something?"

"Do you mind if I ask when you last saw or talked to him?"

"Nearly two months ago. He was on a walking vacation."

"How was his mood when you saw him?"

"It seemed very good." I felt cold, and there swept over me the terrible sense that I had been abandoned. If Randall jumped, then I knew and believed nothing. In panic, my tired brain sent me back to the first question, and my mouth blurted it: "Is Randall dead?"

There was a moment's silence, and then the deputy said, "I'm sorry, Sir? 'Is Randall dead?' Did you talk to Mrs. Lang?"

"Yes, of course. She said he fell and was killed. It's just hard to believe."

Then, before I could frame the question myself, the deputy asked me, "Do you have any idea why it might have happened?"

The panic seized me again. "A terrible, inexplicable accident. Did anybody see it?"

"A couple of kids playing on the tracks. They heard a yell and saw him hit."

"He yelled?"

"That's how they happened to see him falling."

"Is it possible he was pushed?"

"There was no sign of that. No sign of a struggle either up on the bridge or on his clothing. By the way, we'd appreciate Mrs. Lang's permission to proceed with an autopsy."

"I think she's sleeping."

"Have her call me when she wakes up."

"All right." I waited for the deputy to say more, but he was silent. I tried to visualize the scene of Randall's fall, but no version of it was credible to my imagination.

Eventually the deputy asked, "Does anything else occur to you that might help us with the investigation?"

"I don't think it could be suicide," I said.

"And why is that?"

"He was a Christian."

"Anything else?"

"Everything I know about him argues against it. I believe he was quite a happy man, married to a beautiful woman and taking comfort in his religious faith. It's just not reasonable."

"Anything else?"

"Was the bridge he fell from a dangerous one? An easy place to have an accident?"

"Not really. The parapet's about chest-high. You'd have to climb before you could fall."

"Then I don't know," I said. Sleep deprivation overwhelmed me at that moment. I felt disoriented and full of pity, for Randall, for Joanna, for Bartley—of all people!—and for myself. I wanted nothing more than to be alone and praying for the repose of Randall's soul. I thanked the deputy for his information and hung up. My body felt heavy and my mind adrift. I lay back and dozed.

I dreamed that Joanna came down from the bedroom and found me asleep in Randall's chair. I realized that Randall had come back and was waiting at the front door. I tried to get up but I was heavy as death, unable to move a limb. I was letting Randall down, disappointing his expectations of me. Joanna opened the door and led Randall in, and the two of them stood opposite me, hand in hand, smiling like schoolchildren. I wanted to get up and greet Randall but I was asleep and couldn't move. There were many things I needed to say to him, to account for my omissions while he was away. I felt frustrated by my inability to wake up, and anxious that Randall would leave again before I could speak. I struggled to sit up but a great, invisible mass held me down. I tried to cry out to Randall to wait, but no sound came from me. Finally I closed my eyes and waited for the paralysis to pass. Sometime later I was startled by the realization that I had been left alone. I sat up, wide awake, and saw that the room was empty, the late morning sun pouring in at the window. And I remembered that Randall was dead.

The house was quiet. I lifted myself out of Randall's chair and made my way stiffly to the bedroom. The door was ajar; I peered past it and saw Joanna asleep on the bed. I thought I had never felt more lonely. I pulled the door nearly shut. I went back to the living room, knelt bereft in front of the sofa and prayed for Randall.

But my prayers unsettled me. I prayed first that Randall's soul might be at rest, and then that God might provide for Joanna in her widowhood, and that He might forgive her past sins with Bartley. It was the picture of Joanna alone in a world inhabited by Bartley that unsettled me. I would have prayed for Bartley to conceive honorable intentions toward Joanna, so that their companionship might in the long run be blessed by God, but the idea seemed not inspired and of God, but irrational and springing from my own desperation in the face of my failure to guard Joanna for Randall, and the uncertain obligation I remained under on account of Randall's death. I wondered if God wanted me to take up Randall's yoke, in the manner of the surviving sons of Judah with Tamar. But Joanna's aggressive sexuality so frightened me that I imagined coming to grief before God as surely as Onan had.

I trusted that God's wishes for me would appear, whether they matched my preferences or not, and my instant fear gave way to the solace of knowing that I would eventually be called upon to do the right thing, whatever that might be. The immediate task was plain in any case: to protect Joanna and to put Randall's affairs in order, and to bring Randall home to be buried. I thanked God for the reassurance I felt, got to my feet and went upstairs again to peek through the bedroom door at Joanna sleeping there. I pushed my way in as quietly as I could and sat in a chair, unwilling to disturb her.

The scene reminded me of the brief but wondrous moment in my hospital room when I was reborn in God and Jesus—that minute or two between my waking from the coma and Beth's waking to find me restored to life but forever out of her reach. Now I was the one waiting in the chair, and it was the woman in the room that was unconscious on the bed and transformed, perhaps, by desperate circumstances. When finally she awoke I would not burst into tears and throw myself on her; I would maintain a respectful distance and try above all to add in no way to the harm.

Only a few minutes passed before Joanna did in fact wake up. She stirred, uttered a slight moan and opened her eyes to see me sitting a few feet away. She started, confused and evidently frightened, let out a small cry, then lay back and began to weep. I was torn with pity but I didn't move. Instead I prayed aloud. "Dear God," I said, "please be with us and comfort us in this terrible time. Please fold Joanna in the wings of Thine angels and give her the peace and strength to go on living in Thy ways. Help us as we come to grips with all the practical problems around this awful accident. Guide us in honoring and remembering Randall. 'In Jesus' name. Amen." Joanna may have murmured Amen. She kept crying.

"I spoke to the sheriff's office," I said. "I think they need to perform an autopsy to find out what happened."

She was silent for most of a minute. Then she said, "Do they have to cut him apart to do that?"

"I don't know exactly how it's done," I said—truthfully, I thought.

"I have to see him," she said. "I can't do anything until I see him."

"We'll bring him back," I said. "I'm sure they'll send him back very soon. But I take it they have to perform an autopsy first."

"Why?"

"A sudden death in unexplained circumstances. I think it may be required by law." I waited for Joanna to give a sign but she lay still and said nothing. "I'll phone them again," I offered. "Do you trust me to speak for you?"

"Tell them we want him back."

"I will." I left her lying on the bed and went back to the living room to phone the deputy. Whatever test of legitimacy I had been subjected to in our earlier conversation I must have passed, because the deputy knew who I was before I identified myself, and he was ready to talk. I told him Mrs. Lang had authorized me to speak for her.

"Good," he said. "I'll special-deliver some forms for her to sign. You'll witness them and send them right back."

"This is for the autopsy?"

"That's right."

"And without the forms, what would you do?"

"We'd get a court order."

"I see."

The deputy quoted Joanna's address. "Do I have it right?"

"Yes." I paused. "One other question," I said. "Would anything about the autopsy prevent us having an open casket at the funeral?"

"I don't see why. It might depend on how good an undertaker you get. His head is pretty banged up as it is. I'm sorry to have to tell you that."

"I understand. And how long would it be before you could ship his body back?"

"Not more than a day or two after we get your paperwork. You tell us where you want the body shipped and a local funeral home will handle it from here."

When I had put the receiver back on the cradle I heard in my own head Bach's chorale setting from the St. Matthew Passion of the Lutheran hymn about the wounded head of Christ. I saw in my mind's eye the trickling blood and the crown of thorns. I supposed that Randall's wounds must be less painterly, less Holy, less emblematic, less comprehensibly an act of God. I thought they might be hideous, his skull cracked wide open on the steel rail, his excellent brain splashed out on the wooden cross-ties. I remained where I sat, waiting for an idea I could share with Joanna, but none came.

I longed to engage God and Joanna at once in a debate about how and why Randall had died. When I confronted alone the terrible fact, it was inexplicable; it was barely even credible. If Joanna and I were to talk about it without invoking God, how could I be sure that we might not conspire, in the mutuality of our anxiety and our wishfulness, to deny what was true? But God,

Who knew all about Randall's death—and mine and Joanna's, for that matter—would hold the Truth up to us.

I longed also to go away and meet God by myself. I felt the risk that Joanna could suck the life out of me, needy as she was. In spite of my early hope we had never strengthened each other, but only disappointed— she with her sexual voracity, I with my censorious remoteness. It was now early afternoon on Monday; we could be thrown together by necessity until Wednesday or Thursday at least, while we awaited the disposition of Randall's body.

I made my way back to the bedroom and looked in. Joanna, haggard and still wearing yesterday's gray sweatshirt and pants, was seated on the edge of the bed she had shared with Randall. "Is there somebody that can come and stay with you?" I asked.

"Why can't you stay with me?" she said in a flat voice.

"Wouldn't it look better if a woman stayed with you?"

"Are you afraid?"

I had no idea what her question meant, but I said no. She stared at me, her green eyes rimmed with red, a handkerchief crumpled in her right hand. I felt helpless to assist. In Heaven, with God Supreme and Eternal, with the last battle fought and Satan defeated forever, I could have shared all comfort with her. But we were still on earth and a time of trial was upon us. I placed my back against the doorjamb and sank to the floor so that she could see me, as she never had, from a high vantage. I wanted her to appreciate how small and weak I now found myself. My idea was not to contribute to her insecurity, but to make her understand that we were equal partners before God in the enterprise of justifying Randall's death. This was my new dispensation—the idea I had come to lately that priesthood should be outgrown as rapidly as possible. I needed Joanna's intercession as much as she needed mine. I slumped a little lower against the doorjamb and said, "We have a lot to do." Joanna didn't speak. "Would you like to pray together over what's happened? It would help me," I said.

"All right," she said.

I struggled to my feet, walked past her and knelt beside the bed. "Will you kneel beside me?"

"All right," she said, and got down on her knees.

I closed my eyes and began to pray aloud in generalities I no longer remember. I sensed Joanna beside me, although she made no sound. I asked God to be with us and to help us understand His purpose in taking Randall. I prayed that He might hurry the process by which our sorrow over Randall's loss would give way in time to gladness for Randall's life and for the certainty in Jesus that we would see Randall again. As I prayed I felt strength and confidence returning to me for the first time in the weeks since my last sermon. I sensed that this prayer in company with Joanna could accomplish much good and cover much difficult ground. Tormented as I had been with guilt for my failure to guard and guide Joanna, I hoped through this prayer to find expiation for us both. I asked God to help us reflect on sins and failings that might oppress Randall's spirit and for which we needed to ask forgiveness. I heard Joanna stir beside me. Then I felt a tremendous, stinging blow to my left cheek and ear.

"Stop it!" I opened my eyes to Joanna screaming and cocking her arm to hit me again. I threw my arms over my head and she rained down half a dozen more blows, screaming all the time, before she collapsed on the floor in tears. "Stop it," she said again, and wept miserably.

I was astonished, mortified, frightened, embarrassed, and in some small physical pain. My left ear was throbbing and I thought the over-pressure her hand had applied to my auditory canal might have damaged the eardrum. Furthermore, I was at a loss to know what had set her off. Surely we both had wronged Randall. I couldn't believe that I was the only one that saw it. And I had never before been attacked and beaten in the midst of prayer like a Christian martyr. I felt sad and cold. I wondered if Joanna expected an apology, and—if so—for what.

"You're a monster," she said.

My mind reeled. "I don't understand what you mean."

"How can you be so sanctimonious? Do you think my moral improvement will bring Randall back? Do you think you understand how Randall and I loved each other?" She rolled herself into a ball and quaked with sobs.

In my chagrin I turned inward and asked God to help me. I was certain I had been praying for the right things. I had to suppose that Joanna, in her grief, was not ready to accept the truth that she had sinned against us all. It was possible that she had not even accepted the truth that Randall was dead. In my desire to make amends to Randall for our failures, I had moved too fast. As well as I could, I apologized to Joanna for hurting her feelings. "But I still think it's vital that we pray together. Maybe you could choose the words."

She mumbled something. I leaned down and placed my throbbing ear near her mouth. "When I'm ready," she said.

CHAPTER FIFTEEN
FAITH

She wasn't ready until the following day, by which time we had received, signed and returned the permission for Randall's autopsy, and arranged for a local funeral home to accept the body. It was a slow process to get Joanna to focus on the practicalities. I considered offering to conduct the funeral, but I thought I should leave it to Joanna to ask, and I was no longer sure of my ground. What if I were to eulogize Randall innocently in some way that caused Joanna to react as she had while we were praying? I tried to get her to consider whether she wanted a large funeral or a small one. The whole community of the seminary knew and loved Randall. I could even imagine my own mourning appropriately subsumed in a public occasion marked by the tent-revival style of a George Woodrick. It would leave me free to know what I knew, with no obligation to represent Randall to anyone but God.

Monday night I slept on Joanna's sofa, but not before I borrowed her car to drive to my apartment for a change of clothing and some toilet articles. On Tuesday morning I phoned my summer office again to project my absence for another couple of days. I felt I must not leave Joanna alone until we had prayed together and found common ground for mourning Randall.

I pressed her as much as I thought I could do without exciting her natural stubbornness. It seemed to me that our praying together and the planning for

Randall's funeral were parts of a single enterprise, and the tone of the one would determine the particulars of the other. When we had mailed the paperwork and selected the funeral home, Joanna finally knelt with me.

We were silent at first. I waited for her to speak, as I thought I had promised, but the silence wore on. Inwardly I prayed to God to give Joanna a voice that would please Him while it taught me, but the silence continued minutes more, until I broke it myself. I repeated my prayer aloud, certain that it needed to be shared with Joanna, but she only said "Amen." Another minute passed before she began to speak.

"Lord," she said, "why did You take Randall? Why did You take him when I already missed him so much?" These were words that might have been mine. I was glad she had asked them; I squeezed my eyes tighter shut and listened for a reply, but she went on. "How can I live without him? How long will I have to wait to see him again?"

"Make strong our faith," I interjected. "Give us peace."

"Lord," she said, "are You punishing me? If You took Randall away for something I did, it's very cruel."

"Give us strength," I said.

"Bless and keep Randall," she said. "Forgive him if he made my love for him more important than my love for You. Forgive me too, please."

"In Jesus' name," I said.

"Amen," she said, and I repeated:

"Amen."

I kept my eyes shut and my attention on God, and I hoped Joanna was doing the same. I felt the praying had gone well to this point. We had covered important ground, and quickly, but there was more. "Lord God," I said, "forgive me too, for being a coward when Thy yoke threatened to grow too heavy. Forgive me for not keeping my duty of faith to Randall and Joanna. Take Randall to Thy bosom and tell him I tried. I can't forgive myself. I pray one day I may, in Jesus' name."

How might it have affected me if, at that moment, Joanna had reached for my hand and squeezed it? But there was no outward sign of forgiveness from anyone—not from Joanna, not from me, not from God.

And in my suddenly exacerbated loneliness, I had no further doubt that Randall was dead. I opened my eyes and turned my head toward Joanna. She was watching me, her face impassive but her eyes full of sorrow. I looked away.

As it turned out, the funeral packed the seminary chapel, Woodrick officiating. It took place the following Monday, the casket open, Randall waxen and diminished, but with no sign of damage to his head. During the viewing at the funeral home I had tried to acquaint myself with the Randall who had lived between my last talk with him and the fall from the bridge, but it was all a mystery. He lay uncharacteristically surrounded by flowers, and his receptive intelligence, his charismatic vitality and his pipe were all absent. I could no more see the face of the living Randall in the corpse displayed before me than I had so far been able to see the face of God in life or in my dreams. Each frustration reminded me of the other, although they were on separate scales entirely. I had the memory of Randall, and it was precious. I had the promise through Jesus Christ, Him of the iconic human face that didn't interest me so much, that I would live to see God finally. But my need was more urgent than that.

Joanna and I viewed Randall's body together and separately in the days before the funeral. She had run out of tears by the time the body arrived, was prepared and went on display. I think she believed, more than I did, that some essential part of Randall was in that box. She had known him years longer than I had, and his physical body had had authority and substance for her that it could not have had for me. I suppose she looked into the casket and saw wreckage. I saw the specter of anomie.

No coroner's report had been issued by the time Randall's body was interred. I watched it go into the ground with no sense that I understood, aside from the obvious, why my friend was being buried. Every death scenario seemed implausible. An accidental fall over a chest-high barrier seemed impossible; that someone could or would have lifted and pushed him over such a barrier, nearly so. That he might have lifted himself and jumped, almost unthinkable at that moment. George Woodrick's sermon and eulogy contemplated only that Randall was dead in the midst of life, and not whether by the hand of any person. The lesson Woodrick drew was the conventional one that the best and the worst of us die inexplicably and in God's time, and that those present could find joy in the midst of sorrow in the sure knowledge that Randall—as one of the best of us—by dying had gone home to God. What Woodrick said gave me no comfort. It was unexceptionable sentiment, safe and true as far as it went, but I desperately wanted to hear the further truth, as if from Randall himself. I was glad Joanna had not asked me to officiate: I would not have been able to marshal even as much truth as Woodrick had.

At the moment when Randall was lowered into the ground I resisted an impulse to intervene, as if by letting him go I would lose my last chance to hear him explain. Joanna, standing beside me, drew a breath as deep as our remorse and rose on the balls of her feet; I took her arm to keep us both where we were, and the casket sank out of sight. I lowered my head, clutched Joanna's arm, and prayed that the peace of God would be with her, as it was not then with me.

After the funeral I drove her home in her own car, accompanied her into the house and watched for a sign of what to do next. She was quiet. She removed her hat and shoes and sat on the edge of Randall's chair. "I should offer to drive you home," she said.

"No, no," I said. "Rest. There are plenty of buses." She didn't argue. "I'll phone later to see how you're doing," I said, and left.

Joanna and I had yet to discuss the nature of Randall's death. Whether he died by foul play, accident or suicide must surely be at least as important a question for her, I thought, as it was for me, and for me it was crucial. I felt I couldn't rest until I knew what had happened, but I feared I might not be able to rest, either, when I knew. What if my friend was murdered? What if Joanna had lost her husband to a murderer? It would be necessary to find the killer, to punish him for Joanna's sake and to get an explanation from him for my sake. What if Randall killed himself? What could that mean to Joanna but repudiation, abandonment, proof that she was not worthy to keep him alive? I didn't dare to think what it would mean to me.

I haunted the sheriff's office with my telephone presence for a few days following the funeral, until the coroner filed his report. The deputy told me the conclusion. "Officially an accident," he said.

"How were other causes ruled out?" I asked him.

"Absence of evidence," he said. "No sign whatever of foul play. No marks on the body except the ones caused by hitting the ground. No marks of a struggle on the bridge."

"What about suicide?"

"No reason to think so, I guess. He didn't leave a note. I remember you couldn't give us any reason. And the autopsy showed nothing wrong with his health."

"But you didn't entirely rule it out."

"Well, there's no way to rule it out entirely. Anything's possible. Foul play's possible; we just don't think so. One thing: jumpers usually leave property behind. Mr. Lang had a knapsack, but it fell with him—on the body. Point is, the coroner has to come to a conclusion, so he comes to the one that leaves him the shortest distance out on a limb. Murders and suicides need motives. Accidents don't. They just happen."

"But how could Randall have fallen over a chest-high barrier?"

"Climbed up on it for the view? We'd have to have physical evidence or some reason to think he was suicidal before we called it anything but an accident. But I'll ask you again: do you know of any reason why he might have killed himself?"

"No," I said.

"All right."

I hung up the phone and thought about calling Joanna. I believed she had assumed all along that Randall had died by accident. The news of official concurrence might be less welcome than my forbearance to bring up the subject at all.

In the end I didn't.

Instead I found myself fixated on Randall's accident, if that's what it was. I could think of nothing else, although I was at my summer office trying to catch up on time lost during the week after Randall's fall. I phoned the deputy again to ask for a copy of the autopsy report.

"I'll see if I can get you one out of this office," he said. "Might have to come from the coroner's office. And the way things work around here, you might have to pay for the copies."

"That's fine, of course." I gave him my mailing address.

"I'm thinking you might not want to show this stuff to Mrs. Lang," he said.

"Of course, I understand. Very thoughtful of you. Thanks. God bless."

"Good luck," he said.

The taking of steps to confront the mystery let me concentrate once more on my work, but the preoccupation was evident in my dreams. I found myself on the road again with Randall. We were on the bridge he had fallen from, looking over the parapet. I was afraid for my own safety. I clung to the bridge rail with both arms, but it was insubstantial, so that I had to depend on my sense of balance to keep from falling. Far below, on a grassy verge beside the single, straight railroad track, two small girls were seated playing. My unease extended to them. They were too close to the track. A passing train could hit them. I was filled with fear. I knew it was inevitable that Randall would fall and be killed; I knew that he was dead. Every creature was in danger: the little girls, Randall, I. Some of us were doomed to die before I could wake up.

Randall slipped his arm through mine. I clung harder to the railing, certain we were about to fall. "Are those your children?" Randall asked. I squinted and saw that they were.

I awoke then in the dark, momentarily relieved to be out of danger. But loneliness and failure weighed on me. I felt myself becalmed, all headway lost, and with it all steerage. Once again I had reached an end of my life, just as had happened when Marie abandoned me. But I knew that this time I had no choice but to struggle on, according to my promise to God. When He was ready for my struggle to end He would take me, perhaps as unexpectedly as He had taken Randall. But the choice of time was His, not mine.

Somehow the fire that had burned in me to tell God's Truth to the nations—that fire had gone out. Only my stubbornness remained. I still knew and believed God's Truth, but I no longer believed I could convey it. My next sermon, if I could find the courage to deliver it at all, would instruct my congregants to teach God's Truth to themselves. It would constitute my letter of resignation from priesthood after a short, brilliant, failed career. Now I had to consider whether to continue with seminary in the fall. With Randall gone and George Woodrick no longer my model, there was no teacher there I cared to follow. In my dark bedroom, at some unknown hour of the night, for the second time in two years I had reached the end of a skein of hope.

I hesitated to pray for new hope, God Himself having taken away my vocation as unforeseeably as He had given it. I doubted whether He had an earthly purpose for me. He loved me as surely as I loved Him, but I doubted all at once that He liked me. He seemed a hard taskmaster, not enough displeased to punish me, but waiting for me to justify myself. I considered the case of the sinner Bartley, outwardly blessed with a cheerful disposition, worldly goods and the love of women who ought to have known better. For all I knew, of course, Bartley might already be afflicted by demons, and God alone knew what the future held. But I wondered at the difference in our fortunes. Finally I simply prayed to God to let me sleep, and He did.

CHAPTER SIXTEEN
HOPE

At Christmas of that unruliest of years, American astronauts in orbit around the moon read Bible verses by radio back to earth. By then I had delivered my last, failed sermon, dropped out of seminary and been refused the resumption of my former job. But because I had in effect been laid off at the end of the summer I qualified for unemployment compensation, and it was enough to guarantee survival while I huddled in my small apartment and debated with God over what to do next. A new President had been elected, the party of the old one having been discredited by bloody days of anarchy in the streets around their convention in Chicago. The new President claimed to be implementing or about to implement a secret plan to end the war. I hoped it was true. His affect was strange for a public man: there was a systematic disjuncture between his speech and his gestures, as if he were the creature of animators who had not yet mastered their craft. He reminded me of an old film I'd seen of Adolf Hitler reviewing boy soldiers in the last days of that other War, his eyes mad and his purposes unspecified. The new President consorted ostentatiously with Billy Graham. I hoped the country might benefit from that.

I thought daily of my lost friend Randall, and I was assailed daily by feelings of guilt over my failure in my duty to him. I no longer saw or spoke to Joanna; all empathy between us had vanished, in spite of my efforts immediately after Randall died to offer care and protection to her. She was remote and seemed resentful, and my courage failed me. I soon realized that her friendship with Rob Bartley was continuing, and my courage failed again. I was haunted by Randall's ghost watching these events—whose particulars I knew nothing of, and wanted to know nothing of—and I felt guilty and feckless. Would Randall have had me intervene? I felt cold with the realization that I had never understood the nature of the Langs' relationship. It even seemed possible that Randall's ghost, with the perspective of one subsumed in the infinite, might be better pleased with Bartley's care of his widow than with any care I could offer. My chagrin was complete.

I prayed constantly to God to guide me hence and to comfort Randall and me with the fact of my good intentions, but comfort eluded me, at least. I regretted the curiosity that had prompted me to ask for a copy of Randall's autopsy, because now my overriding memory of my friend was a passionless, minute description of the anatomy of his body, its tissues and its internal organs, and a more vivid and distressing one of the trauma to his dear head and his engaging brain. I knew, for example, that whatever the usual practice in preparing bodies for an open casket, there had been no brain tissue whatever inside Randall's skull when Joanna kissed his reconstructed face. I had hoped fervently for a clue to the mystery of Randall and his death, but the autopsy contained none, so I was the worse off for having read it. My only satisfaction was that I had kept it from Joanna.

In my loneliness and isolation in that Christmas season, I went so far as to contemplate a life among people, regardless of my obligation to God. It might have been easy to garner companionship from among strangers, living as I did in a city, and particularly from among women, whom I felt I understood better than men. But I hesitated to attempt a contact, for fear of any number of sorry outcomes. I still felt that any liaison with a woman would have to be directly in the service of God, and in that respect I feared another disappointment like the one with Solveig. I also felt less sure of myself than at any time since my rebirth in the hospital—less sure that I had anything valuable to offer to another person, less sure that I knew how to witness for the Lord. I looked less beautiful in the mirror, too. Something of the golden patina was gone, as if this sign of my provenance from God and my grace in God had been probatively withdrawn, and now I had to win it back.

Many precious people had been taken in the course so far of learning what God wished of me. It was a mystery that grew more profound and spawned more passion in me with every loss. I had no doubt that, once plumbed, the mystery would magnify and validate my passion, and my exaltation would be towering and eternal. My brain entertained this idea with great excitement; my soul contemplated the final triumph with great joy; but my body felt depleted and unable to contribute to the struggle. I had never been more tired.

I ought to have been haunted, too, by the memory of my failed final sermon, except that in retrospect the failure seemed not a loss but a validation. With Randall less than two weeks in the ground I might have used my mourning as an excuse to stand down. But I felt a compulsion to finish what I had begun. With my best audience, Randall, snatched from the world, and my vocation to preach withdrawn by God as emphatically as it had been given, I wanted to say goodbye to my congregation and warn them not to depend on the likes of me, Woodrick and the Apostle Paul to bring them to the Lord. So I told them; they sat stolid in their pews, even when I challenged them to get up immediately, go into the streets without waiting for the sermon to end and the recessional to play, and begin their private searches for the true, the secret, the hidden God. Did they hear me? Did they believe me? To a man and a woman, they sat with their faces upturned benignly and let me speak. But they didn't move. My power to stir hearts had lapsed with my vocation, and I was an object lesson in the truth of my own theme: that God does not occupy pulpits. I preached at them helplessly, no more cogent than a tree falling in an empty wood, and when I received their greetings at the door at the end of the scheduled service, the most perceptive comment offered me was: "Interesting."

In my holiday isolation I reviewed the times I had felt closest to God. None of these was in a church, except for the occasion of my first public sermon, and one or two occasions when I had prayed alone in an empty chapel. I remembered instead some conversations with Randall, the early companionship of Solveig, some dreams. God seemed hardest to find in a crowd, easiest in the enthusiasms of one other person, or in the soul's diffidence. Then the main chance, if I were not to dream my life away, was to find a Godly companion.

I found myself thinking of Rob Bartley, that corrupter of women who might have been my Godly companions, but for Bartley's perverse engagement with the same questions that possessed me. It seemed possible, with Bartley in the world, that every woman that could be brought to an appreciation of the yoke conferred by God's Love would be unyoked again, and easily. I might search for Godly companionship in a woman, find it, then see it dissipate before the secular blandishments of Bartley and his ilk. It was as if, apart from sentiment, the women of the world understood the nature of God only through the apostolic lead of men, and the Bartleys of the world understood the nature of women far better than I did. If I wanted my companion to be a woman, it seemed I had two choices: to acquire her and hide her thoroughly from men, or to disarm Bartley and the people like him. The alternative would be to settle for the companionship of men; but in those days I regarded God as a Man, and a jealous one at that. I could be cloistered and love God or I could be married and love God, but I didn't want to submit my relationship with God to the disruptive force of another male intellect.

I felt a vague compulsion to seek out Bartley and do battle with him, as if I might thereby make the world safe for feminine religiosity. I had Faith without any reservation, mental or emotional; I had confidence in my ability to defend my faith; I had enough confidence in Bartley's intellectual integrity to believe that he could entertain my arguments and be convinced by them. Still I hesitated to call, repelled as I was by thoughts of his relationship—whatever it might now be—with Joanna.

Instead I placed a classified personal ad in a weekly tabloid newspaper that had begun publication only two or three years before. It was not a comfortable venue for me. The editorial content was strictly secular and the point of view was leftist, skeptical and a little angry. But there were many pages of ads placed by people who, like me, must have felt isolated by the anonymity of urban living. It was hard to gauge the sincerity of the advertisers, and among the dozens of ads placed by women seeking men, I read none I thought I could respond to. But I knew my own heart well enough to trust my own sincerity, so I submitted my copy and waited.

My ad, when it appeared, was unique in that issue of the paper. I was the only advertiser specifying religious faith as a qualification. It had come to my attention that the letter "J" appearing in many ads meant "Jewish", as for example in "WJM" for "white Jewish male". But there was no explicitly religious content to any of these ads, so I took the qualification to be no more than ethnic and cultural. I might have styled myself "WCM", but there'd have been no precedent to guide readers away from the misapprehension that I was, for example, "WRCM". I considered "WPM", but there was no precedent for that either, and the "P" seemed to me as broad as the ethnic and cultural "J". Finally I just spelled it out: "Christian." And I made clear that Christian Faith was at the center of my requirements.

In the first week my mailbox at the newspaper received just two replies. One was printed in pencil on lined paper, badly spelled, and more in the nature of a screed than an introduction to a person. If I had wanted to reply to it I could not have, because the writer forgot to sign and gave no address. The other was written in blue ink and a small hand on several five-by-seven-inch sheets of white, unlined, watermarked paper. It read as follows:

Tuesday, December 17

To whom it may concern,

I read your ad with great happiness to know there is a Christian man willing to put his beliefs first in priority. This is such a wicked world, it sometimes seems that everybody is just out for whatever they can get and never mind what is right.

I am a born again Christian woman 34 years old praying for a relationship that would be blessed in the eyes of the Lord. I sinned before I found Jesus and accordingly had a child, a beautiful

little daughter, that I had to give up several years
ago, which is my earthly punishment. As a
Christian I know you will be forgiving if and
when we meet, and so I just come right out and
tell you this.

I work as a secretary-typist with some people in my
office who are very nice, but they are not strong
Christians. I would like to marry a Christian man
and begin a family before much longer. I could
continue to work, but I would pray for the chance to
stay at home and make a happy household for my
family.

I tell you more about myself than necessary at first
because I don't want you to waste time on me if I am
not what you were looking for.

I could send a picture but I don't have a good one,
also I think appearances are a lot less important
than what is in the soul. I am average-looking, but
you could decide for yourself. I am warm and
friendly. I love animals and would have a cat but am
allergic.

I believe the Lord means me to have a family to
replace the one I was raised in, which is now gone
since my father died this year of lung cancer and my
mother a few years ago. I had a twin brother killed in
Korea the Christmas after high school. I know this is

getting ahead of myself, but hopefully you could be the Christian man I have been praying for.

If you would like to meet, I include my telephone number, or you could write and I could call you. If I don't sound right for you I will understand, but I hope and pray it is God's will that we should get together.

Sincerely yours in Jesus,

Sandy Ann Fisher

I read this letter with a growing sense of agitation, and I tucked it back into its envelope with the feeling that it was very unsatisfactory. I wasn't sure what kind of answers to my ad I had hoped for, but this was not it. I was disappointed that there were only two responses—one, really. I could leave the ad to run another week, but it was apparent that not many Christians were reading this tabloid.

I took a copy of the ad out of my desk drawer and reread it for a clue to the reply it had elicited. The ad said only:

Committed Christian man in early 30's, non-smoker non-drinker, seeks female of strong Christian faith for sincere, supportive relationship.

Nothing in this formulation seemed to invite a proposal of marriage, although I saw that I might better have substituted the word "friendship" for "relationship". In fact, on impulse I made a strike through "relationship", penciled in the change and phoned it then and there to the newspaper classified department, and settled back to wait.

But the letter from Sandy Ann Fisher nagged at me and I read it again. It was clearly a call for help from a lonely person under pressure of time. I doubted that I could provide the help she sought, but the fact that she had sought it from me made her impossible to ignore. I formed a mental picture of her as a plain, thin, waif-like woman of medium height and sallow complexion, wearing a housedress and no jewelry except for a Jesus fish. She looked like no sort of intellectual companion for me. I asked myself if I could dedicate my life in Christ to one so lacking in *éclat*. I felt petty and un-Christian asking the question, but I was certain that God wanted to engage my intelligence: it was for this reason that He had made His purpose for me so arcane. What if I were to take this woman under my wing to protect for the rest of our lives at the cost of abandoning the daily struggle to know His will? I might come to the end of my life having achieved a place in Heaven, but I'd have done it without distinction, without the edgy joy of wrestling every day with the Divine. However perverse it seemed to think it, Rob Bartley looked like a better choice.

Christmas loomed. I thought of Sandy Ann Fisher bereft of family or strong Christian friends with whom to celebrate the holiday. It would have been easy and convenient to meet her in time to share Christmas worship and a meal, and my own isolation would have been abated. But I was afraid just then to take up her burden. I prayed for her though, while in my mind's eye there hovered the picture of her solitary life. I may have wept.

The tabloid that carried my ad skipped publication the week of Christmas, so that my corrected copy didn't appear until a few days before New Year's. This time it attracted only one response. But I recognized the small blue hand on the envelope.

Monday, December 30

To whom it may concern,

I see your ad running again and think I may be rebuked for what I wrote last time. A sincere Christian friendship is more than many could hope for and it would be enough for me. It is true that I pray for a family of my own in Jesus and the chance to atone for my previous mistake which I mentioned in my letter, but friendship is precious whether the beginning of something greater or not.

I hope you can consider me as a friend and will get in touch. I have prayed for you already, knowing you are a good man even though we have not met.

Sincerely in Christ Jesus,

Sandy Ann Fisher

I collected this letter from my box on New Year's Eve. The sentimental possibilities of phoning Sandy Ann Fisher immediately did not escape me, but neither could I bring myself to do it. I was lonely, but not so lonely that I would jump without due reflection into a friendship or relationship with so much of its agenda preset by the woman in my mind's eye, or by any woman. I spent the night of New Year's Eve at home, most of it in prayer. I sat up to watch 1969 arrive on television in Times Square. I prayed it would be a better year for the world than 1968 had been, and then I went to bed.

I dreamed that Randall came to a house I lived alone in, bringing my two daughters. It was late at night in winter, snow on the ground, a full moon very high. The three of them sat on the floor playing at some game. Through the window I saw a sleigh parked on the lawn. I realized that all three were alive, or else all three were dead. I waited but no one spoke. Randall pointed the stem of his pipe at the moon. It occurred to me that I might be dead also, but not yet buried or received into Heaven. I listened carefully for a clue to where I was and to what was expected, but the silence was complete. I stared at the moon again. There was no face in it; it looked like a plain disc of white snow isolated in the sky. Something was lost, and I felt a fear of further loss. I sat silent, afraid to move. A wind rose, also silent, and blew snow in swirls around the sleigh. It grew dark then, but I slept on.

CHAPTER SEVENTEEN
CHARITY

Years passed. It would not be easy to say what I did during that time, except that I continued my search. I changed my mind about advertising for the companionship of a Christian woman. After the second letter from Sandy Ann Fisher I cancelled my ad. I struggled over those letters, unwilling to ignore a plea for help, but unable to persuade myself that by entering on an imperfect match I would not cause more harm than good. I wrote a letter designed to keep Sandy Ann Fisher at arm's length, but I never mailed it, afraid that it too would do more harm than good. During the period of this debate, I actually phoned Rob Bartley for advice. It was not as if I had been consulting Satan for the sake of rhetorical balance: I knew that Bartley was only a man, although a bright but flawed one; but my prayers had begun once again to give back the sound of my own voice, and I longed for another debating partner.

"Bring the letters and come over for a beer," he said. "Or something else. What do you drink?"

"Seven-Up," I said.

"I'll lay some in," he said.

Bartley's flat, half underground on the lowest floor of an old brick building on the side of a hill, was substantially larger than mine, but cluttered with books and high-fidelity sound equipment. It did not seem to be geared for entertaining. I took advantage of an opportunity to peer into the bedroom.

"Is that one of those waterbeds?"

"Yeah," he said. "King-size. I couldn't resist, since I'm on a concrete slab. It's got something like a ton and a quarter of water in it. It'd probably bring down a frame building." He smiled happily but I wasn't charmed. It seemed possible—likely, actually—that this was the bed Joanna slept in the first night Randall lay dead. And that it was also a bed slept in by Solveig, by the Jewess I had met on the street, by an unknown number of women gullible, suggestible or corruptible enough to be seduced by Bartley. On one wall I saw a large, horizontal poster that I recognized as a side-view photograph of Bartley's sports car, ingeniously divided into a series of vertical strips of increasing width, so that it seemed to be accelerating. I didn't doubt that Bartley was faster and more headlong than I.

He brought drinks from the kitchen and set them on a coffee table in the living room, waved me into an easy chair and fell backward onto the sofa with the informality of a random accident. "So you've come to me for moral instruction," he said.

"Well, hardly," I said reflexively, but wishing I'd said nothing. In the time I had known him, I'd seen Bartley's self-assurance produce all manner of unpredictable behavior and unwarrantable declarations. If he was making fun of me I felt no edge to it, but neither did I see any advantage for either of us in my abetting him. "Practical, worldly advice," I said. "What would you have done?" And I handed him the letters.

He leaned forward to receive them, then swung his body around and flopped full-length on the sofa, propping his head on a toss pillow and proceeding to study. He read both letters twice, soberly and with seeming respect, and then he said, "Well. What do you think?"

"I doubt she's right for me," I said.

"I'm pretty sure she's not right for me," he said, "but I might be inclined to investigate."

I heard his subjunctive mood but I flinched anyway. The idea of a Bartley incursion deeper into the Christian laity than he had already gone—it filled me with dismay. "Investigate?"

"Yeah. It's been my experience that every woman is a surprise. Many of them pleasant. It's a mistake to approach anyone—goes for men too, I should think—with the idea that you know in advance what your relationship with that person is supposed to be. It kills spontaneity. It also reduces your options and tends to put the other person in a box." He sat up, either because he took Sandy Ann Fisher's case seriously enough to make the effort, or because he wanted to be heard better as he spun out his worldview. "I don't think you can tell from these letters who she is."

"Then I should meet her."

"I would. Find out what makes her tick. Of course, before you can do that you have to know who you are."

"I know precisely who I am."

"Great! Then you don't need to worry about making a mistake." He hoisted a bottle in what was meant to be either a toast or a salute and took a drink of beer directly from it. I poured some Seven-Up.

I had every doubt that Bartley's style could be made to work for me. For one thing, his judgment-less approach to women amounted to promiscuity, as I had seen. For another, my range of choices was narrower than his, because God through my Faith had placed constraints on me that Bartley, for all of his sophistication, could never imagine. I stared at him across the coffee table and marveled that it had been within his scope to corrupt Joanna. I wondered if he were still seeing her and, if not, whether he had broken her heart. I was afraid to ask, not knowing what to do with the information if I got it. If my vocation had not been taken away, if I had a pulpit, I'd have rained brimstone on him without a second thought. But now, if I were to do anything at all to edify him morally, it must be to challenge him, to reason with him, to engage his appreciation of ethical principles. "But," I said, "aren't there some standards of moral behavior that would disqualify certain women *a priori* as candidates? I mean, don't you know in advance that some women are simply beyond the pale?"

"Not until I meet them. You know, it's not as if I were assembling a field hockey team. It's up to them, one by one, to decide what they're good for."

I pounced before I could think. "What did Joanna decide she was good for?"

"That would be violating a confidence," he said.

I was ashamed. I had broached the very subject I meant to avoid, and been roundly rebuked before I had any chance to withdraw or soften the question. I must have blushed scarlet.

"By the way," he said—and I was relieved that he kept talking, "I guess her husband was a good friend of yours. I'm very sorry for the loss of him."

"Thank you," I said.

As ever before, my attempts at the moral improvement of Bartley were going nowhere. He was a maddening farrago of charm, insouciance, generosity, reticence and misdirected talent. For a moment I coveted the rack and thumbscrews of a more theocratic age and place. Had I been able to immobilize him long enough to fix his attention on the true but hidden nature of things, there might have been hope. "You give the impression of not having any core beliefs," I said.

"Really?" Bartley said. "I operate out of a core of assumptions. Doesn't everybody?"

"But what do you believe? Do you have a fixed, definable faith in anything?"

"Sure I have," he said. "I think it's possible to find things out. I think there's an external reality that doesn't depend on what I think."

"I think the same thing," I said.

"That's why we're drinking together," he said, and laughed as spontaneously as if he had just overheard a particularly good joke.

"What's funny?" I asked, genuinely curious.

"What isn't?" he said. It wasn't the first time I'd seen easy rhetorical flourishes from him that did nothing to sharpen the debate. Then he added, "You're religious and you sense that I'm not."

"I more than sense it. I see the deficit in everything I know about your life."

"We're cut from different bolts. But neither of us turns out to be a man of the cloth." He snorted with glee. I got the jape, although I didn't find it terribly apt.

"We both believe in a reality external to ourselves," I said. "Doesn't this reality obligate you in some way? It always looks to me as if you're winging it. Aren't you guided by desiderata?"

"I don't know about 'obligate'. Reality constrains me. Maybe the difference between us is that your truth is revealed and my truth remains to be discovered."

"The same truth, though?"

He shrugged. "I'm inclined to think there's only one truth, but it's big and it's complicated. And not easy to divine. You should pardon the expression. To the extent that you're sure of more of it than I am, you're probably harboring more misapprehensions than I am. No offense."

"You refer to my Christian faith."

"I refer to everything you know for sure but can't prove."

"And how much can you prove?"

"Tentatively, quite a bit. I check my ideas against my experience. The ideas that don't withstand the test are disproved. The ones that do, I keep around to check again."

"I check my ideas against the Word of God," I said.

"As handed down unsigned and un-notarized in that Book of yours. To a neutral observer, not an entirely dependable source. Experience works better."

Bartley's arrogance and indifferentism made me despair for his soul, even as his dismissal of the Scriptures submerged me in a slough of frustration. It seemed we had nothing to teach each other, and that—until I could regain my courage—he was lost. I marveled that I had sought advice from him about a woman, or about anything of God. I left him as soon as I decently could.

In those days I felt a general disappointment with the world that informed my relations with everybody and everything. God seemed to be telling me to withdraw even more than I already had. The meeting with Bartley reminded me how unsatisfactory a life in society can be when the ideas one encounters are uncongenial and the people who hold them are unregenerate. Bartley's suggestion that I should meet Sandy Ann Fisher confirmed me in my conviction that I should not; and my sense of Bartley as an alienating influence also served to extinguish a spark of curiosity I had kept about me concerning Joanna and her understanding of Randall's death. I wondered if she—and Bartley—had come to know more about it than I did; but I found myself more willing to wait for my own passage into the Life Eternal to discover the whole Truth, than to face Joanna again in this one to learn only a little. And so I prayed, but otherwise I kept my own counsel.

It became necessary to take menial jobs in order to support my modest life. I suppose I might have recommenced a career like the one I left to go to seminary, but my dissatisfaction and discouragement in the world made me want to avoid any strong commitment to an enterprise I deemed corrupt. There were jobs as warehouse clerk or deliveryman that paid a living wage and that I could perform conscientiously and with an accuracy and punctuality far out of proportion to their social importance. My various employers must have thought they'd struck gold in me, but I resisted promotion, and they generally came to see, sooner or later, that my perfectionism and stubborn insistence on being guided by my own compass made me unsuitable to be a manager. The modest demands of the jobs I took left me with intellectual and moral space to pursue the important question. Properly, of course, it was not a question. It was the Answer. But the menial jobs let me contemplate that Answer for hours every day.

Remarkable events were occurring in the world I so despised. Having rounded the moon with an obeisance to its Creator at Christmas of 1968, men landed on it the following July, and several times after that. The Vietnam War dragged on and on, and so did the youth rebellion against it in the streets. In the spring of the year after the first moon landing, Ohio National Guardsmen shot and killed unarmed college students. The President of the United States continued to consort with Billy Graham and continued to promise an early end of the war. To me, his affect remained bizarre. I sensed that he was in no way a Godly man. Except for the Reverend Graham, he had surrounded himself with hard-eyed functionaries whose air of amoral efficiency did nothing to humanize the President. His Secretary of State was a Jewish academic who spoke with a German accent and was by birth ineligible for his fourth place in the order of Presidential succession. In my lifetime and before, the genius of my country had been to meld every influence impinging on it from the outside—every immigrant person, every alien ideal, every international challenge—safely into the vital Christian republic of the Founding Fathers. Now we saw division everywhere, distinctions of age, race, sex, class, income, ideology, nationality and denomination vaunted as if they should be the occasion of pride and joy, rather than a source of shame and invidious dissension. Every group capable of identifying itself by its differences immediately claimed to be the victim of some other group or of the civil polity in general. The commonweal historically blessed by God was in willful tatters. An age of assassination that had begun ten years earlier with the death of John Kennedy continued in train, killing or crippling candidates for office, pornographers, labor organizers, social agitators. Kidnappers and hijackers commandeered heiresses and airplanes in the name of political instruction. The group crying loudest—the youth—would be in middle age and putatively in charge at the coming of the Third Millennium a generation hence. It was easy to believe that we were entering upon the End Time of Revelation.

Through it all I continued my lonely dialog with God. From time to time, over a period of many years, I dreamed that I had at last come into the presence of the Lord of Creation and would, on that night and in that very dream, be accorded the bliss of seeing His face. But I never did. Each dream, whatever its particulars, followed a pattern in which, as I drew nearer the Sanctum Sanctorum, delays, diversions and impediments trammeled me and made me desperate with the knowledge that the time on earth to see His face was running out. If I didn't see Him this time, the next opportunity must be in a dream that might never come. And still I met frustration and failure, made to wait alone indefinitely while throngs went into the Presence, or finding that I had forgotten at home some gift or amulet without which I could not enter.

I devoted most of my waking hours when not at work to prayer and Bible study. Besides selected readings for particular occasions, I read both Testaments four times *verbatim et seriatim*. As a consequence, I knew in detail the ways of God as documented in His Book, when He watched and guided at a distance the Exodus of the Israelites and when He appeared on earth in the person of His Son Jesus Christ. For me, such exquisite detail heightened the mystery of His nature. In the Old Testament He took as close an interest in the politics and daily life of His people as if He had been one of the meddlesome lesser gods of Greek mythology, except that He never appeared on the ground. In Jesus, whose identity was subsumed in His, but Whom He forsook and abandoned to a death by torture, He seemed to prefigure my own latter-day struggle to hear and be heard by Him, and to be His witness in the world. It typically happened, when I read the Gospels, that the wish to preach came over me again, Jesus' relations with man and God being so similar to my own. But the memory of my first, failed career pained me. I associated it with the death of Randall, which I had never understood, and the descent of Joanna, which I had failed to prevent. I felt already crucified by these realities, and hadn't the courage or the understanding to justify them to a congregation. I looked at myself in the mirror and saw the progressive softening of my physiognomy, the retreat of my hairline, the blurring of my musculature. I had lived longer on earth than the man Jesus, and would leave less beautiful a corpse than the one racked at Calvary. I stared at my palms, wishing the stigmata were there and my life's battle finally decided.

It was in those years that the President was driven from office by the multiplying evidence of his corruption, and that my country was driven from Vietnam by an inferior enemy more dedicated to their cause than we were to ours. It struck me that adherence to principle might have prevented both defeats. The President was a nominal Quaker who ignored his communitarian tradition of consultation and concordance in favor of aggression and conspiracy, until he was found out and punished by legal and political processes that were without Quaker pretensions of any kind. My country was historically Christian, and the arsenal of the Godly nations, but it fought without conviction and ran away while the triumph of righteousness over Marxist atheism was still in the deepest doubt. I could only pray that we might meet the anti-Christ in a different arena and defeat him there. As for the President, I prayed for the regeneration of his soul.

From the time I left seminary, and throughout the decade of the 1970s, I made a practice of attending a different church every Sunday, or at least of never attending the same church twice in any period of a few weeks. The immediate cause of my diasporic wanderings was the failure, in August 1968, in front of the congregants of my own church, of that final sermon. I had given them the benefit of my best advice and had evidently not been understood. I might have joined them once again in the pews, another suppliant among many waiting for either revelation or reassurance from the pulpit, but I had warned them that they must look for God everywhere else. The exception would be the congregant whose spiritual quest had been fulfilled or that promised to be fulfilled soon in that place. I was not that congregant. It was not wrong to look for God in the churches; indeed it was right to look for Him everywhere; and any Christian house of worship on a Sunday morning was a place where the search was likely to be under way, however ineptly. And so I went everywhere, watching for a sign, but making no effort to rejoin a community. I found preachers I liked well enough to visit their churches by preference from time to time, but mostly I spread my custom as widely as I could.

I had not given up hope, either, of finding a Christian companion, but as the years passed and I surveyed candidates among the women I met in my pilgrimage, my skepticism about each seemed to increase faster than my loneliness, which was nevertheless considerable. I found myself reflecting on the past and looking there for companions I might reclaim. I was in the same city where I had been married and divorced, met Solveig and Bartley, attended seminary and preached, been befriended by Randall Lang. I looked in the telephone directory for signs of these people and events. Randall, dead nearly a decade, was in there, and at the same address. So Joanna was in town, still living under Randall's aegis. Bartley was listed as well. I looked for Solveig's name, but of course it wasn't there. I looked for Marie under the name of her husband but found no listing. I even checked under "Fisher" for Sandy Ann, but she was gone. I hoped she had found a Christian man to marry.

Because I'd been on a quest as long as I could remember, it seemed natural to me then to go to Joanna's house to see what I might see. It was a winter evening in 1977 when I had the idea. I bundled myself against the cold and went immediately, riding a bus and then walking a few blocks to her street. I had not been there since the autumn after Randall's funeral. The house was as I remembered, except that something—perhaps the quality of the light reflected from the snow—made me think it might have had a coat of paint. The downstairs was dark, but there was a light upstairs in the same window I'd seen illuminated the terrible night I realized Bartley had seduced Joanna, and that I knew, from my days in the house after Randall's death, was the bedroom. Involuntarily I looked along the street for Bartley's sports car, although I thought I knew enough of his habits to suppose that he'd have long since moved on, to another woman if not to another machine.

I stood in Joanna's street for a long time, irresolute. There was no question of going to her door. The irresolution came from uncertainty about how I should think of her and the years that had passed since I saw her last. I walked a little to keep warm, reflecting that I was now as old as she had been then, and that she was now as old as Randall. Only God was immune to the passage of time. I walked around the block, to be out of sight of Joanna while I meditated, and said a prayer as I went. I thought: if it had been given to me to see the face of God those several years ago, His face would be the same if I could see it now. I had a momentary fantasy in which I saw His face not ageless but young and playful, hiding from me. In that instant the face was mine as it had looked in a mirror in the years before age had begun to soften it. I felt poor and alone. I could not accept that God, although He had no age and had made man in His image, might look younger than I remembered Randall.

CHAPTER EIGHTEEN
FORTITUDE

Those ought to have been palmy years for a man of my public engagement and religious disposition. Jimmy Carter, the first self-identified born-again Christian ever elected President of the United States, was in office and applying a moral test to the actions of government, where heads of state usually appealed to reasons of pragmatism and national self-interest, however these might be gilded with invocations of Godliness and the right. Like me, Jimmy had experience as a lay preacher, and no diffidence about proclaiming the suzerainty of the Lord. At first I was put off balance by his easy toleration of people and ideas that were vastly more worldly and liberal than contemplated in our tradition. For example, he might have used the combined moral authority of his office and his character to mitigate the effects of the Supreme Court decision permitting abortion, then only a few years old. He might have used the bully pulpit to inveigh against all manner of popular trends and practices abhorrent to a Southern Baptist. Instead, he seemed the least establishmentarian of politicians, and the most willing to overlook the peccadilloes of others. It was as if he fully trusted God to govern in private while he, Jimmy, governed in public. And for a man so worthy he was oddly unsanctimonious. I grew to admire the un-Pharisaical certitude of his faith almost as much as I'd have admired a full-on, four-year tent meeting of a Presidency, complete with remand to Hell for certain malefactors. But those years were not palmy for me in fact. I felt time getting away: regardless of the Godliness of the man at the head of my country, I sensed no progress toward the better world I deemed possible. I didn't suppose that this sublunary world was the one that counted, but I was enough of a meliorist to wish that as a nation we might justify ourselves in the eyes of the Lord.

A few months after my visit to Joanna's street I happened to meet Bartley in a supermarket. It was spring by that time, and a Saturday afternoon. We were both bachelors shopping for the odd foodstuff. I saw him before he saw me; I hid from him in another aisle, not sure I wanted to speak. He looked exactly as I remembered him, but dressed even less formally than usual, in Levi's, sneakers and a polo shirt. I surveyed the area for a sign that he might be accompanied by another of his women, but he had a shopping basket on his arm and appeared to be alone. I temporized in my adjacent aisle, leaning on my shopping cart, and let him find me.

As it happened I had to speak to him first anyway. He came along the row of breakfast cereals where I'd stopped my cart, picking up and studying the boxes as closely as if they had been sacred texts. When he drew near enough to sense my presence, he glanced up without recognizing me, refocused on the shelves and reached for another box. "Rob Bartley!" I said.

Bartley looked up again, recognized me this time, spoke my name in exclamatory fashion and reached to shake my hand. "How are you doing? What are you doing? Nice to see you."

I wasn't sure how much of Bartley's effusion required an answer. He seemed to like me; it was remarkable that I felt a degree of engagement with him after nearly a decade without contact. It occurred to me that this headlong amiability of his might be the implement of his seductions and that I shouldn't approve or be flattered by it. "It's good to see you," I said, temporizing again.

"What have you been up to?" he said. "I've thought about you from time to time and wondered what you were doing. Do you preach?"

"Not in years," I said.

"Really? You were good."

"Beginner's luck," I said. "I lost the vocation."

"I remember you'd dropped out of seminary," he said. "I thought maybe you'd go back. You were very good. What vocation replaced that one?"

What was it about Bartley? All at once I was mute with embarrassment and thought I might even burst into tears. I regretted not running when I'd had the chance. It seemed that Bartley's very existence would always be at cross-purposes with mine. I didn't feel just then like sharing the history of my failure, although I knew that Bartley's capacity to hear about it might be bottomless, and his willingness to offer commentary, judgment-free but unwelcome anyway, might be infinite. "No new vocation," I said. "Just the basic, eternal one to try to know God and do His will."

"The study of a lifetime," Bartley said.

I nodded.

There was a silence. Far from feeling driven to second-guess my life, Bartley seemed to have decided that we'd run out of things to talk about. I felt relief and disappointment simultaneously. No doubt I was lonely and might have enjoyed a conversation with him. "Do you ever hear from Solveig?" I asked.

His face broke into the broad, goofy smile I used to see when they were together. "Yeah," he said, "we write once in a while. I spent a couple of weeks in Sweden with her a couple of years ago. I remember she asked about you when I was there. She always liked you. Thought you were too serious."

"Too serious."

"Yeah. Too hard on yourself."

"I always felt that she was serious too," I said.

"Well," he said, "earnest, maybe. But always able to cut herself some slack. She's a really good doctor, I guess. One of the best women I ever knew." As usual, Bartley's discourse was a vexatious hash of the welcome and the unwelcome. I wasn't sure what he meant by his last remark, but it made me uncomfortable. I tried to change the subject, but ineptly.

"What about Joanna? Have you seen her?"

"Not since—wow!—1969? She kind of went into purdah after her husband died. Do you ever see her?"

"No," I said.

"She had a fixation on you," he said. "Seemed to think you were the Second Coming—if it's okay to say that. I always had the impression she was in love with you. But kind of hoped and expected to see you crucified."

He was doing it again. Bartley's gift for heedless offense was downright preternatural. It seemed that nothing sacred was safe from profanation with Bartley on the scene. I wondered if he was similarly reckless in the company of adherents of other world religions. In my mind's eye I saw him cleft from head to heel with the Saracen's blade. "That's offensive," I said. "Nobody thinks I'm Jesus."

"I apologize," he said. "But she did take you very seriously. Used to rave about how beautiful you were."

"I know she thought that," I said. "I wish she'd found a better reason to take me seriously."

"Oh, I think she did," he said. "She thought you'd turn out to be an important preacher. I kind of thought so too. I took her word for it." He tucked into his shopping basket the last cereal box he had read. "I'm sorry you quit."

"I didn't quit," I said. "I lost my vocation."

Bartley returned a quizzical look. "Not the same thing?"

"No. Were you never religious?"

"No. Well, maybe. As a kid. I think I lost it the year my parents admitted they were Santa Claus. I'm serious."

Serious. It seemed this word had cropped up half a dozen times in different contexts in the short time we'd been standing in front of the cereal shelves. It was not a word I readily associated with Bartley. I marveled at the shallowness of a faith in the Almighty that could not survive the unmasking of Santa Claus, until I remembered that my own childish faith had gone missing for several years, until my spiritual rebirth in that hospital room. "A religious vocation is nothing you can quit," I told him. "If you have it, you follow. If you don't have it, you wish for it."

"Odd," he said.

With that word we confronted each other silently across my shopping cart, seemingly at the end of another of our infrequent and fruitless communications. I prepared to offer my hand to say goodbye. If I had carried through, perhaps I'd never have seen or spoken to Bartley again. But a moment before I could take my leave he said something that surprised me, frightened me, changed everything. "So how bad is it?"

I must have gone pale. "'How bad?'"

"Yeah," he said. "You're not doing what you wish you were doing. You're not doing what most people expected of you. How hard is that?"

I tried to think of an answer. I had rarely felt less comfortable in front of another person, Bartley included. I blanked. Not for the first time, and regardless of his amiability, I felt Bartley threatening to destroy me. I considered turning and walking away, but the burden of my grocery cart discouraged me. If I stayed I'd have to answer his question. As it happened, I couldn't remember what his question was. I watched him staring at me.

"Are you okay?" he asked.

"I'm sorry. What did you say?"

"I asked if you're okay."

"Before that."

"I asked if you're having a hard time."

I was disoriented, as confused as if Bartley's speech had suddenly lapsed into another language. I had no idea what he was talking about. I remembered—or thought I remembered—feeling resentment toward him a moment before; now I felt embarrassed and awkward, wrapped in the worst stage-fright I'd experienced since that time years earlier when I stood tongue-tied in a church basement before Solveig and a cadre of anti-war activists. I heard silence booming in my head. I found I couldn't remember what Bartley and I had talked about in the breakfast cereal aisle, and I was experiencing *déjà vu*: I saw Bartley watching me, and then watching me again. I sat down on the supermarket floor.

Bartley squatted beside me. "You all right? You look awful."

"I'm fine," I said.

"How do you feel?"

"A little panicky."

Bartley laid the palm of his hand on my forehead and peered into each of my eyes. I was in terror all at once that he might try to kiss me. I drew my arms up and folded them in front of my face.

"Do you need a doctor?" Bartley asked.

"I'm sure I don't," I said through my folded arms.

Bartley backed a little away. "Can you get up?"

I nodded but didn't move. Bartley stood and offered a hand, but I picked myself up without assistance and placed a steadying palm on the grocery cart. "How do you feel?" he asked.

"Fine," I said. "I think I'm fine; thank you." I felt considerable embarrassment; I wished I could leave. "I'm sorry," I said. "I have no idea what that was about."

I felt stronger and Bartley must have sensed it, because he stopped hovering like a rescue helicopter and backed away another six inches. "Look," he said, "why don't I give you a lift home. You don't have a car, right?"

"It's only six blocks."

"Same place you used to live?"

"Yes."

"Great! Lemme pick up a couple more things and I'll drive you. We oughta catch up anyway."

"All right," I said.

"I'll meet you at the checkout." He waited a beat, as if he were not sure I'd made up my mind, gave an airy wave of his shopping basket and walked off. Again I considered leaving. But it seemed inevitable that I'd have to come to grips with Bartley in one way or another. He knew where I lived; I was afraid of his officiousness; I had the idea that if I walked away he'd follow me home. So I finished my own shopping and met him at the door.

His car was the one I knew from years before. It seemed remarkable that he hadn't traded it for something newer or larger. On the other hand, like Bartley himself, the car had not visibly deteriorated. I wondered how many women by now had preceded me in the passenger seat. We put our separate bags of groceries in the tiny trunk and he drove me toward home.

In the ten or more years I'd lived in my small apartment I had never entertained a guest or made any provision for entertaining. I could invite Bartley in, but if he expected more than yogurt and constrained talk, we'd have to carry his groceries in as well. I seemed forever doomed to discomfiture when in the presence of Bartley. We arrived in front of my building while I was still trying to think of a graceful way not to invite him, but he preempted me. "I'd hang around and converse," he said, "but I've gotta take a shower and shave before I go out tonight."

Once again I had failed to anticipate Bartley. My feelings were not hurt, but I almost thought they should be; and once again I couldn't decide between relief and disappointment. "I understand," I said. "I really appreciate the lift."

"But there's one subject I'd like to broach, and we could talk about it later," he said, "if you don't think it's too intrusive."

I quailed inwardly. "What is it?"

"Depression. You know—misery. I get the feeling you might be having some of that."

"Why would you think so?"

"Just guessing. I've seen it in other people." Bartley's word "intrusive" seemed altogether apt. Misery was at the core of the dialog I had been carrying on for years with God, as was joy, its counterpart. Now, at this late date, Bartley seemed to be offering to

241

intervene. I could think of no one less qualified by grace or intuition. I didn't know what to say. Finally I blurted, "Are you a therapist?" No one had ever told me what Bartley did for a living.

"Not hardly," Bartley said. "I'm a physicist. But I have a girl friend who's a psychiatric social worker, and she has connections."

Connections to what? I wondered. I felt crowded and oppressed. Bartley reminded me of Christian colleagues I had seen so eager to proselytize that they made themselves unwelcome before they'd had a fair chance to witness. Most likely he was proselytizing for psychoanalysis, that secular religion pretending to be a science. I had never, even at the highest pitch of my own evangelical fervor, offered to harangue an unwilling audience. For the briefest moment, by extension, I had ethical doubts about the propriety of missionizing.

"Think about it," Bartley was saying. "It never hurts to have a neutral set of ears reviewing a problem."

The only response that came to mind was, "Leave me alone." But I didn't say it. I disliked rejecting Bartley, although I had found it necessary to do so on every occasion I could remember since the day we met. Instead I nodded my general agreement with the proposition about neutral ears and climbed out of the car. I fished my groceries out of the trunk and walked around to Bartley's door. "Thanks so much, Rob," I said, and offered my hand.

He reached across himself, poked his right hand through the window and shook mine. "Call me," he said. "We gotta catch up. I want to report on you to Solveig." He drove off. I listened to the fading blat of the exhaust as his car receded up the street and disappeared around a corner.

Indoors I shelved my groceries, then knelt to meditate and pray. Bartley's faculty for putting me on my guard and off my balance was practically sacerdotal. There was no chance that I would admit him into my dialog with God on joy and misery. When I had settled the question with God, then I could carry the answer to Bartley and he could profit by it. I prayed to God to arm me better for these skirmishes with Bartley, because I foresaw that I'd meet him again. He had quickened for me the ghost of Solveig, whose importance I had never settled in my own mind.

My life had become a study in loose ends and unclosed chapters. I had never had the chance to say goodbye to Randall or to ask him why he had died; I had turned away from Joanna without saying goodbye; I had lost my vocation to preach before I could bring any new community to God; now I saw that I had never truly given up Solveig. Memories of childhood came back, as if I had unfinished business there as well. I recalled the naïve belief that characterized my religious life following my first, natural birth, and preceding my youthful apostasy and later rebirth in Jesus. In some way, such childish faith seemed superior to the vexed struggle for perfection that consumed me now. I wished I could have stayed a child forever, in that Eden of the spirit that preceded familiarity with the fruit of the Tree of Knowledge. I wished I could be cradled in human arms.

CHAPTER NINETEEN
TEMPERANCE

I remained agitated for several days after my chance meeting with Bartley, but I resisted phoning him. After a week or two my agitation had subsided into the background of my other preoccupations and I could no longer think of a reason to call. I still found my thoughts reverting to the past, but no more than was usual for me. Then Bartley phoned.

"How you holding up?" he asked.

"Okay," I said. Now that my previous excitement had remitted, his call felt like an annoyance. I found myself reacting to him as often before: alert, distressed and on the defensive, as if he were trying to sell me something I didn't need and couldn't afford. I interposed a silent prayer that Bartley would state his case and hang up quickly.

"I was thinking we ought to call Joanna Lang," he said. "I'll bet she'd be glad to see us. I could take us all out to dinner."

I was seized with fright. I had been right to be alert and defensive, but this idea of Bartley's was worse than I could have anticipated. "Are you serious?" I asked.

"Of course," he said. "It'd be a reunion. She liked us both. Don't you wonder how she's doing?"

I thought I knew how Joanna was doing. She was growing old and she was angry with me. Neither of these was a phenomenon I wanted to see at first hand. "I don't think I'd be welcome," I said.

"Aw, come on," Bartley said. "You've gotta be kidding. You were way too interesting to her not to be welcome."

"I think I let her down."

"That was ten years ago."

"Well," I said, "I haven't forgotten it."

"She relaxes easier than you do. Trust me."

I winced. In his amiable way, Bartley was offering provocations as usual. If I was less relaxed than Bartley, it was nothing I needed to apologize for; I had never felt that relaxation was the way to a moral life. But I disliked hearing Bartley vaunt Joanna's capacity for relaxation; it dishonored the memory of Randall. "Why do you think this is a good idea?" I asked him.

"I told you," he said. "It's a reunion. Didn't we all like each other? Don't we both miss her? Don't you think she misses us?"

"I have no idea," I said. But Bartley's powers of suggestion were great. It may have been true that we all liked each other. Then it might also be true that I missed Joanna. When Bartley proposed it, I almost thought so. "Maybe," I said.

"So are you up for it?"

"Why don't you go see her by yourself?"

"What kind of reunion would that be? She'd just want to talk about you, anyway."

I felt tired and beaten. Bartley's enthusiasms were easy to resist, but Bartley himself was a juggernaut. "You really think she wants to see us?"

"I can find out," he said. "When are you free?"

"Any evening," I said.

"I'll set it up," he said. "Okay?" I didn't reply immediately. "I'll call you," he said, and hung up.

I was in turmoil. I lay on my bed, pulled my knees up against my chest and imagined scenarios that might excuse me from Bartley's reunion. They ranged over the rather small ground from disability to death, and none of them was noble or practical. The only judgment I feared was the judgment of God; nevertheless I shrank from the thought of Joanna hearing what I had failed to do with these nine years of my life.

I recognized my inconsistency. If I had done my best before God, there was no need to feel apologetic before Joanna. But I wished I had good news, some fresh witness to bring to her. Instead, God had so continued to hide His purposes from me that I felt I knew no more about Him, and less about my task, than I did when she and I met. I wished I could explain to her why Randall died, but it was information that I didn't have.

I began to hope that God was—at last—leading me toward a crisis. I had come to Him the first time through a crisis of sin and despair that nearly took my earthly life. I felt I could gladly undergo any such terror in exchange for a revelation like the one that succeeded the overdose. If it was God's will that Bartley should be the agent of my crisis, I could begin to understand His seeming easy tolerance of that unruly servant. To face Joanna's probable contempt, to deflect Bartley's scattershot secularism, to grapple with the ghost of Randall in front of his widow—these might be tests anticipating a new stage in my life of Faith.

I looked at myself in the mirror and tried to gauge whether I had changed since Joanna saw me last. Undoubtedly I had, because I was forty years old and recognizably so. Dark lunules that could not have been there when I was thirty were in residence between my cheekbones and my nose, and more forehead now surmounted my deep-set blue eyes. I tipped my head forward to see more of the scalp. The hair was blond and fine, but thinner than I remembered it, and my hairline meandered a little—fore at the center and aft near the temples. On close examination I could see a single hair occupying one brave follicle half an inch forward of the hairline proper. I was developing male pattern baldness, and this single hair was the geodetic reference mark that proved it.

If God had for a short time made me beautiful and a preacher of His word, He had seen fit to take those things away. I saw with bemusement but without regret that I would never be beautiful again. I sensed that this fading of my beauty might be sacramental— the outward and visible sign of my inward journey toward a deeper, more private, more secret Communion. I had some hope that the forthcoming struggle with Bartley and the past might drive me to a place underground where my Rapture could begin.

Bartley phoned a few days later to say he'd made Saturday night dinner reservations for the three of us at a popular restaurant a little way out from the city center, and he named an hour to pick me up. I prayed, meditated and made ready.

My job at the time was as an inventory clerk in an automobile supply warehouse. The work and the ambience suited my mood. I was largely confined to a desk inside a steel cage on the floor of a ten-thousand-square-foot slab building filled with car parts laid out on what I calculated to be about two linear miles of shelves. Larger components were stowed on pallets hoisted into the rafters. My only human contact in the course of a typical day was with a few rather brusque men who operated forklifts and handed documents in to me through the wire-mesh door of my cage. I kept careful paper track of goods coming and going, to a standard of accuracy that must have impressed anyone reviewing my work. The demands on my intellect were minimal and human interruptions few, so I had a lot of time for contemplation. Something about the way the high ceilings and open architecture of the warehouse contrasted with the small but exposed compass of my work cage seemed emblematic of that stage of my relationship with God. He was large and present and able to see me at every moment, while I was isolated from Him but not sheltered. In the days of my vocation I'd have broken out of the cage, ascended into the rafters and filled the space with my voice and witness. In these days I wished only for God to join me in the cage and shelter me with His wing.

On the appointed Saturday night, Bartley rang my buzzer on schedule and I met him in the vestibule of my apartment building. I had calculated correctly that he would be wearing a sports coat and slacks without a tie, so I was dressed the same. He offered me a hand to

shake. "Come see Joanna," he said, and held the street
door open.

She was in the front passenger seat of a car of the
same make as the one she had owned with Randall, but
a few years newer. Bartley opened the nearside back
door and I climbed in and took the hand Joanna offered
to me over the back of her seat. Her green eyes looked
moist in the late spring twilight. She was fifty years
old, still blonde, small and slender. "You don't look like
a boy anymore," she said.

"You look lovely," I said.

Bartley took the driver's seat and beamed at us
with proprietary zest. "This'll be a treat," he said. He
started the engine and we drove off. I sat quietly, not
confident of maintaining a conversation from my place
in the rear. Bartley and Joanna had their backs to me,
but Bartley's animation was such that I saw him lift
Joanna's hand out of her lap and press it to his lips.
"It's great to be together again," he said. Joanna
glanced over her shoulder at me and smiled—a little
wanly, I thought—and took her hand away.

At the restaurant, which was called La
Bibliothèque, we were given a table in an alcove lined
with shelves of books. Nothing about the menu, which
was large but traditionally American, seemed related
to the French name or the book theme, but the books
were welcome because they deadened the room and
damped the noise of the other diners. The alcove
arrangement reduced the noise too, and gave us a
degree of privacy. I scanned titles but recognized none
of them. The books seemed to be potboiler novels and

self-help manuals a few decades old, arranged in no order. The restaurant management must have bought them by the pound. Still, they gentrified the atmosphere and might have provided diversion for a man or woman dining alone.

Joanna was dressed conservatively in a suit of the type I used to see her wear to church, but she was not, of course, wearing a hat. We made our choices from the menu and Bartley ordered a bottle of wine that he regarded as a match for all three entrees. When it arrived he let Joanna do the tasting. Her diffidence seemed to confirm what I'd have expected: that she had no oenological expertise. I could imagine that Bartley had none either. My own pretensions, of course, were of an entirely other tendency. No objection being offered, the waiter poured three glasses and left the bottle. Bartley proposed a toast. "To continuity," he said. I remembered my only other experience, years earlier, of drinking alcohol in the company of Bartley; this time I barely sipped. Bartley looked from my face to Joanna's and back again, smiling indulgently. "Let's catch up," he said.

Joanna set her wine glass down and stared across the table, perhaps appraising me. I stared back, uncertain where or how to begin the conversation. The book titles behind her head distracted me; it was easier to read them than to choose a topic. I was still trying to marshal my thoughts when Joanna spoke. What she said surprised me utterly. "Do you have children?" she asked.

I wasn't sure I'd understood her. "Children? Yes. I had children when I was married."

"Randall told me you had," she said. "You never talked about them."

"How did Randall know?" I asked.

"You told him," she said.

I didn't remember that. I stared across the table at her and then at Bartley, who gazed back with a slight interrogatory lift of his brow. "Children?" he said. "No kidding! What kind?"

"Girls," I said. "Two girls." I tried to recall any conversation with Randall on this subject but none occurred to me. It was perfectly possible that I had at one time or another, in passing, mentioned to Randall the circumstances of my marriage. But it came as a surprise that he'd have spoken of it to Joanna, and as a greater surprise that Joanna should have remembered.

"Where are they now?" Bartley wanted to know.

"With their mother," I said.

"Around here somewhere?"

"I don't know," I said. "It's been many years."

Conversation ceased for several seconds. I looked from Bartley to Joanna and back again. Both were gazing at me with blank faces that I didn't know how to read. During this hiatus the salad course arrived. Mine was dressed with distractingly pungent Roquefort.

I sat quietly opposite Joanna and browsed my salad plate. I was hesitating to fasten on the subject of Randall, but I badly wanted to know what had happened. Finally I said, "I think about Randall often."

"He thought a lot of you," she said.

"Was there ever any more information about the accident? I mean, how do you think about it?"

"I never think about the accident," she said. "I think about Randall. How good he was. I visit his grave every Sunday after church."

"Do you ask him?"

"No."

Bartley watched us converse, his face an earnest mask of sympathy. It occurred to me again that he had never met Randall, that his only association with Randall was as the seducer of Randall's wife and the abuser of Randall's legitimate expectations of his matrimonial estate. It seemed bizarre that he was now sponsoring our dinner and presiding over our reminiscences as if we were his creatures. By rights, in this universe governed by God it ought to have been I in Bartley's chair, picking up the tab for dinner and directing the three of us toward reconciliation and absolution, the shriving of our sins. As usual I didn't trust Bartley not to be working for the Adversary.

By her last monosyllable Joanna seemed to have foreclosed any further discussion of Randall's death. I tried to formulate some rejoinder that might keep the conversation going on that subject, but my imagination failed me. Instead the idea occurred to me to visit Randall's grave myself, to ask the question that Joanna hadn't.

"Rob says you haven't preached," Joanna said.

"I lost the vocation," I said.

"How can that be? I was sure you had it."

"Yes," I said, "I did have it. But God saw fit to take it away again. He has some other purpose for me."

"How do you know?"

"By my faith. He has a purpose for each of us."

"There's been so much waste," Joanna said. "I always believed my purpose was to be a loving wife to Randall, and Randall's was to know and teach about God. I believed your purpose was to bring people to God by your example. Ever since Randall died I haven't known what the purpose was. And you don't preach. What a waste."

Her tone of despair and defeatism disturbed me greatly. She was physically and morally frail. I surveyed her small figure across the table and felt again that I was failing Randall. The third at our table, Bartley, whose Godly purpose was the most obscure of all, evinced no mark of frailty whatever. Bartley had identified a quality in me that he called misery, and I felt it now. I associated it with something absent in Joanna and absent in me, but present and unwelcome in Bartley. It was as if Bartley were better able than the rest of us to draw sustenance out of the crass world our mortal bodies inhabited—as if he enjoyed a spiritual metabolism capable of finding nourishment in matters and ideas that should have been anathema. His psychic and somatic health in the midst of his apostasy set my teeth on edge.

"Do you realize this is only the second time the three of us have been together?" Bartley said. Certainly I realized it.

"Can that be true?" Joanna said. "When was the other time?"

"The day you and I met, of course. At the Redeemer church for this guy's excellent, spellbinding sermon on sex and sin. Remember? We all had lunch in the church basement."

"Was that really the only time? It's hard to believe."

"Yeah. I saw you. I saw him. He saw you. But never the three of us together. I guess we might have found ourselves at cross-purposes in those days."

"I remember it with mixed feelings," Joanna said.

"Yeah, I know you do," Bartley said. "I remember it with unmixed feelings." He lifted her hand from the edge of the table and put the back of it to his lips. Joanna looked solemn but offered no resistance.

Without a doubt I was the least happy participant at this reunion. It might have been so even if our artless host had not reminded me that he and Joanna had responded to my sermon on adultery by committing adultery. Under the circumstances I regretted having come. Regardless of my hopes, God was not yet showing me by this experience where I should go next. Furthermore, I began to sense an axis of sympathy developing between Bartley and Joanna, as if they'd rediscovered the relationship they shared apart from me—and might even be preparing to celebrate it.

The entrees arrived, prompting Bartley to relinquish Joanna's hand. Once again I found myself out of patience with the man. A few minutes earlier I'd felt inclined to learn all there was to know about him.

I'd been framing a question to steer him into talking about his work as a physicist, and waiting for the apt moment to insert it into the conversation; but now I found I didn't care. Bartley added wine to each of our glasses, although mine took very little.

I was torn between a desire to be elsewhere, working on the questions that interested me, and the wish that I could participate more fully in this reunion. Surveying the plates filled and on the table, I realized that none of us had remembered to offer the blessing. Bartley was already brandishing his silver and Joanna was reaching for hers. "May I offer a prayer?" I said.

"I'm sorry. Of course," Bartley said, and set down the utensils. Joanna bowed her head.

"Lord," I said, "make us worthy to receive what Thou hast provided for us through the generosity of Thy servant Rob. Make us aware of our obligations to Thee and to one another. Make those of us who knew him thankful for the memory of our friend and husband Randall. Amen."

Bartley and Joanna both murmured "amen" and Bartley added, nodding toward me, "Very gracious. Thank you." He lifted his glass. "*Bon appétit*," he said, and sipped.

I wasn't pleased that Bartley had greeted the blessing as some sort of cross-cultural curiosity, but I was glad that I'd been able to include it in the proceedings. To entertain God and Bartley in the same room was an act of faith, and energy-intensive.

"You still have a little of the vocation I guess," Bartley said. "Enough to say grace in a restaurant."

"Vocation and faith are two utterly different things," I said. "I haven't lost my faith. If I still had the vocation, though, everyone in the restaurant would have heard me. And responded." I must have blushed immediately, hearing what I had just said as braggadocio. It was hard to remember, those several years later, whether it had been my diminishing vocation or my fading success from the pulpit that had led the other downhill. If it was the former, God had chosen to take it away and I was reconciled; if the latter, I had met with simple difficulty, lost my courage and failed God. I couldn't accept that it was the latter without admitting that the past decade of menial labor was only that: a decade of purposeless work after a fall from grace, not a decade of searching out God's intention while I enforced my own humility.

"Maybe you have more of the vocation than you think," Joanna said.

"No," I said. "I haven't."

"You're the most stubborn man I ever met," she said.

The rest of the meal passed in conversation about things I don't quite remember. Probably Bartley discoursed on the news of the day and Joanna listened. They may have talked about current movies but I hadn't seen any. If we discussed politics I participated a little. I seem to think that Bartley liked Jimmy Carter as well as I did, but for his rhetoric on human rights rather than his Godliness. Bartley and Joanna shared the balance of the wine.

They dropped me at home. "Let's do this again," Bartley said. I doubted he was sincere, although he seemed so. "I might be able to drum you up a date," he added, "if you were interested." I found myself in a hurry to get indoors. Was I supposed to double-date with the worst rakehell I knew and the suborned widow of my best friend? I couldn't even guess what sort of woman Bartley might try to match me with. But the implication that Bartley had readopted Joanna distressed me most of all. I gave her my hand and said goodnight. "I'll phone you," Bartley said, and they drove away.

CHAPTER TWENTY
JUSTICE

To be dragged nine years into the past as I had been by the meeting with Bartley and Joanna was a trial of the spirit. I was conscious suddenly of having made no progress toward salvation in all that time. All at once Randall Lang was current business again. I sat in my apartment with my eyes closed and tried to find my way in memory to the exact site of his grave. I thought I remembered where it was.

I'd have gone to see him the next day, but the next day was Sunday and I could not risk meeting Joanna. I didn't trust her not to be accompanied still by Bartley, whose capacity for transgression was boundless. Anyway, I wanted no intrusion on our privacy when I sought to communicate with Randall's spirit. The cemetery was open daily until sundown and it was early summer, so I waited to go until Monday after work.

The trip from the warehouse to the cemetery entailed half an hour on buses and a transfer from one line to another. I had delved through drawers of papers until I found the few letters I'd received from Randall on the road, and I carried them with me. There were only three. I re-read them on the bus.

In the letters I heard the voice of Randall speaking to me for the last time in life. All of these words had been written after our final meeting—after I heard his actual voice for the last time, and after I saw his face for the last time until I saw it in his casket. I was haunted by the letters' symmetry. The first announced his departure; the second described him in mid-career; the third reported him at his destination, even though he had explicitly not had a destination when he started. But now I saw that when he set out into the wilderness depicted in his father's painting of Jesus, it was his father that he'd been looking for.

I look at this house, which is the only place I
ever knew my pa, & it's hard to remember he
was ever here, he's so long passed over & the
town is so changed.

So he had not found his father. The idea came to me, although I rejected it, that Randall had despaired and killed himself. And there was a coda:

Tell Joanna I said this trip is also a search for
her. It's a search for everybody & everything I
love.

I shivered. What could Randall have meant by this? He had pronounced himself on the point of turning around and coming home to where Joanna was, and then he had asked me to tell her that a search was under way.

May the two of you care for each other & God
care for us all until we're together again.

On earth? Or in Heaven? I thought again, my heart jumping, my skin cold, my stomach a void, that it was possible Randall had foreseen or even intended his death. And left me with instructions to care for— marry?—his widow.

> The first time I laid eyes on you, I had the feeling somebody had died on you too. It's what I meant when I said something had gotten away from you. You looked like me in the time between my pa dying & me finding Joanna.

And then:

> You've said you don't know what got away. I imagine we'll figure it out sooner or later.

I found myself in great distress. I prayed silently to God to come to my assistance. Was it possible that I had missed another vocation—this one to comfort and protect Joanna until the two of us could rejoin Randall in death? I turned back to the second letter.

> You & she are the two people closest to me in this world. I pray that when we meet next time we'll be closer still & also better & closer to God.

On second reading, this could indeed be seen as the language of transcendence, the passing over into a better world. Was it possible that Randall had gone on the road without the intention of coming back? I prayed, for the sake of his immortal soul, that this was only the language of a man cognizant of his mortality, but prepared to serve God on earth as long as God would have him here. I returned to the first letter, in which he apologized for leaving me with Joanna with no warning, and I drew courage from this line:

I hope to come back a better man & I ask you to pray that I will.

At least he had left expecting to return. But what had overtaken him on the road? According to Joanna, according to the coroner, according to my preference in the matter, he had been overtaken by an accident. It remained possible that he had been overtaken by malefactors, murdered by a person or persons steeped in sin and forever unknown. Or he had been overtaken by despair—to a man of Christian faith, washed in the blood of the Lamb of God, a sin in itself. So he had died by accident or by his sin or by another's. If by accident, the initiative had been God's entirely, and the profoundest mystery.

The bus stopped a block from the cemetery gates and I got down and walked. I felt great trepidation. For reasons I cannot name, I had never come back to Randall's grave. Now I was going to visit him harboring more doubts than I had ever entertained when his death was new. I followed the curved paths past flowering shrubs, rows of headstones, crypts sunk into artificial embankments. The summer sun, still high, shone down on this green suburb of the dead. Vestiges of worldly vanity persisted here. The better-heeled deceased had sponsored themselves into the ground with larger monuments and better style than their neighbors, but it was their last display, and a gesture unlikely to turn the head of God. It struck me that, as large as this cemetery was, surely it was far too small to accommodate the remains of all of the people who must have died in all of the generations of the city I lived in. Where were the rest of them?

After a few minutes I realized I was lost. My recollection of the geography of Randall's burial must have been either inaccurate or incomplete, because when I reached the part of the cemetery that I thought I remembered, no specific feature of it was familiar. I realized also that I couldn't expect to recognize Randall's headstone without reading it, because the headstone had been placed some days or weeks after the interment. I wandered, reading names and epitaphs. I felt like a child separated from a parent in a crowd, staring into faces and finding them all unfamiliar. The illusion of childhood helplessness was so strong that my mouth grew dry and a hint of panic rose in my chest. A quarter of an hour into the search I gave up and sat down on the grass at the edge of the path.

I read names from the headstones I could see from where I sat. Irrationally, I wondered if Randall knew any of these people. Some of them had died many years before Randall; only one or two had died since. Like a lost child, I was afraid to ask any of these bystanders for help. I closed my eyes and tried hard to remember where I had seen Randall last.

I thought I remembered the lay of the land around the gravesite fairly well, and some of the particulars of the walk behind the casket from where the hearse had stopped on the access road nearest the grave. I stood up, but I couldn't relate what I remembered to anything I could see. I knelt on the grass, lowered my head and prayed wordlessly for Randall and for myself.

I may have dozed. At any rate, I saw Randall once more being lowered into the ground, and this time I climbed in after him. I threw one arm around the casket and laid my ear against the wood, hoping to hear Randall speaking from inside. I saw him lying there, eyes closed, his face severe, his head stuffed with rags from the bag my mother kept when I was small. "Randall," I said, but quietly, for fear of waking him, "why did you forsake me?" Randall didn't stir.

I jerked awake, still kneeling on the grass in the lowering sunlight, filled with doubt. If Randall was so deeply asleep, there seemed no point in continuing the search for his grave. I still wanted to go back to it, to reacquaint myself with the place and the events surrounding it, but I felt safe waiting until another day. I stood again and took one last look around. Randall's grave was nowhere to be seen.

Passing the gate on the way out of the cemetery I did what I ought to have done on the way in. I stopped at the caretaker's office and asked for a map. The caretaker found the location of Randall's plot in his files and marked it. I folded the map into the packet of Randall's letters and carried it away.

Riding the buses, I thought some more about Randall's final words to me regarding Joanna. In fact they were Randall's final words to me on any subject: *May the two of you care for each other, and may God care for us all until we're together again.* It was the plainest injunction, but one that I'd been ignoring almost since he made it. God, Who can never be enjoined, had been fulfilling His half of Randall's wish, but I had failed again. I saw his severe, sleeping face. They had every right to be angry with me. I had done nothing in nine years to justify myself, except to stand and wait, full of good will but empty of purpose. I shivered. I had run up against something.

I felt all at once that I had reached a crux. It might be the end of life; it might be only a stymie; it might be an obligation that I sensed but couldn't appreciate. Someone was angry with me; something was required. Sunlight slanted at a low angle through the bus. I bowed my head, closed my eyes and prayed at large, waiting for a sign. I heard blood pulsing and felt the bus sway and bump. I was acutely conscious of my own presence, as if there were two of me, one watching and one being watched, both alone. I felt isolated and menaced at the same time, hearing my own alien voice inside my head. I opened my eyes and stared at the metal roof until the feeling passed and I was just myself again, riding on a bus and resigned to the necessity of offering that self to Joanna. With the decision made, it seemed quite possible.

At home I ate some supper and read Randall's letters one more time. Then I telephoned Joanna and asked her to come to see me.

"Why?" she wanted to know.

"I went looking for Randall's grave today," I said. "I think he spoke to me."

There was a long silence on the line. "I don't understand," she said at last.

"I have much to atone for," I said. "Will you come?"

"Won't you come here?"

"Not to Randall's house," I said.

"Are you sure you're all right?" she said.

"I'm sure of it," I said. "But we have a lot of work to do. Will you come?"

"All right," she said.

I hung up the receiver and walked alone one last time through the scene of my ten years' monasticism. I picked up and tidied a few things. I washed the supper dishes and put them away. I squared the corners of my single bed, brushed my teeth and examined my face in the mirror. The skin beneath my eyes was dark and finely checked. When the bell rang I pressed the button to buzz Joanna through the vestibule door, and when she knocked at my door I let her in.

I was surprised again by how small she was. She gazed at me evenly, wholly self-possessed, and stepped aside to let me close the door behind her. I felt no awkwardness or indecision, but folded my arms around her and pressed her against my chest. She smelled of lilacs or lavender or something. I lifted her by her legs and shoulders and carried her to my bed and deposited her there, and removed her clothes and my own. She had been wearing sandals, dark slacks, a flowered blouse, white brassiere and underpants. Her breasts were small, with pale brown nipples, and her pubic hair was dark blond and very fine. Her body looked much younger than her face and was entirely new to me. I realized that in all my preoccupation with her I'd never considered how she might look naked.

I lay beside her on the narrow bed and drew her against me. My own body, whose every sexual manifestation I had been suppressing for years, was in a state of global tumescence. I remembered the reference to Tantrism in Randall's first letter. He had tried to pair it with our tradition: "Christ intoxication and sexual practice occupying the same space." As I lay there with Joanna, feeling the full length of her naked body arched against mine but shorter than mine, so that her head stopped under my chin and her toes bumped against my ankles, I understood the Tantric part. But the Christ intoxication, the transcendent love of God, was missing. Then Randall must have loved Joanna in a way that I had not yet learned to do. I felt myself compromised. Randall had married me to Joanna without establishing first that I loved her with the whole heart, soul, faith and trust that I reposed in God. I lay with her without embarrassment or guilt, relieved to be working at last toward fulfilling my obligation to Randall, but conscious that our union was not yet blessed. I let her do whatever she was moved to do. I realized that Randall had been a mystic and I was a literalist, such that I found Joanna scrambling over me and drawing me into herself in a way that subsumed the Tantric but bore no coherent relation to the Heidelberg Catechism, the profession of my Faith. I was struggling with this conundrum when my entire physiology veered suddenly, madly, drastically and hyperbolically out of my control. I heard screaming and felt Joanna's fingernails raking my shoulders. Luminous magenta pools like radioactive paint spills spread behind my clenched eyelids and my limbs thrashed wildly. I crushed Joanna to my chest in an attempt to prevent some accident, but it was too late, and I felt us tumble and hit the floor. Still I held on. A series of waves, like heavy surf but in rapid succession, bounced my body and knocked my head against the hardwood. The intensity of the shocks diminished slowly, and after what seemed a minute or two we were quiet, although I twitched for a few minutes more with little involuntary after-quakes. Joanna lay on top of me cooing and muttering like doves on a parapet, her cheek against my chest, her poodle-cut blond hair tickling the end of my nose. I pushed the hair away and scratched. I had no idea what to do next.

"Are you comfortable?" Joanna asked me in a drowsy voice that I barely recognized as hers.

"What do you mean?"

"You're on the floor and I'm lying on top of you."

"Oh," I said. "Yes. I'm comfortable."

We lay there not moving while I tried to measure the significance, both practical and sacred, of this unfamiliar situation. I prayed silently to God, asking once again for guidance. If I had made a mistake and deserved to be tormented for what I had just done, there was no sign. I was enjoying the greatest sense of well-being I'd felt in many years—perhaps since the early, best days of my vocation to preach. I tried to evaluate my feelings. I felt warmed and soothed by Joanna's weight, but daunted by the notion that I might be expected to stand in for Randall. Randall had loved her entirely within the ambit of God, Who evidently had created them for each other. Randall's easy advocacy showed that he had trusted her completely, while I had passed the majority of our acquaintance afraid of her. If she shared my mistrust there was no sign of that either: she had fallen asleep on my chest and was snoring softly. I reached for the edge of the bed, tugged the counterpane away and threw it over her naked body and mine, part of which had been inside of hers but slipped free when I stretched. It seemed to me that a world of besetting service lay ahead.

CHAPTER TWENTY-ONE
PRUDENCE

With the benefit of hindsight I perceive how incompletely I'd considered Joanna's circumstances before I acted, and how woefully little prayer and meditation had preceded the decision. These events happened after many years of waiting for a sign of my next task, and I let myself be rushed by duty to Randall, rather than by duty to God, into what seemed difficult and therefore perhaps of God. In the years that followed I had many opportunities to consider whether the impetus might not instead have come from Satan, that accomplished Deceiver, ingenious enough to disguise temptation to commit an easy sin as obligation to undertake a hard duty, and to seduce me at last into carnality by flattering me with the illusion that I had understood Randall's death.

Doubt assailed me from the first. I lay under Joanna's slumbering weight and polled my feelings. It seemed to me that if I had done what was difficult and right, I ought to feel stronger in virtue than I did. I ought to have felt married to Joanna and committed to protecting her against the forces that had threatened her ever since Randall set out on his walk nine years before. I didn't doubt that I could protect her asleep, but I feared what could happen when she was awake. She was older than I and—for most of the time I had known her—tougher. Maybe Randall had misjudged her capacity to receive when I was the giver.

As if to illustrate, and before I knew she was awake, Joanna suddenly lifted herself off me, pulled back the remaining covers and climbed into bed, leaving me cold and naked on the floor. I wrapped the dropped counterpane around me and knelt at the side of the bed and said my prayers. As through most of my life, my bedtime prayer in those years was a boilerplate to which I subjoined special penance or petitions, according to the events of the day just past or thoughts that might then be occupying my mind. This night I recited the boilerplate and stopped, unsure of what, if anything, I had to regret, or for what in particular I needed to ask God's help. I stayed where I was and wrestled with my doubts. Finally I asked God to bless and direct my union with Joanna. But still I hesitated to get into bed. I got up and put on pajamas. I stood in the dark for several minutes, self-conscious, suspended between the conflicting demands of protocol and habit. At last I compromised by leaving the pajama bottoms on but removing the tops. I slipped into bed beside Joanna. But then I got up again, retrieved the pajama tops and covered Joanna's bare shoulders where they protruded above the bedclothes. Then I climbed into bed and, feeling rather calm, fell into a dreamless sleep.

The hours that immediately followed were among the few peaceful ones I was to know for many years—if "know" is the right word, since I slept through them. When next I was aware, Joanna's hand was inside my pajama bottoms and she had fondled me to erection. I opened my eyes and saw by the window that the sky—

and with it the room—was just growing light. My mind and my body were following separate tracks, the latter eagerly participating in Joanna's activities, the former, barely awake, mulling the propriety of Joanna's behavior. I seemed to think that our relationship should be regularized in some way before we let sexual union become expected practice. The rational part of me wanted to ask Joanna to interrupt what she was doing until we could be married, but the fleshly part rendered the rational part speechless. She scrambled over me as she had the night before, but longer and in more detail, exploring me more closely and kissing me over more widely divergent parts of my body. I didn't resist her but I didn't encourage her either. She could have thought I was indifferent, except that my bodily responses informed her otherwise, I suppose. The upshot (or outcome?—every formulation seems prankish) was the same as the night before, except that we avoided falling out of bed.

Once more I found myself lying on my back with Joanna resting full-length on top of me. She drew a sheet over us, and a clammy odor like that of a seafood store billowed from under it. I was experiencing sights, sounds and smells that I had either long forgotten or never known. I wished I felt more secure.

"What happened to change your mind?" Joanna asked, without lifting her head from my chest.

"I haven't changed my mind," I said.

Neither of us spoke for several minutes. The light spilling through the window grew brighter. I looked at the alarm clock and saw that there were two hours before I had to go to work.

"You went to Randall's grave?" Joanna said.

"I couldn't find it," I said.

"What happened?"

"I re-read his letters."

There was another long silence. I wondered what Randall had written to Joanna, and whether she had long seen my failure to provide comfort and companionship as the explicit denial of Randall's wishes that I now saw it to be. I waited for her to understand and respond, but she said nothing. Finally I asked, "What do you think Randall wanted?"

"What do you mean?" she said.

"When he was on the road. What did he write?"

"He wanted to come home," she said. And after a few seconds she added: "But he died anyway."

This remark, as neutrally declarative as she had made it, nevertheless hovered in the air around us and echoed in my head. I listened to it playing back and thought I detected some hint of blame. "It was God's unfathomable will," I said.

She amazed me by snorting. "Honestly!" she said. "You and Randall!" She lifted her head from my chest and stared into my eyes. "Sometimes things just happen."

"No," I said. "He sees the sparrow when it falls."

"He sees it," she said, "but does He make an issue of it?"

"God is immanent in everything," I said. "Everything is an issue. The fall of the sparrow. The fall of Randall. God has a purpose in all of it. Nothing just happens."

"Then why does a sparrow fall? What's the point?"

"I don't know. God knows."

"And why did Randall fall?"

"I don't know that either. I've wondered. It could be anything. Maybe eventually we'll come to see that it was part of His plan for our salvation. I don't know."

"Randall's plan?"

"No! Of course not. God's plan."

"For our salvation," she said.

"I wouldn't presume to say," I said. "That's just a possibility. What does his death mean to you?"

"That I'm lonely," she said. "That I won't get to see him again until I'm dead too." She lowered her head to rest it once more under my chin. The tip of her nose was cold. Adjacent to it, a warm tear dribbled on my chest.

The pity that I ought to have been feeling was leavened somewhat with frustration. I wanted to offer to marry her but we seemed to be at odds over matters of great importance. If she didn't believe that God oversees all of Creation and cares profoundly about all of our thoughts and deeds, how could she be a wife to me? I might as well leave her to the mercy of opportunists like Bartley.

I had not thought about Bartley since our dinner, and this sudden intrusion into my meditations was not welcome. It occurred to me that I had just had sexual intercourse with a woman who might well have been Bartley's sexual partner as little as forty-eight hours before. Visions of corruption and disease assailed me. All at once the ichthyous vapors issuing from beneath the sheet seemed noxious. Far from believing that I had taken an irreversible step toward the fulfillment of Randall's wishes and the acceptance of God's task for me, I suddenly imagined myself an actor in a low, obscene travesty. I saw in my mind's eye a Hogarthian eruption of chancrous sores on pasty flesh. I believed I had fallen among orgiasts; I recoiled at the picture of Bartley invading my bed. I was desperate to exclude Bartley from Joanna's life, and now I blamed myself for missing the opportunity to do so ten years earlier. If I had not been careless, they might have never met. I was quite agitated. "Will you pray with me?" I asked her.

She sniffled and raised her head. "What about?"

"Chastity," I said.

Her head went back down. "Go ahead and pray," she said. Silently I asked God to grant me the wisdom to put my prayer into words that would command Joanna's heart, and then I began.

"Lord," I said, "now that in Your Grace and Mercy You have brought Joanna and me together, we pray that You'll bless our union by showing us how to be faithful to You and to each other in our minds and bodies, forsaking all others. We thank You for this gift and we thank You for the memory and example of Randall Lang. In Jesus' name. Amen."

Joanna said nothing. She was silent for several minutes, during which I continued to pray inwardly for her favorable construction. At last she said, "Well. You did change your mind."

"No," I said. "Only my understanding changed."

"And now we're married. A week ago we didn't know each other anymore, and now we're married. Don't you think you should have asked me first?"

Her tone was incongruously flat, considering the hint of challenge in her words. I was afraid to ask if she might be angry. For several seconds I was afraid to say anything at all. Eventually the silence became harder to bear than the fear of a false step, so I spoke. "Well," I said, "we're not married, but I think we should be."

"I have to go home," she said.

I felt a quick little jolt of panic. Joanna started to get up. Involuntarily, I threw my arms around her shoulders and pinned her where she was.

"No!" I said. "This is important."

Much later, when I reviewed these events in my mind, I understood this as the moment when I lost forever any mastery I might once have had over Joanna. In contrast with the heady days of my preaching, when Joanna had taken me to be her spiritual guide, I had now been reduced to the merest suppliant, relying on my greater physical strength to keep her from disappointing me. I was learning the frustration of main force without moral authority. She was so small, and I was so strong, that I could have kept her there indefinitely, but I could not have avoided defeat. Even so, I clutched her body to my chest while I tried desperately to think of words that might detain her as effectively. She neither struggled nor resisted, but I knew the argument was lost. "I can't stay here if you're going to ask me to marry you," she said.

"I won't ask you," I said. "But can we talk?"

"Let go of me and we can talk."

In an act of faith I prayed and let go. But for the prayer, I might have held on longer and things might have gone worse. Joanna lifted herself slowly and sat on the edge of the bed and reached for her blouse. There was something forlorn and placeless in the picture of her rising naked from bed and putting on yesterday's clothing. If she had consented to be married to me she'd have arisen in a nightgown, I in my pajamas, and we'd have had breakfast together. But all she now owned under my roof were the clothes she had arrived in. She might as well have been under Bartley's roof. "This is not right," I said.

"I know," she said. "So you feel it too."

"If we don't do something to put it right I fear for our souls."

"We can forgive each other," she said.

I had no idea what she was talking about. Our sin was against God, and if we were not prepared to join ourselves together, it was a sin against Randall too. Joanna seemed to be saying that only the two of us were involved. I felt helpless in the face of what I took to be willful obtuseness. I sat up, found my pajamas and put them on. We sat side by side on the edge of the bed.

"Randall wanted us to be together," I said. "He wrote that in his letters to me."

"Randall loved you," Joanna said. "I don't know why. "

"He asked me to take care of you," I said.

"I guess he didn't realize I could take care of myself."

I turned my head and studied her. She was staring into the middle distance at the floor. It frustrated me to see her isolation and to feel myself isolated in the same way. I sensed that both of us were in the grip of a single, nameless sorrow, and that each of us might be the cause of it in the other. I realized that she didn't love me. It seemed superfluous to ask if she ever had. I understood that I had never loved her either, except as she was a child of God and the wife of Randall. I felt shame. I had abandoned my vow of celibacy on the strength of a delusion that had come from—where? All of Joanna's old attempts to seduce me had failed, and in the fullness of time I had seduced myself. I had lost my virtue and would have to start all over again.

Joanna gathered the rest of her clothes and finished dressing. She folded her brassiere and pushed it into one of the pockets of her slacks. I wondered if she felt as bereft as I now did, and pity made me want to offer to pray for her, but I was afraid. My thoughts were divided between the idea that I would never see her again and the notion that I would yet be the agent of her salvation. And for the first time since the accident, or whatever it was, I felt at last that Randall was truly dead and beyond the reach of everything but prayer. I doubted that I would go back to look for his grave. An age had passed. I sat on the edge of the bed and wept quietly. Joanna kissed my forehead where hair used to be and left the room. I heard the apartment door. Then I heard it click shut, and I was as alone as I had ever been.

CHAPTER TWENTY-TWO
RETREAT

The day that followed was a terrible one. When Joanna left I fell on my knees and prayed to be forgiven for more transgressions than I could count. In my pride I had let my imagined duty to Randall make me forget my duty to God. I had succumbed to the sin of lust, although not with malice aforethought. I had allowed my own fear and sloth to invade the space between my good intentions and Joanna's willfulness. I had—as usual—been lacking in charity for Bartley; I was conscious of this failing even as I prayed, confounded as I was that God should continue to give that sinner so much rope. What was worst, I found myself clutching at faith rather than praying out of what had been a permanent, profound conviction that God loved me and in time would show Himself, whole and unstinting. I struggled up and took a shower, washing away traces of Joanna from my body. I made breakfast and ate it. Gripped by dread, I went to my job.

It was hard to concentrate on the work, but the work was undemanding and I did it well enough. I pretended to be busier than I was, in order to avoid intrusive conversation with the warehouse men. It distressed me more than ever that God could see me but I couldn't see Him. I felt that I had been on a downward course for years, growing ever farther from intimacy with Him. In desperation I tried to think of a means of growing closer to Him quickly. I thought of death, but death was not a permitted option unless it came from God Himself. I saw once more the image of Randall in his coffin, his face severe, his head stuffed with my mother's rags. If God had taken him home, why was I not able to see him anyplace but underground? I remembered the last time I saw him in life, smoking his pipe and lecturing to me about the Kabbalah and *Deus condatus*, God hidden from us. That image too was shrinking into the past, along with the echo of his voice and the memory of his charismatic presence. It had begun to seem possible that he had walked west and simply died, and that neither Joanna nor I would see him again, regardless of our faith. The sin of despair was overcoming me, as if the late mistaken surrender of my virtue had weakened my soul.

As that first post-Joanna workday wore on, my agitation grew. From preferring to avoid contact with the other men, my mood evolved by mid-afternoon to one of great anxiety at the thought of facing them at all. My hands shook when I took papers from them through the cage door, and I couldn't meet their eyes. My pulse and respiration felt fast and shallow, my head light, my chest constricted, the pit of my stomach cold. Once or twice I had to lay my head on the desktop to avoid fainting. In two years at this job I had not missed an hour of work on account of illness, but now I thought I might have to go home early. I watched the clock and tried to ward off feelings of panic. It seemed safer and easier to stay at my post and feign equilibrium than to risk the talking that would be necessary to excuse an early departure. By quitting time I was on the verge of hysteria; I left without speaking to anyone, hurried home and fell into bed.

Joanna had been in that room only twelve hours earlier but no sign of her remained. I felt lonely and distraught at the same time. What had happened was too devastating to contemplate and too grave to be ignored. I wished irrationally that she were there now to undo what we had done, but it was impossible. I wanted to sleep. I got up and lowered the window shade to exclude the daylight, then crawled again into bed. I lay awake for a long time. The yellow light at the window dimmed to gray; sometime later I awoke to find the room black. I closed my eyes again and dozed.

I dreamed I had gone back to the cemetery to look for Randall's headstone. It was night, but I could see well enough to conduct the search. As it happened there were no headstones at all, only acres of rolling hills, with a scattering of trees silhouetted against a starless sky. I hiked over the hills, wishing I had arrived in daylight, fairly sure I was too late and that Randall was gone. In the distance I could see a stone crypt sunk into a rise in the ground, and I realized that this was the grave of Randall and Joanna. Light spilled from a single window. I drew closer and peered in, but nothing was there.

I snapped awake in my darkened room, heavy with the sense that I had arrived at the end of something. I was disoriented and thought the month was February, although in fact it was summer and the month was June. It seemed impossible that I could support the burden of my life much longer. The difference between the world as I'd made it and the world that I wished for—the difference rebuked me and rode me to the ground. The thought of going to work to spend another day like the one just past filled me with dread. I struggled up, went to my desk and turned on a light. Blinking in the glare, I saw by the clock that it was not yet midnight.

I delved in the desk drawers for the savings account passbook from my bank. For years my income had been very modest but my expenses had been even less, the single major one after the controlled rent on my apartment being the tithe to my church. As a consequence I had saved a few thousand dollars. I looked at the passbook balance and saw how the accumulation of occasional deposits and monthly interest increments over many years had yielded this result. I would not have indulged myself in the spending of money kept for an emergency if the present emergency had not made it necessary. I saw that I could stop working long enough to gain relief from the torment and humiliation of having no acceptable account of myself to offer either to God or to my fellow man. I felt more alone and without moral resource than at any time since my near-death years before; even so, the prospect of more solitude comforted me. I left the passbook on the desk, shut off the light and picked my way back to bed, more at ease and expecting to sleep. I knelt and prayed, then climbed under the sheet. I was by no means well enough to go to work.

I did sleep, but I was oppressed by long and complicated dreams in which I hid from Joanna and ran from Bartley. Solveig appeared; I wanted to go to her, but the risk of being overtaken by Bartley prevented me. I crawled into a hamper of tattered rags and would have stayed there, but strangers picked away the pieces until I was uncovered and had to run again. In my dream I prayed to God to take me in, but I realized in the dream that I was dreaming, and that if I stopped dreaming I'd find myself alone and awake in my bed. So I stayed asleep, aware that God would not intervene to take me in or wake me up, and I kept running. When finally I awoke it was morning; the room was light. It was still too early to phone in sick. I lay where I was, fearful before a great chasm of uncertainty, lonely and despondent. I felt depleted, as if something had withdrawn all nourishment from my body and all courage from my soul. Awake, I prayed again to God to take me in. But it wasn't time yet for my release; I saw that I'd have to continue to struggle, regardless of my weakness and my ignorance of God's intentions. I hardly knew how I might carry on, but I knew I must.

Between the time I woke up and the time I could phone the warehouse, my intentions underwent half a dozen changes. At first I thought that, not only could I not go to work on this day, I could never go to work again. But the prospect of having to resign and then explain myself was so daunting that I considered summoning more courage than I possessed and going to work anyway, to carry on indefinitely in timid isolation and secret anguish. Equally I thought of doing nothing: not phoning, disappearing without explanation. But my compulsion to fulfill others' legitimate expectations of me made that option unacceptable, unless I meant to fail outright. In the event, I said only that I was indisposed and would phone again the next day if I was not better. I hung up temporarily relieved but un-encouraged, and I went back to bed.

I lay there for hours between waking and sleeping, weighing whatever options occurred to me and praying for guidance. I seemed to be at the end of my tether, having over many years attempted everything I could think of to do right and to please God. I had gone as far as I could go in the context of the life I'd made. It seemed that there was nothing left but to disconnect and strike out in an entirely new direction. But I had no idea what the direction might be, or what resources I might need to pursue it. I thought again of going home to God—of the peace there would be in abandoning the earthly life that I had prosecuted so earnestly but unsatisfactorily, and reaping the reward that I had earned by the quality of my faith, if not of its execution. But there was no sign that God was ready to take me, and every sign that He was not. I was in Despair, the fallen opposite of the heavenly virtue of Hope, and God would not take as faithful a servant as I when that servant was struggling in sin. I would have prayed to Him to take me, but it was my Christian duty now to continue to be tested. I thanked Him instead. I recalled, however inexactly, some lines of John Donne,

my Trinitarian forebear and the great preacher I might
have been:

> Batter my heart, three person'd God;
> That I may rise and stand, o'erthrow me.
> I, like a usurp'd town, to another due,
> Labor to admit thee, but to no end;
> Yet dearly I love thee and would be lovèd too.
> Take me to thee; imprison me, or I never
> shall be free,
> Nor ever chaste, unless thou ravish'st me.

I thought then and still think: Better half a sonnet
than no prosody at all. Better to aspire and die than to
sleep and die anyway.

I got out of bed about noon, very hungry, and made
breakfast. At that hour every weekday for two years I
had been in my steel cage, at the midpoint of a day's
work, eating a snack from the caterer's truck or a
sandwich I'd carried from home. It seemed sad to me,
even though it was my own choice, that I was not there
now. In my mind's eye I saw the place as it was at that
moment, myself absent, my work being done by others.
I felt lonely, disconnected and expendable, as if I had
been gone for a long time, been replaced, forgotten. The
idea of going there ever again to sit in the cage, at once
trapped and exposed, seemed more forlorn still. I'd
have phoned to say goodbye, but I had no explanation
adequate for the people I'd associated with. I gathered
my courage and phoned to resign instead, because I
could address this formality to anonymous

functionaries in the company personnel office. I said I was ill and couldn't be sure of returning to work in due time, and so I'd have to be replaced. A woman I'd never spoken to advised me that I was being assigned simultaneously to sick leave and two weeks' notice. It was the purest act of mercy—faceless, compassionless, uncontemplated, accidental. Only a corporation, I said to myself, could have done so much good for no reason. A friend might have done it like birthing a calf, with pangs of love and labor, and in that respect Jesus-like. God's mercy, though, is like no other—bountiful, shining from the Face that I so longed to see, beyond compassion, eternal, inevitable. God would not have granted me two weeks of sick leave; He would not have denied it either. His Purposes are immense.

Once I'd resigned, the stress of the world's expectations lifted like a weight. I realized that I'd tried too long to do too much with too little help, and that a retreat was in order. My apartment, not much bigger than the wire cage but dark and private, at first seemed the ideal place to hide. I built an altar and prayed at it. Candles burned there every hour I was awake. I went out only to buy groceries and withdraw cash from the bank. I began my fifth verbatim reading of the Bible.

After several weeks I ventured out on a Sunday and went to church, but I chose a congregation where I was not known, and I sat in a back pew. This was my return to public worship after the longest sequestration since my spiritual rebirth in the hospital room many years before. My style of worship except during my short career as a preacher had always been more interior than demonstrative, and now I found myself distracted by the liturgical forms taken by the religious substance. From where I sat I had a rear view, or a rear quarter view, of every head in the congregation, and a view of what they could see—the altar, the pulpit, the preacher and the choir. There was a show going on, but I couldn't relate it to the private struggle that engaged me at the altar in my apartment. It was hard to believe that the same Being I wrestled with there had presented Himself in this bright, public place and was investing the hearts and souls of these unimaginative-looking people. It was as if He affected a dance hall persona, light, popular and accessible, as a leaven for the personality I knew in private—obscure, censorious, demanding, jealous of my imperfection. He seemed to require more of me than of the mass of men and women: if not, why did no one else appear to be as conscious of failure as I was then? and why was no one visibly as joyous as the knowledge of Him had made me in my best days?

The preacher seemed to me to be trafficking in the airiest kind of soft soap. He addressed the congregation as if he expected nothing transcendent of them, ever. He told them they were sinners, but there was no sign they believed it. They sat impassively, putting in time, while the preacher reminded them of a handful of Scripture, which he tried without visible success to relate to their lives. I sensed nothing moving in the room. God was much closer and much tougher at home. I wished that two or three congregants in the front pews might burst spontaneously into flame, to show that God was present and that He was serious. I bowed my head and offered myself to Him, but I didn't burst into flame either, however much I wanted to. Before the service was over I stood up quietly and slipped out of the church, perhaps taking more of God with me than I left inside. I went back to my apartment and prayed in front of the shrine there.

CHAPTER TWENTY-THREE
REVELATION

During those days I began to reflect on the coming of the next millennium, now only a little more than twenty years away. It would be the third of the Christian era. What was more interesting, it would be the seventh millennium since the Creation as reckoned by Old Testament scholars beginning with Bishop Ussher, who in the Seventeenth century, using clues from the Scriptures, calculated the date of Genesis as October 23, 4004 BC. Many of my coreligionists had begun to consider that the End Time of Revelation could be expected by the year 2000, to be followed by one thousand years of peace during which Jesus would reign over the earth from His throne in Jerusalem, as set forth in prophecy. They reasoned from the admonition of the apostle Peter

> that with the Lord one day is as a thousand
> years, and a thousand years as one day,

that the Second Coming expected imminently by the early church should have been expected in a matter not of earthly days or years but of millennia, and that the number of those millennia should appropriately be six from the Creation, the Millennium of peace corresponding to the Seventh Day, when the Lord rested from His labors. Being in the midst of my fifth full reading of the Scriptures, with their allusions to the End Times scattered all the way from Daniel through the Gospels to Revelation, I was in no doubt as to the events to come; the only thing uncertain was the timing. But if Bishop Ussher's count was accurate and my coreligionists were right, then all the prophecies must be fulfilled before the end of this Twentieth century. And if the count was precise and the schedule rigorous, then all must be fulfilled by October 1997 (6000 years from 4004 BC, there being no year zero between the old and the new eras). That meant the Abomination of Desolation, the Great Tribulation, the Beast and the False Prophet, the Second Coming, the Rapture and the Wrath of God, all before the next twenty years were out! The first time I considered it, it took my breath away. I realized that if I simply lived to the age of retirement I would see Jesus come back to earth. I felt more urgently than ever that I should see the face of His Father, and more despairing that I'd been denied that blessing for so many years, and continued to be denied. What was I to think if, for all my devotion, all of mankind were to be shown the face of the living Jesus before I was allowed to see the face of the living God?

I took out pencil and paper and began my own count of the timeline given in Revelation and elsewhere for the events leading up to the Millennium. I assumed at first that Bishop Ussher had correctly deduced the date of Creation and that the Second Coming could therefore be expected to occur far enough in advance of October 1997 to allow time for the gathering of God's people and the pouring out of the seven plagues upon the earth. From October 23 I made my way backward through the prophecies, assigning a tentative date to each event. In my zeal to anticipate the End Times I lost track of the time in which I was living. I may have stayed awake through whole days and nights, forgetting mealtimes, making notes and diagramming chronologies, studying the Concordance to remind myself of the whereabouts of the Biblical references, which occur throughout both Testaments but most densely in Revelation. I exhausted myself many times, collapsing into bed and sleeping, often dreamlessly, until God restored me to continue the work.

Where Scripture didn't specify the duration of events, I adopted the shortest plausible duration for each, in order to arrive at the latest possible date for the End Times to begin. I was sure that when they appeared I would recognize the End Times for what they were; consequently I was sure that the End Times had not yet begun. I wanted to know how much time I had to order what was still chaotic in my life. I dealt first with the seventh and last of the plagues of the Wrath of God, the final event before the establishment of the Millennium of peace. John describes it this way:

> There were flashes of lightning, loud noises, peals of thunder, and a great earthquake such as had never been since men were on the earth. The great city was split into three parts, and the cities of the nations fell, and every island fled away, and no mountains were to be found; and great hailstones, heavy as a hundredweight, dropped on men from heaven,

till men cursed God for the plague of the hail,
so fearful was that plague.

It seemed to me that the worldwide scale of these events, and the geologic size of their effects, would require several days at least to be realized. If all of the world's islands were to sink and all of the world's mountains to be laid low, it was Divinely-inspired understatement to say that the earthquake that was to do it would be greater than any seen before. It would be immense, and understandable only as the act of an angry and omnipotent God, but it would progress at a rate appreciable by men. For a single mountain to collapse would take hours. Even if all the mountains on earth were to collapse simultaneously, the interaction of neighboring mountains collapsing into the same adjacent lowlands would complicate the picture and protract their disappearance. I estimated that the shortest time for the geologic events of the seventh plague to be completed would be ten days. The last feature, the plague of hail, if not actually contemporaneous with the leveling of the earth, could still be fulfilled in a matter of an hour or two. If men were to curse God for the hail, I supposed it must come after the geologic events and be regarded as the last straw and the surest sign, pelting down in prodigious mass, of intentionality by a wrathful God. It appalled me to think that men could see the earth leveled and still find it in their hearts to curse God for the weather, as if He were susceptible of correction. But it was written so.

I counted back the ten days from October 23, adopting October 13, 1997, as the tentative date of the beginning of the seventh plague. At this point, curiosity prompted me to consult an almanac for a perpetual calendar to calculate on which days of the week the dates were to fall. The first day of the Millennium of peace seemed scheduled for a Thursday, the first day of the great final earthquake perhaps a Monday. I was aware that Bishop Ussher, in the face of small uncertainty, had settled ultimately on October 23 because in 4004 BC that date was a Sunday, and that—what with discrepancies between the Julian calendar of Ussher and the Gregorian calendar of our latter days—I could as well have preferred a Sunday for the beginning of the great Millennium; but for my purposes the canonical date was close enough.

The sixth plague presented more of a problem, the Revelation accounts being evidently more figurative than the plainly physical descriptions given of the seventh plague. Consider this from Chapter 9:

> Then the sixth angel blew his trumpet, and I heard a voice from the four horns of the golden altar before God, saying to the sixth angel who had the trumpet, "Release the four angels who are bound at the great river Euphrates." So the four angels were released, who had been held ready for the hour, the day, the month, and the year, to kill a third of mankind. The number of the troops of cavalry was twice ten thousand times ten thousand; I heard their

number. And this was how I saw the horses in my vision: the riders wore breastplates the color of fire and of sapphire and of sulphur, and the heads of the horses were like lions' heads, and fire and smoke and sulphur issued from their mouths. By these three plagues a third of mankind was killed, by the fire and smoke and sulphur issuing from their mouths.

I looked also at the separate description of the sixth plague given in Chapter 16:

The sixth angel poured out his bowl on the great river Euphrates, and its water was dried up, to prepare the way for the kings from the east. And I saw, issuing from the mouth of the dragon and from the mouth of the beast and from the mouth of the false prophet, three foul spirits like frogs; for they are demonic spirits, performing signs, who go abroad to the kings of the whole world, to assemble them for battle on the great day of God the Almighty. And they assembled them at the place which is called in Hebrew Armageddon.

It was obvious to me that these accounts, especially the former one, had to be reinterpreted from the imagery of the visions John acknowledged them to be. Surely God's angels, at the end of the Twentieth century, would not loose a mutant cavalry to kill one-third of the five billion inhabitants of the earth when the nuclear weaponry to do the same thing was already in place. I was prepared to read "heat and blast and radiation" for "fire and smoke and sulphur" and the names of Leonid Brezhnev and Deng Xiaoping—or whoever their heirs might be a few years hence—for "the kings from the east". John gives the number of combatants as two hundred million; I had to accept that number because John says he was told. I supposed it referred to the number of men under arms of all countries. That they could not all be assembled at Armageddon, a hilltop in the Holy Land not much bigger than a football field, showed that that part of the prophecy was figurative and probably anticipated the outcome of the final battle, when Jesus, preparing for His Millennial reign in Jerusalem, might easily in such a small expanse accept the surrender of the heads of all the warring states. But my immediate interest was in judging how long, at a minimum, this sixth act of God's Wrath might take to run its course. It was generally conceded that an all-out nuclear war could kill one-third of humanity in a few hours; the toting up would take much longer. And for the survivors to notice the depredations of the seventh plague as a new set of facts, enough time would have had to pass after the last nuclear exchange for there to be the appearance of stability. In the end, I estimated that all of these things could not occur in a period of less than six weeks. I counted back from October 13 and assigned the beginning of nuclear war, the sixth plague, to September 1, 1997, or thereabout.

The duration of the fifth plague is explicit:

> Then came locusts on the earth, and they were given power like the power of scorpions of the earth; they were told not to harm the grass of the earth or any green growth or any tree, but only those of mankind who have not the seal of God upon their foreheads; they were allowed to torture them for five months.

So the plague of human-stinging locusts might begin on or about April 1, 1997.

Both descriptions of the fourth plague involve abnormal behavior of the sun, and in Revelation 8:12 the moon and stars are affected as well. The sun is dimmed by a third, and yet (Revelation 16:8)

> it was allowed to scorch men with fire; men were scorched by the fierce heat, and they cursed the name of God who had power over these plagues, and they did not repent and give him glory.

I estimated a month minimum for the fourth plague: long enough to encompass a lunar cycle and long enough for its effects to be appreciated as something more than a brief anomaly. One day's sunburn could pass as an accident; a month of sunburns regardless of precautions taken might easily prompt the unrepentant to curse the Lord. So I assigned the beginning of the fourth plague to March 1, 1997.

In the third plague a star, perhaps a meteor, falls to earth and contaminates a third of the fresh water supply, killing many people. The scripture doesn't make clear whether this plague abates completely before the fourth begins. I estimated the shortest duration for the third plague—that is, the least time for the contaminated waters to be substantially restored by natural processes—at two months. I noted with bemusement and fear that this calculation pointed to a date very near Christmas 1996 for the falling of the star; I thought of the Star of Bethlehem and the slaughter of the innocents. This time the slaughter would be largely of the guilty.

Working backward, I noticed for the first time in all my many readings that the second plague prefigured the third in an odd way. Here (Revelation 8:8,9),

> something like a great mountain, burning with fire, was thrown into the sea; and a third of the sea became blood, a third of the living creatures in the sea died, and a third of the ships were destroyed.

Another meteor, or something larger: an asteroid or a comet. But again the effect was to contaminate the water and to kill creatures dependent on it. In Revelation 16:3, the contamination kills not a third but everything. I didn't know how to account for the difference, but I was glad that if God let me live and I had understood the calendar aright, I would get to see the answer for myself. As for the time frame, this plague sounded like something that could happen almost instantaneously; it would need to continue only as long as it might take for the effects to reach all corners of the globe. I thought one day might be enough. We were still speaking of events occurring in the Nativity season of 1996.

I had now arrived at the first plague of the wrath of God. This one is described incompletely in each of the Revelation accounts, but taken together the picture is of a storm of hail, fire and blood that burns a third of the earth, a third of the trees and all of the grass, and an outbreak of foul sores on the bodies of "the men who bore the mark of the beast and worshipped its image." In my previous reading I had not noticed that in the first plague all of the grass on earth is burned, but by the time of the fifth plague the locusts are specifically commanded not to harm the grass. I perceived that the grass must have grown back in the interim, in spite of the activity of the intervening plagues, with their poisoned water and scorching sun. Here was a possible clue to the duration of the first plague, or a hint that I had allowed too little time for recovery of the earth between plagues. After long consideration, because I meant to calculate the latest date for the first sign of the End Times, I left the time line as I'd estimated it before, and I assigned a minimum duration of two months to the first plague—time for fires to consume all of the grasslands and a third of the forests, and for a simultaneous outbreak of ulcerating sores on all those guilty of apostasy. And so it seemed plausible finally to adopt the period of one year, from late October to late

October, for the duration of the seven plagues of the wrath of God. In nature, burned grass recovers very rapidly. And even if it didn't, still God could make it so.

When I was satisfied with my picture of the final twelve months preceding the Millennium, I stopped to catch my breath and look around. I didn't know the day, although I was pretty sure the month was September. I checked my watch. The time was 3:45, but I didn't know whether a.m. or p.m. until I looked past my desk lamp into the bedroom and saw that it was dark. I'd been indoors continuously for several days and felt like stretching, so I got up and went out, opening and closing doors quietly to avoid disturbing my neighbors. The air in the street felt mild on my skin and ineffably salubrious, as if something had passed through the city during the night and cleansed everything in it. I thought of ambrosia, the food that was supposed to have sustained the pagan gods of old, before Christ came to earth and showed what Divinity in human form would really look like. God had made the world so fine and beautiful that sometimes the experience of it could break the heart. But I had been so immersed for days or weeks in His coming wrath that the terror He was capable of had made me forget. I looked about me and saw no hint yet of the End Time.

I stepped off the curb and walked eastward on the empty pavement, under street lamps, past parked cars. Ahead I saw a crescent moon framed between buildings, its horns pointing upward, and between the horns a dark presence like Satan. This was the moon that in twenty years or less, in company with other signs, would make manifest His wrath. Only five years before, men no more Godly than I had been walking on it, and one of them had essayed to play golf. We had danced all over Creation without improving or appreciating it, and now we hadn't long to await the Judgment.

When I'd stretched enough I didn't stop walking. I thought of Randall, years before, walking in the opposite direction out of this city, westward, in quest of something. My back was to his destination and to the great mystery of why he had died. Ahead of me was the horned moon and, not yet visible beyond it, the dawn. I understood once more, as I had after my fall from grace with Joanna, that I had given up hope of knowing anything at all about Randall. I felt trapped between the past and the future, between Randall's and my death on the one hand, and the dark of the moon and that day's dawn and the Last Days, on the other. Elsewhere in the city my worst failure, Joanna, lay asleep, and in yet another quarter—or so I hoped and prayed—lay the faithless Bartley, ignorant of and indifferent to the Wrath to come. I walked on, afraid to turn my back to the moon, but reluctant to see the sky grow light.

CHAPTER TWENTY-FOUR
DOUBT

Ifound my way back to my apartment about six a.m., the moon having climbed higher and grown pale and innocuous in the brightening sky. I made some breakfast, prayed and crawled into bed, out of phase with the world I had just visited and come back inside to avoid. I kept my shades drawn and put plugs in my ears to shut out any disturbance from those souls in jeopardy going about their earthly business, and I slept for several hours. I dreamed I was in Heaven in the End Times before the throne of God, waiting for the angels to pour out the plagues of His wrath onto the world below. But something was wrong. Although I knew where the throne stood I couldn't see it, and although I was surrounded through the length and breadth of the air by the elect—the risen dead in Christ and those living in Christ who had been Raptured—I realized that no one could see me. I searched among the risen for the face of Randall, but I saw him not. And although we Christian multitude were there according to the Biblical promise that we should escape the Wrath, there seemed to be a stoppage. The Wrath was not proceeding. If the angels had their bowls or trumpets they were neither sounding flourishes nor pouring out the plagues. There seemed to be an understanding throughout Heaven of an indefinite delay, but I had no communication with the others and could not ask. I knew that Christ had come again, descending from heaven with a shout, with the voice of

302

an archangel, with the trumpet of God, as foretold in First Thessalonians, and brought us here, but I couldn't remember the event. Somehow I had missed it. I began to weep. On every side, stretching to the infinite distance, the people waited; but I was alone.

I awoke in the dimmed daylight of the drawn bedroom shade, fearful and disheartened, and looked at the clock. It was a little past one p.m., date unknown— and immaterial, until I should have finished working out the timing of the Last Days. My dream seemed to reinforce the urgency of pinning down the prophecy, as if the fulfillment of the End Times depended on my monitoring its progress. I couldn't afford to miss any of it, or I might miss it all. I said a prayer, climbed out of bed hungry and ate another breakfast.

My next task was to fit the Coming of Jesus and the Rapture of His people into the time line. I sat again at my desk, under the lamp, and studied Revelation. I had determined to set aside, temporarily, the Old Testament and its many allusions to the Second Coming—in Job, Isaiah, Jeremiah, Daniel, Joel and Zechariah—as well as the New Testament accounts in the Gospels and the Epistles, in order to concentrate on John's visions of the events attendant on Jesus' return. Most of them occur entirely in Heaven, which I took to be a place asecular, outside of time, as ageless, dimensionless and infinite as God Himself. Only the handful of Heavenly events affecting the earth directly could be dated, but this would be an important start.

For the first time in all my reading I was struck by how unequal were to be the impressions made in

Heaven and on earth by the moment itself. In fact, I
had to read closely to realize that the Second Coming
occurs invisibly in Revelation at the opening by the
Lamb, Who is Christ, of the sixth seal. I deduced this
from the fact that at the opening of the fifth seal the
souls of the martyrs cry out to the Lord, "How long
before Thou wilt judge and avenge our blood on those
who dwell upon the earth?" and are told to be patient,
and the further fact that, before the account of events
following the opening of the sixth seal is completed, we
read this:

> I looked, and behold, a great multitude which
> no man could number, from every nation, from
> all tribes and peoples and tongues, standing
> before the throne and before the Lamb, clothed
> in white robes, with palm branches in their
> hands, and crying out with a loud voice,
> "Salvation belongs to our God who sits upon
> the throne, and to the Lamb!"

Obviously, these were the raptured of the church, the
multitude I'd found myself among in my dream only
hours before, brought to Heaven by Jesus to deliver
them from the coming wrath. So the actual
reappearance of Jesus on earth was as absent from the
Revelation account as from my dream, but it was
implied in both. I looked again at Paul's marvelous
description in 1 Thessalonians 4:16,17:

For the Lord Himself will descend from heaven with a shout, with the voice of an archangel, and with the trumpet of God. And the dead in Christ will rise first. Then we who are alive and remain shall be caught up together with them in the clouds to meet the Lord in the air. And thus we shall always be with the Lord.

While the Lamb in Heaven was busy opening the seven seals, He would simultaneously, in His human form, be descending from heaven to fulfill the promise of the Gospels: "They will see the Son of man coming on the clouds of heaven with power and great glory." I now understood that the Second Coming of Jesus would be a mystical event—sudden, global and virtually instantaneous. There would be no time for press coverage or media analysis. If Christ as the Lamb and the Son of Man were to be in Heaven and on earth at the same time, then He would be everywhere on earth at the same time. And the rapture of His people would have no logistical dimension at all: it would just happen, occupying no more of the time line than the minute or two required for each of the elect to appreciate that he was being whisked away. And so it seemed that the Second Coming and the Rapture would occur suddenly and quickly, after the appearance of the signs foretold, not later than October 1996.

Now I backtracked to the signs.

When he opened the sixth seal, I looked, and behold, there was a great earthquake; and the sun became black as sackcloth, the moon became like blood, and the stars of the sky fell to the earth as the fig tree sheds its winter fruit when shaken by a gale; the sky vanished like a scroll that is rolled up, and every mountain and island was removed from its place.

I began to feel discouraged. I had been at work on the time line for days or weeks, and now I was finding precursors of events that I had already weighed and placed later in the chronology—events of such global effect and destructive magnitude that it seemed anomalous that they could happen more than once. Could every mountain and island be removed from its place in—say—the third calendar quarter of 1996, and then, in plague number seven, which I had calculated for the ten days following October 13, 1997, all of the world's islands sink and all of the world's mountains be laid low once again, with never a mention in the interim of islands being restored or mountains raised back up? I began to doubt that I knew how to read the Bible after all. In a single passage were descriptions of signs that might appear without producing any physical effect on the earth, and descriptions with the very same rhetorical weight but contemplating global destruction. How could I deduce the duration of events that seemed to be half minatory and half extirpative?

I bent over the passage following the opening of the sixth seal and felt my head begin to hurt. The sun as black as sackcloth suggested an eclipse; the moon becoming like blood could be an eclipse as well: I remembered once, years earlier, seeing the moon turned a ghastly, metallic red by an eclipse. For a moment I wished I had enough astronomy to know whether eclipses of the sun and moon could take place simultaneously, or whether some minimum time had to pass between one and the other; and then I realized that signs from God didn't need to follow any rules but their own. To the extent that the signs in the sky were signs only, they could occur in as little time as it might take for them to be seen and appreciated, and this included the vanishing of the sky like a scroll that is rolled up—an event I couldn't even visualize. But the geologic phenomena still asked to be weighed and accounted for, along with the response to them of the kings and potentates and everyone, slave and free, who

> hid in the caves and among the rocks of the mountains, calling to the mountains and rocks, "Fall on us and hide us from the face of him who is seated on the throne, and from the wrath of the Lamb; for the great day of their wrath has come, and who can stand before it?"

Before I could come to grips with these passages, my eye slid down the page to the verse immediately following—a verse that invariably made me think of Bartley, who had challenged me with it on that fateful day in 1968 when I introduced him to Joanna:

> After this I saw four angels standing at the four corners of the earth, holding back the four

winds of the earth, that no wind might blow on earth or sea or against any tree.

I remembered how I had met that challenge from Bartley. In the purity of my faith, I had told him simply that I accepted whatever the passage said, including— if it were the plain sense of it—that the earth is flat. I felt sick. Whatever had happened in the years since to batter my faith, it had led me to the enterprise I now regretted to find myself embarked upon, of snipping, parsing and schematizing the Biblical account as if it were the ledgers of a small business. Faith was easier when it inhered in the beauty of the Scripture and the unexamined upwelling of the heart. In ecstasy the earth could be flat without a doubt, and mountains could be raised up and laid low in a matter of seconds. But my coreligionists and I had insisted on the Bible as history and plain prophecy, and now I had to struggle to understand it. Bartley had told me he was a physicist. I supposed he knew some astronomy too. If it happened that God had chosen to synchronize the revealed events of Scripture with the predictable events of His natural world, then I might even get help with the End Time chronology by asking Bartley for the dates of future eclipses. But I could never do that. The spiritual journey that I was on and that still threatened to defeat me was mine to struggle with alone, except for the help of God. I closed my eyes and rested my forehead on the open pages of Revelation and prayed for assistance.

I dozed and dreamed that Solveig had come back from Sweden to read the Bible with me. She was as tall and blonde as I remembered; I watched her saffron-colored hands moving on the text. She read aloud, with her lilting accent, but in a language I didn't understand. This was not the gift of tongues; the tone was calm and narrative, not ecstatic or hortatory. I looked into her face, which glowed with light reflected from the page, and realized that I was excluded. The page illuminated her face; her face illuminated the page; the purling of her voice subsumed the truth of what she read in perfect, circular self-reference. I knew that what she knew was unspeakably beautiful and unbearably remote. I reached to stop her hand from moving on the book, but there was nothing material there to touch. My hand passed through hers; it gave me vertigo; surprise woke me up. I raised my head off the Bible and cradled my temples in the heels of my hands.

For the first time since I had begun working on the End Time chronology I doubted the value of the exercise. What if the scriptural passages in which time was an imponderable so far outnumbered or outweighed those that could be understood in secular terms, that the uncertainties in my calculations turned out to be larger than the time line itself? What if the experience of my dreams were truer than any work I could accomplish through my waking effort? The image of Solveig reading by her own light tantalized me, but I feared it. If Christians could find salvation in their sleep, then what was the point of being born? In such a case, intellectual and moral rigor would be superfluous; the world might as well be an opium den and its saints addicts. But I was tired. I laid my head down again and fell asleep.

CHAPTER TWENTY-FIVE
PROPHECY

A s it happened I did not abandon the time line project. Awake and rested, with my strength about me, the idea of Christ coming again in my generation loomed like a prodigy. The struggle to interpret its particulars could not be anything but worth the cost. I stuck to my original plan—to estimate the least time necessary for the fulfillment of each of the elements of the prophecy, in order to determine how old I would be, at the very most, at the appearance of the first signs. Over a period of weeks stretching into the winter of 1978, praying often for strength and guidance, I backtracked from the place where I had first been stymied, between the Rapture and the Wrath, through the sealing of the 144,000 representatives of the twelve tribes of Israel (recognizing that these people must be already alive somewhere on earth, wondering who they might be, and afraid to hope that I might be one of them), through the Second Coming and the rapture and sequestration in Heaven of God's people (certain that I would at least be one of these), through the reign of the Beast and the activities of the False Prophet—the time called the Great Tribulation—back to the event that I must learn to watch for and which would signal the start of the End Time: the Abomination of Desolation.

Of the whole chronology, the only piece whose duration was easy to deduce was the period of the Great Tribulation, given in Daniel as 1,260 days. I divided by thirty and got forty-two months, or three and a half years. So even if the other events preceding the Wrath of God were to happen instantaneously, the End Time must begin no later than April 1993. I imagined the Abomination of Desolation being set up at Easter of that year—the paschal decorations torn down by order of the Beast, and some attractive nuisance instituted in their place by the False Prophet. It was easy to picture a commercial subversion of Jesus' passion as thorough and hideous as the one that had already overtaken the celebration of His birth.

But it was clear to me that the Abomination of Desolation could be expected even a little sooner than April 1993—just fifteen years from the period when I was carrying out my research—because the prophesy foretold events at the coming of Jesus that would require some finite time to make their impression. Matthew quotes our Lord Himself:

> Immediately after the tribulation of those days
> the sun will be darkened, and the moon will not
> give its light

—Jesus' own description of the signs I had interpreted in Revelation as possible eclipses—

> and the stars will fall from heaven, and the
> powers of the heavens will be shaken; then will
> appear the sign of the Son of man in heaven,
> and all the tribes of the earth will mourn

in anticipation of the wrath to follow, occasioned by their mistaken adherence—regardless of the evangelism of Christians despised and persecuted throughout the Tribulation—to the Beast and his works. I assumed that a little time—days at least, or more likely a week or two—would be required for these lost souls to appreciate their predicament. There would be discussion in the news media, initial disbelief in the halls of power, consternation among apostates and the adherents of false creeds, and, finally, mourning for the loss of their eternal lives and the inevitability of the punishment to come. A couple of weeks. We Christians would have this time to say I told you so, and then would be seen

> the Son of man coming on the clouds of heaven with power and great glory; and he will send out his angels with a loud trumpet call, and they will gather his elect from the four winds, from one end of heaven to the other.

This would be the Rapture. It might take no time at all, because Christians would be ready for it, their preparation having taken place over a lifetime in their hearts and souls. And then the way would be clear for God's wrath to be poured down on those left behind. I now felt that I had backtracked far enough, and that the Abomination of Desolation, the unmistakable first sign of the End Times, could be expected not later than, say, the Spring Equinox of 1993.

Nothing remained but to wait, pray and be vigilant. For the first time in all my years of seeking after the face of God, I was confident of seeing Him by a date certain. The very fact of my months-long siege of the Scriptures to gain this awful knowledge—hidden, I supposed, from virtually everyone else on earth—fortified me. I read these words of Jesus in Matthew 24:36:

> But of that day and hour no one knows, not even the angels of heaven, but the Father only.

Had my scholarship not been a mighty act of faith, I could have read this passage as a rebuke to presumption. Instead, it confirmed for me the extreme arcaneness of what I had teased out.

If the Beast was a man who only fifteen years hence would initiate the Great Tribulation by driving the Church underground and setting himself up as the false Christ, then he must already be on earth and working toward that end. I combed through Revelation again, looking for clues that might help me to identify the Beast, the Antichrist, sooner rather than later. It seemed possible to me that he was already in public life, visible as a political or religious leader, but not yet detectable as Paul's "man of lawlessness, the son of perdition". If I could spot him early, I could watch his public actions and anticipate the Abomination of Desolation. The event was inevitable, of course, but I might be able to warn my fellow Christians, and many of us might situate ourselves in the best way to survive the Tribulation, and so be among the living elect and there to see with our own eyes the Second Coming of the Lord.

The clues I was able to find in Revelation were scanty and abstruse. The physical description given in Chapter 13 was evidently allegorical:

> And I saw a beast rising out of the sea, with ten horns and seven heads, with ten diadems upon its horns and a blasphemous name upon its heads. And the beast that I saw was like a leopard, its feet were like a bear's, and its mouth was like a lion's mouth. One of its heads seemed to have a mortal wound, but its mortal wound was healed.

The allegory is made explicit, but not transparent, in Chapter 17, where the angel explains to the prophet the mystery of the Great Whore, Babylon, seated on the scarlet Beast:

> The seven heads are seven hills on which the woman is seated; they are also seven kings, five of whom have fallen, one is, the other has not yet come, and when he comes he must remain only a little while. As for the beast that was and is not, it is an eighth but it belongs to the seven, and it goes to perdition. And the ten horns that you saw are ten kings who have not yet received royal power, but they are to

receive authority as kings for one hour, together with the beast.

If there was a clue in any of this to the physical identity of the man who would be revealed to be the Beast, it had to be the head wound—a feature evoked again in the passage describing the offices of the False Prophet:

It exercises all the authority of the first beast in its presence, and makes the earth and its inhabitants worship the first beast, whose mortal wound was healed. It works great signs, even making fire come down from heaven to earth in the sight of men; and by the signs which it is allowed to work in the presence of the beast, it deceives those who dwell on earth, bidding them make an image for the beast which was wounded by the sword and yet lived.

The head wound was a solitary clue but an arresting one. How often might the survivor of a wound that ought to have been mortal be expected to become prominent in public life? This century had been marked and changed by examples of head wounds that had emphatically been mortal: I thought immediately of President Kennedy and his brother, either of whom, had he survived, might have been a candidate. The Beast would be hard to detect, but I believed I had two advantages. I knew what to look for, and I knew how soon it must appear.

CHAPTER TWENTY-SIX
WITNESS

By the time I finished my research into the Last Days it was the dead of winter, cold, gray and enervating. I had barely noticed the passage of Christmas. I felt at once listless and anxious, exhausted by the mental effort of my close reading, but agitated by the epochal importance of what I had learned. I hungered for an interlocutor to share my knowledge, but Randall was long dead and I had lost contact with every other friend or acquaintance. The memory of Joanna mocked me. In spite of myself I thought again of Bartley, my seeming equal in the seriousness with which he regarded questions of eschatology and things unseen. I had no doubt, if I should try to talk to him, that he would listen; but I had no confidence that in the end the experience would not mock me too. I would have saved Bartley if I could—sooner, by preference, than I'd have saved almost anyone else, but my courage flagged. I stared at myself in the mirror and judged that I had aged visibly since last I looked. The youthful beauty that I'd once taken as both a mark of God's favor and a means (by making me more liable to assault on my virtue) of testing my fidelity to Him—that beauty was no more. My face had gone soft and sallow and I was definitely balding. I looked for signs of an inward beauty but they were absent. My eyes looked back at me inclemently. They were blue, hooded and severe, peering out as from the face of one that loved no person. It seemed bizarre to me that I could have spent so much of my substance in devotion to the good, only to appear as a friendless man, alone in the winter, with fewer marks of God's love than ever. And the End Times were coming.

I went out and bought a small, second-hand television set and installed it in my apartment. I had not had one since the days when I was married, but now I felt the need to watch world events as well as read about them. Sometime soon the face of the Beast would appear on my TV screen and I would know him for what he was—not immediately, perhaps, but quicker than if I only read. I switched on the set and twisted the channel selector. Of the four stations I could find, three were showing commercial messages, the fourth a documentary about narrow-gauge railroads in central Asia. I turned the volume down to full silent and left the screen to run. If something important were to happen, it would come to my attention.

The presence of the television, with its small window moving constantly, seemed to exacerbate the sense of irresolution that had been tormenting me for some time. It reminded me that outside my apartment there was a world hurtling toward ruin and Judgment. Without a vocation, I no longer knew my duty to that world. With not much more than ten years to go before the reckoning would surely be upon us, I could take advantage of the time that remained to go outside and cry Cassandra-like through the streets, or, because I was weary, I could stay inside and pray to God to move the date forward. Faces, products, titles, interiors, exteriors, machinery, undecipherable activity flickered on the screen. If I had ever truly wanted a career in that world, the short time remaining meant that there was no longer a reason to begin. Even so, ten years was a long time to wait in forlorn inactivity.

Prayer walking occurred to me as a useful compromise. This was a practice then gaining popularity among some evangelicals. It entailed walking through the neighborhoods of a city and stopping in each street to pray for the salvation of its residents, or the reform of its institutions if they were not Christian. Some walked in pairs or small groups; some prayed aloud, some silently. When prayer walking was organized by whole congregations, it was possible to plan the intercessional coverage of an entire town in the course of a day. I realized that with a main effort it should be possible for committed Christians, in the few years remaining before the Rapture, to pray on-scene for the enlightenment of every misguided soul and every erroneous sect and school on the face of the earth. I realized, too, that I could no longer spare the energy that would be required to be counted among the organizers of such an effort. But it was well within my capabilities and the limits of my vocation to prayer walk, even if I ended by doing it alone. According to my experience, every street in the city needed salvation. I took out a map and studied the grid. Joanna was represented there, as was Bartley. The campus of the local university sprawled across blocks where materialist notions of the creation of the world by an uncaused explosion and of humanity by an unimaginably long series of biological accidents had for decades been crowding out Godliness. A section of the downtown that I had never visited was the terrain of prostitutes and pornographic bookstores. Surveying this facsimile of my city spread across several square feet of desktop, I imagined thousands of pinpoints marking the locations of sexual misbehavior rampant at that very moment. There was no shortage of sin, scandal and disgrace to pray over.

I refolded and put away the map, and then I delved in another drawer for my financial accounts. Without a windfall there would be no chance of husbanding my savings to support me unsalaried into the End Time. I remembered my teacher George Woodrick's aptitude for harvesting money from the very fields of the Lord where grazed the flocks he served. Had I retained my brief vocation, I might have done the same, and been as well a mighty thorn in the side of the Beast when he appeared. As it was, I had to think of becoming a mendicant, or else compromising my last purpose in the world by enduring the distraction of a job. From childhood I'd seen cartoons of the stereotypical prophet, unkempt, in sackcloth and wearing a sandwich board proclaiming the end of the world. Now I threatened to be that character.

It goes without saying that I prayed assiduously and for hours to know how to proceed. I had spent years in devotion to the God Who loved me but continued to hide His face from me. I was unsure of the nature of my failure to be worthy in His eyes; I still sensed that He was angry with me, that He disliked me, that at my core I was without grace, that He perceived me guilty of some great negligence. I tried to deny a phantom that I sensed intruding into my life with God: a wish of long duration that He would comfort me, as Marie—and Beth before her—had comforted me: with a sheltering hand. I wished that He would reach into the world and touch me. Except for my terrible mistake with Joanna, I had gone years without a love that contemplated the existence of my physical body and its claims to nourishment, warmth, sleep and comfort. I didn't remember choosing asceticism, but I had ended up with it.

As much as I prayed, I still felt no reassurance in my body. But my mind and heart, well conditioned by my recent studies and undoubtedly guided, however invisibly, by the Lord, settled on prayer walking. Initially I would do it by myself, depending on my own resources. When and if I depleted them I could reconsider. But if my prayer walking were effective, it might lead to alliances with those I prayed for, and a self-supporting movement could begin. For all I knew, there were large numbers of prayer walkers already abroad and we would recognize one another. In a corner of the room the TV screen was busy with images I would be confronting outside. I walked closer and looked. A sedan with a small flashing light on top was weaving at high speed down a city street. I saw no reason to think this might be the Beast.

I sat at my desk and considered how to go about my first day of prayer walking. I took the map from the drawer and spread it out again. The city stretched nearly one hundred blocks west to east and nearly eighty north to south. My first impulse was to choose a corner, probably the northwest, and begin walking that quadrant. At first glance it was a daunting prospect. The border of the city on its near suburbs was rectilinear but arbitrary, so that the residential streets, not laid out on a square grid like those nearer the center, wandered across the city line at random angles and intervals. Even restricting myself to neighborhoods inside the city limits, it would require considerable attention and ingenuity to pray in every street. I was conscious again of a moral exhaustion that had assailed me from time to time for years—at least since the death of Randall and my retirement from the seminary. Each time I flagged I used prayer to reassert my determination to act out my faith with or without encouragement from my physical body, whose energy seemed to continue its downward trajectory. Whatever might happen to my health, whatever disappointments might befall me in my daily life, I was determined not to yield my spirit. I'd promised myself to God and I would work as long and as hard as necessary to please Him, even if it were not in His timetable to acknowledge my sacrifice in this world. So there was no question of not prayer walking, and over the hardest ground, at that. I bent over the map and studied the rapid transit routes to the fields I meant to cultivate.

I laid out warm clothing, set my alarm clock for six a.m., and went to bed to pray. Relative strength and courage suffused me again; I fell asleep before long and dreamed that I had earned my way into Heaven. The sun shone on green, rolling hills dotted with the white figures of souls that had arrived ahead of me. The silence was perfect, the air still, tepid and odorless. I wandered, hoping for a glimpse of something that would inform me of my status. I realized I had no address, no knowledge of the place I was in, and no certainty about how long I was to stay. I had arrived at last at the abode of God, but I didn't see Him yet. As on earth, He must be immanent in everything. But His throne was in Heaven, and there it should be possible to see His face. I walked over the hills, never drawing closer to the other souls, although I followed them hopefully. I grew tired and sat down on a park bench. Randall had arrived before me and was sitting at the opposite end smoking his pipe, his head broken. I took fright. He looked at me directly and said either "I am not the Beast" or "I am the Beast"; I couldn't tell which. "How did you die?" I asked him. He stared at me with a look that bespoke a terrible effort to be heard, but no sound came. Fear swelled in me. I stood and tried to walk away, but my feet were planted. I knew that if Randall spoke he would say something too awful to hear. He lifted one hand to the opening in his skull and pushed something into it.

I awoke in near panic, clutching at the bedclothes and afraid to open my eyes. I was amazed and discouraged to think that I had had a nightmare—my first in many years. A wind had come up and was blowing audibly, whistling against the side of the building and rattling my bedroom sash. The weather had been cold for several days; I guessed it must be getting even colder. Prayer walking would be hard. I opened my eyes, turned on the bedside lamp and read awhile from Psalms. I avoided looking at the alarm clock. I didn't need to know what time it was. I would prayer walk regardless of the weather, with or without sleep.

The alarm woke me at six. The lamp was on, the Bible resting open on my chest. I closed it, climbed out of bed and knelt on the cold floor to pray. The time of terror was approaching for the world; I would go out and meet it. I wondered what Randall had known, and why the image of him had come to frighten me.

I made breakfast. The TV screen in the corner of the living room showed a weather map with temperatures between five and fifteen degrees sprinkled over it. A news reader's head and shoulders appeared, and behind her a still photo of a dysphoric-looking old man, his head wrapped, and the caption "Khomeini". I turned up the sound. Khomeini was an Iranian cleric in exile in France. He didn't seem a likely candidate for the Beast, although the headdress could have been concealing a wound. I noted his name.

I dressed, then began bundling into the warm outer clothes I'd need for the first day of my crusade. I had an old parka with a hood trimmed in artificial fur, fleece-lined gloves and boots, and a woolen scarf. The parka had unlined patch pockets on the sides large enough to accommodate the smaller of my two Bibles, and flannel-lined slash pockets big enough for my gloved hands, should I need the extra warmth. I stuffed my city map into the second patch pocket, turned off the

TV sound and went out to catch the first of three buses that would take me to my mission.

The weather was colder than I expected. The air stiffened in my nostrils; the wind was blowing hard enough to sweep surface snow along the street. The walk to the first bus was only three blocks, but I stopped to wrap the scarf across my face, tie it at the back of my neck and cinch snug the hood of the parka. The sun was still low behind buildings to the southeast. I hoped it would warm up later in the day, but I prayed only that God would make it possible for me to carry out the work.

Nearly an hour passed before I got down from the third bus at its final stop before the city limit. The wind had not diminished and the weather had not warmed, so I covered my face again and cinched my clothing tight. The first building I noticed when I looked around was a large synagogue. I felt glad. With the End Time in sight, the center of world events would soon be Jerusalem, and the tribes of Israel figured critically in the prophecy. I prayed the first prayer of my first prayer walk that God would open to Jesus the hearts of many of this Hebraic citizenry, so that some of them might be among the 144,000 sealed against the depredations of the Beast. And then I moved from the synagogue and into the neighborhood around it. I worked my way north along the western edge of the city, praying in each street for the salvation of its residents. The names on mailboxes and house fronts revealed that nearly everyone here was Jewish, which made obvious what I had to pray for. But I didn't settle for easy formulations or unconsidered superficialities. I was so determined that my prayers should count, that I kept my back turned to the adjacent suburb, leaving the salvation of those citizens to some other Christian, while I concentrated all the force of my faith and all the purpose of my orisons on the people inside the city limits.

The irregular layout of the streets in this neighborhood complicated the process of achieving full coverage. Each time I reached an intersection I peered along the streets in all directions, not including the one I had just come from, and determined whether I could see to the ends of the nearest blocks. If so, I judged by appearances what sort of people might be living there and I prayed for them accordingly. Then I marked that intersection on my map with a pencil and moved to the next one northward, my strategy being to reach the northern city limit, turn two blocks east, then return southward, praying at each intersection as I went. But because the streets often crossed at other than right angles, I had to be careful not to overlook any that might not communicate with at least one of the intersections I reached. And because some of the streets were curved, I had to refer to the map often to be sure I was not missing the occasional neighborhood tucked away in a cul-de-sac. The grid irregularity sometimes forced me into dead ends from which I'd have to retrace my steps, and when this happened I didn't pray again for those double-covered; I prayed instead for the enterprise itself, that God would give me the strength and stamina to carry it out and a mind alert to the signs of what needed to be prayed for.

God seemed to be testing me with the cold; I prayed about that too. After half an hour my toes and fingertips grew painful; after an hour the pain in my toes subsided but the pain in the fingers remained. Between intersections I pushed my gloved hands into the slash pockets of my parka, which kept them warm enough to function when it was time to use the map and pencil. The wind had not stopped blowing; it chilled my legs from the hem of my parka to the tops of my boots. I regretted that I had not provided myself with thermal underwear. My legs were the least dressed part of me, being covered with only one thickness of trousers, and the chill that the wind imparted to them seemed to invade the insulated parts of my body as well. I found myself shivering all over.

My discomfort was such that, had I not promised God and myself to devote the whole of the daylight to the prayer walk, I might have gone home then. But I pressed on, marking the map as I went, reading as well as I could the clues to the spiritual needs of the neighborhoods I passed and offering what I hoped were the appropriate prayers. I grew drowsy; my mind wandered and I began to have trouble matching prayers to the immediate circumstances. I considered sitting down in the snow to rest, but just then God led me into a small zone of retail establishments, and adjacent to a convenience store selling lottery tickets, where I stopped to pray for the deliverance of the citizenry from the snare of gambling, I found the glass front of a donut shop. I went inside, bought a cup of hot tea at the counter and sat in a booth several feet away to warm up. I was chilled through; I thought I might fall asleep where I sat, but I took the Bible out of my pocket and opened it on the table. My fingers stung, and after a few minutes my toes began to hurt again. I wrapped my hands around the teacup to warm them, bowed my head and considered the novelty that the addition of the cup worked on this familiar attitude of my head and hands. I had always prayed with my hands clasped and nothing in them; the warm cup felt as if it might have been put there by God to reassure me that He was listening. I almost understood the practice found in some other religious traditions of praying through palpable or visible objects—beads or flags, for instance. I thought of fashioning some thing that I could hold in my hands when I prayed—not a graven image, but a shape plain and smooth like the perfection of God, yet finite and graspable—a microcosmic epitome of God as He might have been before He sent His Son to earth to give human form to His mystery, and to be sacrificed. It was the brutality of this sacrifice that prevented me just then from thinking of praying with the Cross in my hands. The Cross was not like a warm teacup, but angular as an implement of war, and the comfort it offered was not the comfort of the womb but the promise of victory after a vexed birth and a life of pain. With my eyes closed, in my fantasy I saw my hands clasped around the warm, poodle-trimmed head of Joanna, as may have been the case on the night or morning when she and I unfortunately made love. Startled, I jerked upright and realized that I had begun to doze; I had barely avoided falling into the tea.

The time was about eleven a.m. and I seemed to have the attention of the counter man. There were only three other patrons in the donut shop: two in a booth together talking, the other alone and reading a newspaper. I may have been behaving strangely; I was chilled through and having trouble staying awake. I had also begun to shiver so uncontrollably that in order to sip the tea without spilling I had to leave the cup on the table and lower my face to it. I felt disoriented and detached, as if I only partially inhabited my body. If Satan had been tracking me, this would have been the moment to invade. I tipped the cup enough to empty it into my mouth.

I sat upright, still shivering, and saw the counter man watching. I felt vulnerable and in need of help. I tried to enlist the counter man by hoisting the teacup with my left hand and pointing at it with my right.

"What does that mean?" he called.

"Another cup of tea?" I said. "And a donut?"

"What kind?"

"Glazed," I said.

He turned and created another cup of tea out of a bag and water steaming from the urn, put it on the counter and set a donut on a plate adjacent. "Come and get it," he said.

"Could you bring it?" I asked.

"No booth service," he said.

"I'll get it in a minute," I said. But I was shivering too violently to risk carrying the tea. I waited where I was until embarrassment prompted me. I went to the counter, sat there on a stool and dipped the donut, biting down on the moistened part with chattering teeth.

"You okay?" the counter man asked.

"Cold," I said.

"You left your book in the booth," he said.

"It's the Bible," I said.

"Whatever," he said.

I felt that I'd wandered from my country and fallen among pagans. I was desperate to get warm, uncertain whether I'd ever feel secure again, and counting on the bulk of the donut and the hotness of the tea to restore a little of my strength. I looked into the eyes of the counter man and realized that his was the first face I'd actually seen of all those I'd been praying for that morning. At close quarters a human being is enigmatic: an entire person, with a history peculiar to himself and a relationship with God of unknown quality and intensity. To pray effectively for the counter man would require a text less generic than the ones I'd been reciting in the intersections. But the look he returned was blandly uncommunicative. Like virtually everyone else, he seemed unaware that time was running out. I continued to dip and chew the donut until it was gone, and then I chanced picking up the teacup with both hands to drink from it. I felt steadier; I drank it down. The counter man had moved off and was puttering at a distance.

I went to the booth to collect my Bible; I even bused the first teacup back to the counter for the man's convenience. I sat on the stool and studied the street map, which I'd folded to expose only the area of that day's prayer walk. I had made good progress, praying for every street within a space roughly four blocks wide and ten blocks deep, tucked into the northwest corner of the city proper, and I'd marked the map accordingly. I had no doubt that the work was good, but I wished for some means of measuring its effectiveness—something like before-and-after polls to count conversions or awakenings. But the work was an act of faith, and the measure of its success would have to inhere in the strengthening of my own Faith. The counter man came back. "Anything else I can get for you?" he said.

I looked once more into his unsympathetic eyes; I lowered my own and prayed silently, "Dear Lord, if this man's heart is hard, please soften it." Then I said to him, "May I ask if you are saved?"

"Excuse me?" he said.

"Are you saved? Have you accepted Jesus Christ as your personal Savior?"

"Look," he said, "I don't want any trouble. Could I get you to pay up and leave?" He was neither loud nor truculent, but his attitude surprised me. I hesitated. "You've been acting really weird since you came in here," he said. "Do you mind?"

"I pray that you'll consider the welfare of your immortal soul and let Jesus in. There isn't a lot of time."

"Please," he said. "Don't make me call a cop."

"Please think about it," I said. "I'll leave. I'll pray for you."

"One dollar and thirty-nine cents," he said.

I took the money from an inside pocket and paid him. My hands were shaking badly, partly from emotion and partly from the chill, which I hadn't yet completely overcome. He gave me eleven cents change from a dollar fifty and I felt around in my pocket until I found a quarter, which I placed on the counter as a tip. "God bless you," I said to him, and I left with my Bible and my map.

Outdoors the wind was still blowing and the air seemed barely warmer than when I'd left my apartment. The sun was as high as it would get that day, but it gave no detectable warmth. The stinging had gone from my fingers while I was in the donut shop but my toes were still a little painful. I made myself as snug as possible in the clothing I had, consulted the map and selected a route that would broaden eastward the rectangle of my prayer coverage, then I set off.

The neighborhood immediately to the east of the shopping area where I'd stopped for tea was easier to pray through than the newer neighborhood to the west, being of two- and three-family houses fronting close on streets that intersected at right angles. The way into the neighborhood took me past a large Roman Catholic church; I stopped opposite the entrance to the nave, cognizant that a degree of idolatry flourished there, and prayed for the perfection of Christian practice everywhere in the world. Then I asked God to give me the strength to endure the discomforts of the frigid afternoon before me, and I moved on to pray in the nearby street.

CHAPTER TWENTY-SEVEN
PROVIDENCE

I must have lain down in the sun sometime early in the afternoon with the mistaken idea that by presenting a smaller target for the wind and taking a catnap I might warm up a little and overcome a growing drowsiness that was interfering with my efforts to keep track of my line of march and to pray cogently at the same time. Afterward I was never able to recall how I came to grief, or to learn exactly where or at what time I was discovered lying in the snow in a public park a few yards from the nearest street. Evidently it was still daylight when God sent one of His angels to find me there dangerously cold and unresponsive, and to call an ambulance.

Thus it happened that for a second time I was driven *sub specie mortis* through winter cold into the care of medical emergency workers, and once again I was kept whole for tasks that God alone knew the nature of. I awoke to severe pain in my hands and feet—frostbite that might have cost me some appendages, but by the grace of God did not. There was a mask of some sort over my nose and mouth, and I was naked except for a jacket with water tubes passing into it wrapped around my chest and abdomen; and— as I eventually realized—I was inside the same hospital I'd fetched up in eleven years earlier, after my overdose. Once I was out of danger and out of intensive care, the bed they installed me in may even have been the same: the room looked familiar.

I tried to fathom the irony—if that's what it was—of this situation. My religious journey, as long and awkward as it had been, had brought me back without warning exactly to the place where it began. But I had no sense of coming home. Instead I felt as if every dubious gain had been lost and all credit for the dedication of my life had been expunged. God had let me invest my every hope in Him, had set me to work for Him, had received my devotion in every waking hour, but He had never offered any sign of His favor. Now I was back where I started, but the life of service I'd looked forward to with joy I now anticipated with chastened faith. I was no longer sure that God would show me His purpose while I was on earth. It even seemed possible that God had no purpose for me on earth except to test me as long as I lived.

While I was still in intensive care, lying in a hospital bed connected to equipment that was re-warming me to human temperature, I considered what it meant to live a life whose sole purpose was to be tried for one's faith. This was martyrdom of the purest sort: to be scourged not by the enemies of God but by God Himself. In truth, the idea thrilled me. To be set upon by forces that were clearly Satanic and to resist in the name of God—that was easy compared to being set upon by God Himself and clinging nevertheless fiercely to one's faith. It seemed obvious which victory would please God more. In spite of the pain in my extremities and the quaking cold in my body's core—or perhaps because of them—I was happy.

I had not been long out of intensive care and installed in the familiar-looking room when I was visited by a man in street clothes asking questions and recording my answers on a clipboard. The hospital had identified and admitted me on the basis of documents found in my wallet, but there was no evidence of my next of kin, and the medical insurance card I carried belonged to a group where I was no longer employed. The hospital was concerned that I might not be able to pay for my care. I was similarly concerned, but the remarkable circumstances that had brought me there—the act of Faith that had put me at risk of freezing to death, the ambulance ride to the scene of my earlier rebirth—so outweighed the practicalities that I wasn't inclined to worry just then. I saw that God had provided everything to that point; He would provide the rest. The hospital administrator pressed for the name of my next of kin, but I had none unless it was Randall, and he was dead. The administrator went away.

A nurse came in soon afterward and asked me how I felt. Except for some sensitivity where my toes came in contact with the sheet covering me I felt fine and—although I didn't say it—glad of her company. But then she caused me great embarrassment by taking my temperature both orally and rectally, and I gave up the idea of a friendship. She wrote the numbers on a clipboard similar to the administrator's, took my pulse and measured my blood pressure, wrote those numbers down as well, and left me alone. On a wall bracket mounted above my bed a color television was playing silently. I lay and watched it, still alert for the first manifestation of the Beast.

My recuperation was medically uneventful, although I was subjected over a period of three days to a great deal of monitoring and examination. After one day I was moved to a room containing a second bed, but there was no patient in that bed, so the degree of privacy I enjoyed was unaffected. Whatever time I wasn't being examined or fed I spent in prayer and contemplation, trying to understand why I had been chastened so drastically for my prayer walking. The map and the Bible I'd carried were beside me on a table; I looked at the map and saw by its pencil marks that I had covered more streets than I could remember; but the park where I was found unconscious was three blocks away from the nearest pencil mark, so it seemed I'd grown disorganized before I collapsed. The percentage of the city I'd been able to pray over was discouragingly tiny. I asked if that discouragement were of God or of Satan, and I feared that it might be of God. Satan moves in the world to trap the unwary, but he doesn't control the weather. I had to decide by any prayerful means whether on the one hand God simply did not want me to prayer walk, or on the other He intended such a stern test of my resolve that if I passed it I'd have discovered a vocation to replace the one I'd lost. My mind whirled.

There was a telephone in the room on a table between the two beds, and it surprised me by ringing. I picked up the receiver and was further surprised to hear the distinctive voice of Rob Bartley. "I saw you on page eight of yesterday's paper, below the fold," he said. "How's your health?"

As had so often happened in my relations with Bartley, I felt excited and oppressed at the same time. To be in his company always made me think that something of moral significance was about to happen, but I always feared that the significance might be to my moral detriment. Furthermore, I had put Bartley behind me along with Joanna; to have him cropping up again threatened to blight a future already fraught with risk and challenge. I didn't see how the companionship of Bartley could help me cope with the dangers of the End Times, or contribute to my vigil against the Beast. "I'm fine," I said. "A touch of frostbite."

"How did you get caught out like that? Something else wrong?"

"No, no," I said. "I was out evangelizing. I guess I wasn't dressed well enough for the cold. I thank God somebody got me to the hospital."

"So do I," he said—whether out of generosity or hypocrisy, I couldn't tell. "Are you entertaining?"

"Sorry?"

"Can you have visitors? Do you want visitors?"

I did and I didn't. I wished for human company, but I felt too unsure of my state of grace at that moment to subject myself to moral combat with Bartley. His use of the plural "visitors" disturbed me too: what if he wanted to bring Joanna? It occurred to me that the last time I laid eyes on her I had been on a bed and humiliated. The thought that she might come back and see me again on a bed and humiliated was really unbearable. "I don't think I'd want to see Joanna," I said.

"Yeah," Bartley said, "I discussed it with her."

"You did."

"Yeah. For reasons unknown, she seemed kind of fed up."

"With me. Yes."

"So she turned us down. But I'm not fed up; I'm more—I'd say—mystified. You need anything? I could run some errands for you."

I recognized this as Bartley at his headlong, disarming, seductive best. If he was manipulating me it was impossible to know why, and consequently I could think of no good reason to refuse him. "No," I said, "I don't need anything. Very kind of you to ask."

"Book? Magazine? Something from home? I could probably get the super to let me into your place."

"Really, nothing."

"I'll drop around after they feed you, if that's okay. Seven? Seven-thirty?"

"That's fine."

"See you then. Keep well. Stay indoors." And he hung up.

"Stay indoors." A certain inconsequential jocularity was a feature of Bartley's personality that I'd noticed from the day Solveig introduced us. I imagined it was a feature that could unhinge me if I spent enough time in his company. He seemed constitutionally incapable of sobriety for more than a few minutes at a stretch, as if he suffered from an attention deficit that caused him to lose track of the fundamental seriousness of the human enterprise, which is to do right and to please and fear God. From time to time he seemed intent on doing right, but I worried that the rest of the enterprise was forever beyond him. His moral reconstruction remained on my list of miscarried projects, yet he now appeared intent on rescuing *me*.

It unnerved me to think that Bartley might be coming to meddle with whatever balance I had thus far achieved in my life. On at least one occasion he had tried to refer me to a psychiatrist, as if he supposed I had no spiritual resources. I wondered about Bartley himself: if he had spiritual resources I couldn't imagine what they might be. He seemed too unaware of his guilt to be consulting anyone or anything. I tried a thought experiment in which Bartley, with a salary and no natural enemies, inhabited a world with no beginning, no end and no God. In such a case his insouciance would be perfectly explicable but his life would be as bereft of nobility as I had always suspected. I saw him alone and content at the center of a blasted heath, without attachment or duty, and I felt great sorrow for him. He populated his heath with sexual companions, but there could be no salvation in that.

He turned up in my hospital room soon after seven as promised, carrying a single white rose in a slim vase. "From Solveig," he said.

"What do you mean?"

"Nothing coherent," he said. "I just think she'd have brought this." He placed it on the bedside table next to the telephone and sank into a chair. "How you doing?"

"I'm all right. It's good of you to come. I'm surprised you heard I was here."

"Serendipity," he said. "Did you see the article?"

"No."

"'Local Man Hospitalized for Exposure'. Two or three column-inches on page eight."

I felt mortified, but glad that few people I knew could have read about this lamentable misadventure. The majority of exposure victims in our city in any winter were homeless or drunk, and I prayed never to be either of those. I wondered how I had been characterized in the newspaper but I couldn't think of a graceful way to put the question. Had Bartley clipped the article and brought it with him I might have wanted to read it, but as things were I was satisfied to let it go.

"So what do you have to say for yourself?" Bartley asked me.

"What do you mean?"

"Well," he said, "you put yourself in harm's way to the extent of ending up in the hospital."

"I guess I misjudged the weather," I said.

"You'll think I'm silly," Bartley said, "but when I phoned Joanna to see if she knew what'd happened, I flashed on the case of her husband—Randall—wandering into trouble. Nobody's quite gotten over that."

"No," I said.

"In fact I think Joanna made the same connection. Until I got my story out she was sure I was going to tell her you'd been killed."

"Really? How odd."

"Yeah, she was really upset."

I had no idea what I should make of this revelation. If I had died in the park, I supposed, the same ambiguity that had surrounded the death of Randall would now surround mine. I remembered very well the nature of the upset when Joanna got the news of Randall's death. Bartley had played a role in that occasion as well; he had a propensity for dancing whole through the disasters of others. If I had died in the park, would Joanna have thought it an accident, as she seemed to believe Randall's death was an accident? If I had read about my own death, would I have shrunk before the possibility of suicide? The remaining option was foul play, but the only marks on Randall's body had been those of potential energy turned kinetic; there would have been no marks on my body at all, no evidence to support a theory of murder by hypothermia. I couldn't tell exactly what Bartley thought. It seemed possible that he was accusing me of something; in that case he would certainly have been wrong. Still, because he held himself out to be a great rationalist, it would have been interesting to hear his opinion of the relations among the three of us who had survived Randall. But I wouldn't ask. Bartley seemed to volunteer a partial answer anyway: "I worry that you're not giving yourself a fair shake," he said.

"What do you mean?"

"What were you doing out in the cold?"

"An activity called prayer walking." I could see by the look on Bartley's face that the words meant nothing to him. "It's a kind of unorganized evangelism," I said. "A form of ministry with no overhead costs. It just involves walking and praying."

"Does it have to be done in life-threatening circumstances?"

"Certainly not."

Bartley surveyed me with a level gaze for several seconds, not speaking. "You know," he said at last, "when I first met you, years ago, I found you very exotic."

"Exotic?"

"Yeah. Kind of a cabinet of strange intellectual artifacts, unfamiliar passions. Interesting like a woman, but without the pheromones." He paused. "You're giving me a look of offended puzzlement."

"Well," I said, "I am puzzled."

"But not offended?"

"I don't think so. I don't know. I can't be offended until I know what you're talking about."

"Well, okay," he said, "forget the woman thing. Let's just say I remember you packing a certain amount of charisma, and it seemed to be based in a big idea. Now I get the feeling that you've spent years whittling away at the idea, foreclosing its implications, narrowing your scope. It's kind of the difference between exotic and peculiar. If you were a woman you'd be frigid."

I think at this point in Bartley's disquisition I did take offense. His repeated allusions to women annoyed me and I found the vagueness of his language frustrating. If by "big idea" he meant my religious faith, it had grown not narrower but deeper. Yet Bartley sat before me smug, imperturbable and oblivious of the judgment awaiting the world, while my toes still stung from the damage they'd received on an evangelic mission that Bartley now sought to second-guess. It occurred to me then, wounded and confined, that God had sent this man to me in my captivity to be evangelized. Bartley had presented himself over many years as the plainest challenge to be grappled with, and I had shrunk again and again from meeting him. This time, thank God, he had me cornered, and I had no choice but to do the work. "Rob," I said, "if I speak, will you listen to me?"

"Of course."

There was a silence in the room that made me think first of the silence in Heaven that happens at Revelation 8:1, at the opening of the seventh seal, and then, because I didn't know where to begin, of the terrible seconds preceding the amazing moment years before in the church basement in front of Solveig, Bartley and a room full of war resisters, when I discovered the voice that for a time had made of me a preacher. I prayed to God for the wisdom of His presence and then I said, "Mr. Rob Bartley, a time of trial and judgment is at hand."

"Elucidate," he said. There was no hint of doubt or resistance in his tone; the word meant only that I had all of his attention, and I believed that his attention was all that I would need.

"Biblical prophecy and the logic of history and the tenor of the times we're living in all point to a culmination in the near future—ten or twenty years at most. It's not much time to repent for all we've done or failed to do up to now. I've always regarded you as a good man profoundly deserving of and in need of salvation. I hope you'll open your mind and heart to what God has asked me to say."

"I promised to listen," he said.

"Do you ever pray?" I asked him.

"Not since I was a kid."

"Why not?"

"I have a mechanistic view of the world. I don't contemplate the existence of anything that would respond to a prayer."

"But I do. Would you consider praying with me?"

"Of course I'd consider that, but I'd need specific instruction in how to do it."

"You don't remember from childhood?"

"I remember the forms. But I gather there's more to it than that."

"Yes. There's a lot more to it than that. But it can begin in form and ritual and grow deeper."

"Yeah," he said. "I think I'm aware of that. What else?"

"What do you mean by 'What else?'"

"I mean, what do you want to do besides pray with me?"

"I want to reason with you, show you what I've learned."

"That's right up my alley," Bartley said. "What else?"

"I want to share my faith with you and see you saved."

"That sounds like the hard part. Am I right?"

"For me it's the easy part," I said. "Living up to it is the hard part."

"What if I were to tell you what I know about living?" Bartley said. "Would you give me a hearing?"

I hesitated. I was fairly sure I already knew what Bartley knew about living, and to a man of faith it was pure atavism. I understood hunger, want and lust very well, but I wouldn't be guided or governed by them. I couldn't imagine what else Bartley might have to offer. "I would listen," I said.

"Good," he said, "because I worry as much about your life as you worry about my soul."

"You needn't," I said.

"We'll see," he said.

I exulted inwardly and thanked God for this beginning. He had sent Bartley to me at last as a willing interlocutor—the Bartley who had been the agent of my disappointment at every turn: the lover of Solveig when I had wanted her to be my ally, the seducer of Joanna while Joanna had been in my protection, an accessory in the death of Randall, a witness to the mocking of my lost vocation.

"They asked me at the reception desk if I was related to you," Bartley was saying.

"Really? Why?"

"I can't be sure, but I think they may be trying to figure out how to get paid."

"What? That's outrageous."

"Well, they didn't hold me up or anything. I take it your insurance coverage is deficient."

I may have winced. "It's non-existent," I said. "It went with my former employment. I'll be employed again and I'll pay them then."

"Soon enough for me," Bartley said. "I worry a lot less about their survival than I do about yours."

"I'm in good hands," I said, meaning God's. Evidently Bartley understood me, because he didn't object. Instead he sat before me like a mountain to be climbed. My own rebirth had happened virtually while I was unconscious, and I'd spent tens of thousands of hours since then in reflection, confirmation, study, dedication, recommitment. It would take Bartley years to know what I knew, and the process could begin only after lightning had struck to alter the confident landscape of his mind. I wished for God to send the lightning then and there, but I knew the task was mine—not to send the lightning, but to create the potential that would bring the lightning. My toes hurt. "What can I say to you to convey the truth of what I know?" I asked him.

"You have to connect the dots."

"All right," I said. "God created the universe out of the void and populated it with us, fashioned in His image, but finite, fallible and potentially disobedient. We disobeyed and were punished with what you would probably describe as the human condition. But we were offered a way back to grace when God sent his Son Jesus Christ, in human form, to sacrifice Himself on the cross. All we had to do was believe in Him. Some of us do and are saved. Many of us do not and are lost. But the offer stands, and while it does, any of us can come to Jesus. But time is running out."

"I got ahead of myself," Bartley said. "First you have to validate the dots. Let's start with God. What can you tell me about His nature, and what can you show me by way of evidence?"

"I can show you nothing that you're not prepared to see."

Bartley annoyed me by smiling. "Is it my turn yet to tell you what I know?"

"It's always your turn," I said, and I meant it.

"Okay," he said, "I've observed the following about living: it begins when you wake up and it ends when you fall asleep."

"What about dreams?"

"That's not living," he said. "Those are stories."

"Then you discount the life of the spirit?"

"Making certain assumptions about your terminology, and for the purposes of this discussion, yes. There is no life of the spirit. There's only life."

"A forlorn prospect," I said.

"Not really," he said. "Life's got it all: sex, drugs, rock and roll, love, comedy, pain, surprise, death. And the illusion of spirit, since you seem to value that. I love life. How about you?"

"I love God."

"Are you sure? How does He feel about you?"

My toes were hurting terribly and I felt oppressed by an awareness of something insuperable, as if, regardless of all sacrifice, sin would be forever in the ascendancy and dysphoria was the only condition I could expect for myself in this world. I longed for His coming. "God is a hard taskmaster," I said.

"But why?" Bartley asked.

"I don't know," I said.

Neither of us spoke immediately. I had lost track of what I wanted to say to Bartley, and Bartley's curiosity seemed satisfied for the moment. I felt as tired as I had ever been. I tried but was unable to reconstruct in my mind how I had gotten to this place, and the prospect of moving on from it seemed forbidding or impossible. I saw the ten or fifteen years that stretched ahead from that moment until the End Time as my last task, and one I could carry out only if my toes stopped hurting and Bartley went away and let me sleep. I remembered that God had sent Bartley to me to be evangelized; I would do that, but I would sleep first.

"I wish you'd give yourself a break," Bartley said at last.

"I will," I said. "I'll get some rest."

"And then another break tomorrow," Bartley said.

But I couldn't think about it just then.

CHAPTER TWENTY-EIGHT
ANNUNCIATION

I didn't give myself a break, but I did retreat into my own counsel for a while. The hospital released me—perhaps a little sooner than would have been the case if I'd been able to leave behind cash instead of only my signature–and I rode buses back to my apartment still dressed in my prayer walking gear, the map in my pocket but the Bible in my hands. The extremely cold weather had passed, but I didn't consider prayer walking again immediately. From the bus window I saw block after block waiting to be prayed over, public schools where anti-Scriptural versions of the world and its Creation were taught as undisputed fact, convenience stores where women, children and the chaste were exposed to open displays of magazine pornography, liquor stores profiting by the dependence of the weak and unregenerate on the illusory sustenance of alcohol, libraries where promiscuously secularized collections promoted the mongrelization of human understanding. But I made no attempt to pray over these as I passed: God had brought me up short in my initial effort; I needed to contemplate and pray to understand His will before proceeding. When I came into my apartment the television still flickered silently in one corner; I shut it off and left it off for several months. Bartley phoned once or twice in the first few days I was home to inquire after my health and to offer assistance, but I kept him at bay. Regularly I received in the mail billing statements from the hospital. I re-read Chapter 25 of Leviticus and took prospective comfort in God's injunction to His people to celebrate the Year of Jubilee with the forgiveness of debt. I might have gotten a job, but it was more important to me to devote whatever energy I had to preparing myself morally and spiritually for the coming time.

Through most of that year, 1978, I concentrated on reducing my already slight involvement with a world marching toward destruction. I began to winnow my personal property, of which I owned very little in any case. I kept the small television set, although I never watched it, because I expected to resume my vigil as the advent of the Beast grew nearer. I kept most of my books on religious subjects, but I took others from my shelves, including many that I'd acquired in college, and put them outside for the trash pickup. I cleaned out my desk drawers, retaining very little of what I found there. In the bottom of one I rediscovered the pornographic picture that had fascinated but not seduced me years earlier. I destroyed it immediately, as I had destroyed its mates the night I encountered them on the street. I burned old correspondence, including the two letters sent to me by that forlorn woman who had answered my ill-conceived personal ad. I picked old clothing from drawers and closets, boxed it and put it out. I had no clear idea of what I hoped to accomplish by ridding myself of these things, but I foresaw the possibility that in the maelstrom of the End Time I might be homeless and needing to travel light.

Eventually I lost interest in discarding things. I seemed by that point to own little enough, and none of what I owned any longer oppressed me. To conserve money I disconnected my telephone and used electricity sparingly, leaving all lights off at night, with the exception of the single lamp I might be reading by. My only extravagance was the television, which—once I turned it on again toward the end of that year—I never turned off, although I kept the sound muted except when I needed to identify some person whose face had appeared on the screen.

One afternoon in the week following Christmas, as I returned from an errand to buy groceries, I found a young woman standing in front of my building, bundled against the cold. By her size, shape and mode of dress I took her to be about twenty. As I arrived at the door, reaching into my pocket for the key, she met my eyes and I stopped. "Are you my father?" she asked. I looked closely into her face. I was startled, even frightened. I saw immediately her resemblance to Beth, my wife. "I'm Katie," she said, and burst into tears.

I hardly knew what to do or say. She had come back before I was ready to meet her. The work that I'd foreseen for myself when I left home was all undone; I was immobilized with frustration and embarrassment. I was certain that she was lovely, although her face was contorted with anguish, red with emotion and the cold, and streaked with tears. I hesitated to embrace and comfort her; I had no resources for that purpose. I stood there awkward and irresolute, the bag of groceries clamped precariously in the crook of my left arm. "Can I come in? I'm cold," she said.

"Of course," I said. "Of course."

I opened the outer door, which was unlocked anyway, and let her follow me inside. I used my key to open the vestibule inner door to the hallway and she walked through ahead of me, not speaking. I had been overtaken by the passage of time, run to ground, found out. Katie stopped directly in front of my apartment door; afterward it occurred to me that she had read the number earlier from the mailbox and call button. I unlocked that door for her too, and she went in. Except for Joanna, whom I had mistakenly invited once, Katie was the first guest I'd ever had. She looked around, drawing the back of a gloved hand across her eyes. "Is this where you live?" she said.

"This is it," I said.

She walked to the corner where the television was and looked at the picture playing silently on the screen—a mouthwash commercial. There was no explaining to her just then what I was up to: I hadn't gotten far enough with it yet to justify the cost. I set the bag of groceries down in the kitchen and put only the perishables into the refrigerator. "I'm glad you came to see me," I said, although I had nothing else to offer her.

"I didn't tell Holly I was going to do this."

"Your sister."

"She doesn't actually remember you," Katie said.

"Does your mother know you were coming?"

"No; nobody knows. I'm home from college for Christmas vacation. I borrowed the car."

I took off my coat and sat down. A hundred questions might have occurred to me, but I resisted

pursuing any of them. Katie had removed a knit cap
and scarf; I saw that she had brown hair of Beth's
shade, a little darker than I remembered it, and Beth's
brown eyes. She sat tentatively on the edge of a chair,
perhaps waiting for me to talk. I asked where she went
to college. She named a well-respected one, but without
any religious affiliation. "I'm a freshman," she said.
There was another silence, and then she said, "I never
knew why you left."

"Your mother didn't tell you?"

"Not exactly."

If nobody had told her why I left, it was up to me to
do so, but I was having trouble remembering the
particulars. I tried to organize in my mind an account
of my reasons that would be as true and complete as I
could make it without being hurtful to Katie, but
nothing came to me immediately. My only certainty
was that I had had no choice, and that leaving had not
been a mistake. "Did she say anything at all?"

"She thinks you had a girl friend."

"Oh, no, no—I didn't. That's not the reason." As I
write this down I see that my answer may have been
misleading. There had been Marie, after all; but I
didn't so much as think of Marie when I spoke; even
now I'm sure that Beth had not been referring to her
either. "Oh, no," I said, "I could not have left my family
for another woman. How sad that she could think so!"

"What, then?" Katie asked. She was still sitting on
the edge of the chair, still bundled in her coat.

"I had a religious calling," I said.

"You went to a monastery?"

"No! No, I stayed in the world."

Katie seemed pained and embarrassed; I was afraid she might start to cry again. I was embarrassed too; I think we both felt awkward in our roles: she asking personal questions of a stranger, I being interrogated by my own daughter. "I guess I don't understand," she said.

At that moment I didn't understand either. It should have been possible to have a religious vocation and a family at the same time; plenty of Protestant divines had done so. But I couldn't imagine waging the struggle I had waged through these years from within the bosom of a family. The idea seemed ruinous. If I had tried it, I'd surely have brought my family as low as I now perceived myself to be. I looked around my poor apartment and saw it with what might be Katie's eyes. She was dressed smartly enough and had found a car to use in her search. It was possible that her embarrassment grew in part from her recognition of our financial inequality. "It's hard to explain," I said.

"Didn't you tell Mommy?"

"I'm sure I did."

Katie gave a kind of helpless shrug and stared at the floor. When the silence grew awkward I broke it by asking how her mother was doing. "She's okay I guess," she said, and was quiet again.

"And Holly?"

"She's okay too. She's still in high school. She doesn't remember anything about you."

"I guess she wouldn't," I said.

She looked up. "I remember you being really tall, so it was hard to see your face, and Mommy crying a lot after you left."

"It was very sad," I said. "I thought I had important work that I couldn't do at home."

"Yeah," Katie said, "I don't get that."

"It's hard to explain." I realized I was repeating myself, but I had yet to conjure up a better answer.

"I used to think you left because of something I did, and then I used to pick on Holly because I was mad."

"Oh no," I said, "it had nothing to do with you."

"Maybe I'd feel better if it did." She stared at the floor again. I searched for some remark to reassure her, but confusion prevented me. She went on: "I came to see you because I could never understand why I didn't have a real father. I guess Holly thinks of Doug—that's our stepfather—as her real father. But I never could." I sat and listened, still unable to formulate a satisfactory account of myself. I hoped Katie would say something instructive or revelatory. I felt I should invite her to take off her heavy coat but I didn't want to interrupt. She stopped talking anyway; there was another awkward silence. After a minute she said, "Are you mad at me for coming?"

"No," I said. "I'm glad you came." But I was far from sure it was true. I was being forced by the pressure of her inquiry to stretch after knowledge that had eluded me for years. I had no secrets from her but I had no answers either. I should have been able to explain everything, but something had gotten away from me. As now and then happened when I tried to think constructively but was stymied, my interior voice re-formed my thoughts and repeated them like an incantation: "Something has gotten away from me." Unbidden there flashed in my mind an old image of Randall silent in his grave, his broken head stuffed with my mother's rags, and I heard the eerie echo of his voice speaking to me from the days before he disappeared into the wilderness: "Something has gotten away from you." Taken by surprise, I sat upright and stared across the small space separating me from Katie. She seemed tentative and distracted, as if our meeting were going badly and she was thinking of leaving. "I wish I could explain," I said. "I guess the deepest experiences are the hardest to share." And once again Katie began to cry.

I felt quite helpless, unable to explain anything, and without the least idea of how to comfort my child. It occurred to me suddenly that Katie's frustration with me must mirror my frustration with God. This was a novel idea: I hadn't thought until that moment that I was frustrated with God. I tried to appreciate how God might be looking at me then, and how He might have justified the years of His neglect. I could draw no conclusion. It seemed there was no comfort anywhere to give or to take. "God loves you," I said to Katie.

"Big deal," she said.

I was shocked. College or some other baneful influence had corrupted the simplicity she was born with. The same thing had happened to me at the same age, and I had had to wait a decade or more and survive a sinful and unhappy love affair, and an equally sinful brush with suicide, to be born again. But un-preoccupied with God as I may have been at my worst, I don't believe I was ever so dismissive. "Oh, Katie," I said. "You'll come to see it's the biggest deal there is."

"I guess," she said.

I perceived a fine irony in the fact that I'd left my family in order to know God better and eventually to lead others to Him, but that I couldn't with certainty name a single person I'd led to God, while my own daughter, deprived of my example, had gone astray. For whatever reason, it felt too late to correct this mistake—if mistake it was. God had thus far hidden His face from me and didn't seem close to revealing it. I was deep in study of the End Time, alert for the first public signs of the Beast, and convinced that God wanted something more of me than to be His witness. If He were to show me His face and order me to minister, I would do it immediately and well. Whatever His purpose, He had but to reveal it and I'd have carried it out, no matter its nature or the attendant difficulty. But until I knew what He wanted I couldn't interrupt my study for an invidious struggle with Katie over her moral instruction. Without a clear sign of His will I'd have to content myself with praying for her and trusting God to send some other of His servants to her rescue.

Under the circumstances I couldn't understand why God had seen fit to let Katie confront me in this way. The more I tried to fathom His purposes, the more I seemed to be trammeled with distractions. If my search had gone as I had hoped, I might have been able—in triumph!—to reclaim my family years before, secure in my vocation as I was sure in my Faith. Katie and Holly might have been the daughters of a preacher, and religious missionaries in their own right, and Beth the reconciled wife of a man established in the church. Katie still sat opposite me, still in her coat, her face still streaked with tears. I wanted to warn her of the coming judgment—not because she was my daughter, but because the coming judgment was the most urgent business of my mind. Yet I dreaded to warn her—or anyone else—until God had shown me clearly how He expected me to proceed. I wished Katie could go away until I was ready to speak.

She snuffled, breaking a long silence. "I feel awful," she said. "This isn't working the way I hoped."

"I wish I could help more," I said.

"Don't you care that I'm your daughter?" she asked in a subdued voice.

"Of course I do," I said. "I feel a great responsibility that I don't know how to discharge."

"Did you ever wonder what I was doing?"

"I guess I must have," I said. "I've given thought and study to everything over the years."

"Would you have come looking for Holly and me? If I hadn't come looking for you?"

"Yes. As soon as..." But I was stopped by my continuing inability to explain. The image of Randall dead made its way into my brain again, as if it were business that had to be finished before I could concentrate on whatever Katie and I were trying to talk about. My frustration was nearly complete. It seemed to me that I had never, in my entire life, succeeded in a task in such a way that I could call it both good and finished, and leave it behind. Instead, new tasks presented themselves, to supersede or interfere with old tasks. The television sat silent and flickering in the corner, ready sooner or later to offer up the first image of the Beast. But I was scarcely prepared, because now Katie was in the way, demanding an account of my life that would justify an abandonment undertaken for the best of reasons, however failed. Nor had I ever said goodbye to anyone: not to Randall, not to Solveig, not to Marie, not even to the poor woman who'd answered my personal ad years before and whose name I no longer remembered. As a consequence, none of the work of those people was finished either: I had to bear them in my mind like St. Christopher shouldering the Lord. I looked helplessly at Katie sitting opposite, a picture of isolation and dejection that must have mirrored my own, and considered that I was here presented with an opportunity for closure that—characteristically—I would not be able to take. I might have said goodbye to her then and there, except that I clung to the hope that God would show me His purpose in time to gather my family back into His bosom and mine, where they could enjoy the benefit of my hard-won knowledge, and we could be together at the Rapture. "There's so much left to do before I can help," I said.

She looked ineffably sad and apologetic, her eyes downcast, as if I had chastened her for some misfeasance that she alone could name. "Before I came," she said, "I had this fantasy that everything would work out and I'd tell Holly I'd seen you, and she'd want to see you too. Now I guess not."

"Maybe it's not time yet," I offered.

"Then when? I was afraid you wouldn't remember me." This sounded like a non sequitur; I could only let it pass.

"Don't you want to take off your coat?"

"I'd better get back," she said, and stood up. I stood up too, wishing I could think of something to say to comfort her. It can have done her no good at that moment, but I felt reassured in the knowledge that I'd pray about her as soon as she left. "I'll write my phone number at school," she said, and penciled it on a scrap of paper she found in a pocket. She handed me the scrap; I put it on my desk.

I walked her from the apartment back to the vestibule. Standing with her head uncovered she reminded me again of Beth, as her mother had looked when I met her more than twenty years before. Outside, the winter sun was poking long shadows down the street. Katie wrapped the scarf around her neck, fitted the knit cap over her hair and said goodbye.

"You're very pretty," I said.

"Holly's really pretty," she said, and opened the exterior door. Cold air fell in on us in a mass. "Happy New Year," Katie said. She smiled a little wanly, I thought, and went out.

CHAPTER TWENTY-NINE
FELLOWSHIP

The night after Katie's visit I had a dream, lugubrious in its content but elegiac in its mood, that Katie and Holly had found Randall's body on the Midwestern railroad track under the viaduct where he had fallen to his death. In the dream Randall was naked but sexless, and Katie tried to piece his broken head together and hold it intact by clamping it between her hands. She was of college age and looked as she had during her visit; Holly may have looked like Joanna. If I was in the dream I had no acting part, yet in the capacity of observer I tried to will events to reveal what had happened to cause Randall's death. But it was never explained: he was simply dead.

In the first weeks of 1979 I redoubled my efforts to pick up the thread of the End Time. Initially I prayed over Katie and the question of her evident unhappiness, because I sensed that she was now part of the puzzle. But as the weeks passed, the image of Katie dejected and weeping in my apartment moved to the periphery of my mind. I found the scrap of paper with her college telephone number in the clutter on my desk and copied it into a memo book. I spent part of every day watching the TV screen for a hint of how the Great Tribulation was to come about, and much more of it in prayer and Bible reading. I reviewed the notes I'd made in calculating the End Time chronology, and I felt sure my projection was pretty close to right.

Had it been humanly possible to speed up the playing out of prophecy, I'd have done everything in my power to that end. I longed for the coming of the millennium of peace, regardless of the horrors that must precede it. As I reviewed my notes I looked for any sign that I might have been too conservative in my estimates, but I was careful not to let my desire for the early fulfillment of Revelation lead me into self-delusion. I had calculated 1993 as the latest date for the Beast's *coup d'état*; certainly there was a chance that it would come sooner—perhaps a lot sooner. I prayed for such an eventuality, if it might be God's will; but I reckoned on the possibility that fourteen more years might have to pass before the crisis that would put me once and for all into the role of guerrilla. By that time I would be nearly sixty years old and not so able-bodied; but unless I were too lame by then to leave my apartment, nothing would discourage my sacrifice with other Christian soldiers on the barricades.

In my surveillance of the TV screen, too, I was conscious of the risk that in my zeal for the coming of the End Time I might think I saw the Beast or the False Prophet where neither was. The Ayatollah Khomeini, the Iranian cleric I'd noticed a year earlier when he was an exile in Paris, had by this time gone back to Teheran, driven the Shah into exile in his turn, and established a Moslem state. His trajectory made him a candidate: in a short time he had risen from obscurity and displaced a de facto ally of the Christian nations of the West, and now he was declaring a kind of moral war on my country and her culture. I had sympathy for the Ayatollah's critique of the crass Godlessness that seemed to inform much of our national life, but it was easy to imagine this superficial appeal shrouding a whole body of False Prophecy. Thenceforth I made it a point to watch and listen carefully to Khomeini.

Once or twice that summer I returned to the corner of the city where I had prayer walked disastrously a year and a half before, and waited for some sign that I should recommence that mission. My vocation to preach had been so clear and emphatic when it came to me in wartime that I was sure a call to prayer walk would be similarly unmistakable. But I heard no vocation. I prayed in that part of town nevertheless, but without any sense that I was moving souls.

I had to entertain the idea, however uncongenial the prospect of social interaction had become to me in recent years, that it might be necessary to seek God's purpose for me through Christian fellowship. Months of solitary prayer and meditation had not shown me clearly what was expected. At the thought of going into company I resorted once again to the mirror, to vet my person. Earlier in life I had assigned some importance to my appearance, if only as a variable in the calculus of my usefulness to God, but I no longer took my body seriously. I judged that I was presentable enough. Clothed, I was inoffensive and unremarkable, although there was a look of severity about my eyes that probably arose from unrelieved seasons of excogitation and self-criticism. My hairline had retreated some more and my skin was pale, but I supposed I could still go abroad in the world without exciting undue fear or pity.

I began my reintroduction to Christian society by returning to the last church I'd visited, two years earlier, before I retreated to pray at the altar in my own apartment and to parse the chronology of the End Time. The month was August, when many churchgoers are away from home on vacation, but I was shocked at the meager attendance. Had I wanted to avoid human contact, it would not have been necessary to sit in a back pew; I could have sat almost anywhere. There was a perceptibly greater density of congregants toward the front though, and these were biased to the side of the hall where the pulpit stood. I took my seat in an empty pew immediately behind the greatest density of congregation, so that I could add to it without being drawn unwillingly or prematurely into a social connection. As far as I could tell, the preacher was not the same one who had so signally failed last time to convey the urgency of Salvation—or of any of the rest of the existential enterprise—to this flock. This preacher was younger, perhaps standing in for the regular one, as I used to do. Even the choir must have disbanded for the summer: the only guidance for our singing of the hymns came from a young woman with a thin, tremulous soprano voice and an acoustic guitar. The fragility of this connection made me think of the Apostle Paul in his tours of the Christian communities of Asia Minor, keeping the flame in a hostile world and exhorting the faithful to be ready for Jesus' imminent return. Yet it had not been God's intention that Jesus should return in those days; Paul's exhortations were for all times, and most particularly—as I knew quite well—for ours. The church had been destined after the time of Paul to burst forth from her cradle in the Mediterranean to transform the whole world, and now that the transformation was as complete as it would ever be without God's direct intervention in the human polity, it was time for Jesus to come again.

I surveyed the congregation, thin on the ground, and thought how insubstantial His reception would be if the attendance on this Sunday morning were typical of Christian churches everywhere. But I reflected that in the whole world only 144,000 were to be sealed against the plagues of the Wrath of God, and it occurred to me that the numbers taken in the Rapture might be much smaller than I had previously imagined. In fact, I realized that in my life I had met only a handful of people whom I could regard as likely candidates. The great mass of men and women were evidently lost.

I sat through the service without much hope that I was in human company whence the revelation I so hungered for might be forthcoming. The preacher mentioned, and so did the notes at the bottom of the Order of Worship, that a prayer brunch for men of the congregation was held in the church basement every Saturday at eleven a.m. In spite of my discouragement I promised God that I'd look into this, since He had contrived to bring it to my attention, and in the short reception line at the door after the service I introduced myself to the preacher and declared my intention to be at the next brunch. The preacher seemed delighted. He gripped my hand and held me with a level, blue-eyed gaze that reminded me of my own look when I had been a preacher. I thought he could be a friend.

Whatever sectarian predilections I may have entertained early in my religious career, I was no longer bound by such narrow definitions. I cared far less whether my interlocutor professed the Heidelberg Catechism than that he adhered relentlessly to the darkling God with whom Jesus Christ had promised I should be reconciled. The congregation I now thought of attaching myself to called itself simply the Church of God—a name that seemed to comprehend my needs. If in the crisis of the End Time it would be necessary for Christians to travel light, then the acoustic guitar could be a liturgical instrument as good as any, and a piping tremolo could be the voice of prophecy fulfilled.

The first prayer brunch reminded me once again of the precarious condition of the early church. We met underground, though not in secret, and we were a mere handful. The kitchen facilities at our disposal had been designed to cater for potluck suppers of one hundred guests or more, overseen by the church ladies, so they ran heavily to steam tables and chilling trays. But there was a gas stove and a large refrigerator stocked with the necessities for a masculine breakfast, and since there were only half a dozen of us participating, one of our number could easily cook for all. In fact the cooking was done by the preacher, named Reverend Larry, who demonstrated a considerable flair for it, chopping and dicing ingredients with impressive grace and speed, and tossing omelets that seemed to fold themselves neatly in the air above the frying pan.

When we had all been served, Reverend Larry led us in giving thanks, then suggested that we eat quietly and meditatively, in order to be ready when we'd finished to share our thoughts in the form of prayer. I looked around the table from face to placid face. We numbered only half as many apostles as had been present at the Last Supper of Our Lord, but whatever crisis awaited us was likely to be less immediate. We appeared to range in age from about thirty years to about sixty, and four wore wedding rings. So far I knew nothing of the inner life of any of these men, but I found myself drawing inferences about their character from their looks. I thought it might be a useful exercise to make predictions about one or two of them that could be either falsified or confirmed later, when they revealed themselves. But I hesitated to sit in any kind of judgment, generous or invidious, for two reasons: first, because judgment is the province of God alone; and second, in my life I had already misunderstood so much.

Nevertheless, we had been asked to meditate. Meditation in solitude had been my occupation for years. In the company of strangers, though, curiosity prevented me from turning inward. Instead I surveyed my tablemates, and inevitably I had thoughts about them.

For example, although he was darker and a little shorter than I, and had a square face and rather thick lips that in repose turned downward in a pout, because

Reverend Larry was a young preacher I readily projected my own personality onto him. Later I learned I was wrong.

The man whose face I most liked was also the oldest: John, about sixty. He was ruddy, blue-eyed and nearly bald; what hair he had was white; there were lines around his mouth and at the corners of his eyes that suggested a lifetime of smiling. But that judgment proved not quite right either.

Next oldest was a large-headed, jug-eared man in his mid-fifties—also named John, as it turned out— with thin, brown hair combed aft and laterally across a bald scalp. He had nothing of the physiognomy traditionally associated with strong character: his chin was ablated, his forehead receding, his eyes small and dun-colored, his nose knobbed at the tip. Everything about his appearance bespoke an essential stolidity. But once more I was deceived.

Anyone observing our group would have identified me correctly as the next oldest, and might from my appearance have misread the nature and depth of my preoccupation: I don't know. If anyone cared, the prayers I had to offer would speak for me.

Younger than I by about five years was Wilfred, a short, wiry man with reddish-brown hair, bright, black, wide-set eyes, broad nose and a large mouth. He looked like a ventriloquist's dummy; he even had some of the nervous animation with which ventriloquists invest their dummies to misdirect attention from the real source of the voice. But I didn't doubt that Wilfred's voice, when I came to hear it, would be his own.

The last man, in his late thirties and younger than any of us except for Reverend Larry, was Rudy, a sandy-haired, blue-eyed mesomorph, remarkable only for the height of his forehead, which consigned his ears and the area of the face containing his other features to well less than half of the available territory. The arrangement hinted at a very large brain, but evidence from his later conversation failed to bear out the hint.

It could be said aptly that we all ruminated. Reverend Larry's cuisine was quite good, and much less plain in the realization than the ingredients that made it up. With the omelets we had both bacon and sausage on the side, with orange or vegetable juice to start, and coffee and Danish pastry to sustain us when it came time to pray.

I supposed I was the only stranger in the group, but each of us identified himself anyway, by first name, before Reverend Larry invited us to offer prayer or testimony. I remembered the parting shot of my career as a preacher, when years before I had urged a congregation to spill into the streets and search for God, and nobody moved. I had spent the time since then looking everywhere, and the search had now brought me back indoors—albeit on a Saturday and in a basement, and to consult members of the laity. I was torn between the hope that one of these men had seen God and could talk about it, and the fear that in the event I wouldn't understand what was being said. In such a case it would require superhuman discipline not to be envious, and envy could only retard my progress more. Something about the low ceiling and the

company of people whom I incompletely understood—
something about it oppressed me. I was more conscious
than ever of the tightening race between my aspiration
and the coming of the last days.

Wilfred was the first to testify—in a high, twanging
voice that reinforced the impression he gave of being
part of a showman's kit. He delivered a preamble in
general language about the currency of ungodly
practices, and then he asked us to pray with him. I
closed my eyes, lowered my forehead onto my folded
hands and supported the weight of my head on my
elbows. Wilfred prayed for the souls of the unborn
victims of legally sanctioned abortion, and he prayed
that a new government of the righteous would end
forever this holocaust of the innocent. He went on
longer than I might have expected, painting vivid word
pictures of deceived young women, slaughtered infants
and greedy physicians with blood on their hands. My
brunch-mates and I prayed with him, but I couldn't
help thinking that it was late in the day to worry about
the foreclosing of lives that would barely have passed
their adolescence by the time Jesus returned and the
game was up anyway. It was true that a fraction of
these lives, if not aborted, might have survived the
gantlet of the Wrath or, if baptized and dutiful in
childhood, been raptured with their Christian parents
to wait in Heaven for Jesus to take His place on the
Throne of Peace in Jerusalem, there to reign a
thousand years. Somehow these stakes seemed small
beside the prodigious Truth of what was to befall those
of us already born and grown up before God, whether in

fear, in ignorance or in despite. I wondered if Wilfred had considered his priorities.

For me the prayer brunch was off to a disappointing start. If I had ever been much concerned with the political ramifications of my faith, I no longer was. God had invaded the hearts of men and (I supposed) women in times and places of such political strangeness and diversity that it seemed impossible that He could care very much about the particulars of secular governance. He had seen fit to let corrupt princes thrive indefinitely, while saints like the one I wished to be kept their Godly counsel in obscurity. My mind wandered from the secular message of Wilfred's petition. I worried that in the end none of the group would command words capable of revealing so much as a glimpse of the personal God abiding in the undiscovered heart.

The older of the two Johns was next to offer a prayer. A kind of merriment seemed to reside permanently in his face, as if he had never been unhappy, and anything he might say would be edifying without being cautionary. A smile danced around his mouth and in his blue eyes, but when he prayed it was to thank God that he was a delivered alcoholic. Evidently this had been his theme in other weeks, because he wove into the prayer new biographical material about trials and temptations befalling him in the previous seven days. I was satisfied that John's God was personal and not political, but I felt an unrighteous twinge of envy that the God I'd been pursuing so assiduously and unsatisfactorily for so long

IMPERISHABLE BLISS

was working closely with this other man. I considered the possibility that I had not yet fallen low enough to deserve His specialized attention. God had saved me once from suicide without ever showing me His face, but He had not let me forget my quest. As long as He continued to make demands on me I could continue to hope.

With the amens and the lifting of heads at the end of John's prayer, my eyes involuntarily caught those of Reverend Larry. He nodded as if I had asked him something. I had not, but I realized, although I hadn't prepared and there seemed to be no prescribed order, that it was my turn. I looked around the circle, met all of the eyes there and lowered my head. Prayer, since the day I adopted it after my spiritual rebirth, had always come to me easily, and although it had been more than a decade since I'd last led more than one other person, I felt no stage fright and no diffidence. I closed my eyes and began to speak. "Dear God," I said, "I thank You for the company of these new Christian friends. I pray that through their faith and experience You will show me how I can know You better and be given the gift of seeing Your face. I have been Your loving servant for many years but I have not been deserving in Your eyes. I have been both Your shepherd and Your sheep, Your witness and Your acolyte. I have tried to follow the example of Your Son Jesus Christ, but I have misstepped and misunderstood. I have sought You in the marketplace and in the privacy of my heart. I have forsworn wealth and recognition in order to know Your purposes better.

I have studied Your word and I know that Your Son is coming soon and that the days of this recreant world are numbered. I pray for Your grace to shine on me and Your will to be my will, so that in the End Time I may be Your soldier and know Your face when it commands me. I pray for the understanding and support through their faith in You of my new friends assembled here. I pray for all this in the name of Jesus Christ. Amen."

I kept my eyes closed, thinking that something might now happen. There was a beat and the other voices at the table said, "Amen." Silence followed. I waited, retreating into wordless, interior prayer, straining to reach beyond what I'd been able to articulate. I felt that I had marshaled more forces to my cause than in a very long time, and I hated to release them. I closed my eyes tighter and lowered my head onto my hands, which I held clasped on the tabletop. I willed a Face to appear in the darkness behind my eyes, but nothing came. I felt time running out.

CHAPTER THIRTY
PASSION

I think I knew by the end of that first prayer brunch that the fellowship of this company would not yield the breakthrough I so craved. The God invoked by each of them was as hidden from me as my own, and less identifiable as the font of love and protection that I hungered for. Either they had misunderstood God, or I had, or God's will was far less prescriptive than I wanted it to be. None of my brunch partners was as spiritually latitudinarian as the promiscuous Bartley, for example, but as a group they displayed a hermeneutic range that argued a disquieting lack of rigor in the nature of things. They all professed to be Christians but their testimony gave an inconsistent picture of who the Christian God must be. Some wanted Him to mediate the behavior of their neighbors as if He were a local constable; another wanted to be blamed for everything and the neighbors given a pass. The second of the two Johns, whose beige anonymity and lumpish features led me to expect less, gave us glimpses of a theology of considerable depth and subtlety, in which justification by faith trumped justification by works, good works pleased God more than good intentions, and a charitable heart outweighed the narrow claims of faith. It made me think of the game called "rock, scissors, paper", in which the two players try to anticipate each other in invoking one of those implements for its ascendancy over another; but no choice is safe, because for each implement there is one superior antagonist. Reverend Larry seemed to underwrite at least part of John's construction when he thanked God for sending His Son to earth in human form as a reminder of the pity of our condition and the need for us to tolerate the fallibility of others. Rudy, the man with the large forehead and small face, prayed for the safety of the United States of America.

In spite of my failure to break through I kept attending the prayer brunches. The fellowship, whether theologically coherent or not, at least provided me with sympathetic company, and it gave me the opportunity I hadn't had since my brief career as a preacher to challenge nominal Christians with my ideas. In much the same manner as I'd prepared my Sunday sermons in the seminary years, I composed the prayers I meant to offer each Saturday at brunch. The sermons had run twenty or twenty-five minutes and I'd rehearsed them well enough that I probably could have delivered them without a copy of the text at the pulpit; but to be effective at brunch, if not before God, the prayers had to be much shorter and so well-crafted that they would come to me *verbatim*. I faceted them like crystal. They were prose poems, never more than a minute or two to recite, tiny exhortations on a single theme. Others' prayers ran longer, but I think we remembered them only while they were being said. My prayers were meant to resonate. It was my hope each week that my prayer would resonate loudly enough to interrupt the proceedings.

In fact it happened more than once that a long silence would follow my prayer, and Reverend Larry or one of the more imaginative members of the group would begin to expatiate on what I had said. If the subject were the End Time, another of the fellowship, when his turn came, might pray more fervently than usual for his own salvation. Thinking I heard specific echoes of my prayers in the prayers of others, I waited for a sign that God was preparing for me a new vocation.

I attended Saturday prayer brunches and Sunday services at the Church of God regularly through the fall. After Labor Day the size of the congregation underwent a small seasonal increase, but no more than half of the pews were ever full. By choice I maintained a certain aloofness even from the members of my prayer group. I half-expected Reverend Larry to invite me to assist him as a lay preacher, even though I'd never actually apprised him of my history, but he never did. I felt relieved. I didn't think God would call me a second time to preach, although He might call me to recite prayers truly capable of moving the souls that heard them.

Christmas came again and went. As always, I treated it as a religious occasion, not a social one. I attended services and met with the prayer group, but I didn't arrange to be invited to Christmas parties. My notion of what was trivial had grown broader and deeper with the passage of time. Christmas parties had always been trivial, and the birth of Jesus had always seemed to me much less a prodigy than did His passion. Now, with His second coming no more than a decade and a half away, even the Easter season began to feel like a diversion, if it were to be observed without a powerful sense of the imminence of the Last Days.

I began 1980 dissatisfied and with a growing feeling of agitation. My prayers had excited enough admiration within the group that Reverend Larry proposed having them privately printed in Xerox and made available to the general congregation; but I hesitated, seeing that they had not wrought the revolution in understanding that I'd wished for. If I could recite them with full urgency among receptive men and see them admired but not reckoned with, I had little hope that they could command the hearts of people left to read by themselves. In Iran, where the Ayatollah Khomeini, my early candidate to be revealed as the Beast, had consolidated his Islamic revolution, young men acting in his name had invaded the American embassy and taken hostages whom they continued to hold more than two months later. I believed I shared the frustration of Jimmy Carter, my President and coreligionist, with the temporary intractability of the world in the face of his and my Godly intentions.

That was a cold, gray, long and unfriendly winter. I thought again, as I frequently did at that season, of the odd circumstance of living in a part of the world where the two major Christian feast days bracketed the most malign passage of the year. By the calendar, Jesus' life from His birth almost until His death on the cross was one cheerless epoch of physical discomfort and weak, slanting, inadequate light. It seemed to me as I grew older that it was harder each year to bear that dark season. In the midst of it I found myself arrested in the task of justifying my own life. I harbored the notion that if I could wait, my strength and purpose would be renewed with the coming of bright sun and warm weather, and then I would catch up. My best days, those of my greatest strength, had been the first warm ones of 1968, after I'd learned to preach and before Randall had walked westward. I could hope for another such dispensation, but only with the coming of warm weather, much as a man exhausted at the end of a day can hope to be restored by sleep and another dawn.

Easter 1980 fell on April 6. On Monday of Passion Week I was surprised to find in my mailbox a personal letter. I turned it over several times without opening the envelope. I thought I recognized the handwriting as that of my ex-wife, Beth. I carried the letter back into my apartment and sat with it at my kitchen table, certain that its contents would be unwelcome. After a few minutes I unsealed the envelope and read this:

Friday Mar 28 p.m.

I am writing to tell you that Katie died about one week ago. I am so sorry. She had told me she saw you sometime in the past couple of years, so maybe you were in touch with her.

Everyone is very upset as you can imagine. I can't stop crying and Holly is so angry that it almost makes me afraid. My husband blames himself, saying he knew Katie was depressed, and faulting himself for not insisting that we bring her home. This has been the worst week of our lives.

I don't know whether you want to come to the memorial service, which is on the Saturday between Good Friday and Easter. If you do, it will be at the address on the card.

I'm sorry to give you this terrible news.

Sincerely,

Beth

I laid my head on my arms and simply wept, knowing there would be time to pray for Katie's soul. As slight as was the information contained in Beth's note, I knew what had happened, if not why. Some disappointment had overtaken Katie, and God had seen fit to let her succeed in killing herself, where He had seen fit to save me for a purpose He had yet to reveal. As I wept I thought about love, intention and jealousy, and how by careful study of real suicides I might infer the role that longing played in God's relation to the world. I was all exigency, hungry to understand, for the first time sorry that I had survived to be so confused. I wanted to know why God had received Katie but kept me at bay.

I prayed, asking God to forgive Katie and to take her unto Himself. He felt closer than in many months, as if this emergency were forcing Him to give attention to my plight. I pleaded with Him to show me where I must go and what I must do, lest more things should be lost that I might yet have saved. I prayed for guidance in deciding whether to go to Katie's memorial service, and I prayed for time, but not too much. I felt I had His attention in a way that was unfamiliar and I was eager to take advantage of this boon. Yet I seemed to be of two minds about everything; or perhaps God was arguing with me. I was sure, for example, that I must go to Katie's service, but something told me that I shouldn't be seen there, that my presence would be unwelcome. I wanted the End Time to commence and Jesus to return, but I was no longer sure I wanted to live to see it happen. I felt myself bound with bronze fetters and grappling with God, like Samson blind at the mill in Gaza. Yet I felt energized, glad to be fighting, exultant that I might live to see Him, intoxicated with the idea that I might be killed in the attempt.

I spent the rest of that day talking to God. Some of the time I spoke aloud, challenging. Some of the time I read Scripture, either aloud or silently, skipping about through the text, letting God decide where the Book should fall open. Everything I read was familiar, and all of it meant that God had engaged me in debate. This was the week when Jesus had entered Jerusalem to be crucified and I was there with Him, prepared for sacrifice, Christ the Tiger, Christ the Lamb. I forgot meals. Late in the evening I made a sandwich and ate it at the kitchen table, still reading. Afterward I washed and got ready for bed, certain that I was on my way to seeing God at last. I stood down from the debate and prayed as simply as I could: the Lord's Prayer.

I dreamed that Katie, Randall and I had met at night on a long, down-sloping meadow. The sky was black and so brilliant with stars that the grass glistened under our feet. We held hands and walked downward, Randall on my left and Katie on my right. I looked from one to the other but they kept their faces forward. The stars shone clear to the horizon; overhead they spangled the sky in iterations of greater and greater depth, like a schematic illustration of infinity. I peered upward and saw that there was no end of stars, but no chance of touching them either. We hiked lower. In the crystalline darkness I could see Bartley's sports car parked on the grass. I looked inside: it was Bartley's sports car fettled for war, with harnesses draped over the seat-backs and white helmets resting on the bolsters, but Solveig wasn't there. Holly, though, sat nearby in the grass, small and blonde as I remembered her, turning the pages of a picture book. I realized I was dreaming; I tried to stay asleep; I tried also to keep Randall and Katie from leaving me. But there was no more room in Bartley's car. I snapped awake abandoned, my heart leaping in my chest, the will to fight that had sustained me gone utterly. I kept my eyes clenched shut, afraid, if I opened them in the semi-darkness of my room, of what I might see.

I lay awake the rest of the night, unwilling to open my eyes to look at the clock, despondent that He had retired from the field. I was alone definitively, with nothing but duty to my Faith to keep me on earth. I might or might not live to see the Millennium; God might spring forth sooner and without warning to reveal Himself to me, to explain why He had taken Randall when He did, to show me how I might be forgiven for my negligence, to tell me what I must do. I understood that I could not avoid Katie's memorial service, nor the task of watching for the manifestation of the Beast, even if I should prove to be the last Christian on earth to recognize it. I could only strive to do the right thing; God expected no more; to presume to know His will entirely was the sin of pride.

The memorial service for Katie was a forty-mile bus ride from where I lived. I dressed in the soberer of my two old suits and set out early, unsure of distances and connections. Spring had come again; it was the weekend of Jesus' death and resurrection; the weather on Saturday was generous and mild, much more Easter Sunday than Passion Friday. I was forgoing the weekly prayer brunch without having mentioned my absence to Reverend Larry: God at least knew where I was, and why; that was enough.

I arrived well before the time of the service, went inside and sat in a corner at the back. We were in the chapel of a Unitarian church; this was perhaps the denomination of Katie's stepfather, Doug. There were flowers on the altar but no casket. I realized I had no knowledge of Katie's whereabouts or of how she had succumbed, except that she was certainly a suicide.

While I waited, people I had never seen before entered and sat, some whispering, most silent. Many of them were young—perhaps college and former high school friends of Katie. Five minutes before the appointed time, Beth, Holly and Doug came in and sat at the front, facing the altar. I recognized Beth; except that her face seemed a bit softer, she looked much the same as when I had left her fourteen years before. I deduced the identities of Holly and Doug by her company. Holly was blonde and graceful, and as beautiful as Katie had said. Her coloring was the same as mine at the same age. I had no strong impression of Doug. The three of them sat, Beth in the middle, and held hands.

Promptly on the hour, the minister entered through a door on the right, not in robes but in a dark suit, mounted a raised lectern facing the assembly and began to talk about my daughter. He seemed to have known her fairly well; he told stories that I could believe were true of the young woman who had come to visit me. I listened carefully, hoping to learn from the minister's experience. I gathered that he'd known Katie as a Sunday school pupil and later as a church congregant. He had been responsible in part for her spiritual development. All at once I wondered if the minister had ever seen God. For two reasons, I doubted that he had. First, the minister was a Unitarian—no doubt a Godly man, but of a denomination much preoccupied with the secular; and second, a man who had seen God could have conveyed the majesty of his experience to a young girl and she would never have died by her own hand. It had been a dream of mine to see God and be instructed by Him to reclaim my family; how terrible to think it even possible that another man could have experienced my epiphany, lived to guide my daughter's growing up, and then have seen her sink into despair and kill herself. I was sure the minister had not seen God, and that he was better equipped than I to withstand the disappointment. If he had not been, far from seeking to console us at this moment, the minister himself would have been inconsolable.

I considered getting up then and leaving, because I thought I knew how the rest of the service would go, and that nothing about it could either give me comfort or appear to justify my neglectfulness, unavoidable as it may have been, irremediable as it now was. I felt myself a stranger among these people and before what I imagined was their Unitarianism. If they could know what was in my heart, the chances were they wouldn't understand. If they could know my history as Beth did, the chances were they'd have no sympathy. Nevertheless I stayed where I was, believing I was inconspicuous, and reluctant to begin the forty-mile trip back home with so little accomplished.

The minister stepped away from the podium and sat on a folding chair nearby. There was a stir in the front seats; Holly rose quietly and went to the lectern, a folded sheet of paper in her hand. She spread the sheet before her. "This was my sister's favorite poem," she said. Holly's face was beautiful but melancholy, framed in hair blonder than mine, and with eyes whose blueness was striking even at that distance. Her smile must have dazzled. She looked once over her audience; I thought her gaze fixed on me for a moment; I looked down. "'Thanatopsis'," she said, and began to read.

She read well, in a clear, steady voice, intelligently inflected, without flourish or superfluous drama. It was a touching performance; some in the congregation were moved to tears by the language of the young Bryant. I recalled the first time I had preached and moved people to tears—and with my own words, not with those of a poet. I was glad Holly was only reading: I could not have borne any sign that Holly had a vocation—not before my own case was settled. I kept my eyes lowered while she read, afraid to meet her gaze a second time. When she finished I raised my head and watched her go back to sit beside her mother, whom she appeared to kiss on the cheek. A moment later Beth's head turned in my direction. I looked down. I had been discovered.

The voice of the minister resumed, this time on the subject of organ donation and the other-directed generosity of a stricken family. Later I came to wonder about the method and the sequence of events in Katie's death, and which and how many of her bodily components had been "harvested", in the chilling parlance of that soteriologically dubious enterprise; but at this moment I had to consider whether I ought to withdraw. I felt culpable, embarrassed, unwelcome and unprepared to face strangers. I rose as quietly as I could and slipped away.

CHAPTER THIRTY-ONE
EPIPHANY

I said at the outset that I'd offer no apology for the strength of the faith that has brought me this far. When I retreated from Katie's funeral I believed that the purity of my purpose was being tested again: I was being shown what I'd forfeited in the name of my quest. I might have stayed to explain myself to Beth, and to let Holly see where she had come from, but even at that late hour I hadn't gathered the experience I'd need to justify so much loss.

I went away feeling that the body of my work to that point had turned to ashes. Although the agency of prayer is invisible, and thus it is possible that in my diligence I have guided the souls of multitudes, to the best of my own poor knowledge I had brought no one but myself to God, and incompletely. I was glad of the well-made prayers I'd contributed to the Saturday brunches, but now they were old and had perhaps changed nothing; I no longer cared to refuse Reverend Larry if he wanted to publish them. Once more, as when I had fallen with Joanna, I felt all progress lost and no option for me but to start over.

I went to God then in prayer and acknowledged the sins of omission that had caused me to despair, and I acknowledged the despair itself as a sin of commission. I did all of this gladly, believing that He forgives. A burden passed from me: I had set out on my spiritual journey so many times, each of them with a smaller expectation of success while I dwelt on earth, that the hardest taskmaster could not have challenged my sincerity. I was now satisfied to live in Faith, without pretension to any achievement that could justify my life in the eyes of another human person. My natural asceticism overtook me entirely and I surrendered to it without regret.

It suited me after that to revert to my old practice of visiting churches where no one knew me. Reverend Larry encouraged me to remain in his congregation and especially in his Saturday prayer group, where I knew he valued my contribution, but I explained my decision as a form of spiritual retreat from which I expected to return. He knit his brow.

"The Lord comes to our aid in our depression if we ask Him," he said.

"I know that," I said. "Thank God."

"I'm available to pray with you whenever you like," he said.

"I know that too," I said, and thanked the Reverend. When it came to my attention about 1983 that he'd been forced by the progress of some wasting disease to give up his pulpit and move back to the place of his birth to be cared for by his parents, I made it my business to pray for him regularly. I asked God to give me insight into Reverend Larry's case, to let me understand His will in removing from the pulpit at such an early age another of those He had called as His servants—and not just from the pulpit, but, as I heard later, from this earthly coil altogether. It was another mystery that must stay so until my own passing over.

In the several years since Katie died and I understood that my life could never be justified by any of my acts, but only by my willingness to bear witness forever to the joyous Truth that lies hidden beneath the melancholy surface of things, I have kept faith. I watch the fateful pageant marching toward its preordained conclusion, and I wait to be called again for the first time. Something very like the Beast has sprung up lately in the Soviet Union: an amiable, plausible, urbane and well-spoken First Secretary, oddly capable of outflanking the skepticism of our other world leaders. His head wound is almost naïvely emblematic: a red birthmark that looks painted, and which he makes no effort to hide. He dresses as smartly as anyone on Wall Street, and he seems willing and able to ingratiate himself with crowds. He has none of the coarse manner and bureaucratic reserve common to Soviet leaders of the past; he could have been designed by a committee of international power brokers intent on raising an effigy satisfactory to every secular interest, though not to God. The man Gorbachev could be revealed as the Beast without changing a single one of his characteristics: a little further evolution of international politics could be enough. We shall see.

My own life—the material part of it—is straitened and stingy, but it hardly matters. Time is short now, and the way will be steep. I look in the mirror and all the evidence of my preferred asceticism stares back: my face is pale and china-like, my hair a wispy aureole, my eyes a wary, startled blue. I have eked out the means of my survival far longer than would have been possible for a man with stringent expectations of the natural world.

Apropos of that, I saw the natural man Bartley on the street the other day, although he didn't see me, and I didn't speak to him. He looked a little thicker through the waist than when Solveig introduced us more than twenty years ago, but dressed the same, as if he had yet to grow and yet to learn. He was alone, but he wore the giddy expression of someone engaged with friends in pointless banter. I watched him tramp along the street, thinking as usual that if I studied him long enough he might reveal some mystery, but he only turned a corner and disappeared.

While I await the cleansing tumult of the End Time, I review the people and events of my life of Faith. For example, I think of Marie more frequently than at any time since the terrible days beginning with the failure of our affair, and ending with my self-inflicted near-death and my God-inflicted rebirth as the man I now am. Except that I don't know where she has gone, I might try to see Marie—but only to observe her at a distance, not to interact with her in any of the many ways that I now deny myself. However fearful her memory may be to me, perhaps she is sanctified as the agent of the fall that enabled me to rise again. I should seek her out for God's sake and for the sake of remembering how for our instruction He may in His time drive things delusional across the path, or permit the Adversary—pending his imminent consignment for a thousand years to the fiery pit—to do the same. If she lives, Marie is in her forties, almost certainly with a grown child or two and some younger ones, and attached to the husband we deceived.

I think often of Solveig too, whose alliance with me was another of my delusions—but the occasion of God calling me to preach, though only for a season. She is less iconic in my memory than she must have seemed in person, tall, blonde and joyful as she was. It's part of the mystery surrounding my vocation that she should have called me so powerfully, even though she had no use or purpose for me, just as God called me through my association with her to preach, even though He finally had no pastoral use or purpose for me either. If Sweden were not so far away I might think of going there to inquire, believing that causes adequate to their effects lie hidden beneath the surfaces of things.

I think of Randall, my best friend, whom I knew for less than one year. If he had lived, what might he have been able to tell me? When I see him next there will be no mystery left for him to parse; we'll meet in Heaven and he'll say, "Here is what we talked about—you see?" He'll have been raised incorruptible and his head will be whole.

Joanna is another matter. The impatient, sullen, intractable emblem of my failure, she hovers in my memory like a hawk on a thermal. It may be that I'll never see her again on earth or anywhere else. It occurs to me that Heaven, like the contemplative life, could be a place of isolation, though inhabited by God and His angels. Many people important to us in our lives will not be there, and although we shall have come to understand everything, rapprochement with those lost souls will not be possible.

And so the clock of my days runs on. I live only by the grace and with the indulgence of the God Who must come soon to remake the world. When He does, I may be still here or I may have passed, but I shall be in Him in either case, having made sainthood and humility the study of my life. Then the mystery of my failure will be revealed, and I'll know at last why, regardless of my steadfast love and boundless faith, He is profoundly angry, why He despises my work, why He hides from me.

These days I dream but rarely—unusual for a man of my spiritual preoccupation. But the dream that I dream of, in that vast gray space, shadowless, with its low horizon and its echoing sense of some soul's departure, is God: a Voice, deliberate and unmistakable, prescriptive, loving, speaking to me with meticulous care through the pervasive silence.

-END-

LaVergne, TN USA
04 December 2010
207368LV00002B/133/P